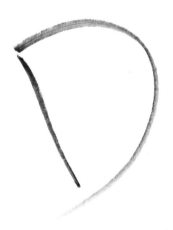

MOUNTAIN HOMECOMING

Center Point
Large Print

Also by Sandra Robbins and available from Center Point Large Print:

Angel of the Cove

This Large Print Book carries the Seal of Approval of N.A.V.H.

MOUNTAIN HOMECOMING

SANDRA ROBBINS

CENTER POINT LARGE PRINT
THORNDIKE, MAINE

This Center Point Large Print edition is published
in the year 2013 by arrangement with
Harvest House Publishers.

The text of this Large Print edition is unabridged.
In other aspects, this book may vary
from the original edition.
Printed in the United States of America
on permanent paper.
Set in 16-point Times New Roman type.

ISBN: 978-1-61173-833-9

Library of Congress Cataloging-in-Publication Data

Robbins, Sandra (Sandra S.)
Mountain homecoming / Sandra Robbins. — Large print edition.
pages ; cm.
ISBN 978-1-61173-833-9 (library binding : alk. paper)
1. Mountain people—Fiction. 2. Homecoming—Fiction.
 3. Reputation—Fiction.
 4. Great Smoky Mountains (N.C. and Tenn.)—Fiction.
 5. Large type books. I. Title.
PS3618.O315245M68 2013b
813′.6—dc23
                                        2013009492

To Guy
for your love, encouragement, and support.
I could never have achieved my dream
without you by my side.

MOUNTAIN HOMECOMING

Chapter 1

Cades Cove, Tennessee
June, 1914

Rani Martin stared through the cabin window at the Smoky Mountains rising above the valley she loved. Usually the sight of the foggy mists curling around the hills made her happy. But try as she might, she couldn't find anything to cheer her up today.

There had to be something that would take away the misery gnawing in the pit of her stomach. Poppa always told her she could do anything she set her mind to, but she didn't know how she could be happy about losing the best friend any girl could ever have.

After today, there would be no reason for her to visit this cabin. Tomorrow Josie Ferguson and her husband, Ted, would load their belongings in their wagon, take their baby, and do what many of their friends and neighbors had already done —move out of Cades Cove. Josie, the one she'd shared secrets with all her life, would be gone, and Rani would be left behind with only memories of her best friend since childhood.

She didn't understand what any of the folks

who'd left the Cove were thinking. How could they leave the most beautiful place on God's good earth?

It was springtime, the best time of year in the Cove. The winter snow had melted and the mountain laurel was in bloom. It wouldn't be long before rhododendrons dotted the mountainsides and azaleas reappeared on Gregory's Bald. This year, however, Josie wouldn't be with her to share the wonder of the Cove coming back to life after a hard winter.

To Rani the prospect of living anywhere except the mountain valley where she'd been born scared her. She'd had an opportunity to see what existed in the outside world when she spent a year attending school while living with Uncle Charles in Maryville. It had been enough to convince her that life wasn't nearly as good anywhere else as it was in the Cove. But others didn't share her thoughts, and they'd left. And now Josie was going too.

With a sigh she turned back to the task she'd abandoned moments ago, helping pack up the kitchen utensils. Her throat constricted as she pulled the cake plate she and her mother had given Josie from the kitchen cupboard. She wrapped her fingers around the pierced handles and stared down at the hand-painted red and yellow roses on the delicate china dish. She'd thought it the most beautiful plate she'd ever seen when she first spied it at the store in Pigeon Forge.

Tears filled her eyes, and she loosened her grip with one hand so she could trace the gold band on the fluted rim. "I can't believe it's been three years since your wedding."

Josie Ferguson bit down on her lip and nodded. "Ted's always said this was his favorite of all our wedding gifts. It reminds him of the molasses cake your mother let him and his sister help make the day George was born."

"I've heard Mama tell that story so many times. But she has one about every baby she's helped deliver."

"She's been a blessing to the women she's helped birth their babies. Everybody loves Anna Martin." Josie's eyes grew wide. "And of course your father too. I don't think I can ever love another pastor like I do your pa. I've listened to him on Sundays ever since I can remember."

"But you won't be there anymore." Rani set the plate down on the table and glanced at the baskets and tubs scattered across the kitchen floor. Pots, pans, and cooking utensils protruded above their sides. The tears she'd been holding back poured down her face, and she covered her eyes with her fingers. "First my brother decides to spend the summer at Uncle Robert's farm in Strawberry Plains instead of coming home from school, then my cousin Annie gets married and moves to

Townsend. Now you're going too. What will I do with all of you gone? I'm going to feel so alone."

"No, you won't."

Rani dug her fists into her eyes to stop the tears and gritted her teeth. "Why couldn't Stephen have come home when school was out at Milligan College instead of spending the summer on Uncle Robert's farm?"

Josie propped her hands on her hips and tilted her head to one side. "You know why."

"Yeah," Rani sighed. "He didn't want to hear Poppa talk to him all summer about following in his footsteps. I don't know why Poppa can't see that Stephen doesn't feel led to preach even though he agreed to that year at Milligan College. He wants to go to medical school. Of course that's what Mama wants too. I'm glad they don't have that problem with me. I don't want to live anywhere but right here in Cades Cove . . . even if I am going to be alone."

Josie rolled her eyes and shook her head. "Like I said, you won't be alone. You'll have your ma and pa, and Stephen will be here for a visit in July." Josie wrapped her arms around Rani's shoulders and hugged her close. "I'm the one who's going to be alone. I won't know anybody over at Townsend. You know Ted never has taken to farming, and there's nothing else for him in the Cove. His new job pays real good. They're going to furnish us a house too."

Rani drew back in shock and gaped at Josie. "House? Have you seen what that high and mighty Little River Logging Company calls houses? I went with Poppa to Townsend last month, and I couldn't believe what the workers were living in. They call them setoff houses because they bring them in on railroad cars and set them off on the hillsides or even right next to the railroad. They're nothing more than one-room shacks with tar paper roofs. When the lumber company gets through cutting all the trees in one place, they load the houses onto a train and ship them to the next spot for their workers."

Josie's lip trembled, and her forehead wrinkled. "I know." Her voice was almost a whisper. "But what can I do, Rani? Ted is my husband. We have to go where he can find work."

Rani gazed past Josie to the cradle in the next room. "I can't stand to think about you living in one of those things, especially now since you have a baby. Can't you convince Ted to stay in Cades Cove? This is the only life you know."

Josie pulled the corner of her apron up and wiped her eyes. She took a deep breath. "We'll be fine. I'll come back to visit, and you can come to Townsend to see me."

Rani snorted and shook her head. "No thanks. I have no desire to share a one-room setoff house with you and your husband, not to mention your baby. I can't believe Ted would be so disloyal to the Cove to go work for a company that's trying to destroy our mountains."

"Are you accusing my husband of turning his back on his friends?" Josie's eyes flared and grew dark with anger.

Rani had seen that look before and realized she'd gone too far. She really needed to follow her mother's advice and not be so outspoken about the company she thought was using the Smokies as a quick way to make money. Her opinion of Little River Lumber differed from that of many who'd left to work for the logging company. Now she had sounded like she believed Ted to be a traitor to his friends.

She reached out and grasped Josie's arm. "I'm sorry, Josie. I didn't mean to criticize Ted. It's just that I've been so upset over what Little River's doing to our mountains. Colonel Townsend has bought 86,000 acres of forest land all the way from Tuckaleechee to Clingman's Dome. I don't care if he does own the company, he's a foolish man. They're cutting every tree in their path. If somebody doesn't stop them, the Smokies will end up as barren hillsides."

Josie waved her hand in dismissal. "As usual, you're being overly dramatic. That's not going to happen. Like I said before, they pay well, and we need the money. End of discussion."

Rani opened her mouth to respond, but the set of Josie's jaw told her it would be useless. With a sigh, she picked up the cake plate from the table and handed it to Josie. "I hope you'll think of me every time you use this."

Josie took the plate and clasped it in her hands like she held a priceless treasure. For the first time Rani caught a glimpse of fear in Josie's eyes, and the truth struck her. Josie didn't want to leave Cades Cove, but she had no choice.

"I will," Josie whispered. "I wanted this to be the last thing I packed. After all, you're my best friend."

Rani burst into tears and threw her arms around Josie. "We're more than best friends. I think of you as the sister I never had."

"Me too." Josie pulled back and wiped at the corner of her eyes. "But you know we could really be sisters."

Josie's words shattered the mood of moments ago and swept all the sadness from Rani's mind. She took a step backward and wagged her finger in Josie's direction. "Oh no. Don't start that again."

"Why not? George is crazy about you. All he talks about is how he wants to marry you, and you won't give him any encouragement. If you married him, we'd be family. Sisters-in-law."

Rani couldn't believe they were having this conversation again. "I've told you at least a hundred times that George is a good friend, but I don't love him. Even if I did, I don't think I'd marry him."

A skeptical expression crossed Josie's face. "What's the matter? Isn't he good looking enough for you?"

Rani's mouth gaped open at the ridiculous suggestion. "Oh, Josie, you know I would never think that. The truth is George is the youngest child in his family, and he's spoiled rotten. If he doesn't get his way, he sulks for days. I wouldn't want a husband that I have to coddle and give in to all the time."

Josie dropped her gaze to the cake plate she held and wrapped a burlap sack around it before she tucked it in the side of one of the baskets. "I have to admit you're right. As a matter of fact, Ted told me George had an awful argument with his pa the other night. It seems he's upset because he's going to be left behind in the Cove after we leave."

Rani held up her hands in exasperation. "You see what I mean. George can only see what he wants. He doesn't realize what a great opportunity he has to work with his father on one of the best farms in the Cove."

"But, Rani, you know he's in love with you. That ought to be enough to make him a good husband."

"Maybe it would be for somebody else, but not for me. I'm just eighteen years old. I have plenty of time to think about getting married. When I do, it's going to be because I love a man so much my heart aches when I'm away from him."

Josie turned to Rani and propped her hands on her hips. "Yeah, you've always had those romantic ideas. I think it must come from all those stories about how hard it was for your pa to get your mother to marry him." She leaned closer to Rani. "Well, for those of us who don't have a great love like that happen in our lives, we have to settle for the next best thing. It's not like there's a lot of men to choose from in the Cove. Being married to George is better than ending up an old maid."

Rani flinched at Josie's words. She remembered how Josie had cried four years ago when Charlie Simmons left the Cove, bound for California. At the time she'd thought it was because he was Ted's friend. Now she wasn't so sure. "Is that what you did, Josie? You settled for the next best thing?"

Josie's face drained of color, and she put her hand to her throat. "Rani, I didn't mean . . ."

"What's goin' on in here?"

At the sound of her husband's voice at the back door Josie's body stiffened, and she glanced over her shoulder. Rani's heart lurched at the lack of expression on Josie's face. She might very well have been looking at a stranger who'd come to her door instead of her husband. "I need to check on the baby," she said, and hurried from the kitchen.

Ted Ferguson frowned and gazed after his wife as she hurried into the next room. His eyes darkened, and the look in his eyes told Rani he longed for something he would never have from Josie. After a moment he took a deep breath and smiled at her. "You two havin' another one of your friendly arguments?"

Rani forced a laugh from her throat and wiped her eyes. "No argument. We're just a little emotional over the two of you leaving the Cove. It seems all my friends are taking off for different places. My family may be the only one left before long."

Ted shook his head. "Naw, you won't be. They'll have to drag my pa out of the Cove to get him to leave. He says he intends to be buried at the church he's gone to all his life."

"That's what my pa says too." Rani picked up the empty basket sitting on the table. "I left you some fried chicken and a fresh loaf of bread that Mama sent. She thought you might get hungry on your way to Townsend tomorrow."

"She always thinks about other folks. Tell her I'm mighty obliged, and I hope I see her soon."

"I will."

Ted followed Rani into the next room where Josie was holding her son. No one spoke for a moment, then Josie swallowed and handed the baby to Ted. "Take care of Jimmy a minute while I walk Rani out."

As Rani stepped onto the front porch, she glanced down at her dog lying next to the door. She snapped her fingers, and he jumped to his feet. He shook his shaggy body, wagged his tail, and awaited her command. It was so easy to communicate with animals. Give them love, feed them well, and reward them for good behavior, and they'd do anything you asked. Too bad people weren't like that.

Josie had a husband who did all that for her, but today Rani had discovered the secret Josie had kept so well hidden—she would never be able to return Ted's love. Rani didn't want to end up like that.

With a sigh, she reached down and stroked her dog's head. "Good boy, Scout. You did what I said. Now let's go home."

With Scout at her heels, she and Josie walked to the road that ran in front of the cabin. As they neared the edge of the yard, Rani turned to Josie. "I'm going to miss you."

"I'm going to miss you too. We're leaving early in the morning. So I guess I won't see you again. I hope you will come visit me in Townsend. We'll make room."

Rani nodded. "We'll see. You take care of yourself. And Ted and little Jimmy too."

Josie smiled, but Rani could see the tears she was fighting to control. "Goodbye, Rani."

Rani started to speak, but the words froze in

her throat. She pressed her lips together and hugged her friend before she turned and started the long walk home. Scout trotted along beside her, and she didn't look back. She wanted to, but she didn't think she could stand the sight of Josie watching her walk away.

She glanced down at the dog and smiled. "Well, Scout, it's a two-mile walk home. Do you think you can make it?"

The dog stared up at her and yelped a reply without breaking his stride.

"I think I can too."

She didn't mind walking. It had always been her way of getting around the Cove, and it gave her time to think. Today she had a lot to mull over. Her discovery about Josie's feelings that she had settled for the next best thing still bothered her. She'd never imagined that Josie might have been in love with someone else.

Now that she thought back to four years ago, she remembered Josie seeming happy all summer. At the time, all she would say was that she'd had her first kiss and was in love. Rani thought it had to be Ted because he had been in love with Josie for years. But it must have been Charlie Simmons, and things hadn't worked out. And soon after Charlie's departure from the Cove, Josie had agreed to marry Ted after putting him off for so long.

Today she had learned the truth. Josie had

settled for something—some*one*—she didn't want. How could she have done that? She must have thought she was doing the right thing, but she'd been wrong. And she was wrong about something else. Being an old maid wasn't the worst thing that could happen to a woman. To Rani's way of thinking, being married to someone you didn't love was far worse.

She squared her shoulders, clenched her fists at her side, and looked down at Scout. "I promise you, Scout, I will never settle for second best, even if it means I never get married."

From the moment he rode into Cades Cove a peace like he hadn't experienced in years came over Matthew Jackson. He pulled his horse to a stop and breathed in the sweet scent of mountain laurel drifting on the air. It smelled like home. He was back where his heart had remained.

Had it really been twenty years since he left the Cove? He closed his eyes and tried to recall every memory of the days following the death of his drunkard father. Even now the thought of the life he, his mother, and his little brother had endured made the old anger he'd tried to bury resurface. With his father drunk most of the time, survival had been hard. But his mother had seen to it that there was always food on the table. Then their lives had taken a turn for the worse when a tavern brawl had ended with his father lying dead of a gunshot wound.

Matthew had been almost ten years old at the time, but overnight he became the man of the family. He'd turned to a newcomer in the Cove, Anna Prentiss. Of course she was Anna Martin now. But to him she'd always be the angel who'd found a place for his family to live and had seen they were taken care of.

He even remembered the last words he'd spoken to her the day they left the Cove. She stood beside the wagon loaded with his family's few belongings, and he'd said, "I'll be back here someday." And now, thanks to the money he'd saved working for the Little River Company, he had returned with the deed to his old homestead in his pocket.

But would the people of the Cove welcome the return of Luke Jackson's son? His father had been a troublemaker and a bully, not to mention an abuser of his wife and children. The sturdy mountain folks didn't have time for a man who didn't take care of his family. As his mother used to say, people have long memories, and he was sure they could recall every one of his father's misdeeds. Now he was about to see if those memories had labeled him a ne'er-do-well like his father.

He could count on one hand the folks who would welcome him back. Simon and Anna Martin. Granny Lawson. They were the ones who made his childhood bearable, and he could hardly wait to see them. But first things first. He had to go to the place where he was born and fulfill a promise he'd made to his dying mother fifteen years ago.

He'd leaned close to her frail, fever-ridden body to catch her last words spoken in that familiar mountain twang: "When you git back to the Cove, see if'n my mountain laurel bush is still there, the one yore pa planted for me when we was first married."

After all the heartache his father had put her through, she still held to the memory of the early days of her marriage when she'd been so happy. Even now the thought of how her eyes had sparkled for a moment, reliving a happier time, made him feel as if a hammer had crushed his heart. His mother and little Eli, his brother. Gone too soon.

He cleared his throat and swiped at his eyes. No need to think about those things now. This was homecoming day, but it was different from what he'd dreamed about when he was a boy. He'd come back alone.

Straightening in the saddle, he spurred the horse forward and concentrated on the road twisting through the valley he loved. All around him were the sights and sounds he'd longed for, but he focused on getting home and seeing the place he'd left twenty years ago.

When he pulled the horse to a halt at what had once been the cabin where he'd lived, his heart dropped to the pit of his stomach. It was worse than he'd expected. The skeleton of a cabin sat near the tulip poplar tree he'd climbed as a boy —bigger now than he remembered. The house's roof had long ago succumbed to the forces of nature and had caved in. A few timbers marked the spot where it had once been. Weeds grew across what had once been a yard.

Even in its best days the cabin hadn't been much, but it could have been if his father had concentrated on making a life for his family instead of spending his time in a drunken stupor. The old hatred welled up in his heart, and he whispered the plea he'd prayed every day since he could remember. "God, don't let me be like him. Make me a better man."

The promise he'd made his mother flashed into his mind, and he climbed down from the horse and tied the reins to a sapling. Taking a deep breath to slow his racing heart, he headed around the side of the house. Had the mountain laurel plant survived the years?

His gaze drifted to his feet, and a warning flickered in his head. The weeds along what used to be a path had been trampled. Someone else had passed this way not long ago.

With hesitant steps, he inched forward. The knee-high weeds swished against his legs. He caught sight of his mother's plant that now towered higher than his head, and he stopped in amazement. It wasn't the bloom-covered bush that made his breath catch in his throat. It was a young woman who appeared unaware of his presence. With her arms outstretched and her face turned up to the sun, she whirled in circles in front of the mountain laurel bush while saying something in a language he didn't understand.

Her bare feet hammered the hardened earth around the plant in a pounding rhythm. Pink blooms from the mountain laurel bush ringed the top of her head and several more protruded from the mass of black hair that reached below her shoulders.

She moved with the grace and elegance of a queen, and he thought he had never seen anyone more beautiful. He tried to speak, to alert her she wasn't alone, but he felt as if he had come under her spell and had been forbidden to move.

Suddenly the air crackled with frantic barking, and a dog emerged from the other side of the bush. His hackles raised, he positioned himself between Matthew and the girl. She jerked to a stop and stared at him, wide-eyed. The dog snarled and inched forward.

Her dark eyes narrowed, and with one snap of her fingers she quieted the dog. She didn't move, and her arched eyebrow told him his company wasn't welcomed. "Stay back, mister, or I'll sic my dog on you."

He glanced down at the dog, whose body still bristled as if he was ready to attack. "I don't mean you any harm, miss."

"Then why did you sneak up on me?"

He shook his head. "I didn't. I stopped when I heard your voice. What were you saying?"

"Just some words I learned from a Cherokee woman." She frowned and glanced past him. "Are you alone?"

"I am. I just rode into the Cove from Townsend."

Her body stiffened, and her lips curled into a sneer. "Townsend? Are you with the Little River Company?"

"I have been."

"It figures." She spit the words at him as if they were distasteful. "We get a lot of Little River workers checking out the Cove. You people are always searching for another stand of timber to cut down, aren't you?" She bent down, grabbed her discarded shoes, and slipped them on her feet. Then with her arms rigid at her sides and her fists clenched, she took a step toward him. "Well, you can go back and tell your bosses we don't sell our land and our trees to outsiders who want to clear cut their way through the Smokies."

The defiant look in her eyes shot daggers at him, and they felt as if they poked deep holes in his heart. This girl's words echoed the fierce pride shared by all the Cove residents for this valley, his valley, the place he called home. He wanted to tell her he agreed with her, that all he wanted was to live again among the people he remembered. Instead, other words emerged from his lips. "I worked for their railroad, not the logging company."

She shook her head, and one of the blooms tumbled to the ground. Her eyes widened, and she glanced up as if she'd forgotten she wore a crown of flowers. A flush covered her cheeks, and she yanked the blossoms from her thick hair. "They're the same to me. Maybe you didn't cut our trees, but you carried them away."

Matthew swallowed hard. There was something so familiar about this girl. Her brown eyes, dark complexion, and the high cheekbones reminded him of someone. It wasn't possible he could have met her before. She probably hadn't even been born when he had left the Cove. But still, there was something. He took a step closer, and the dog growled. With a smile he stopped and held up his hands. "I'm not coming closer."

"Good." She sniffed and snapped her fingers again. "Let's go, Scout. It's time we got home."

He didn't move as she strode past him, her head held high and her dog at her side. He turned and watched her disappear around the side of what had once been his home. Her straight back and determined stride reminded him of the spirited mountain women he'd known. They attacked the harsh life in the Cove and planted the seed of unyielding loyalty to the land in their children. Just like his mother had done with him.

Someone had instilled that same devotion in this girl. He hoped he'd get to meet the person who had done that, for he had just encountered the fierce mountain pride that had ruled his life. And it thrived in the most beautiful woman he'd ever seen.

Chapter 2

With each step she took toward home, Rani's anger grew stronger. Why wouldn't Little River Lumber stay out of the Cove? The stranger she'd encountered at the old Jackson farm wasn't the first one who'd been sent to find tracts of timber to buy. Her father had even been approached about the forest on their land, but he'd told them no.

Now another Little River worker had arrived. She hoped what she'd said had convinced him he was on a futile mission. If truth be told, though, she wasn't sure what some of the other families in the Cove would say. Life was hard here and money was scarce. An offer from a big logging company could lighten the day-to-day problems of living in this remote valley.

Rani sighed and shook her head. No use thinking about what other folks would do. She only knew what her parents would do, and she was proud of them for their stand against the stripping of the mountainsides.

She smiled when the cabin she'd lived in all her life came into view, and her stride increased. The sun had begun to sink toward the west. That meant it wouldn't be long until supper. Mama probably needed her help.

She dashed into the house and hurried into the kitchen. Mouthwatering smells drifted from the iron cook stove in the corner. Spring greens from the mountainsides simmered in a pot on the back burner, and sliced ham ready to be placed in the frying pan lay on a plate on the table. But it was the sweet odor coming from the oven that tickled her nose. She couldn't resist a peek and opened the oven door to catch a glimpse of the apple pie bubbling on the rack.

Closing the door, she turned and glanced around. Where was everybody? "Hello? Anybody home?"

"Out here, darlin'."

The familiar voice came from the yard, and she peered out the back door. Granny Lawson, her Bible in her lap and her cane resting against her chair, sat under the big oak tree behind the house. Rani stood still a moment and studied the woman she'd known all her life.

Granny, as everyone called her, had dedicated her life years ago to serving the people she loved as a midwife. There was hardly a person Rani's age or younger in the Cove who hadn't been delivered by the legendary granny woman. Although not related by blood to her family, Granny had been a second mother to both her parents, and she was the only grandmother Rani had ever known.

Rani's gaze drifted to Granny's hands. Healing hands, they'd always been called. Now they were gnarled with arthritis. Rani ran down the back porch steps and plopped down on the ground next to Granny.

"Supper smells good. Who picked the greens?"

Granny closed her Bible and smiled. "Your pa picked 'em this mornin'. Your ma was just 'bout to put 'em on to cook when she remembered she wanted to go check on Lizzie Morton and her new young 'un. I told her to go on. I'd take care of supper. Your pa drove her over there in the buggy, so they ought to be a-gittin' back soon."

"Good. I can hardly wait to have a piece of that pie you made. But I wish I'd been here to help you. I know how painful it is for you to use your fingers."

Granny frowned and shook her head. "No, child. I made out just fine. You needed to be

over to Josie's a-tellin' her goodbye." Granny
tilted her head to one side. "How's my girl
a-doin'? I know she hates to leave her folks."

Rani sighed. "She does, but she's being brave."
Her voice broke, and she laid her cheek against
Granny's leg. She placed her fingers on the Bible
in Granny's lap and caressed the leather cover
of the book Granny had read to her all her life.
The tears she'd tried to hold in since leaving
Josie's ran down her face. "Oh Granny. What am
I going to do? All my friends are leaving the
Cove. I'll be so lonely."

Granny stroked Rani's head. "No you won't.
You gonna have your folks and me, and you got a
lot of friends at church."

Rani raised up and stared at Granny. "I know
that, but sometimes I feel so . . . so empty inside.
Like something's missing from my life. What's
the matter with me?"

"There ain't nothin' wrong with you. You've
just grown into a woman with feelin's you don't
understand, but you'll figure 'em out. You're
'bout the smartest girl I ever seen." She leaned
closer. "Maybe even smarter than your ma, and
that's sayin' a mouthful."

Rani shook her head. "You're wrong. Mama
knew from the time she was a little girl she
wanted to deliver babies and take care of sick
folks. I'll never be able to do anything that comes
up to her." Her lips trembled, and she paused

before continuing. "And I'll never be able to make up for what I've taken from her."

"Oh, child." Deep wrinkles furrowed across Granny's face. She reached out and caressed Rani's cheek. "You can't grieve the rest of your life over what happened in the past. You gotta look to the future and what God has planned for you."

"I try to do that, but I can't forget. It was my fault."

A sad look flickered in Granny's eyes, and they stared at each other lost in their own thoughts of the past. "I've told you over and over it warn't your fault. What's it gonna take to convince you?"

Rani blinked back tears. "I don't know," she murmured.

Granny exhaled a long breath. "I know life can be hard sometimes. I got my own regrets 'bout things I wish I'd done different. But I cain't stand to see you a-punishin' yourself for somethin' you couldn't help." She pointed toward the mountains in the distance. "You need to think about all that God's already done for you. Look around and see His work, Rani. He blessed you by puttin' you in the purtiest place on earth."

The sight of the smoky mists hanging over the mountains sent a thrill through her. "I know that, and I love the Cove. I don't think I could ever live anywhere else."

Granny smiled and grasped Rani's hand. "I never seen anybody in all my years that loves this here valley like you do. I know sometimes your ma and pa get outdone with you 'cause you a-rantin' about the logging companies, but I just see that as a sign that you got a deep love for this here place. Maybe God's got some plan for you right here."

Rani stared at the hills in the distance for a moment and let Granny's words soak into her mind. With a sigh, she turned back to Granny. "But what could it be?"

Granny shrugged. "I don't know, child. That's just a notion I got in my head. You the one gonna have to figure that out."

Rani pushed to her feet and brushed off her dress. "Well, until I do, I wish I could come up with a way to keep Little River out of the Cove." She frowned at the sudden thought of the stranger she'd encountered earlier today. "That reminds me. I stopped by the old Jackson place to pick some mountain laurel on my way home and ran into another Little River employee. I told him our timber wasn't for sale."

Granny's forehead wrinkled, and her eyebrows drew down across her nose. "Child, you gotta be careful 'bout who you go a-talkin' to. You've grown into a right purty woman, and you never can tell how strangers are gonna react. I couldn't stand it if something happened to you."

The man's image flashed in her mind, and her skin warmed at the way he had looked at her. At the time she had told herself that he was a Little River employee who only wanted to curry favor with a mountain girl who might help him in his search for timber. Now that she thought about it, she wasn't so sure. He'd been courteous even when she hadn't been.

It didn't matter. She would probably never see the handsome man again, and a part of her was sorry about that. She glanced up at Granny who appeared to be waiting for a reply about her concern for Rani's safety. She patted Granny's hand and smiled. "Don't worry. I'll be careful. Besides, I had Scout with me today, and the man appeared harmless. He tried to tell me he worked for the railroad, but it's all the same to me. I watched to see if he followed me, but he didn't."

Granny shook her head. "Just the same, I don't like you talkin' to strangers. It ain't safe." She glanced around the yard. "By the way, where is that dog of yours?"

Rani laughed. "He took off after a rabbit a ways back. Don't worry. He'll turn up for his supper."

The rattle of a buggy pulling off the road in front of the house caught Rani's attention. Ever since she was a child she'd thrilled to the familiar sound of her parents returning home from one of their medical or spiritual missions to those in Cove. "Mama and Poppa are home."

Her parents' laughter could be heard as her father pulled the buggy to a stop on the path that ran beside the cabin to the barn. Poppa reached over and straightened Mama's bonnet and whispered something in her ear. Her mother laughed and swatted at his hand, but there was no anger on her face, only love.

Rani's gaze drifted over the two, and her heart swelled. Poppa's dark features offered a sharp contrast to Mama's blonde hair sparkling in the afternoon sunlight. Together they made a tireless team that served the needs of their friends and neighbors. As she watched them, she knew if God never gave her anything else in her life, He had blessed her beyond measure by allowing her to have such wonderful parents.

Her mother climbed to the ground and glanced back up at her father. Rani waited for the look that would pass between the two, and she wasn't disappointed. She had watched the silent messages their eyes had conveyed for years, and it still made her heart beat a little faster each time she saw it. The Look, as she secretly called it, summed up the love they had for each other, and it was still as strong after twenty years of marriage as it had been when they first knew each other.

That's what she wanted when she fell in love and married, a man whose love for her could be seen in his face every day. She couldn't settle for anything less than what her parents had. No, she wouldn't settle for anything less.

Her mother reached back into the buggy for the black leather bag with brass trim that she took whenever she was attending a patient, then turned to face Rani and Granny. "What are you two doing out here?" she asked.

Her father straightened in the seat and inhaled a big breath before he grinned at Granny. "I do declare I think I smell apple pie. I'll take Anna off more often if it means you'll cook supper while we're gone."

Granny chuckled and pushed to her feet. "Hush your mouth, preacher boy. You know I done taught Anna to cook all your fav'rite foods. I 'spect she's 'bout the best cook in these here parts now."

Her mother laughed. "I may be able to cook a decent supper, but I'll never be able to touch your pies, Granny."

"I'd better take care of the horse," her father said. "The sooner that gets done, the sooner we can eat!" He winked at Rani, snapped the reins across the horse's back, and headed toward the barn.

Rani ran to her mother and reached for the bag. "Do you want me to put this up for you, Mama?"

Her mother reached up and smoothed Rani's hair back from her face before she handed her the bag. "Thank you, darling. How was it over at Josie's?"

"It was hard. Josie asked me to come visit her, but I doubt if I will."

Her mother stared at her for a moment. "Don't worry. I know you feel alone now, but you won't always be. God has a plan for you. He's going to fill your life with wonderful things that you can't imagine right now."

Leaning on her cane, Granny hobbled over to them. "That's what I've been a-tellin' Rani. She just has to be patient and pray." She stopped and leaned both hands on her cane. "Rani, did I ever tell you that I prayed for three years for God to send a woman to the Cove for Simon before Anna came?"

Rani laughed and rolled her eyes. "About a hundred times, Granny."

Granny's eyebrows arched. "Well, my point is, you cain't rush God. He moves in His own time."

"I'll remember that," Rani said.

Her mother started to respond but stopped and frowned. "Did you hear that? It sounded like someone knocking at the front of the house."

Rani listened for a moment, then shook her head. "I didn't hear anything."

"I'd better go check. It might be someone needing help."

Her mother rushed across the yard and into the house with Rani and Granny following behind. They had just stepped into the kitchen when she heard a surprised squeal come from the front of the house.

Rani glanced at Granny. "Was that Mama?"

"Sounded like her."

"Granny, Rani, come here quick!" Her mother's shrill words ended in a loud screech.

Leaving Granny to hobble behind her, Rani bolted through the house and out the front door. She skidded to a stop at the edge of the porch and stared open-mouthed at her mother. She stood on the ground facing a tall man, her arms wrapped around his middle. His arms circled her back, and his face was buried on her shoulder.

As Rani watched, he raised his head and gazed at her. His eyes widened in surprise, and she gasped. The man she'd encountered earlier at the mountain laurel bush was standing in front of her home. And he was hugging her mother.

Her mouth gaped open, and she turned to Granny, who stopped beside her and grasped the front porch post. Granny clamped her free hand over her mouth, and tears glimmered in her wide eyes.

Rani glanced in confusion from her mother to Granny, whose gaze didn't waver from the man at the foot of the steps. "Thank You, Lord," she whispered. "Thank You for answerin' my prayer."

The man now stood next to her mother, his eyes fixed on Granny. He swallowed hard and nodded. "I did what I said I'd do, Granny. I've come home."

Tears rushed down Granny's checks and she held out her arms. In an instant he was up the steps and locked in Granny's embrace. Soft sobs came from Granny's mouth, and Rani turned to her mother and frowned.

"I don't understand."

Her mother laughed and rushed up the steps. She put her arm around Rani's shoulders and turned her to face the stranger. "You've heard us speak about Matthew Jackson. Well, this is Matthew. He's come home."

It took a moment for the words to register. Matthew Jackson, the boy she'd heard about all her life? The one who'd left the Cove with his mother and brother when his father was murdered? She'd often wondered what he looked like, and now he stood next to her on the front porch of her home.

He pulled away from Granny and turned to face her mother. "I can't believe I'm here after all these years."

Joy covered the faces of her mother and Granny, but she still couldn't believe it. Matthew Jackson had returned to the Cove? And he was the man she'd met this afternoon? Her mother gave her a gentle nudge forward. "Matthew, this is my daughter, Rani."

His dark eyes stared into hers, and she

remembered how she'd thought only minutes ago she would never see this man again. Now he stood next to her. His eyebrows arched. "Your daughter?"

A tingle of pleasure rippled through her at his penetrating gaze. Before she could question what she was feeling, a thought popped into her mind. She needed to be logical about Matthew's sudden return to the Cove. Her mother had known him years ago when he was a boy. But a boy hadn't returned. A man had. And that man worked for Little River Lumber. Had he come back in hopes his ties to the past would convince the Cove residents to sell their land? If that was his intention, he had another think coming. She'd make sure that never happened. She opened her mouth to tell him so, but the look of joy on her mother's face stopped her. There was time later to discuss such matters.

Instead of speaking what was in her heart, she held out her hand. "Hello, Matthew. I've heard about you all my life."

Matthew couldn't believe his eyes. No wonder the girl at the mountain laurel bush reminded him of someone. With her dark hair and brown eyes and the tilt of her mouth when she smiled, like she was doing now, she looked exactly like Simon. Somehow, though, he had the impression her smile was more for her mother's benefit than his.

He grasped her outstretched hand and smiled at how his big hand enveloped hers. The feel of her cool fingers in his palm set his pulse to racing. He glanced at her mother. "I should have known this was your daughter. She looks exactly like Simon."

Granny chuckled. "That's right. And her twin brother looks just like Anna."

Reluctantly, he released Rani's hand and turned to Anna. "I remember hearing you and Simon had twins, but I can't believe they're grown."

"They are, but Stephen's not here right now. He's in school at Elizabethton. He'll be home for a few weeks in July." A frown pulled at her forehead. "Will you still be here? I haven't even asked you how long you're going to stay."

He smiled. "Forever. Mr. Howard owned our old farm, and he lived over at Townsend until he died about two years ago. When I found out, I approached his son about buying the place, and I've been paying on it. I made the last payment a few weeks ago and left my job yesterday to come back home."

He glanced at Rani to see how this news affected her. A skeptical look flickered in her eyes, and he swallowed back his disappointment. For some reason he wanted her to approve of his return, and this thought puzzled him. It shouldn't matter to him what a young girl thought. She had to be at least eleven years his junior.

He tried to shake the notion from his head and turned back to Anna. "Where's Simon?"

Anna looped her arm through his and drew him toward the front door. "He's in the barn, but he'll be back soon. Come in. You're staying for supper."

Matthew drew back and shook his head. "No, I didn't come by this late for an invitation to supper. I just wanted to see you."

Granny took his other arm. "You don't need no invite to set down to our table. You've always been practic'ly family anyway."

He halted and glanced down at Granny. "Do you live with Simon and Anna?"

Granny chuckled. "For 'bout three years now. They decided I didn't need to stay by myself any longer." She straightened her shoulders. " 'Course, I think they was bein' a little bit cautious, but I do have to say I enjoy the comp'ny."

Anna smiled at Granny. "And we enjoy having her here. After all, she's a second mother to both Simon and me."

Matthew glanced from one to the other. "Both of you are to me. The memory of you waving to us as we left the Cove that day has stayed with me all these years. And it's what's brought me back."

Anna squeezed his arm. "We're glad you're home." She glanced over her shoulder at her daughter. "Rani, run out to the barn and tell your father to hurry. He'll be so excited to see Matthew."

Without saying a word, Rani hopped off the porch and ran around the side of the house. Matthew turned his attention back to Granny and Anna as they led him into the house. He stopped in the front room and let his gaze drift over the interior. The house still had the familiar rustic look he remembered from childhood, but time had worked its changes.

Simon's long rifle still hung over the stone fireplace, but only a woman would have added the crocheted doilies that adorned the lamp table. Vases containing bouquets of wildflowers sat on either end of the mantel that also held family pictures.

He picked up the photograph made on Simon and Anna's wedding day and smiled. "I remember that day. We came with Mrs. Johnson from Pigeon Forge so we could see you two married."

Anna nodded. "I remember." She walked to a rocking chair that faced the fireplace and picked up a quilt draped over the back. She held it out for him to see. "Do you remember this quilt? The women of the Cove gave it to me as a wedding present. Your mother made one of the squares. She wanted to be there to see me open it."

He reached out and trailed his fingers across the still-bright words emblazoned in the center square. "Angel of the Cove." He glanced at her. "Do they still call you that, Anna?"

She chuckled and hung the quilt across the chair back. "Not so much anymore. I'm just Anna to everybody here. We have a doctor in the Cove now, but he likes for me to deliver the babies. A lot of folks still come to me when they're sick, and I send for him if I think it's serious."

He took a deep breath and glanced around. "I can't believe I'm finally back in this room. I visited Simon here so many times. It looks the same . . . and yet different. Does that make any sense?"

Granny chuckled and eased down into one of the rocking chairs. "I reckon Anna's to be thanked for that. She turned Simon's cabin into a real home."

Anna hurried over and helped Granny settle herself. A slight flush rose in Anna's cheeks as she glanced at him. "Twenty years brings a lot of changes. This is the home we made for our family."

Matthew set the picture of Anna and Simon back on the mantel, picked up one of Rani and a young man, and studied it. Rani's dark hair and eyes and the young man's light-colored features gave no hint that the two could be twins. He glanced at Anna. "Is this Rani's twin brother?"

"Yes. That's Stephen. He's ten minutes older than Rani."

The rocker creaked as Granny repositioned herself. "I do believe that was the longest ten minutes I ever lived through."

Anna laughed. "But we got through it and came out with two beautiful babies."

A frame with the picture of a man he remembered well caught his attention, and he picked it up. "And here's your uncle. Doc Prentiss we called him. I'll always be indebted to him for taking us to Pigeon Forge after my father's death." He rubbed his thumb over the glass, and thought of the man Anna had asked to arrange work for his mother at Mrs. Johnson's inn. He had done that and then seen that they were settled in the little cabin behind her business. "Is Doc still practicing?"

"Not in the mountains," Anna said. "He nearly wore himself out traveling the mountain roads and tending the people he loved. He retired about five years ago and moved to Maryville. He still sees a few patients and teaches some classes at Maryville College, but mostly he enjoys retirement. I miss having him in the mountains, though. He's coming for a visit while Stephen's here, so you'll get to see him then."

"Good. I have a lot to thank him for." Matthew set the picture back down and was about to turn away when he spied a frame sitting to the side of the others. The solemn face of a young boy of perhaps five years old stared at him.

"Who's this?" he asked.

The silence that followed his question sent a warning flashing into his mind. He turned and stared at Anna who stood next to Granny's chair. Her lips trembled. "That's Willie," she whispered. "He died soon after that was taken."

Matthew glanced at the child once more before he stepped away from the mantel. "I'm sorry. I didn't know."

"Of course you didn't," Granny said. She reached out and grasped Anna's hand. They both stared at the picture as if lost in thought. After a moment Granny broke the strained silence. "He was a sweet boy," she murmured, "and we miss him a lot. He would have been 'bout fifteen now."

Before Matthew could respond, footsteps thudded in the back of the house and Simon rushed into the room. He stopped, his eyes wide, and stared in unbelief. "I couldn't believe it when Rani told me you were here."

Matthew stared at the man who had been more of a father to him when he was a child than anyone. Some gray sprinkled the dark hair he remembered so well, but the warmth in Simon's eyes hadn't changed.

He tried to speak, but all he could do was think about how good it was to be back with people who shared his past. Before he could say anything, Simon enveloped him in a bear hug.

Matthew closed his eyes for a moment and let

the welcome flow through his soul. He'd debated for months whether or not he should come back, but now he knew he'd made the right choice.

He glanced over Simon's shoulder and spied Rani standing behind her father. As their eyes locked, she crossed her arms and arched an eyebrow. The expression of distrust on her face sucked the breath from him.

For some reason, Rani didn't like him, and the thought saddened him. Maybe he had just encountered his first resistance to his home-coming. Her opinion might be the result of having heard stories about his father. If a girl who didn't even know him could judge him on what others said, then how could he ever be accepted by the people in the Cove who had actually known Luke Jackson?

Perhaps he'd been wrong. What if he'd made a mistake in coming home? His mother could have been right about people having long memories. If that was true, then there was no place for him in the Cove.

Chapter 3

Rani didn't remember when there had been such lively conversation during supper. Usually after a hard day of work, her parents were content to enjoy their time around the kitchen table as they talked about the events of the day and what they planned for the morning. Not tonight. Her parents and Granny had laughed and talked more than she'd seen them do in the past month. And it was all because of their unexpected guest.

"Have some more of this here pie." Granny picked up the pan from the middle of the table and scooped another big piece onto Matthew's plate.

Rani cast a glance at the man sitting across from her. The smile on his lips extended to his dark eyes as he glanced at Granny. She had to admit Matthew Jackson seemed to be enjoying his time with her family. For their sake, she hoped he was sincere and wasn't just pretending so he could approach them later about his employer buying their timber.

She propped her elbows on the table and tented her fingers. "Well, Matthew, after living so long in the outside world, what made you want to come back to our valley?"

Matthew had just raised his fork with a bite of pie on it, but he lowered it back to his plate and stared at her with the same penetrating gaze he had directed at her earlier. It was as if he directed some kind of silent plea toward her. Her skin warmed under his intense scrutiny, and she leaned back in her chair to distance herself from him. She lowered her hands and clasped them in her lap.

After a moment he smiled, and she swallowed hard as his gaze drifted from her eyes to her lips and back again. "This is home, Rani. All I've thought about for years was getting back here, but I knew I had to have a place to come to. When my old farm went up for sale, I knew God had answered my prayers."

"But didn't it bother you working for Little River Lumber when you knew what they were trying to do to our mountains?"

"Rani," her father interrupted. She glanced at him, and he frowned. "It's not our place to question Matthew's motives. We don't know what his life's been like."

Matthew shook his head. "No, it's all right, Simon." He leaned forward and smiled at Rani. "I told you earlier today I worked for their railroad company. Yes, I knew how they were stripping the mountains, and it made me sick. But at the time, I needed a job, and the only one I could find was with the railroad."

Mama turned a questioning glance toward Rani. "I don't remember Matthew telling you he worked for the railroad. When did that happen?"

Rani fidgeted in her seat and dropped her gaze to her plate. She picked up her cup of water and shrugged. "Oh, I met Matthew on my way home from Josie's today."

Her mother's mouth gaped open. "Where?"

Matthew chuckled. "I stopped at my farm. I wanted to see how the place had changed, and I'd promised my mother the first thing I'd do was check on her mountain laurel bush. Rani was there."

"Land's sakes," Granny said. "So you're the feller Rani came home all upset about 'cause she thought he was after timber in the Cove. Why didn't you tell her who you was?"

Matthew laughed, and he stared at Rani again. "I tried to, but she threatened to sic her dog on me if I came any closer. And the way he was barking, I figured it was best to keep my distance." His eyes softened, and he tilted his head to one side. "There was something about you that looked so familiar, though. Now I understand—it was because you're so much like Simon."

The mellow tone of his voice flowed over her, and her heart pounded. What was wrong with her? She'd never experienced such strange feelings before. It could be the fact that she'd heard stories about how hard Matthew's life had been before his father died. But now that she'd met the flesh and blood person who'd survived those events, she needed to be careful. Her parents might believe his reasons for returning to the Cove, but he still hadn't convinced her that he wasn't secretly representing Little River.

After a moment he picked up his fork again and shoveled a bite of pie into his mouth. He closed his eyes, swallowed, and groaned in satisfaction. "Oh, Granny, I've missed your cooking."

She reached over and patted his arm. "Well, now that you're back you're gonna have a chance to eat a lot of it. And that reminds me. You're back just in time for a big shindig."

Matthew lowered his fork and turned toward her. "What?"

"Well," Granny said, "it's not really a *big* thing, hardly worth mentionin'. But the folks in the Cove seem to think it is."

Matthew pushed his plate away and crossed his arms on the table. He looked from Granny to Anna, whose face was beaming. "It sounds important. Is somebody having a party?"

Granny nodded. "I guess you could say that. The folks are havin' a dinner after church for me next Sunday. To celebrate my birthday."

Matthew's face broke into a big smile. "Your birthday? Then I *am* back just in time! I wouldn't miss that for anything." He darted a glance at

Anna and then back to Granny. "And how old will you be? Surely not more than fifty, because you had to be about thirty when I moved away."

Granny laughed and swatted his arm. "Boy, you shore do make an old woman feel good. You know good and well I warn't no thirty when you left. Next Saturday I'm going to be seventy years old."

Anna laughed, scooted her chair back from the table, and began to stack the dishes. "And she can still do more work in a day than I can."

Simon jumped up and began to help her. "And next Sunday's going to be a very special day at church. Not only will we celebrate Granny's birthday, but you'll get to see all your old friends." As he carried the dirty dishes to the dry sink, he glanced back over his shoulder. "What are your plans for fixing the old place up?"

Matthew rubbed the back of his neck and sighed. "From the looks of things, I have my work cut out for me. I wanted to see what I needed to do before I bought anything, so I came on to check things out. I'll take a better look around tomorrow. Then I'll head back to Townsend and buy what I need to start rebuilding. One of the first things I need to do is get that field next to the cabin cleared and corn planted."

Simon nodded. "That sounds about right. You'll need that corn for your animals next winter. You think you can do that and get the cabin built too?"

"If I work at it really hard, I figure I should have the cabin in pretty good shape by winter."

Anna hesitated in retying her apron and turned from the dry sink to stare at Matthew. "Where were you planning on sleeping while you're rebuilding?"

"At the cabin, I guess."

Her eyes widened, and she propped her hands on her hips. "You can't do that, Matthew. Stephen's room is empty right now. You'll stay there until your cabin is ready."

Matthew rose to his feet and shook his head. "No, Anna, I'll be all right. I've slept in worse places."

She held up her hand and frowned. "There's no arguing about it. We want you to stay here."

A feeling of panic fluttered in Rani's stomach. She jumped to her feet and reached for the empty pie plate. "Mama, I'm sure Matthew knows best. If he wants to stay at his farm, let him."

She glanced up at Matthew, and her heart constricted at the flicker of sorrow in his eyes. He took a deep breath. "Maybe it would be better . . ."

Simon reached out and clamped a hand on Matthew's shoulder. "Matthew, even when you were a child you were independent. I know you grew up too fast after your pa died. But you're a man now, and a man accepts help when it's offered in love and friendship. We want you to stay here." He directed a stern glare at Rani. "All of us do."

Rani flinched not so much from the look on her father's face but from the tone of his voice. He had spoken like that when she was a child and had misbehaved. Had she embarrassed her parents by her less-than-warm welcome of Matthew? If so, she would have to make amends.

The memory of Matthew's cabin popped into her head. There was no way he could stay there until he'd made some major repairs. Their home had always been a refuge for anyone needing help, and Matthew was no exception.

She forced a smile to her face. "Of course Mama and Poppa are right. Your cabin isn't fit to live in yet. You should stay here."

Matthew's eyes narrowed, and he searched her face as if he was trying to decide whether or not she was being honest. After a moment he nodded. "It sure would be better to sleep in a bed than on the ground."

Anna laughed and swept him into a hug. "As long as we're around you won't be sleeping on the ground." She glanced at Granny. "Why don't you and Simon take Matthew into the front room? Rani and I will wash the dishes, and then we'll join you."

"Sounds good to me." Granny nodded, planted her hands on the table top, and tried to push to her feet.

Rani grabbed her arm to assist her, but before she could help Granny up Matthew stepped to the other side of Granny and looped his arm through hers. "Let me help you, Granny."

His gaze moved to Rani, and they stared at each other across the top of Granny's head. Rani's breath caught in her throat, and she grasped Granny's arm tighter. He was so close she could smell the scent of her mother's homemade soap he'd washed up with before supper. For the first time she noticed how his hair covered the top of his ears, a sign he hadn't had a haircut in a while.

A smile pulled at his mouth. "Let's lift her together."

She nodded and directed her attention back to Granny. They pulled her to her feet, and Rani released her hold. Granny chuckled, grabbing her cane with one hand and Matthew's arm with the other. "Land's sakes, this is 'bout one of the best nights I've had in a long time. I've got loved ones 'round me and a handsome young feller is a-holdin' my hand. What more could any woman want?"

Matthew laughed as he and Granny followed Simon into the next room. "I know I couldn't ask for more, Granny."

When they'd disappeared, Rani turned toward her mother. The frown on her face told Rani she was about to experience her mother's seldom-seen anger. Red splotches dotted her cheeks. She crossed her arms, and her toe tapped the floor like it used to do when she reprimanded her misbehaving twins.

"What is the matter with you, Rani?" Anna spluttered. "I've never seen you act so rude to a guest in our home before. Why does Matthew's staying here bother you so?"

Rani moved closer to her mother and lowered her voice. "I thought you should get to know him again before you brought him into our home to stay."

"Get to know him? I've known him since he was nine years old."

Rani shook her head. "You knew him *when* he was nine years old. He's a man now, and he's worked for Little River. How do we know he's still not working for them? If word gets around that he's staying at the preacher's house, folks will come nearer to trusting him. Maybe he'll use that trust to get them to sell their timber to his company."

Her mother's eyes grew wide. "That's ridiculous. You heard him say he doesn't work for Little River anymore. He just wants to come home."

Rani crossed her arms and frowned. "That's what he says, but we don't know if it's true."

Moisture appeared in the corner of her mother's eyes, and she blinked. "When I came to this valley twenty years ago I was so scared no

56

one would like me. Many of the people were unfriendly to me at first. Granny and Simon kept telling me I had to keep making the first move toward friendship with everyone I met. It wasn't easy, but eventually I became friends with everyone."

Rani sighed. "I know, Mama. You've told me the story many times."

She reached out and grasped Rani's hand. "You've never felt that. You were accepted from the day you were born because you were our daughter. Matthew hasn't had that. Folks in the Cove remember what his father was like, and many of them will judge Matthew because of that. He must have been scared, but still he came back. He knew we'd welcome him, but you made him feel like an intruder. I think you owe him an apology."

Disappointment flickered in her mother's eyes, and Rani bit down on her lip. This afternoon Josie had accused her of judging Ted's motives in trying to provide for his family, and now her mother had done the same with Rani's suspicions about Matthew.

Judge not, that ye be not judged. The Bible verse that her father had preached on a few weeks ago flashed in her mind, and her heart pricked. All her life she'd tried to be as trusting and loving of others as her parents, but today she had failed miserably.

She squeezed her mother's hand. "I'm sorry, Mama. I let my dislike for the logging company get in the way of welcoming Matthew to our home as you and Poppa and Granny did. I'll apologize."

Mama smiled, leaned over, and kissed Rani on the cheek. "I understand how you feel about what's happening to our mountain forests. From the time you were born you had an attachment to the land like no one I've ever seen. I kept hoping you'd decide to follow in my footsteps, but I'm about to give up."

Rani's eyes widened in horror. "Oh, no, I could never be a midwife. I'd faint and wouldn't be any good to anybody."

Her mother laughed. "We all have our gifts, and working with sick people just isn't one of yours."

Rani shuddered at the thought of having her hands covered in someone else's blood. "No, it's not. But I'm thankful there are people like you and Granny and Stephen who enjoy it. I just wish I could figure out what my gift is."

Her mother put her arm around Rani's shoulder and guided her back to the dry sink. "You know what yours is, but you refuse to recognize it. I don't know what it's going to take to make you accept the fact that God has given you a great talent."

"You're just saying that because you're my mother." Rani picked up a dish towel and turned to Anna. "There's nothing special about the pottery I make."

"Yes, there is. You'll realize it someday. For now, all I want is for you to live each day like God wants you to, and to be kind to everyone you come in contact with. And that includes Matthew."

"I will."

Her mother poured some hot water in the big pan she used to wash dishes. As they began to work, Rani thought back over the day. When she'd left Josie's she'd felt so alone, and then a handsome man who stirred strange feelings in her had appeared. Now he'd be at their house every day.

Although she would never admit it to her parents, the truth was that Matthew Jackson intrigued her more than any man she'd ever met. Maybe it was because of the stories she'd heard about him all her life or the dark eyes that seemed to stare into her soul. Or maybe it was because she was lonely.

She shook her head to rid it of her silly notions. She was acting like a schoolgirl. Matthew had to be at least eleven years older than she, and he'd worked for Little River Lumber. Both of those were very good reasons to keep her distance.

A quiet peace filled Matthew as he sat in a straight-backed chair next to Granny. The creak of her rocker reminded him of childhood after-noons when he would escape to her home and sit beside her while she told him stories from the Bible. How he'd wished he could stay with her forever in those days. After a few hours, guilt that his mother and little brother might be facing one of his father's drunken rages would tear him away from the safety of her small cabin. He'd never forgotten those times, and the desire to regain those lost moments had kept him focused on his goal to return.

Now he was back, and the fear he'd once experienced in the cabin where he'd lived no longer existed. He was the only one who had survived, but the memories of those years still haunted his dreams. Tonight he was with friends who knew about his past, and they had welcomed him to their home. At least most of them had. Rani didn't appear to share her family's acceptance of him.

He still couldn't figure out her aloof attitude toward him. She'd ignored him most of the way through supper and had seemed to be lost in thought. He couldn't help stealing a glance at her every once in a while, though. Her dark eyes with their long lashes captivated him, and his pulse raced every time she looked at him.

"It's good to have you back, Matthew." Simon's voice broke the comfortable silence and startled Matthew from his thoughts.

He glanced up at Simon, who stood with one arm resting on the mantel and one foot on the stone hearth. For some reason the memory of Simon and his brother, John, building his father's coffin popped into his head, and his heart warmed. Simon had been the only man in the Cove who had befriended his father. Even when his father's actions didn't warrant being loved, Simon had never abandoned his desire to bring Luke Jackson to the Lord.

"Being here with all of you brings back a lot of memories." He reached over and squeezed Granny's hand and nodded at Simon. "I haven't forgotten how good you two were to my pa. He didn't deserve your friendship."

Simon frowned and straightened. "Don't say that, Matthew. I know it was hard to live with him, but God loved him." He paused for a moment, and Matthew saw the regret in Simon's eyes. "Not reaching Luke was one of the biggest disappointments of my ministry."

"I know." Matthew's gaze wandered past Simon and settled on the picture of Rani and her brother on the mantel. Behind the glass frame, Rani appeared to be smiling directly at him. His eyes narrowed as he studied her face and wished that it were so. When he worked for Little River, he'd often seen his friends' wives smile at them that way, but he'd never had a woman respond to him in kind. He pushed himself up straighter in his chair and swallowed hard. "You've got two fine-looking children, Simon."

Simon turned his head to look at the picture and smiled. "We're proud of them. You'll get to meet Stephen later."

Granny chuckled to herself, and the rocker creaked. "When Simon first held that baby girl, I heard him whisper somethin' in her ear. When I asked him what he said, he told me about Ranita bein' a Hebrew word for *my joy, my song.* He knowed right off she was gonna bring lots of joy to him and Anna. I reckon he was set on that name, but we've never called her anything but Rani."

My joy. Matthew remembered how he'd felt the moment he saw Rani at the mountain laurel bush. Now he understood. Her name suited her well.

He was about to tell Granny and Simon that when he was interrupted by the frantic barking of a dog followed by a knock at the front door. Granny gripped the arms of her chair and started to push to her feet, but Simon stepped away from the mantel and headed across the room. "Don't get up. I'll see who it is." He opened the door, chuckled, and snapped his fingers. "Scout, hush up! George, get in here before that dog eats you up."

Matthew rose and faced the door as a young man stepped into the room. "I don't know why that dog don't like me. I never done anything to him."

Granny laughed. "Don't worry 'bout it, George. Scout's mighty choosy when it comes to the folks he likes. He don't take up with many people."

He nodded. "You can say that again."

As he had when he first saw Rani, Matthew sensed something familiar about the young man's appearance. His neatly combed red hair lay plastered to his head, and freckles dotted his nose and cheeks. He gripped a battered straw hat in one hand and stuck out his other hand to shake Simon's. "I just thought I'd stop by and see how ev'rybody's doin'." He walked to Granny's chair and smiled down at her. "Ev'nin', Granny. How you doin' tonight?"

She smiled up at him. "I'm fine, George." She pointed toward Matthew. "This here's Matthew Jackson. He used to live in the Cove years ago. He just bought his old homestead and is a-comin' back to live. He's gonna be a-stayin' here until he can get his cabin fixed up."

George grinned at him, stepped around Granny's chair, and stuck out his hand. "Pleased to know you, Matthew. I'm George Ferguson, Pete Ferguson's boy. I reckon you knowed my pa when you lived here."

Now he understood why George looked familiar. He had the freckles and wiry body just like all the Fergusons he'd ever known. Matthew grasped George's hand and smiled. "Yeah, and your sister, Lucy, and your brother, Ted. You were just a baby when we moved away."

Simon walked up beside George and slapped him on the back. "Well, he's not a baby anymore. He and his pa raise some of the best corn in the Cove."

George nodded. "I reckon we do all right."

"Did I hear someone come in?" Anna's voice drifted into the room before she stepped through the door. Her eyes grew wide, and a smile pulled at her mouth when she spotted George. "I thought you'd be over at Ted and Josie's tonight helping them get ready to leave in the morning."

He shook his head. "Already done that and said my goodbyes. I just wish they weren't goin'. But you know Ted. He's always been independent. Wouldn't farm with Pa and me. Had to try on his own. When he couldn't make it, he decided to go to Townsend. Ma sure hates to see them leave. Especially now that they have the baby."

Anna walked over to George and hugged him. "Well, we're glad you're staying right here in the Cove." She turned to Matthew, her arm around George's waist. "Matthew, George was the first baby I helped Granny deliver when I came to the Cove. He's always been my special one."

George glanced down at Anna, and the love he had for her shown in his eyes. Matthew knew how George must feel. He'd felt that way since childhood too. He was about to say so when another voice interrupted.

"George? What are you doing here tonight?"

Matthew glanced around to see Rani standing in the kitchen door. A dishtowel dangled from her hands. The look George had flashed at Anna intensified as he stared at Rani. "I thought I'd come by and set for a spell."

The meaning behind his words hit Matthew like a brick. The real meaning of George's visit wasn't to visit with Simon and Anna. He was here to see Rani. He had come to court her.

Matthew clenched his fists at his side and bit down on his lip. Suddenly he felt like an outsider. He'd been gone for years and knew nothing about what had happened in the Cove during his absence. People had lived and died here. Those he'd known had married and had babies that were now grown. He'd missed being a part of life in the Cove. So why did he care that a young man had come to court a woman he hadn't even known existed until today? He might not understand why it bothered him, but he knew it did.

As he stared at her a slight flush colored Rani's cheeks, and she darted a quick glance in his direction. Before he could say anything, Anna motioned to Simon. "Come help me finish the dishes so Rani can visit with George."

Granny reached for her cane and grasped the handle. "And I reckon it's time I was a-gettin' to bed." Anna and Simon helped Granny to her feet and held to her for a moment as she struggled to get her balance. When she'd steadied herself, she smiled at George. "It's good to see you, boy. Tell your folks hello for me."

He nodded. "I'll do it, Granny."

Anna glanced over her shoulder at Matthew as she and Simon led Granny toward the kitchen. "Come with us, Matthew. I'll show you to Stephen's room. It's in the addition Simon built on the back of the cabin."

Matthew nodded and glanced at George. "It was good meeting you, George. I hope I'll see you again soon."

George grinned again, and Matthew was struck by the young man's friendly manner. "Me too. If'n you need any help a-gettin' your cabin and barn rebuilt, let me and Pa know. We'd be glad to give you a hand."

"Thanks. I'll remember that." He turned and followed Simon and Anna. Rani had stepped into the room and stood next to the kitchen door. As he approached she backed away, her hands clasped behind her back, and stared at the floor. He stopped beside her. "Goodnight, Rani."

"Goodnight, Matthew." Her icy words sent a chill down his spine.

He'd hoped she'd say something else. When she didn't, he hurried into the kitchen and followed Simon and Anna down a narrow hallway to the left of the back door. Simon, who'd picked up the oil lamp from the kitchen table, held it high to light their way.

"John and I built this addition when Stephen and Rani were born," Simon was saying. "We built four rooms back here in hopes we'd have a larger family." His voice cracked on the last words, and he and Anna exchanged quick glances. After a moment he continued. "Anyway, Rani and Stephen each had a room, and Anna uses one for all her herbs and medical supplies. And now Granny has the other one."

An awkward silence followed Simon's words, and Matthew cleared his throat. "I'm sorry I haven't asked you about your brother and his family. Do they still live in the Cove?"

Simon nodded. "Yes. Besides my duties at the church, I help John farm the land our parents left us. He and Martha have three children. Annie married and moved to Townsend where her husband got a job. Rachel and Daniel are still at home."

Matthew chuckled. "I guess I have a lot of catching up to do. But for now I really appreciate you letting me stay in Stephen's room."

"You're welcome as long as you need a place," Simon said. He and Anna came to a stop, and he leaned over and kissed Granny on the cheek. "Goodnight. I hope you have sweet dreams."

A soft chuckle rumbled in her throat. She turned and patted Matthew's arm. "I reckon I will. Having this boy back is some of the best medicine I've had in years."

Matthew's eyes burned, but he forced the tears back. He swallowed, leaned forward, and hugged Granny. "This is the best day I've had since I lost my ma and Eli."

"And we's got lots of good times a-comin'. I know the Lord's gonna bless you, Matthew."

"He already has just letting me be here with all of you."

She smiled again and hobbled into her room. The light from an oil lamp on a table by her bed sent a soft glow across the room and cast her shadow on the far wall. His heart pricked at her stooped shoulders. Granny had always seemed invincible to him, able to tackle any task and be successful. But the years of hard living in the Cove had taken their toll, and even she wasn't immune to their effect.

Anna closed the door and pointed to the room across the hall. "This is where you'll sleep. Rani's room is on the other side of Granny's, and my herb room is next to yours. I think you'll find everything you need, but let me know if you don't." She turned to Simon. "Why don't you light the lamp on the bedside table for Matthew?"

Simon nodded, walked into the room, and pulled the chimney from the lamp. Within moments, light filtered across the room. "There you go, Matthew."

Matthew glanced through the doorway at the bed covered with a patchwork quilt. He could see some books on a shelf on one wall and a hunting rifle hanging on another. He couldn't help feeling a little envious of the boy who'd been lucky enough to grow up here. He shook the thought from his head and smiled. "Thank you both for letting me stay in your son's room. I'll try not to be a bother while I'm here."

Simon waved his hand in dismissal. "You're always welcome here. It's like having long-lost family return." He reached for Anna's hand and started to walk back to the kitchen, but he paused at the doorway. "I may not see you in the morning. John and I are going to cut wood for the cook stoves. I should be back by noon, but you may be gone by then."

Matthew nodded. "I'm going back to my farm in the morning and look things over. I've got a lot to do there, and I have to figure out where the best place is to start. After I do, I plan on going back to Townsend to buy what I need."

"But you'll be here tomorrow night?"

"I doubt it. I may leave tomorrow."

"How many days you think you'll be gone?" Simon asked.

"About three, I guess. I want to be back by Saturday so I can be here for Granny's birthday."

Anna smiled. "Good. And try to get back in time to help us celebrate her family birthday Saturday night."

He nodded. "I will."

They turned and disappeared through the doorway that led into the kitchen. After a moment Matthew entered the room. He walked to the shelf and trailed his fingers across the books' spines as he read the titles. *The Count of Monte Cristo, The Three Musketeers, Moby Dick.*

Matthew smiled. So Simon and Anna had a son who liked adventure and read about what was happening in other parts of the world. But their daughter seemed very different. She appeared to be more concerned about what was happening to the valley she'd lived in all her life.

He sat down on the edge of the bed and let his gaze travel over the small room. It came to rest on the lamp Simon had lit. A round, clay bowl streaked with orange and black sat on the table next to it. He picked up the container and stared at the arrowheads it held inside. He could imagine Simon taking his son on a walk through the fields as they searched for remnants of the Cherokee people who had once lived in this valley.

He held up one of the arrowheads to the light and studied it before he placed it back in the bowl and set it on the table. There was no doubt in his mind that Simon and Anna's son had lived a happy life here with his parents. Nothing like what he had endured at the hands of his father.

He undressed, lay down on top of the patchwork quilt, and put his hands behind his head. As he stared up at the ceiling, Rani's face drifted into his mind. Ever since he'd encountered her at his farm, he hadn't been able to get her out of his mind. It was as if she had some kind of hold on him, and he didn't understand it.

Maybe what he needed was a good night's sleep. He might feel differently in the morning. Like his mother always said, you never could tell what a new day would bring.

Chapter 4

Anna read back over her journal entry for today. She closed the book and rubbed her hands over the smooth leather cover. How many journals had she filled with her thoughts since coming to Cades Cove over twenty years ago? She smiled as she remembered how the first one had contained Granny's instructions about the medicinal uses of herbs. In the years since, she'd written of her life with Simon and their children. Someday she would pass them all to her grandchildren.

Smiling, she laid the book in the desk drawer and pushed herself up from her chair. She walked to the bedroom door and peeked out to see if Rani and George were still talking. The low buzz of their voices drifted from the front room. Smiling, she closed the door and walked back to sit on the edge of the bed. As she pulled the brush she held through her long hair, her gaze traveled over Simon in the chair next to the lamp table.

For the last fifteen minutes, he'd been absorbed in the Scripture passage he was reading. She liked this time of night when they could be alone in their bedroom without the normal distractions of family life.

The muscle in her husband's jaw flexed as it did whenever he was concentrating, and a slight frown puckered his brow every so often. Through the years she'd come to know and love all his little mannerisms. His facial expression told her that he was committing something to memory. Probably a passage he'd use in his sermon next Sunday.

Her gaze traveled to the gray streaks in the hair around his ears. She smiled softly in spite of herself. He had been concerned when the first ones had appeared, but she assured him it gave him a more distinguished look. To her he would always be the young man whose laughing eyes had captured her heart the day she arrived in Cades Cove and stepped from her uncle's buggy.

After a minute he shut his Bible and placed it on the table. He closed his eyes and pinched the bridge of his nose before he looked up at her. "Is George still here?"

She nodded. "I could hear them talking in the front room."

Simon picked up his pocket watch he'd placed on the table beside him, looked at it, and frowned. "Doesn't that boy ever know when to go home?"

Anna laughed and laid her brush on the bedside table. "I'm sure he'll leave in a little while." She stood up, stretched her arms over her head, and yawned. "I wonder if he's going to propose soon?"

Simon's eyebrows arched, and his eyes widened. "Propose? Why would you think such a thing? Rani's not old enough to get married."

A laugh rumbled in her throat, and she ran to him and settled herself in his lap. His arms encircled her, and she leaned her head against his shoulder. He tightened his embrace and nuzzled her ear.

She reached up and stroked his cheek. "So you think Rani's too young to think about marriage. Did you ever consider the fact that she's the same age I was when we married?"

His lips grazed her cheek. "That was different. You were more mature."

She pulled away from him and stared into his face. "Why, Simon Martin, I didn't have any idea what life was all about until I came to the Cove and fell in love with you."

His eyes lit up with a teasing glint. "Yes, I did have a time persuading you that you could be happier living in a cabin in the mountains than you could be in a bustling city."

She swatted at his arm. "You make it sound like I was a spoiled girl."

His dark eyes narrowed. "Have you ever been sorry you stayed instead of going to New York to nursing school?"

Her hand cupped his cheek, and she leaned forward and brushed his lips with hers. "How could I be sorry? I found the greatest love any woman could ever have, and you've made me happier than I could ever have thought possible."

He swallowed, and his Adam's apple bobbed. "The first time I saw you I knew God had sent you here for me. I love you more today than I did the day we married."

"And I love you too." She smiled and settled back against him. "Life hasn't been easy here, but God has gotten us through some rough times."

They were both silent for a moment before he whispered, "I saw you staring at Willie's picture tonight. It doesn't get any easier, does it?"

"Easier? I don't think it ever will." Tears filled her eyes, and she shook her head. "I try not to question why God took him, but sometimes I do anyway."

Simon let out a long sigh. "So do I. Some days I wake up hoping I dreamed he's gone, then I know it's real." He was silent for a moment. "A preacher is supposed to be a man of faith, and I pray every day God will give me strength to bear that great loss. Then it's as if God speaks to me and says His Son died too, and I realize He knows how I feel. That helps."

She cuddled closer to him. "One of my sweetest memories is how quickly Willie could memorize a Bible verse you taught him."

Simon chuckled. "Yes. I told him he was going to know the whole Bible before he was grown. I thought God had given me a son to follow me in the ministry."

She reached up and covered his hands with hers. "Is that why you've been so insistent on Stephen going to seminary?"

"Maybe . . . but it's only driven him away from us. I'm sorry about that, Anna. God has been dealing with me, and I've come to understand Stephen isn't Willie. When Stephen comes home in July, I'm going to tell him I support his decision to go to medical school."

Anna sat up straight, threw her arms around Simon's neck, and hugged him. "Oh, I knew God would make you see what Stephen's path should be." She leaned back and smiled at him. "You are a good husband and a good father. Now you need to realize Rani is growing up too. Don't be surprised if she wants to get married soon."

75

Simon rose to his feet, stood Anna in front of him, and wagged a finger at her. "Now even if George is your favorite of Rani's friends, don't you go matchmaking. I don't think he has the right temperament for Rani."

Anna frowned and propped her hands on her hips. "Temperament? What are you talking about?"

Simon rubbed his chin. "You've always been blind where the Ferguson children are concerned. I know you care deeply about them, but you have to admit that Pete and Laura let them get away with a lot when they were growing up."

Anna rolled her eyes and chuckled. "And you have to admit that you thought they were spoiled rotten."

"They were," Simon said. "George is the worst of the bunch. Pete's never been able to do anything with him, and Laura makes excuses for everything he does. Pete tells me that George acts like a child when he doesn't get his way. He says sometimes George will sulk for days without speaking to him or Laura. He's about at the end of his rope with the boy."

Anna's eyes darkened. "Does Rani know this?"

"I think she does. At least I haven't seen any indication that George is anything more than a friend to her. Rani is headstrong, and she has a sharp tongue sometimes. Can you imagine how she would react when George got into one of his feeling-sorry-for-himself moods?"

Anna laughed. "Well, then, what kind of man do you think she needs?"

Simon thought for a moment before he answered. "She doesn't need a man who's going to give in to her all the time. She needs somebody who loves her so much he'll let her share his life and work but who'll stand up to her and tell her when she's wrong."

Anna's mouth gaped open. "Why, Simon Martin, you have really surprised me tonight. I've never heard you talk this way."

He screwed his mouth into a grimace. "Well, I've never heard you talk about our daughter getting married before either."

They stared at each other for a few moments before Anna burst out laughing. "It's really a treat living with you, Simon. I never know what you're going to say or do."

He grinned and winked at her. "A little spice in a marriage is always good. And these last twenty years have been the best of my life."

She leaned over and blew the lamp out. "And they just keep getting better."

A clock chimed somewhere in the house and woke Matthew out of a restless sleep. He bolted up into a sitting position and clutched the edge of the bed. It took him a minute to realize he wasn't in the room he shared with other workers in Little River's company town. He was in Simon and Anna's home.

He raked his hand through his hair and pushed himself to his feet. He'd had enough sleepless nights in the past to know it would be a long time before he'd drift off again. Usually a walk helped relax him.

He pulled on his clothes and stepped into the hallway. No sounds came from Granny's room. He eased into the kitchen, but Simon and Anna weren't there. The door to their bedroom on the other side of the kitchen was closed, and no light filtered underneath the doorway.

Convinced all the family was asleep, he crossed the kitchen and was about to enter the front room when he stopped at the sound of voices. "And Pa says we gonna have a good crop this year, Rani. If'n we do, Pa's gonna build me a cabin on that piece of land next to where we live."

"That's nice, George." Rani's voice drifted through the door.

Matthew stood frozen in place. George was talking about building a cabin? Matthew might have been gone from the Cove for twenty years, but he knew what that meant. When a family built a cabin for their son, it was so he could get married and have his own starter place.

Matthew's heart slammed against his chest. George wanted to marry Rani. She must be considering it, or George wouldn't be calling on her. Suddenly it seemed as if the walls were closing in around him. He needed to get some air.

Gasping for breath, he stumbled through the backdoor into the yard. He stood in the dark trying to calm his racing heart. There was no moon tonight, and the darkness surrounded him. He squinted to make out the mountains he knew were in the distance. Only a dim outline shadowed the horizon. After a few minutes, his pulse slowed, and he walked around the side of the cabin and into the front yard.

A large tree sat at the front corner of the cabin, and he remembered seeing a chair on the end of the porch when he'd arrived earlier. He could imagine Granny sitting there in the afternoons "soaking up the mountains" as she used to say. He put his foot on the first step to the porch but stopped when a low growl rumbled nearby. The light filtering through the cabin window revealed Scout standing next to the chair, his teeth bared.

"Easy boy." Matthew eased onto the porch and came to a stop in front of the dog. He knelt down and held out his hand. "I'm not going to hurt you. I just want to be your friend."

Scout growled again and took a step forward. Matthew didn't move. "Don't be afraid. Come to me." Scout hesitated a moment before he took a step forward and sniffed Matthew's hand.

"Good boy." Matthew moved his hand closer, placed it on Scout's head, and rubbed the soft fur. "Yeah, we're going to be great friends."

Scout whined, licked at Matthew's hand, and lay back down beside the chair. Matthew smiled as he eased himself into the seat and closed his eyes, reaching over to stroke Scout.

Rani's muffled voice could be heard coming from the front room of the cabin. He couldn't tell what she was saying, but just the sound of it had a calming effect on him. He leaned back and sighed.

Even with all the strange emotions he'd experienced today, it was good to be home. And he knew it wasn't just because of seeing those he'd left behind years ago. The most pleasure had come from meeting a dark-eyed girl who stirred him in ways no woman ever had.

Rani stifled a yawn. It was getting late, but George didn't seem to notice. She glanced at the clock on the wall and wondered if he hadn't heard it chime a while ago or if he had ignored it. Usually she could let him ramble on about his crops and what he and his father had planned for next year, but not tonight.

For some reason she felt restless and wished he would hurry and end his visit. The thought made her feel guilty, and she straightened in her chair. After all, George's family was well respected in the Cove, and they'd been close friends and members of her father's church ever since she could remember. She had played with George and his brother and sister all her life, but as she'd told Josie this afternoon, she wasn't in love with him.

"Are you list'nin' to me, Rani?" George's voice pulled her from her thoughts, and she blinked.

"I'm sorry. I guess my mind is wandering."

His bottom lip drooped. It reminded Rani of the young children in the Sunday school class she taught. "Well, I was a-talkin' to you," he whined. "Maybe you ain't too interested in what I was sayin'."

She reached up and smoothed her hair away from her face. "Don't be ridiculous, George. I'm a little tired after going over to Josie and Ted's cabin today."

His eyebrows arched. "Did you walk over there and back?"

"I did. You know I walk everywhere I go. It gives me time to think."

The pout disappeared and was replaced by a big grin. He propped an elbow on his knee and leaned forward. "I hope you was thinkin' about me."

"I had a lot on my mind. You know, like Little River Lumber and what they're doing to the Cove. And Ted and Josie moving away. I still can't believe he's gone to work for that company."

He slapped his knee and jumped to his feet. "I declare, Rani," he snarled, "I don't understand you at all. Most girls your age are thinkin' about gettin' married and settlin' down, but not you. All you think about is takin' on the biggest company in this part of the country and runnin' 'em out of the mountains."

Rani bristled at his words, and her eyes narrowed. "And why shouldn't I want them to leave? They're stripping our hills of trees that have been growing here for hundreds of years. And they're not replacing them. We won't live to see those hillsides covered in trees again."

"Well, what's that to me? By that time we'll all be dead and gone. All we can do is live for the right now, and I want to do that." He paused, straightening up and adjusting his posture. "And I want you to do it with me," he declared.

His words infuriated her. How could anyone who'd grown up in the Cove be so uncaring about its future? She stood up and faced him, her hands clenched at her sides. "George, you've been my good friend ever since we were children, but we think differently about a lot of things. I know you're going to find a girl who wants the same things from life that you do."

He took a step back from her and let his gaze rove over her face as if he couldn't believe what she'd just said. "Are you sayin' that you're not that girl?"

She took a deep breath. "I'm saying we're never going to be anything but friends. You need someone who loves you and wants to share her life with you."

He nodded. "I see." He turned his back and faced the fireplace. He stood there a moment before he turned and stared at her. The anger she'd seen before when he'd been denied something lined his face. "I've been callin' on you for months, Rani, and you ain't never said nothin' like this before. Why did you wait until tonight?"

She frowned and started to protest that she'd tried to tell him for weeks. But before she could speak, Matthew Jackson's face flashed in her mind, and she remembered how her heart had pumped when he'd stared at her across the table at supper. She shook the thought from her head and lifted her chin. "It's time we got on with our lives, George. You'll always be one of my best friends, but you need to look somewhere else for a woman who will love you."

His face grew red, and he raked his hand through his hair. "I cain't believe you're turnin' me down." He pointed a finger at her. "I'm warning you, though, I ain't givin' up. I'll keep comin' back until you change your mind." He rammed his hat on his head. "Now I guess I'd better be gettin' on home. It's late."

Rani followed him out the door and stopped at the bottom of the front porch steps. George strode to the horse he'd tied to a small tree in their yard and grabbed the reins. He was about to climb into the saddle when he shook his head and led his horse back to where she stood. He raised an arm and gripped her shoulder.

"I reckon I ain't ever come out and said the words, Rani, but I want you to know I love you. Don't that mean anything to you?"

She wiggled in his grip. "Please, George . . ."

He tightened his grip on her shoulders. "We're alike, and we got lots in common. We grew up here, we've been in church together all our lives, and my folks would welcome you into our family."

She blinked back tears. "I know they would."

He released her and stepped back. "I ain't givin' up, Rani. Like I said, I'll keep comin' back 'til you change your mind. I want you for my wife, and I intend to have you." He gripped the reins in his hand tighter and swung into the saddle, then looked down at her. "That's a promise."

Without another word, he turned the horse and disappeared into the thick darkness. She stood still, her shoulders slumped, and listened to the hoofbeats recede in the distance before she trudged back to the cabin.

She'd just stepped onto the porch when a noise to her right caught her attention, and she whirled. The dogwood tree next to the house cast dark shadows over the end of the porch. She squinted to see what had made the sound, then gasped and covered her mouth with her hand. She didn't know which shocked her more—the fact that Matthew Jackson was staring at her from the porch chair a few feet away or that Scout lay at his feet as if they were best friends.

She started to speak, and then her face grew warm. The truth hit her. Matthew's presence and Scout's attachment to him were the least of her concerns right now. Of all the people in the world, Matthew was the last one she would have wanted to overhear her conversation with George, and that bothered her most of all.

Rani and George had been too involved in their conversation to notice him when they came out of the cabin, and Matthew tried not to move as she came back up the steps. Just as she reached the top of the porch, Scout stirred in his sleep and whined.

Matthew's hopes that Rani would go back into the cabin without seeing him died when she turned and stared at him. Darkness shielded her face, but he could hear her gasp. He rose to his feet and took a step toward her. Beside him, Scout raised his head, looked from Rani to him, then lowered his head again.

She spoke before he could explain why he was on the porch. "What are you doing out here? I thought everybody had gone to bed."

He shoved his hands deep in his pockets and nodded. "They have. I guess I was still too excited over being back home to sleep. I thought I'd get some air, but I wasn't spying on you and your friend."

Rani walked closer, and now the light coming through the window lit her face. She glanced down at her dog. "It looks like you've made friends with Scout. How did you manage that?"

He chuckled. "I don't know. It seems like we just kind of drifted into a mutual agreement that we liked each other. He's a fine dog. I noticed that right away when you threatened to sic him on me this afternoon."

Her eyes narrowed, and her gaze flicked over his face as if searching for some assurance he could be trusted. She arched an eyebrow, propped her hands on her hips, and nodded toward the sleeping dog. "I don't guess I can threaten you with that from now on."

"I guess not."

"Scout's always been a good judge of character. You should feel honored he took to you like he did." Her mouth opened as if she was about to say something else, but she hesitated. She bit down on her lip and took a deep breath. "I need to apologize to you, Matthew."

His eyes grew wide. "Why?"

She tilted her head to one side. "For one thing, I haven't been very friendly to you since you came. My dislike for Little River made me jump to conclusions about you this afternoon."

"I'm glad to hear that. Maybe you're beginning to think I may not be the enemy in disguise out to buy up all the timber in the Cove. I assure you I'm not." A slight frown pulled at his forehead. "Thank you for apologizing. I haven't known many people who would do that."

She didn't flinch from returning his gaze. "Well, I didn't decide to apologize on my own. Mama told me to do it."

At her words he threw back his head and laughed. When he'd calmed, he glanced at her, and her eyes seemed to sparkle in the lamplight. A slight smile pulled at her lips. "Then I suppose I have your mother to thank for getting to see that pretty smile on your face."

He couldn't be sure in the dim light, but he thought he detected a slight flush on her cheeks. Her smile deepened, and she glanced down at her feet. "I suppose so, but I really am sorry. It shouldn't bother me that you used to work for Little River."

"I told you I don't anymore."

"I get so angry every time I think about those people and what they're doing to our mountains. What made you go to work for them?"

With a sigh, he walked to the edge of the porch and leaned up against one of the posts. He stared into the distance and at the dark outline of the

Smokies. "I love these hills, Rani. All I've ever wanted was to come back here, but at times I thought I wouldn't make it." He pushed himself up to his full height and faced her. "I lost my mother and Eli, the only family I had. You're a young girl. You've always had parents who loved you and took care of you. You can't begin to know what it's like to be alone."

She stepped closer. "You're right. I don't. Do you want to talk about it?"

Something in the tone of her voice pierced the deep part of his heart where dark memories lay. How he wished he could rid himself of them, but he couldn't. He'd tried to bury them just like he had his mother and brother, but they returned to remind him of who he was and what he'd come from.

He shook his head. "You don't want to hear about my past and what I've been through. I'll just say this: When you're hungry and nobody's willing to give you a chance, you'll take whatever job you're offered. I took Little River's job, and it brought me home. I'm thankful for that."

"I see," she said. "You're right. I can't know what's happened to you since you left here, and I was wrong to judge you so quickly. But you're also wrong about something."

"What?"

"I may be young, but I'm not a girl. Some folks think of me as a woman."

The lift of her chin relayed the challenge of her words, and he smiled. In that gesture he saw a fleeting glimpse of his mother and the way she'd stood her ground at times against his father.

"George seems to think so. I couldn't help overhearing your conversation."

She sighed. "George was upset with me."

Matthew nodded. "I could tell something was wrong, but he sounded like he's mighty taken with you."

"That's what he says, and I don't like hurting him." A sad look flickered across her face. "He's been a friend all my life, but we don't think alike on lots of things. I know he's going to find someone who'll love him."

Matthew's heart pounded. "Are you saying that someone isn't you?"

"Yes. All I want is for George to be my friend."

A slow smile pulled at his mouth, and he let his gaze drift over her face. "I hope you'll be my friend too, even if I am a lot older than you."

She tilted her head to one side and studied him. "I don't think there's any age limit on friendship. I was trying to figure out earlier how old you are, and I decided you must be about thirty."

"I will be soon. And you?"

"I'll be nineteen on my birthday."

He tried to remember where he'd been and what he'd been doing when he was nineteen, but it seemed like ages ago. Some of the things that had happened to him back then were too shameful to remember, but he couldn't change the past. All he could do was try to make the future better. But no matter how much he didn't want it to, the past did influence the future.

He took a deep breath. "Well, if George isn't the one, I'm sure there are other young men in the Cove who are just waiting for their chances with you. You'll find somebody."

"Maybe, but I'm in no hurry." She took a deep breath and stepped backward. "But it's late, and I need to get inside. Are you coming?"

He shook his head. "Not yet. I'll stay out here with Scout a little longer. I'll see you in the morning."

"Goodnight, Matthew."

"Goodnight, Rani."

He watched her enter the cabin and then sat back down. He stared down at his shaking hands and clasped them in front of him. The conversation he'd just had with Rani had his mind whirling.

What was it about Rani that fascinated him? She was beautiful, to be sure, but there was something else that intrigued him: She shared his love of the Cove. From the moment he'd first seen her, she had occupied his thoughts. No other woman had ever done that. And even if he had called her a girl, she was right. She was a woman.

He shook his head. He shouldn't be thinking like this. Rani was Simon and Anna's daughter, and that was reason enough for him to keep his distance. The fact that she was so young also presented a problem.

There were already many obstacles to over-come if he was going to rebuild his life in the Cove, and he didn't need to complicate matters more. There was only one thing to do—thank Simon and Anna for their hospitality and insist on staying at his farm. If he was away from her, he could focus on other things.

A groan rose in his throat. He was only deceiving himself. No matter where he was, he knew he would never forget how the breath had almost left his body when he first spotted her by the mountain laurel bush.

Chapter 5

Rani came to a stop outside the henhouse door and counted the eggs in her basket. Satisfied with the number she had gathered, she turned toward the house but stopped and gazed into the distance.

This morning the hazy mists that hung over the mountains were not as dense as usual. She shaded her eyes with her hands and stared toward the hills that rimmed her valley. Today the trees that blanketed the hillsides glimmered in the sunshine, and it looked as if their branches were lifted in gratitude toward heaven and their Creator. With scenery like that and the sweet scent of wildflowers, like the honeysuckle that grew on the post at the end of their clothesline, you couldn't find a more beautiful place to live than Cades Cove.

She'd never seen a picture of another place that could compare with the sight of the sun filtering through the low-hanging clouds that gave the Smokies their name. She remembered sitting in her father's lap when she was a child and asking him what made *her* mountains smoke. He'd told her that even though she couldn't see God, she could be assured He was nearby every time she looked at the mountains. Then he'd taught her the words from the Psalms that she'd never forgotten. *He looketh on the earth, and it trembleth: he toucheth the hills, and they smoke.*

Her father's words had proven true through the years. Even when she felt the sadness creeping back into her soul, she could look at the mountains and know God hadn't forgotten her. She closed her eyes and thanked Him for giving her that visible sign of His presence.

When she'd finished praying, she opened her eyes and turned toward the house. The whinny of a horse near the barn caught her attention, and she glanced over her shoulder. Her fingers tightened on her basket as Matthew Jackson, leading his saddled horse, emerged from the barnyard and walked toward her. Scout trotted alongside him.

His steady gaze locked on her, and he didn't waver as he approached. When he was a few feet away, he came to a stop, but Scout ran to her and jumped up on her. Rani pulled her gaze away from Matthew, leaned over, and scratched Scout behind the ears. "How are you this morning, boy? I thought you were probably off chasing a rabbit."

She looked up slowly and stared into Matthew's face. He pushed the hat he wore back on his head and nodded. "He's been keeping me company at the barn." His somber expression gave no hint of whether he was glad to see her or not.

Rani straightened, shifted the basket of eggs in front of her, and grasped the handle with both hands. "Are you leaving already?"

"Yes." He squinted up at the sun. "I'm later getting off than I meant to be, but I got carried away visiting with Anna and Granny during breakfast. I was just on my way back to the house to tell them I was leaving."

"Then I'm glad I saw you before you left. Will you be back tonight?"

He shook his head. "I don't think so. I'm going to take a better look around my place this morning and see what I need to get for repairs. I'll probably go on to Townsend this afternoon to buy what I need."

"I don't mean to sound discouraging, but from the looks of the cabin you're going to need a lot of materials. And it's going to take a good amount of work."

"I know, but I'm up to it. Coming back and making a go on that piece of land is what's kept me going for years. Besides, I've already had an offer to help rebuild."

"You have? Who?"

A smile erased his impassive expression. "George volunteered last night. Of course that was before you broke his heart. If he's changed his mind, I may have you to blame."

Her cheeks burned as if they were on fire, and she started to make one of her biting retorts. Then she saw the teasing glint in his eyes and laughed. "Well, don't expect me to take his place. I'm helpless when it comes to using a hammer."

"I'll remember that, but I'm sure there are lots of other things you're good at."

She sighed. "That's what Mama and Granny keep telling me, but I don't know what they are. Maybe I'll find out some day."

"Maybe so." His horse tossed her head and snorted. Matthew reached up and placed his hand on the mare's neck without breaking eye contact with her.

He was doing it again—letting his gaze drift over her face while a slight smile pulled at his lips. And it was producing the same effect in her it had last night. She took a deep breath in hopes of calming the increased pumping of her heart. "So, did Mama fix you some food to take with you?"

"She did. I have it in my saddlebags."

"Then I'd better let you go so you can get on with your work." She started to back away but stopped. She couldn't let him leave without asking the question that burned in her mind. "When will you be back?"

"I hope I won't be gone longer than three days, so I should be back sometime Saturday afternoon. I want to be here for Granny's birthday celebration."

"She would be upset if you were to miss her shindig, as she calls it. She's really been looking forward to this for months. Besides, you'll get to see all your old friends."

A frown flickered across his face. "I wouldn't call them friends, Rani. Our family didn't have friends in the Cove. I doubt if anybody besides Granny and your parents will be glad I'm there."

The sad look on his face pricked her heart, and she took a step toward him. "You're forgetting me. I'll be glad you're there."

His gaze drifted over her face for a moment. "Will you? Have you changed your mind about me?"

Her pulse hammered, and she pressed the basket she held closer to her body. "If I remember correctly, I apologized last night, and we agreed to be friends. I look forward to getting to know you better."

He swallowed, and his Adam's apple bobbed. "I'd like that, Rani. I haven't had any friends in a long time."

She smiled. "Then it's good you came home."

"Home." He almost whispered the word. "That's a mighty sweet word."

"Yes, it is." She cleared her throat and glanced toward the house. "Now you should get going, and I need to get these eggs inside to Mama before she comes after me. She's already upset with me because I overslept this morning and missed breakfast."

A laugh rumbled in his throat. "Yeah, she did say something about that. I'll go with you and tell them goodbye."

He tied his horse to the clothesline and fell into step beside her. Rani glanced at him out of the corner of her eye. He was taller than George, and the top of her head appeared about level with Matthew's shoulder. The outline of rippling muscles beneath his shirt sleeves sent a surge of pleasure through her. Her breath caught in her throat at the thought niggling in the back of her mind. Without a doubt Matthew Jackson was the most handsome man she'd ever met, and just being near him stirred her in ways no one else ever had.

Her face grew warm, and she hurried forwar
to open the back door. Just as she reached for the
latch, his hand reached around her and grabbed
hold of it. They stood so close together her
shoulder touched his chest. "I'll get it," he said.
With a shove he pushed the door open and
stepped back for her to enter.

Granny still sat where she'd been when Rani
had left to gather the eggs. A cup of coffee sat on
the table in front of her, and she raised it to her
mouth as they entered the kitchen. Rani hurried
to her mother who stood at the sink washing
dishes. Behind her she heard Matthew approach
Granny.

"Here are the eggs, Mama." She set the basket
on a shelf beside the stove and inhaled. "Mmm,
something smells good. Did you make more
biscuits?"

"I had some dough left over and cut out a few
for you." She arched an eyebrow. "Since you
missed breakfast."

"Thanks. You are too good to me. I'm starved
this morning." Rani put her arm around her
mother's shoulders and gave her a hug. As she
turned toward the table, Matthew leaned over
and planted a kiss on Granny's cheek. She
reached up and patted his cheek.

"I wanted to say goodbye before I took off. I
should be back in a few days."

Granny swiveled in her chair and stared up

him. "Now you be careful, boy. And you come back here as soon as you can."

"I will, Granny," he said. "And take care of my new friend for me while I'm gone."

Granny tilted her head to one side and stared up at him. "What new friend?"

Rani's eyes grew wide and her body tensed. He glanced at her, and the twinkle in his eyes set her heart to racing. "Scout."

Mama turned and propped one hand on her hip. "What? That dog doesn't like anybody outside of our family. How did you manage that?"

Matthew shrugged. "I sat out on the porch after everybody went to bed last night, and before I knew it Scout was lying beside me. He followed me to the barn this morning too."

Granny shook her head and laughed. "Then you oughta feel real special. You the first person I've known him to take a likin' to."

"Yeah, I remember how he barked at George last night." He looked at Rani, and a teasing smile pulled at his mouth.

Her face burned, but she managed to smile. "I can't figure out why Scout doesn't like George."

"Well, I'll sure try not to do anything to cause him to mistrust me. I like it better when he's licking my hand than when he's trying to attack me." He straightened his shoulders and backed toward the door. "Now I'd better be on my way.

Much as I'd like to, I can't stay here all day and keep company with you three lovely ladies."

Granny waved her hand in dismissal. "Now quit that butterin' us up. We already right taken with you."

"That's also good to know, Granny." Matthew laughed and directed one last glance at Rani before he turned toward the door.

"Goodbye, Matthew. Hurry back!" her mother called out.

"Bye, Anna."

Rani hurried to the door and stared after him as he walked toward the clothesline. He untied his horse and started to mount, but he turned and looked back at her. He smiled and tipped his hat before he pulled himself into the saddle and galloped from the yard.

Rani closed her eyes. Before yesterday, Matthew Jackson had been someone she'd only known from the stories her parents told. Now that had changed. He had come into their home, and his brooding eyes and quick smile had touched her soul. Was it possible you could meet someone and know right away there was some kind of special bond between you?

Whether that was true or not, she knew that after the time she'd spent with Matthew last night and this morning, something in her life had changed. As of now, however, she had no idea what it was.

Her father pulled the buggy to a stop in front of Cecil and Pearl Davis's cabin and glanced over at Rani beside him. "I'm glad you came today. I know Pearl will be glad to see you."

Rani's chin trembled, and she stared down at her hands. "I wish I was a little girl again, and I was coming to play with Josie. It still doesn't seem real that she's not in the Cove anymore."

"I know. There are a lot of familiar faces gone now." Her father straightened and smiled. "Then there are some new ones, like Matthew."

Rani's skin warmed, and she reached for the basket her mother had sent to Mrs. Davis. Setting it in her lap, she lifted the cover and busied herself checking the contents. "I hope nothing spilled on our way over here. The roads seemed a little bumpy today."

Her father hopped out of the buggy to tie the horse to a tree, and she breathed a sigh of relief. She hoped her face hadn't disclosed how much the mention of Matthew's name excited her. He'd been gone for two days now, and all she could do was think about him. Maybe this trip to visit Josie's parents would give her something else to occupy her mind for a while.

As she climbed down from the buggy, Mrs. Davis ran out the front door of the cabin. A big smile covered her face, and she wiped her hands on her apron. "Cecil," she yelled. "We got comp'ny. Come see who done come a-visitin'.'"

The words were barely out of her mouth before Mr. Davis ambled around the side of the cabin from the back yard. Ever since she was a child, Rani had thought him the tallest and one of the strongest men she'd ever seen, but his size deceived many who didn't know him. Those who took the time to get to know the man behind what appeared to be an impenetrable façade found he had a tender heart for his friends and family. He was always the first to help when problems arose in the Cove.

His mouth cracked into a half smile when he spotted Rani coming toward him. His wife ran from the porch and reached her first. She threw her arms around Rani and hugged her. "It's so good to see you, darlin'. It seems like you ain't been over here in months." She held Rani at arms' length and glanced over her shoulder at her husband. "Don't she look good, Cecil?"

He nodded. "She shore does."

Rani wriggled out of Mrs. Davis's grasp and held out the basket. "Mama sent fresh bread and some of the dumplings she made last night. And Granny stuck in one of her apple pies."

Mrs. Davis's eyes lit up. "Did you hear that, Cecil? One of Granny's pies."

"Tell her we be beholden to her."

Her father walked up behind Rani and put his

arm around her shoulders. "No need for that. Not with all you've done for us. After that bad storm last spring knocked part of our chimney down, I don't reckon we'd have one now if you hadn't laid the bricks."

Mr. Davis stuck his hands in his pockets and nodded again. "Glad I could help out, Simon."

Mrs. Davis grabbed Rani's hand and pulled her toward the cabin. "Let's me and you go inside and visit while the men folks talk. I want to know all that's been a-goin' on with you since I last seen you."

Rani followed Mrs. Davis into the cabin and to the kitchen. Through the years very little had changed in this house where she'd spent so many hours when she was growing up. There were still few furnishings, and at times Rani knew there had been little food. One thing the home had never lacked was love. Josie had always been the bright spot in her parents' harsh life.

"Now you set right down at the table, and I'll cut you a piece of Granny's pie."

Rani slid into the chair and folded her arms on the table. "No thanks. Poppa and I can't stay long, and Mama will have dinner ready when we get back. I just wanted to come see you. I miss visiting here."

Tears glistened in Mrs. Davis's eyes. "I miss you too. It don't seem right that you and Josie are all grown up. And I cain't hardly believe Josie is a married woman with a baby." She smiled at the mention of her daughter's name. "But I reckon she's got a good husband, and Ted's gonna take care of her."

"I'm sure he will. Have you heard from them since they left for Townsend?"

She shook her head. "Don't think we've hardly had time for a letter to get back to us, but maybe soon. I shore do miss that baby."

Rani laughed. "He was so cute the other day when I helped Josie pack."

Mrs. Davis dropped down in the chair across from Rani and grinned. "That was real sweet of you to go help Josie. I remember when me and Josie saw you for the first time after you was born. Josie was about three years old, and she said right then and there that you was gonna be her baby. She loved you from the start, and I reckon you and her been best friends ever since."

"Yes, we have. I'm sure going to miss her. Maybe one of these days I'll get over to Townsend to visit her. Or maybe she'll come home for a visit."

Mrs. Davis shook her head. "I don't know when that will be. I 'spect Ted's gonna be busy workin'. But he did say his folks might go over to Townsend for a visit sometime this summer. Maybe you could go with them."

"Oh, I wouldn't want to intrude on a family visit."

Mrs. Davis waved her hand in dismissal and chuckled. "Intrude? From what Josie been a-tellin' me you're practic'ly family with the Fergusons since you thinkin' about marrying George. That shore would be nice if'n the two of you could be sisters."

Rani's mouth dropped open, and she shook her head. "I don't know where Josie gets her ideas sometimes. She's the one who wants me to marry George. I don't want that."

"Why not? He's a good boy."

"I know he is, and he's a good friend. But we're not getting married."

Mrs. Davis tilted her head to one side and directed a penetrating stare at her. "You could do a lot worse than George. He comes from one of the nicest families in the Cove."

Rani sighed. "I know. Josie's tried to convince me."

Mrs. Davis reached over and patted her hand. "Then think about what she's said."

"I know." Rani straightened in her chair and smiled. "Mrs. Davis, I've changed my mind. I think I'll have a small piece of Granny's pie."

"I knowed you couldn't pass it up." She jumped to her feet and hurried to the cupboard to get a plate.

Rani tried to concentrate on what Mrs. Davis was saying as she cut her a piece of pie, but it was impossible. All she could think about was how sad Josie had looked when Rani discovered that Josie had married a man she didn't love. She wondered how often Mrs. Davis had told her daughter what a good husband Ted would be. And he was a good husband. The sad part of it all was that Josie's heart belonged to someone else.

She didn't want to live like that. She wanted a man who made her heart race every time she looked at him—the way it had when Matthew tipped his hat to her the morning he left for Townsend. She took a bite of the pie when it was placed in front of her, but even Granny's cooking couldn't pull her thoughts away today.

Thirty minutes later Rani breathed a sigh of relief when her father called out that it was time to leave. Her visit with Josie's mother had proved unsettling. It seemed everyone close to her had decided she would marry George. Even her own mother had hinted at it several times.

As she stepped into the buggy to leave, she couldn't help wishing for the first time in her life she hadn't come to the Davis home today. But as much as she missed Josie, she knew the turmoil she was feeling wasn't because of her friend's absence. It was because of the strange emotions just the thought of Matthew produced in her.

They'd only gone a short distance when her father glanced at her and smiled. "Cecil and Pearl seemed happy to see you today."

"Yes."

A frown pulled his eyebrows across his nose. "You don't seem very talkative. Did something happen?"

She ran her perspiring hands down her skirt to smooth it out and then clenched her fists in her lap. "Sort of."

Her father pulled the horse to a stop and turned to face her. "Rani, if something's bothering you, I want to know what it is."

"Oh, Poppa," she said, "why do people think they have the right to tell you what you need to do?"

A surprised look flashed across his face, and he leaned back in the buggy seat. "I don't know. I guess that's a question people have been asking since the beginning of time." He pushed his hat back on his head and propped his foot on the dash rail. "Maybe they think they're giving you good advice. Your mother and I have always tried to help you make good decisions because we don't want to see you get hurt."

She pounded her fists on her knees and gritted her teeth. "But what if you knew you'd end up getting hurt in the long run if you followed their advice?"

"Then I suppose you should make your own choice." He exhaled and shook his head. "Rani, are you going to tell me what's bothering you, or are you going to keep me guessing?"

A tear rolled down her cheek. "Everybody

seems to think I should marry George, and I don't love him. He's a good friend, but I can't stand to think about living the rest of my life with somebody I don't love." She swiveled in her seat and stared at her father. "I want a man that I love so much that we look at each other like you and Mama do."

He lowered his foot to the floor of the buggy and met her gaze. "And you don't look at George that way?"

She shook her head so hard her hair whipped against her cheeks. "No."

Her father reached over, covered her hand with his, and sighed. "Oh, darling, it's so hard for me to think about you being old enough to talk about getting married. But I have to face the fact you're growing up." He cleared his throat. "But if my opinion means anything, I don't think you should marry George. You're young, Rani. You don't have to marry the first man who comes along. God is going to send you someone that He's picked out especially for you. Be patient and wait for him to find you."

She blinked back more tears. "Then you're not disappointed."

He threw back his head and laughed. "Disappointed? I'm thrilled. I've never thought George was the right man for you." He reached over and chucked her under the chin. "Besides, I'm not ready to lose my baby girl to another man. And I doubt if I ever will be. You can be an old maid for all I care."

Rani laughed and threw her arms around her father. "Oh, Poppa, I love you so much."

"I love you too." His voice choked on the last words. He released her and snapped the reins across the horse's back. "Now, we'd better be heading home. Your mama will wonder where we are. But first I'd like to stop by Matthew's place."

"Why?"

"I want to see how much needs to be done to get the cabin in shape. Cecil said he'd organize a group to come one day when the men are caught up in the fields. If Cecil can get a crew to join John and me, we ought to get Matthew's cabin rebuilt soon."

"I'm sure Matthew will appreciate that."

On the other hand, she didn't know how she felt about Matthew being able to stay in his cabin. That would mean he wouldn't be at their house as much, and that troubled her. She sat up straight and gritted her teeth. *Stop it, Rani Martin. You don't need to be thinking about a man you've just met.*

Even as the thought drifted through her mind, she knew it was impossible. She couldn't get the image of him tipping his hat to her out of her mind.

Late that afternoon Simon walked from the barn toward the house. His talk with Rani earlier had occupied his thoughts most of the day. Although he wasn't ready for his little girl to grow up, he knew he couldn't keep it from happening. Sometimes he could hardly believe that she and Stephen weren't racing around the cabin like they had when they were children. No doubt about it, he missed those days.

As he approached the house, he spotted Anna sitting under the tree in the back yard. She had her back to him, and he crept up behind her. When he stood behind her chair, he leaned over and kissed her cheek.

She jumped and swiveled in her seat to look up at him. "Simon! I didn't realize it was you! Why, I almost cut my finger."

He walked around to face her and glanced down at the pan of June apples in her lap. The skin of one dangled between her finger and the blade of her knife. He chuckled. "Maybe I could find something to bandage your cut like you did mine the first day we met."

She laughed and shook her head. "You still haven't forgotten that, have you?"

He dropped to the ground and crossed his legs. "I haven't forgotten a thing about the most important day of my life."

She held out a piece of apple. "Here. Eat this. I know your sweet talk is just a way of getting me to give you one of my apples."

He accepted the offered bite and popped it into

his mouth. "Thank you, Mrs. Martin, for taking such good care of your husband."

She laughed again, then settled back in her chair and picked up another apple. "I didn't get a chance earlier to ask you how Pearl and Cecil are doing."

"They're fine. Cecil is going to help Matthew with his cabin."

"That's good."

"Rani was upset when we left, though." He pulled a piece of grass from the ground and stuck it in the corner of his mouth.

Anna paused in cutting the apple and looked up. Concern shadowed her face. "Did something happen?"

He rubbed the back of his neck and wrinkled his forehead. "I guess she and Pearl were talking about Josie, and the conversation turned to Rani and George getting married."

Anna scooted to the edge of her seat and arched her eyebrows. "And?"

"It upset Rani. We talked about it on the ride home. She's concerned because she thinks everybody is trying to push her to marry George, and she doesn't want to."

"I suppose everybody in the Cove knows that George has been calling on her for months. Anybody can look at him and tell he's in love with her. Did she say why she didn't want to marry him?"

"Because she doesn't love him."

Anna propped her hands on her hips and frowned. "Well, I haven't seen any other young men coming around here. What did you tell her?"

"You know how I feel about this, Anna. I told Rani I didn't think she should marry George."

Anna set the pan of apples on the ground and started to rise. "You know I don't agree with you about George. Rani has loved him since they were children."

Simon grabbed her arm and pulled her back down into her chair. "Listen to what you're saying, Anna. It reminds me of a girl who grew up with a friend on the next farm. Paul Sparks was his name, I believe. Paul and all her family thought she should marry him, but she didn't want that. Do you remember why?"

Anna smiled sheepishly. "Because I didn't love him like a woman needs to love the man she marries. I loved him like a brother."

"Exactly. And that's why we have to leave Rani alone to make her own choice."

She clamped her lips together for a moment before she exhaled. "But George is so special to me because . . ."

"Because he was the first baby you helped deliver. But that's no reason for Rani to marry him." Simon arched an eyebrow as he looked at his wife. "Promise me you won't interfere in this."

She frowned and crossed her arms. "All right. I won't. But you make me sound like a terrible mother. You know I only want what's best for her."

"I know."

"Did she mention any other man she might be interested in?"

"No. I think she just wants to be left alone to make her own choice." He stood up and pulled Anna to her feet. He wrapped his arms around her and drew her close. "She did say something that touched me, though."

"What?"

"She said she wants a man she loves so much that they look at each other the way you and I look at each other."

"Oh, Simon, how sweet," she said. She wrapped her arms around his neck and pulled his face close to hers. "And I hope she finds someone she enjoys kissing as much as I like kissing you."

He covered her lips with his. He didn't know what he had done to deserve Anna, but he'd thanked the Lord every day for the last twenty years for sending her to the Cove. She'd worked by his side to minister to the people in this valley. In time she had earned their love and respect, but with him it was different. She'd taken over his heart the day she climbed out of her uncle's buggy.

Chapter 6

Since her visit to the Davis cabin yesterday, Rani had tried to keep busy so she wouldn't dwell on Matthew's absence. But when she'd gotten out of bed this morning her first thought had been that it was Saturday. Matthew was expected back today. Now with supper over and the setting sun barely visible on the horizon, she had begun to doubt he'd arrive after all.

She finished putting the last of the supper dishes away and walked out to the front porch. Scout, who'd lain beside the chair most of the day, jumped up the minute she stepped out the door and ran to her. She knelt down and patted his head. He whined and looked down the road, then back at her.

It was as if he was telling her he wanted Matthew to return too. She shook her head and wrapped her arms around his furry body. "Sometimes I think you're almost human," she said. "I've never seen you take a liking to anybody like you have to Matthew."

She rose and sank down in the chair where Matthew had sat the night they had talked about George. Scout settled beside her, and she dangled her hand down to rub his head. He looked up at her, and she smiled. "I'm sorry. I don't know what's keeping him."

Even though she'd tried to tell herself he could have been detained for any number of reasons, it was no use. He'd only been in their home a short time, but everyone, including Scout, had felt his absence. And the fact that she missed him surprised her more than anything.

The front door opened, and her father stuck his head out. "Rani, I'm back from the barn. We're going to cut the cake."

She glanced down the road once more and sighed before she stood up. "Coming."

As she started in the front door, Scout jumped to his feet and began to yelp. She whirled, and her heart leaped at the sight of a horse galloping toward their house, Matthew crouched over the saddle. She walked to the edge of the porch and watched him rein to a stop in the yard.

"Mama, Poppa, Matthew's back!" she called out.

Scout dashed down the steps and stopped beside the horse. His bark grew louder, and his tail wagged back and forth in a frantic rhythm. Matthew swung out of the saddle, dropped down beside Scout, and grabbed his wriggling body. He threw back his head and laughed in an attempt to shield his face from the dog's licking tongue.

"It looks like somebody's glad to see me," he said. He stood up, and Scout ran back up the steps and barked at Rani as if he wanted her to welcome Matthew.

"Hush, Scout," she said. The dog quieted and lay down at her feet.

She started to speak just as the front door burst open and her parents rushed out. Matthew's gaze swept all of them, but it lingered for a moment on her before he turned his attention back to Anna and Simon. He smiled as he stared up at them. "Did you think I wasn't going to come?"

Simon hopped down the steps and slapped him on the back. "We'd just about given up on you."

"I got back to my place this afternoon, but I had a lot of supplies to unload. It's a good thing my barn isn't as dilapidated as the cabin. I put everything in there and took care of the mules and cow I brought back with me. It took longer than I thought."

"It's about time you was a-gittin' here," Granny called from the front door. "You're just in time for a piece of the cake Anna baked for my birthday."

Matthew chuckled and nodded. "Then I'm glad I got here when I did. I'll take care of my horse and be right back."

"We'll be waiting for you," Simon called over his shoulder as he and Anna reentered the house.

Matthew didn't say anything, just stood there looking at Rani. She wanted to tell him how glad she was he had returned, but she couldn't

115

speak those words. She searched her mind for some-thing to break the silence between them. After a moment she cleared her throat. "How was everything in Townsend?"

"Busy. There were lots of people everywhere."

This wasn't the kind of conversation she wanted to have with him. She wanted him to tell her he'd missed her and couldn't wait to get back. Instead, their conversation had all the excitement of two farmers discussing the weather.

Unable to come up with a witty reply, she swallowed and followed up on his response. "There were people everywhere when Poppa took me to Townsend. Especially around the mill."

"I think they have more people working now than ever before. The Little River trains seemed to be coming in from all directions."

That information struck a warning in Rani's mind. More trains meant more trees were being cut. The day she and her father had been there, they'd watched the mill workers unloading a train from one of the lumber camps. "I saw a train come in with logs from Elkmont while we were there. It made me sick when I thought of all those trees that had been cut."

"From Elkmont? I know that place. I helped lay the eighteen miles of track from there to the mill. I saw one of the bigger trains they've got now for the long haul back to Townsend. They're coming in every day."

She sucked in her breath and gripped the porch post. "Every day? And the smaller trains are coming in all the time from the logging camps nearer to Townsend." The thought of all those trees being cut and the fact that Matthew worked on the railroad that transported them there made her stomach roil. "How did it make you feel seeing those logs arrive and knowing you laid the tracks that got them there?"

His eyes grew wide with surprise, and his body stiffened. He glared at her. "Not good, Rani. But then . . . I've done a lot of things I'm not proud of."

She knew she should be careful what she said, but she couldn't stop. She stomped down the porch steps and came to a stop in front of him. She stared up into his angry eyes. "I know you've had a hard time since your mother died, but you're a product of these hills. How could you stand by while your friends destroyed the place where you were born?"

"Friends?" He almost spat the word at her. "There's not one person there I'd call a friend. Maybe there aren't here either. You're mighty quick to condemn me for something you know nothing about. Maybe you need to get away from the protection of your parents and see what goes on in the rest of the world. Then you might understand what some people have to do to survive."

His words hit her like a slap in the face, and she flinched. Before she could respond, he whirled and led his horse around the corner of the house toward the barn. Rani wanted to call him back, but she hesitated.

Tears flooded her eyes, and she groaned aloud. What had she done? For three days all she'd thought about was how she wished Matthew would hurry back. Then when he arrived, the first thing she did was attack him. She'd be lucky if he ever spoke to her again.

Poppa had said they couldn't know what Matthew's life had been like, and he was right. The look on his face when he'd said he had no friends sent chill bumps down her back. And her angry words had proved she wasn't a friend. She only hoped there was some way she could repair the damage her wagging tongue had done.

What Poppa had said in his sermon had proven to be true. *Judge not, that ye be not judged.* She supposed it was her time to be on the receiving end of judgment, and she didn't like it at all.

She wanted to run after Matthew and beg him to forgive her thoughtless words, but her feet were rooted to the porch. Scout barked at her and ran to the corner of the house as if he wanted her to follow. She took a deep breath and ran after the dog.

Matthew had just reached the gate of the barnyard fence when she rounded the house.

Fighting back tears, she called out to him. "Matthew, wait."

He turned and watched as she ran toward him. She came to a stop facing him and stared up into his smoldering eyes. "What do you want, Rani?"

"I—I want to talk to you." She took a deep breath to control her racing heart. "I'm so sorry for the way I talked to you. I can see by the look in your eyes that I've hurt you, and for that I'm truly sorry. I shouldn't have spoken to you like that."

He pressed his lips together and shook his head. "It doesn't matter. I've had worse said to me."

"But I don't want you to hate me because I have trouble controlling my tongue sometimes. I want you to like me."

"I do like you, Rani. And I understand how you feel about the forests. I share that with you. I hope in time you'll come to see that." He reached for the gate and opened it. "Now I need to take care of my horse, and you need to go inside before your folks wonder where you are. We'll talk later."

He turned and led his horse into the barnyard. When he entered the barn, Rani looked down at Scout, who hadn't moved since they caught up with Matthew. She took a deep breath. "Well, boy, I think I've made a terrible mistake today. I just hope Matthew won't hold it against me."

In her heart, though, she feared that was exactly what would happen.

• • •

It wasn't long after that Matthew was sitting at the kitchen table and swallowing the last bite of Granny's cake. He pushed the plate away, picked up his coffee cup, and stared over the rim at Anna.

"That was mighty fine jam cake, Anna. I don't know when I've had as good."

She smiled and leaned back in her chair. "I may have baked it, but it was Granny's recipe."

Granny reached over and squeezed his arm. "And I'm right glad you got back to share some of it with us. Anna's baked a pie to take to the church tomorrow, and I reckon she'll be up early gittin' everything else ready to go. I hear it's going to be a mighty big shindig."

Simon laughed, pushed back from the table, and stood. "That's what I hear too. With Lavinia Davis in charge, it ought to be."

Anna nodded. "I don't know if you remember her or not, Matthew. She's married to Cecil Davis's brother. They've been coming to our church for several years now, and she's organized the whole celebration tomorrow."

Granny cocked an eyebrow. "And with Lavinia, I'm sure ev'rybody's a-doin' just what she says."

Simon turned to walk away from the table, but he whirled and came back. "I forgot to tell you something, Matthew. Rani and I went over to Cecil's cabin yesterday. He's going to get some men together to help rebuild your cabin. With

John and me helping you, I figure if Cecil can get about two or three to join him, we'll have your cabin ready in no time."

He stared at Simon in disbelief. "Do you really think there are men who'd leave their own work to help me?"

"Of course. Just leave it to Cecil. He'll get a crew together."

"I—I don't know how to thank you. All of you have been so kind."

Anna laughed and began to stack the cake plates. "It's easy to be kind to a nice person."

Simon reached out to stop her. "Leave that until later, Anna. I think this would be a good time to give Granny her presents. Why don't we all go sit in the front room?"

Granny frowned. "Presents? Now you shouldn't have gone and done that." Then her eyes twinkled, and she grinned. "But I shore am glad you did."

Matthew rose and grabbed Granny's arm to help her up. Rani stood on her other side. She hadn't said anything since they'd sat down at the table, and now she didn't look at him as she had the last time they helped Granny to her feet. When Granny had steadied herself, Rani took her arm and led her into the other room. She didn't look back.

Matthew watched her go, and sadness flooded through him. What did he expect? All day he'd looked forward to getting back and seeing her. Then she'd turned on him without warning. But he had to admit, he had snapped back at her too. He bit down on his bottom lip.

He'd never known a woman so passionate about a cause as she was about protecting this valley, and he admired that in her. She might speak before she thought sometimes, but he'd never known anyone to ask forgiveness as quickly. That was something he hadn't encountered in others. No doubt about it, she was some woman, and she hadn't been out of his mind since he first saw her at the mountain laurel bush.

But besides the fact that she was much younger than him and the daughter of two old friends, there was another problem—he was the son of Luke Jackson. It made his skin crawl to think how much he'd sounded like his father when he spoke in anger earlier. He doubted if he could ever overcome the hatred he felt for the man he sometimes feared he was just like. For twenty years he'd been struggling to rid himself of his father's influence but instead had found himself becoming more like him all the time. That thought scared him more than anything. But if it was true, then he didn't need to pursue a friendship with Rani. She didn't deserve somebody like him in her life. Someone like George—someone easygoing and dependable —would be better for her in the long run.

He walked to the door leading into the front room and stopped. Granny sat down in her chair, glanced up, and said something to Rani. She laughed, and the sound of it made his heart lurch. She might not need him, but she was exactly what he longed to have in his life.

Simon, who sat in the chair next to Granny, stood and motioned to him. "Come on and sit down beside Granny, Matthew. I'll go see what's keeping Anna. She went in the bedroom to bring out Granny's gift."

Rani smiled at Granny. "I have something for you too. I'll go get it."

She brushed past Matthew and hurried back into the kitchen and down the hallway to her room. He only waited a minute before he turned and followed her. He caught up with her just before she entered her room. "Rani, wait."

She turned and faced him. "What do you want?"

Her eyes narrowed, but it was her trembling lips that made his heart slam against his chest. "I wanted to explain about earlier."

She shook her head. "You don't owe me any explanation. I was awful to you when you first came, and I said some terrible things to you today. I don't blame you for holding it against me."

"But I don't. You didn't deserve the way I answered you when you tried to apologize, and I want you to know I'm sorry. It's just that old habits are hard to break."

A frown wrinkled her forehead. "What do you mean?"

"I haven't trusted anybody for a long time. But you're different, and I don't want to hurt you. I thought about you a lot while I was gone, and I was excited to see you."

Tears filled her eyes, and it was all he could do to keep from wiping them away. "I thought about you too," she said. "Then when you got here I ruined it. Sometimes my tongue gets ahead of my brain, and I say things I wish I hadn't."

"I know," he said.

She laughed, and the tears disappeared. "I guess you've learned that because you've been on the receiving end enough." Her eyelashes blinked, and his heart jumped.

He licked his lips. "I figure I can hold my own with you."

Her gaze traveled over his face. "I think you're the first man who's ever been able to." She tilted her head to one side and stared into his eyes. "I think you have a lot of other good qualities too. I look forward to getting to know you better."

"I want that too." Her words sounded sincere, and he smiled. "Then everything's all right between us again?"

She nodded. "As far as I'm concerned, it is."

"Me too." He backed away toward his bedroom. "I put my saddlebags with Granny's present in here. I'll get it and go back with you."

"I'd like that."

Matthew hurried into the room and pulled the small box containing Granny's present from the saddlebags. When he stepped back into the hall, Rani was there waiting for him. She held a basket that was covered with a cloth.

"What's that?"

She shrugged. "Not much. Just something I made."

He smiled. "Then let's go give Granny her presents."

When they reentered the front room, Anna and Simon had already arrived and were seated in chairs on either side of Granny. Two others, side by side, faced Granny, and she motioned for them to have a seat. Matthew waited for Rani to sit before he slid into the chair next to her.

Anna handed Granny a small package wrapped in brown paper. "This is from Simon and me. We hope you like it."

Granny held the present in her hand for a moment and looked from Anna to Simon. "I 'spect this is 'bout the best birthday ever. It would be perfect if Stephen was here."

"Yes," Anna agreed.

Rani and Simon leaned forward and watched as Granny pulled at the gift's paper. For some reason Matthew glanced at Anna. She stared past him, her blue eyes glazed and sadness lining her face. He knew without turning she was staring at Willie's picture on the mantel. She wiped at her eyes before she took a deep breath and looked down as Granny pulled a knitted shawl from the paper.

"Just what I needed," Granny said. "This'll keep me mighty warm when those cold winds blow across the mountains this winter." She smiled at Simon and Anna and then looked at Rani. "Rani, did I ever tell you I prayed for three years for God to send Simon a wife before Anna came to the Cove?"

Simon, Anna, and Rani all burst out laughing. "Yes, Granny," Rani said. "And I sure am glad you did. If you hadn't, I wouldn't be here today."

Matthew smiled and leaned back in his chair. This was what being a family was like. He'd never had that. He hoped Rani knew how lucky she was.

He cleared his throat and thrust the small box he held toward Granny. "I got this for you while I was in Townsend, Granny."

"Oh," Granny breathed as she accepted the box. "You didn't have to go and do that. Just having you here is present enough."

"Happy birthday. I hope you like it."

She opened the box and pulled out a small circular brooch set with pearls. "Matthew, this is 'bout the purtiest pin I ever saw. I'll wear it on my dress tomorrow, but tonight I want it on my shawl."

Anna laughed and proceeded to attach the brooch to the shawl. She draped it around Granny's shoulders. Granny pulled the shawl tight around her and reached up and trailed her finger over the pin.

Rani leaned over and placed her covered basket in Granny's lap. "Here's a little something I made for you, Granny."

Granny smiled and squeezed Rani's arm. "Anything from you is a treasure, darlin'."

Her eyes grew wide as she reached inside and pulled out an egg-shaped clay bowl. Streaks of black and rusty red swirled through the cream-colored clay. It reminded Matthew of the bowl on the table next to the bed in Stephen's room.

"You made this?" He knew his face must reflect the disbelief he was feeling.

Rani nodded. "Yes."

Granny picked up the bowl and held it up to examine it closer. "Oh, darlin', you outdone yourself this time. This here bowl is the best yet."

Rani laughed. "I guess all my practicing is finally paying off."

Matthew shook his head and turned to her. "Tell me how you made something that beautiful."

Rani's cheeks flushed, and she glanced down at her hands. "It's really not as difficult as it looks. I get my clay from a pit in a hollow not far from here. Then I mold my pot with my hands and bake it in a fire pit that I dug in the field next to our cabin."

He leaned over and slid his fingers down the side of the bowl. The fired clay felt cool to his touch, and he let his fingers wander over the indentations decorating the clay. "How did you make these designs?" he asked.

"I use different things, depending on what I'm making," Rani replied. "On this one I used a fork and a peach seed to make the design in the wet clay. Sometimes I wrap a piece of string around a stick and press it against the pot, or I might even coil clay into designs and press them on before I fire it."

"But the colors. Do you paint those?"

"No. As the wood burns the flames leave the color on the pots. I never really know what color they're going to be until I take them out of the pit." She laughed and shook her head. "The Cherokee have been making their pottery like this for hundreds of years. I'm just copying what they did."

He glanced around the room, and for the first time noticed several clay bowls and vases scattered about the room. "Did you make all the ones in here and the one in Stephen's room?"

"Yes." She laughed. "Don't act like they're something special. They're just pit-fired pottery."

Matthew shook his head. "No, Rani, they're

special. When I worked for Little River, I couldn't believe how many resorts were opening up in the mountains. People are beginning to visit the Smokies, and they want to buy mountain crafts. Your pottery is just what a lot of resort owners are looking for."

Rani shook her head again. "No, my work isn't good enough for that. Besides, pit firing is very risky. You never know how the pots are going to turn out." She glanced at her father and smiled. "But I can make other things too."

Matthew's brow wrinkled at the teasing glint in her eye. "Like what?"

"I made the bricks for our chimney when a storm blew part of it down, and I'm going to make the ones for the fireplace and chimney at your cabin. Poppa and I looked at it yesterday and decided how many we'll need. Mr. Davis is going to lay them for you."

"Y—you can make bricks? And you're going to make the ones for my cabin?"

They all burst out laughing, and Matthew felt his face grow warm. Granny reached over and squeezed his arm. "I been a-tellin' this girl for years she's got a gift, but I cain't convince her. Maybe you can."

"Maybe I can." Rani blushed and lowered her eyes to gaze at Granny's bowl. He had thought when he first saw her at the mountain laurel bush he'd never seen anyone more beautiful.

Tonight, though, with the light from the oil lamps casting a soft glow on her pink-tinged cheeks, she took his breath away. His gaze raked her, and he knew that vision would be tucked away in his memory forever. He glanced back at Granny. "She sure made you a beautiful present."

Granny nodded and set her bowl back down in the basket. "This one here is the favorite of all the ones she's done." She leaned back in her chair and glanced around at each of them. "And thank you for givin' me such a good birthday. You done made me real happy."

Tears filled Anna's eyes, and she kissed Granny on the cheek. "No, you're the one who's made all of us happy. I hadn't started to live until the summer I came to stay with you. You taught me about life and what's important." She gazed at her husband, and Matthew could see the love they shared in their eyes. "And because of you I have Simon and Rani and Stephen. I'll never be able to thank you enough for that."

Simon put his arm around Granny's shoulders and hugged her. "And thank you for praying for a wife for me. God sent me the best woman in the world."

She grinned and raised an eyebrow. "Now that Matthew's back, I 'spect I'm gonna have to be a-prayin' for a wife for him too. That is unless he's already got some young lady picked out over to Townsend."

Everyone turned and looked at him, and he felt his face grow warm. "N—no," he sputtered. "I doubt if I could ever find a woman crazy enough to marry me."

"Oh, don't say that," Anna cried out. "There are several young women in the Cove who might like for you to call on them. In fact, Granny and I will make a point of introducing you to them tomorrow after church."

Granny nodded. "We shore will."

The happiness he'd felt moments ago disappeared in a flash. He cast a quick glance at Rani, but she didn't look at him. He shook his head. "No, really, I don't think . . ."

Anna held up her hand to interrupt him. "I won't take no for an answer."

Simon chuckled, stood up, and stuck his hands in his pockets. "Matthew, you might as well give up. All women think it's their duty to turn single men into married ones. You're fighting a losing battle here."

He looked from Granny to Anna, and the determination on their faces told him Simon was right. Out of the corner of his eye he tried again to see Rani's reaction, but now she had turned to stare at the fireplace. Maybe she didn't care if her mother introduced him to some eligible young women. He exhaled and nodded.

"All right. Whatever you say."

Rani jumped to her feet and picked up the bowl

from Granny's lap. "Let me put this in your room for you."

"Thank you, child. I shore do like it."

She turned and headed toward the kitchen, but glanced over her shoulder when she got to the door. "I think I'll go to my room, Mama, unless you need me to help you with the dessert dishes. I need to study the lesson I'm teaching at Sunday school in the morning."

Anna shook her head. "I'll take care of the dishes. You go on and study."

Rani nodded. "I'll get up early to help you with the food for the church dinner. Goodnight."

Matthew heard everyone else reply to Rani, but he couldn't voice the word. He wondered what she thought about her mother's attempt at match-making. Did it upset her, or did she approve of the plan?

The most troubling thought to him, though, was that Anna apparently hadn't thought of her own daughter as a possible match for him. Would she approve if she knew how his heart raced whenever Rani was around?

Anna knew everything about his family when he lived in Cades Cove, but she would never see that as an obstacle to a relationship with Rani. It had to be his age. She must think he was too old for a girl only eighteen, and she was probably right. The effects of his hard years of living made him an unsuitable choice for any innocent young woman—especially one like Rani Martin, the daughter of two of Cades Cove's most beloved residents.

Tomorrow he would be cordial if Anna introduced him to anyone, but that was as far as it would go. He'd decided years ago he was destined to be alone, and that's what he intended to do. Starting right now, he would put any foolish notions he had about Rani out of his mind.

Chapter 7

With the sun beaming down and a slight breeze blowing down from the mountains, Rani decided it was a perfect morning to take her Sunday school class outside for their lesson. Now with the Bible story of Daniel in the lions' den completed and questions answered, the young children in her group sat on the church steps and munched the cookies she'd brought.

As they ate, she silently counted the heads to make sure no one had slipped away. It wasn't unusual for one of the boys to decide he'd rather stay outside than go back in for the church services. Today they all seemed content. The teacake cookies she'd made probably were the reason.

The sound of an approaching horse caught her attention, and she glanced around. Matthew rode into the church yard, dismounted, and tied his horse to a tree at the edge of the grounds. Today he wore dark pants and a white shirt, not his usual work clothes, and she thought him more handsome than ever. She couldn't take her eyes off him as he ambled toward her.

Several of the children looked up and hesitated before shoving the next bite in their mouths, but most hardly gave him a glance. He stopped beside her and smiled. "It seems you have everything under control."

"For the moment. But you should have been here about fifteen minutes ago. I decided I'd better get the cookies out early."

Matthew's dark eyes sparkled. "I'd get quiet for one of your cookies too."

"Would you like to have one?"

She held up the basket with a few cookies still inside, but he grinned and patted his stomach. "No, I'm still full from that breakfast your mother cooked, and I sure don't want to ruin my appetite for Granny's big dinner."

"I'll take his if'n he don't want it."

Rani held out the basket toward the young boy who'd gobbled his cookie up before most of the children had taken their first bite. "All right, Noah. Have another one."

Several other children jumped up and rammed

their hands into the basket before Rani could set it down. Matthew stared down into the now-empty basket and laughed. "I guess I missed my chance to have one of your cookies. Maybe I'll get one next time."

Her heartbeat quickened at the teasing glint in his eyes, and she smiled. "Maybe so."

The door of the church opened at that moment, and her father peered out. His face broke into a smile when he spied Matthew. "So you got back from feeding the animals over at your place. How was everything there this morning?"

"Fine."

"Good." Simon directed his attention back to Rani. "It's almost time to start. You need to get the children back inside."

She clapped her hands, and the children grew still. "It's time to go inside." A groan arose from the group, and she saw Matthew cover his mouth with his hand. She propped her hands on her hips and frowned. "None of that. Now swallow your last bite of cookie, and go inside and find your folks."

With a whoop the children jumped up and ran into the church. Noah stopped before entering and looked back at her. "Miss Rani, will you bring some more of them cookies next time?"

She smiled. "I will, but I have a secret just for you."

His eyes grew wide, and he hopped back down

the steps to where she stood. "What is it?" he whispered.

She leaned forward and stared into his face. "I brought an extra batch of cookies for you to take home today. When you and your ma get ready to leave, let me know, and I'll get them for you."

His mouth gaped open, and he shook his head in disbelief. "Honest, Miss Rani? You brought some just for me?"

"Just for you, Noah. But don't tell the other children. I don't have any for them."

He threw his arms around Rani and hugged her before he charged up the steps and into the church. When the door closed behind him, Matthew touched her arm. "That was mighty nice of you, Rani. You sure made him happy."

She didn't know if her skin warmed from his touch or for her concern over Noah. The child had been on her mind a lot lately, and she prayed for him and his mother every day. "Noah has a hard time. His father doesn't stay home much, and his mother struggles. I wish I could have brought them more food, but his mother's too proud to accept it. But she won't turn down anything I bake if I say it's for Noah."

He exhaled and withdrew his hand. "Sounds like Noah and his mother have a lot in common with my family."

"I've never thought about it before, but I suppose they do." She glanced back at the church door. "We'd better get inside before Poppa comes looking for us."

Matthew laughed and swept his arm toward the door. "Then let's go. I'll follow you inside."

Matthew stopped inside the door of the church and stared at the people already seated. Before he could take a step down the aisle, John Martin, Simon's brother, jumped up from his seat and headed toward him.

He grabbed Matthew's hand and pumped it up and down. "Simon told me you was gonna be here today. We sure are glad to have you back home, Matthew. I'll be over in a few days to see how I can help you out gettin' your farm up and running again." He motioned to a man sitting in the back row. "Hey, Joshua, do you remember Matthew Jackson?"

The man rose and extended his hand. "It's been a long time. He may not remember me. I'm Joshua Whitson."

Matthew nodded. "I do remember you. My mother often spoke of your wife."

"Yeah, your ma was a good woman. We missed her after she moved away. Let me know if you need any help at your farm," he said as he headed back to his seat.

"We'll talk later," John said, and walked back to the pew where his wife Martha sat. She smiled and waved at Matthew before she scooted down to make room for her husband.

Matthew glanced down at Rani, who'd been silent during the exchange. A satisfied expression covered her face, and she leaned forward. "Now you see that folks are going to be friendly with you."

He was about to agree until he looked past her to where George Ferguson sat beside his father. George glared at him before he leaned over and whispered something to his father. Pete darted a glance at Matthew before he frowned and looked away.

The old feeling of being the outsider washed over him, and he almost turned and left the church. Then he took a deep breath and forced a smile to his face. "At least some people seem glad to see me."

When they entered the church, Rani's mother was already at the pump organ. Her father bent over her as they discussed the songs the congregation would sing today. The sight of them together always filled Rani with happiness, but today she held her head a little higher—Matthew walked down the aisle behind her.

She stopped at the pew near the front where Granny sat and dropped down next to her. Matthew followed, and before she realized it, she sat wedged between Granny and Matthew. He was so close their shoulders touched.

Her father strode to the pulpit. "Everybody, get a hymnal and turn to one of our favorites, number fifteen."

The congregation rose as her mother began to play the opening chords of *Old Time Religion*. Rani grabbed a hymnal, opened it to the page, and held it up so Matthew could see it. He spread his fingers across the back of the book, his fingers brushing hers. Her hand tingled. She knew she should pull it away, but instead she inched her fingers closer until they rested next to his.

He didn't look up, but his fingers lifted and slowly descended to settle atop hers. The movement sucked the breath from her, and she almost gasped aloud. One gentle touch was all she felt before his fingers relaxed and moved away. Had the caress been accidental or intentional? The stony look on his face betrayed nothing. In confusion, she let go of the hymnal and dropped her hand to her side.

Rani had no understanding of the words she sang or those spoken by her father in his sermon. All she could think about for the next hour was how she had felt when Matthew's hand touched hers.

When the last song was sung and the benediction complete, Matthew stepped into the aisle and waited for her to follow before he moved back to Granny and helped her to her feet. She patted his arm and smiled, "How did it feel to be back in your home church today?"

"It felt mighty good, Granny. Now I'm ready to enjoy your birthday shindig."

Rani felt a hand tugging at her arm, and she turned to see Lavinia Davis beside her. "Come on, Rani," she said. "I need you out to where we're gonna spread dinner. There's lots to do, and I have a job for you."

"I'll be right there, Mrs. Davis." She glanced back at Matthew, but he appeared to be occupied with assisting Granny.

Her mother hurried over from the organ and grabbed Rani by the arm. "Come on, Rani. Lavinia needs us. Matthew can help Granny outside."

Matthew glanced up at the sound of Anna's voice and nodded. "You two go on. I'll bring the birthday girl."

He didn't look at Rani, and her heart dropped to the pit of her stomach. She'd been foolish to read too much into what had happened earlier. She whirled and followed her mother from the church.

Outside women carried large baskets of food toward the tables that had been set up under the trees. Rani and her mother joined them, and before long platters and bowls filled with the Cove's bounty lined the tables. Out of the corner of her eye, Rani caught sight of Matthew easing Granny into a chair one of the men brought for her, and then her father called out for everyone to be quiet.

Simon stood next to Granny's chair and laid his hand on her shoulder. "We've come together today to honor one of the most beloved women in our community. Matilda Lawson, better known to all of us as Granny, was born in this valley seventy years ago yesterday. Her mother taught her how to be a midwife as her mother had done before her. I'd like for you to raise your hand if Granny delivered you into this world."

All around, hands shot into the air. Rani held hers up. So did Matthew and her father.

"I thought so," Simon continued. "Granny has been more than a midwife to us, though. She's been a doctor when we didn't have one, a mother when ours was gone, and a spiritual advisor in our lives when we needed her. Because of her, I've been the pastor at this church for going on twenty-five years, and it's because of her that I have my wonderful wife and family."

Her father choked up, raised his hand to his mouth, and coughed. "Before we eat, I want to say a prayer of thanks for this woman who has meant so much to us." The gathered friends bowed their heads. "Father, You know all that Granny has meant to the people of Cades Cove. I thank You for her, for the healing hands You gave her, for the dedication to Your work she's taken with her into every home where she was needed,

141

and for the influence she's had on all our lives. I pray You will continue to bless her and give her many more years with the people who love her. Amen."

Amens rang out across the group as they raised their heads. Then one after another they came forward to hug her or to shake her hand. Most of them whispered to her, and Granny's eyes glistened with tears. After they spoke with her, they stepped to the tables and piled their plates with food.

By the time Rani finished serving, most of the crowd had scattered across the churchyard in small groups. Matthew sat on the ground next to Granny, his full plate on his lap. Granny balanced her plate on her legs and laughed from time to time at something Matthew had said.

Although she didn't feel as if she could eat anything, Rani put a piece of ham, some corn bread, and a spoonful of peas on her plate. Before she could decide where to settle, a familiar voice beside her interrupted her thoughts.

"Hello, Rani. I ain't had a chance to talk to you today. How about us settin' under that tree over yonder and eatin' together?"

Rani turned to face the man beside her. George. She started to excuse herself, but the hopeful look on his face made her feel guilty. She glanced at Matthew once more in hopes he'd look her way, but he didn't.

She forced a smile to her face. "I'd like that, George."

Matthew's mind had been in turmoil ever since he'd entered the church earlier today. Besides his fears about how the people who'd known his father would accept him, he'd worried about what Anna had said last night about introducing him to some young women. He didn't want that, but he didn't want to hurt Anna either.

"What you thinkin' 'bout, Matthew?" Granny's voice startled him.

He shook his head and chuckled. "Just about coming home, I guess. And about how good your birthday party's turned out. I haven't eaten this much in years." He set his plate on the ground beside him.

Granny put her fork in her plate and leaned forward in the chair where she'd sat since they came out of the church. "I guess you was a-feared of seeing folks today who knew your pa."

He shook his head in amazement. "Granny, how do you know exactly what's on my mind? It was that way when I was a boy too."

She laughed. "I guess I'm just an old woman who pays attention to what's a-goin' on around me."

He reached for her plate and set it on top of his. "Well, I'd better be careful when I'm near you. You might not like reading some of my thoughts."

She swatted at his arm. "I don't have no fear 'bout that. But I thought ev'rybody acted real friendly to you."

"They did. A few people didn't remember me, but most did. Do you think I was wrong to worry about folks holding a grudge against me because of my pa?"

Granny's eyes clouded. "It's hard to know how folks are gonna think, but there ain't no need to go a-worryin' about things like that. Most of the Cove folks know you ain't like your daddy." She leaned over and patted his arm. "Fact is, you more like your mother than anybody. She was a sweet woman, and I thought a lot of her."

His eyes misted, and he blinked. "She loved you, Granny."

Granny straightened in her chair and smoothed her dress over her lap. "But it's too purty a day to be a-talkin' 'bout such sad things. Why don't you take our plates back over to Lavinia before she has a conniption? That woman shore do like for things to run on schedule."

He grinned. "I'll be back in a minute."

As he rose, he glanced around for Rani. He hadn't seen her since she'd finished serving. His heart dropped to the pit of his stomach when he spied her and George together some distance from the group. He gritted his teeth and tightened his grip on the plates when she laughed at something George was saying.

The thought of their fingers touching in church returned, and he wondered if she'd been offended. He hoped not.

"Matthew?" Granny said.

He pulled his attention back to her. "Yes, Granny."

She pointed toward the table. "The plates. Remember you supposed to be a-takin' 'em back."

He nodded. "Sorry, Granny. I'm on my way."

He hurried to the table and handed the plates to Mrs. Davis. As he turned back to Granny, he swallowed back the panic rising in his throat. Anna, her arm around the waist of a young woman, stood beside Granny. The moment he'd dreaded had arrived. He cast another glance in Rani's direction, but she still seemed intent on what George was saying.

Anna waved to him. "Matthew, come here. I want you to meet somebody."

"Coming, Anna." He forced himself to smile and trudged back to stand beside her.

A slight smile pulled at Granny's lips, but Anna beamed as he came to a stop. She nudged the girl a little closer to him. "Matthew, this is Becky Ledbetter. You may remember her father, Howard Ledbetter. Their farm is on the west end of the Cove."

Matthew nodded. "I do remember." He smiled at the young woman. "It's nice to meet you,

Becky. I spoke to your pa earlier. He remembered me too."

The young woman smiled and ducked her head. "It's right nice a-meetin' you, Matthew. Welcome back to the Cove."

"Thanks."

Matthew's mind went blank, and he suddenly felt tongue-tied. He shot Anna a pleading look to fill the awkward silence. Becky glanced from Anna to him and shifted her weight from one foot to another for a moment before she wiggled from Anna's grasp and backed away. "I better be goin' now. I think my ma needs me to help her git our basket to the buggy." She glanced down at Granny. "Happy birthday, Granny. I had a fun time."

Granny nodded. "Me too, Becky. Tell your ma I shore did like that strawberry cake she baked."

"I'll tell her." Becky turned and hurried away.

A pleased expression on her face, Anna turned to Matthew. "Well?"

He arched his eyebrows. "What?"

"How did you like her?"

Perspiration popped out on Matthew's forehead, and he tugged at the collar of his shirt. "I liked her fine, Anna. I'm sure she's a nice young woman."

Anna sighed and glanced at Granny. "He didn't like her, did he?" She narrowed her eyes and let her gaze drift over the people scattered across the grounds. Her eyes widened, and she snapped her fingers. "I know. Charity Hopkins. I need to find her. I'll be right back."

"Anna, please don't . . ." But before he could finish his sentence, Anna had already left in search of the girl.

Ever since they'd sat down under the tree, George had droned on and on about what he'd done on the farm for the last three days. Rani tried to appear interested, but she felt as if she'd been right there with him from sunup until sundown every day. When he finally paused for breath, she spoke. "It sounds like you've been busy."

"I have been, but I've been thinking 'bout you too. I hope you did the same for me."

"I have," she said. "In fact just this morning I was wondering if your family had heard anything from Ted and Josie since they moved."

"That ain't what I meant, Rani, and you know it," he snarled. "I don't know why all of a sudden you done started actin' like some stranger who don't have time for me."

"George, please . . ."

His eyes narrowed, and he held up his hand to stop her. "Don't say nothin' else right now." He glanced back toward the tables. Lavinia was motioning for everyone to bring their plates back. He reached over, took her plate, and stood.

"I'm gonna take these back, then I'm a-comin' back to have a real important talk with you. It's time you started takin' me serious."

The anger on his face alarmed Rani, and she jumped to her feet as he strode away. She looked around for her mother and caught sight of her standing next to Matthew, her arm around Becky Ledbetter's waist.

Her mother had carried through on her promise. Rani's eyes filled with tears when Matthew said something to Becky. The smile on Becky's face probably meant she already had her sights set on snaring Matthew. And who could blame him for being interested in Becky? After all, she was known as the prettiest girl in the Cove. But Rani didn't think she could stand it if Matthew thought so too. She didn't want to watch them laughing and talking together, and she didn't want to have the conversation George had just mentioned. All she wanted was to get away and be alone for a while.

Before George could turn and come back, she ran around the church and into the cemetery in the field next to it. She raced to the far side as fast as she could and stopped at the place she'd come many times in the past few years. She dropped to her knees beside the small headstone and balled her fists. For a moment all she could do was stare at the name etched into the stone. William Prentiss Martin.

She crossed her arms, hugged her body, and toppled forward. She landed face-down on the grave. Her fingers dug into the hard earth, and she sobbed.

Matthew didn't want to meet any more young women, but he didn't know how to tell Anna. He pulled his attention away from her retreating figure and cast a glance in the direction of Rani and George, but they no longer sat where they had a few minutes before. He searched the crowd, but they were nowhere to be seen. He glanced at Granny, and a smile curled her lips.

"You ain't interested in meetin' no girls, are you?" she said.

He started to deny Granny's accusation, but he couldn't meet her steady gaze. He looked down at his feet and shook his head. "No."

Granny straightened in her chair. "Well, in case you're interested in where Rani went, I saw her run around behind the church when George took their plates back to the table. I 'spect he's a-lookin' for her right now, but you might find her first if you'd go to the back of the cemetery."

He opened his mouth to protest, but the glint in Granny's eyes told him she'd already guessed his secret. "You've done it again, Granny. You can tell what I'm thinking. How did you know?"

Granny sniffed. "I may be a-gittin' old, but I ain't blind. I seen how you and Rani look at each other. I guess Simon and Anna ain't seen it yet, but they will. It's hard to hide something like that."

Matthew shook his head. "Granny, I would never do anything to hurt Simon or Anna."

"I know that, boy. But you ain't a-hurtin' nobody but yourself when you pretend. I been a-prayin' for you all these years you been gone, and I've prayed for Rani since the day she came into the world. I reckon I'll be prayin' now that God will show both of you what He has planned for you." She reached out and grabbed his hand. "But remember, Matthew, His plans aren't always what we want."

"I know that, Granny." His heart felt like it would burst. He bent down and kissed Granny on the cheek. "I've missed you and your wisdom all these years."

He turned and strode around the church. As he entered the cemetery, he remembered the last time he'd been on this ground—the day of his father's funeral. It had rained that day, and he had stood by his mother and supported her in her grief, but he couldn't cry. Not for the man who had made their lives so miserable.

He walked past the spot where they'd buried his father but didn't look down. He kept walking to the back as Granny had said. His gaze swept the gravestones, but he didn't see her.

Then he heard a sound—a woman crying. He

spotted her lying across a grave. Her fingers scratched at the earth, and her body shook with deep sobs. He eased up, knelt beside her, and touched her shoulder.

She bolted into a sitting position and scooted backwards. Her eyes, red from crying, reminded him of a frightened animal. He bent closer. "Rani, are you all right?"

"M—Matthew, wh—what are you doing here?" A hiccup escaped her mouth.

"I noticed you'd left and wanted to make sure you were all right." He glanced at the tombstone. "Is this your little brother's grave?"

She nodded. "Yes."

He eased into a sitting position facing her. "I lost my little brother too. I know how much it hurts."

Her chin trembled, and she took a deep breath. "But your brother died from getting sick. It was my fault Willie died."

He drew back in surprise. "What?"

Another tear rolled down her cheek, and she wiped at it. The dirt on her hands mixed with the tears left dark smudges on her face.

"Willie always followed me everywhere I went, even when I climbed the big tree in the field behind our house. He'd beg me to let him climb, but I always told him he was too little. He'd get mad and tell me someday he'd show me he was big enough. Then he'd run back to the house."

Matthew smiled. "That sounds like the way brothers and sisters argue. But that doesn't mean they don't love each other."

"I know. I loved Willie so much, and he loved me too. Then one day when I was nine years old, Mama was busy canning peas from our garden. She asked me to watch Willie while she worked. I got angry because I wanted to go over to Josie's and play, so I treated Willie awful. I told him to leave me alone, that I didn't want to watch him, and I ran off and hid from him."

Sorrow lined her face, and he wished he could say or do something to ease her pain. He swallowed hard. "Then what happened?"

"Sometime later I got really scared when I couldn't find him. So I ran and got Mama. We found him lying under the big tree I climbed all the time. I guess he decided he'd show me he was big enough, but he fell and broke his neck." Her last words were lost in her sobs.

Matthew grasped her by the shoulders and pulled her to him. She pressed her face against his chest and moaned as she cried out her grief. He pressed his lips to the top of her head and kissed the dark hair that had intrigued him from the moment he first saw her. He tightened his embrace and whispered in her ear. "Let it all out, Rani. I'm here with you."

He didn't know how long he held her. All he wanted was to comfort her, and he would stay with her as long as needed. After a few minutes, she calmed, but she kept her face pressed against him.

Finally she pulled away, sat up straight, and wiped at the tears again. "I must look a mess."

He touched her face to help wipe away the muddy streaks, but his fingers lingered a moment before he trailed them down in a light caress. "No, you don't. You're the most beautiful woman I've ever seen."

Her dark eyes stared into his, and his heart pounded. "Am I?"

He grasped her hand and laced their fingers together. "I thought so the first minute I saw you at the mountain laurel bush."

Her chin quivered. "Prettier than Becky Ledbetter?"

He smiled. "I don't remember what Becky looked like. All I could think about was finding you."

Her hand trembled in his. "Thank you for coming to look for me. It . . . it means a lot to me."

"I'm glad." He glanced back at the tombstone. "But you can't blame yourself for Willie's death. You were a child at the time, and it was an accident."

"That's what everybody tells me. I can't quit thinking that if I'd watched him like Mama asked, he'd still be alive."

He squeezed her hand tighter. "Don't say that. I can't stand to see you hurting like this."

She stared into his eyes, and his pulse raced. She leaned closer to him, so close he could feel her breath on his face. "What's happening with us, Matthew?"

"I don't know," he whispered.

"I feel like there's something between us. Is it just me, or do you feel it too?"

His head told him to tell her he felt nothing, but he couldn't. He swallowed hard. "I feel it too." He slid his hands up her arms and pulled her nearer until she was so close their lips almost touched. "But you're so young, Rani. You need friends nearer your age—like George."

"I don't want George," she said.

He started to pull her closer, but he stopped when the angry tone of a man's voice shattered the air. "So you don't want me, huh? Is he the reason you snuck off from me?"

Rani gazed over his shoulder, her eyes wide. Matthew turned and stared into George's face. Red splotches covered his cheeks, and rage filled his eyes.

Matthew pulled Rani to her feet and stepped in front of her to shield her from George's anger. "Rani didn't run off from you. She wanted to visit her brother's grave. I found her here."

George glared at them, and a fleck of spittle escaped the corner of his mouth. "Yeah, it looked like the two of you found each other all right. I guess I know now why you ain't got no time for me anymore, Rani. If you wanted somebody dif'rent, why didn't you try to do better than Luke Jackson's son?"

Matthew's hands curled into fists, and his body stiffened. "I don't take that kind of talk from any man." He took a step toward George, but Rani's hand on his arm restrained him.

She stepped in front of Matthew. "I'm sorry you're angry, George, but I told you I only felt friendship for you. I know tomorrow when you get over being angry you'll be sorry for your . . . your hateful words."

He shook his head. "You're wrong 'bout that, Rani. I ain't the only one thinkin' Luke Jackson's son don't have no place in the Cove. I reckon you'll come to your senses in time, but don't expect me to be waitin' for you."

George whirled and stomped across the cemetery. When he had disappeared from sight, Matthew groaned and raked his hand through his hair. "I'm sorry, Rani."

Her eyebrows arched. "For what?"

"For making George so angry with you. I didn't mean to ruin your friendship."

She didn't say anything for a moment. Then she reached for his hand and covered it with both of hers. "I've seen George's temper before. He'll sulk for a few days because he didn't get his way, then we'll be friends again. But that's all there's ever going to be between us."

"But you heard what he said. There are people in the Cove who never will forget the things my father did. I would do anything before I would let you or your family be hurt because of that."

She reached up and pressed one of her fingers against his lips. "Don't talk like that. You have to show everyone that you're not like him. You're not like your father. I know you can do that."

He almost gasped aloud at the thought that Rani believed in him. He hadn't felt trust from anyone in years, and it thrilled him that he saw it in her eyes. "Rani, I'll try, but sometimes I believe I'm just like him."

"I know you're not. And so do Mama and Poppa and Granny. We'll pray that you come to know it too."

"Thank you." He gave a slight nod, but in his heart he doubted he would ever reach that conclusion.

As he stared into Rani's face, he knew George was right about two things. He had come between her and George, and he was glad. There was something that thrilled him and scared him at the same time happening between him and Rani. Was that how love began? If so, he needed to tread lightly because George had been right about something else—Rani deserved somebody a lot better than Luke Jackson's son.

Chapter 8

Three days after Granny's birthday Rani woke up early. She shivered in the predawn chill of her room and pulled the covers up to her chin. With Matthew leaving early every morning and getting back late, she'd barely seen him since Sunday. As she huddled under the quilt, she tried to remember everything she and Matthew had said to each other that day at the cemetery.

Had he really meant it when he said he'd thought her the most beautiful woman he'd ever seen? He'd certainly been on her mind ever since that day at the mountain laurel bush when she'd opened her eyes in the middle of the prayer . . .

She bolted upright in the bed and clamped her hand over her mouth. The prayer. He'd heard her! But he didn't understand the words. In fact she couldn't even be sure she'd pronounced them correctly. She hadn't uttered those words in years until that day when she'd felt a need to speak to God in the language of the people who'd lived in the Cove long before her. But she knew the intent of the prayer. And so did God.

Suddenly restless, she jumped out of bed and hurried to the window. As she did every morning, she pulled the curtain back, closed her eyes, and gave thanks to God for the dawning of a new day. When she opened her eyes, she sucked in her breath. The sight of the sun coming up over the mountains always thrilled her, but today she felt happier than she had in a long time. She wrapped her arms around her waist and leaned against the window frame. There was no need to wonder what caused this new joy in her heart, but it still amazed her. Although she hadn't admitted it at first, it had been there since the moment she whirled to see Matthew at the mountain laurel bush.

Poppa had said many times how he knew the minute he saw her mother she was the woman he'd been waiting for. She'd never believed it could happen to her. Until now. Maybe it had happened to her just like it did Poppa.

She tiptoed to the door and listened for sounds of anyone stirring in the kitchen, but she heard nothing. The door creaked as she opened it, and the sound echoed in the quiet house. Easing the door open wider, she stared into the hall. The door to Granny's room was closed, but Matthew's stood open. He must have gotten up early and left for his farm.

She dressed quickly and pulled a light shawl from the peg next to the door. As quietly as she could, she slipped from the house and into the backyard. She breathed in the crisp morning air that was laced with the sweet smell of honeysuckle. A horse whinnied from the direction of the barn. She held her breath as Matthew stepped into the barnyard and led his horse toward her.

When he stopped in front of her, she wondered if he could hear her heart beating. His horse pawed at the ground, and Matthew tightened his grip on the reins he held. "What are you doing up so early?"

"It just seemed like a good morning to get a head start on the day. I haven't seen much of you the last few days. Have you been avoiding me?"

His long eyelashes blinked, and he smiled. "No. I have a lot to do at the farm, and I've been trying to get an early start."

Rani pulled her shawl tighter and tilted her head to one side. "I'm glad I got to see you before you left today."

He stuck a finger under the brim of his hat and pushed it back on his head. "Did you want to tell me something?"

"I haven't talked to you since Sunday, and I wanted to thank you for the things you said. About Willie's death not being my fault."

"I hope you'll come to believe it wasn't."

She sighed. "Maybe in time, but I'm also sorry about the things George said. He was angry, and he was wrong about folks in the Cove being sorry you're back."

He shook his head. "I doubt if he is, but I'm glad you think so." He glanced up at the sun that had climbed higher in the sky. "I need to go. I have a lot to do today."

She held out a hand to stop him. "I know you do, but would it interrupt your work too much if I came over there today? I need to check some things."

He regarded her with a skeptical expression. "What kind of things? I have a feeling you know a lot more about my place than I do."

Her face warmed, and she glanced at the ground. "I need to make sure I've gotten an accurate count of the number of bricks you need for your fireplace and chimney. I want to get started right away."

"Are you sure you want to make those bricks? It sounds like a big job to me."

"It's going to take some time to make all of them. That's why I want to get started as soon as possible. The base of the chimney is still there, but I'm not sure how many of those bricks will need to be replaced. And with the chimney starting at ground level and going up the side of the house, it's going to take more bricks than most of the ones in the Cove."

"Will Simon come with you?"

She shook her head. "I doubt it. I heard him say last night he had some visits to make today."

"What time do you think you'll be there?"

Rani hesitated before answering. The prospect

of being alone with Matthew tempted her to suggest the idea that had formed in her mind the minute he walked out of the barn, but she didn't know how he would accept the notion. She took a deep breath. "How about if I come about noon and bring some food for us? Do you think you'd have time to sit down and eat with me?"

His eyes twinkled. "Just the two of us?"

"Yes," she murmured. Her stomach fluttered at the thought of how brazen she was to suggest such a thing. What if Matthew thought she was throwing herself at him? She squirmed under his intense gaze and pulled her shawl tighter. "If you don't . . ."

His grin grew larger. "I can't think of anything I'd rather do than have a picnic with you. I'll look forward to it all morning."

"Me too," she whispered.

Matthew tugged on the brim of his hat and climbed into the saddle. "I'll see you then."

She nodded and waved as he guided the horse around the house and into the road, then ran back to the cabin. When she dashed into the kitchen, she came to a skidding halt.

"What you so happy about this morning?"

Granny sat at the kitchen table with her Bible open in front of her. Rani shrugged and grabbed the water bucket from the dry sink. "Nothing. I was just enjoying the day." She held up the bucket. "I'd better go get some fresh water from the well before Mama comes to cook breakfast."

"No need to do that yet," Granny said, and motioned for Rani to sit down. "Your mama left before sunup to go over to the Jordan place. Wilma's done gone into labor, and her husband come for Anna. She and Simon both went."

Rani frowned. "I didn't hear them leave. I must have been sleeping pretty soundly. And Matthew didn't say anything about them being gone either."

Granny's eyebrows arched. "Matthew? Where'd you see him?"

"I was outside when he left, and we talked for a few minutes."

Granny nodded. "I see." She studied Rani for a moment. "I reckon you talked some at my birthday gatherin' Sunday too. Seems like the two of you was gone for a long time. Must have been a right in'trestin' conversation."

Rani turned and placed the bucket back on the dry sink. "It was. I enjoy being with Matthew."

"And I reckon he likes bein' with you. He shore didn't want to meet any of those girls your mama had lined up for him. So I told him where to find you."

Rani slowly faced Granny and swallowed. "He found me at Willie's grave."

"That's where I figured you'd be. Later I saw George come a-runnin' over to his pa. He looked like he could spit nails, and the next thing I know he's on his horse a-gallopin' off. What happened to make him so mad?"

Rani sank down into the chair next to Granny. "George wants to marry me, but I'm not in love with him. He found Matthew and me at Willie's grave, and he said some awful things."

"Like what?"

"He said if I wasn't interested in him I should have tried to do better than settle for Luke Jackson's son. He said there were lots of folks in the Cove who didn't want Matthew back here."

Granny pursed her lips. "I was a-feared there might be some people who wouldn't forget. I shore do hate that for Matthew's sake. He couldn't help what his pa did."

"That's what I told him. He has to work to prove to everybody that he's not like his father. I know he can do that."

Granny reached over and clasped Rani's hand. "Darlin', it sounds like you got a lot of faith in that boy."

Rani nodded. "I do, Granny. I didn't want to like him at first. I think I was so awful to him because I didn't understand . . . well . . . why I couldn't get him out of my mind. He's a very kind person, and there's something about him that draws me to him."

"I was a-feared of that too."

Rani's mouth gaped open. "But what scares you? I thought you loved Matthew."

Granny frowned and leaned back in her chair. "I love him, but he's got a lot of bad mem'ries that've been eatin' at him for years. We don't know what his life's been like, and he may have scars that will make it hard for him to have a normal life. I love both of you too much to see you get hurt."

Rani gave a nervous laugh. "Granny, you're talking like Matthew and I are in love. I don't know that it's love. It's just—we like each other. But it seems we argue a lot. My mouth says something before I think, and he lashes back at me."

A sad look darkened Granny's eyes. "That's what I'm talkin' about, darlin'. You need to pray real hard 'bout this before you get too attached to Matthew. Better to walk away 'fore one of you says or does somethin' that hurts the other one."

Rani started to protest that Granny was wrong about her feelings for Matthew, but she knew she would only be trying to convince herself. There was something about Matthew that excited her and attracted her to him. She'd never felt this way before.

It made no difference what Granny or anyone else said. She intended to find out what this feeling was. If she got hurt in the process, she'd have no one to blame but herself. It was worth risking a broken heart to find out what the future held for her and Matthew.

● ● ●

Matthew hadn't been able to concentrate on his work all morning. Although Rani was familiar with the farm where he'd grown up, he wanted her to know more about the place that held so many memories for him. He wanted to tell her about his mother and what he was like as a boy. His father was a different matter—he didn't know if he could ever share all the memories he had locked away about him.

He chided himself for letting his mind wander when he had work to do and threw himself into the repair of the animal cribs in the barn. He'd just pounded the last nail into the sagging partition between two stalls when Scout's bark broke the silence. He stepped out of the stall into the middle aisle of the barn just as Scout and Rani appeared at the open door. When Scout saw him, he ran to him and jumped up on his leg.

Matthew laughed, dropped to his knees, and hugged the wriggling dog. Rani leaned against the side of the door and smiled. He stood up and walked toward her. "I can always expect a warm welcome from Scout. Maybe you should take a lesson from him."

She held up a basket covered with a cloth. "I suspect you would much rather have what's in this basket instead of my welcome."

He closed his eyes and sniffed. "You may be right. I smell something good. What is it?"

"I brought the rest of last night's squirrel stew. Granny made us some cornbread, and I made you some teacake cookies like I promised I would."

He closed his eyes and groaned. "You read my mind. I'm starving."

She arched an eyebrow and studied him from head to toe. "Well, you need to get cleaned up before you eat. Go do that and meet me under the big oak tree over there. I'll have everything ready for you."

His heart pounded at the ease with which they teased today. Maybe they had passed the point of taking exception to everything the other one said. As she walked away, his eyes took in her every movement. Strange how a few days could change the way a person looked at the world. He hadn't been this happy in years. He reached down, scratched behind Scout's ears, and laughed. "Come on, boy. Let's get ready to eat."

Whistling a tune, he hurried to the bucket on a bench at the entrance to the barn and poured some water into the pan beside it. For several minutes he scrubbed his hands and arms and then scooped up water to wash the grime from his face. As he wet his hair and slicked it back from his face, he glanced down at Scout.

"Do I look good enough to eat with a pretty woman?"

Scout tilted his head to one side as if trying to decide, and Matthew laughed. What would the men he'd worked with at Little River think of Matthew Jackson talking to a dog and trying to impress a woman? It didn't matter. At the moment nothing mattered except being with her.

She sat on the ground under the oak tree, and his heart beat a little faster as he walked toward her. His gaze traveled over the plates and forks she'd pulled out of the basket beside her, but he stumbled to a stop when he spied the small vase in the center of the cloth.

With the streaks of red and black that ran up the sides, he knew right away it was one of her pit-fired vases. But it was what the vase held that sucked the breath from him. She had picked blossoms from the mountain laurel bush and arranged them inside for a bouquet to decorate their simple meal.

Her hands fluttered to her lap, and a pink tinge lit her cheeks as she followed his gaze to the flowers. "I picked some. I like to enjoy them as long as they bloom."

The memory of his mother walking out of the cabin the day they left the Cove flashed in his mind, and he almost groaned. He could still see her clutching the small can that contained a cutting from her mountain laurel bush. Now when he looked at her bush, he not only thought of her but of his first glimpse of Rani also.

He took a deep breath and smiled. "They make it look like we're having a fancy meal."

She ducked her head and motioned for him to sit down. "There's nothing fancy about squirrel stew, but it does fill you up. One good thing about living in the Cove is all the wild game we have for our tables."

He nodded and dropped down beside her. "There are a lot of good things about living here."

She picked up a dish, spooned some stew onto it, and handed it to him. "There are. I'm glad you came back to enjoy them."

His heart leapt, and he smiled. "I am too."

As they ate, Matthew related story after story about his childhood days when he roamed the forests and streams in the Cove. He took care to only mention happy times, never anything about his father. Rani's eyes lit up with laughter when he told of the time he'd tried to catch a bear cub to keep as a pet. He'd had to run for his life when the mother showed up.

"What did your mother say when you told her?"

He grinned. "Nothing. I never told her. I thought it was better keeping it to myself instead of worrying her."

"That sounds a lot like me when I was little. Stephen always did what Mama and Poppa wanted, but it seems I was in trouble all the time." She laughed and held out the plate with her cookies on it. "Have another?"

He shook his head and rubbed his stomach. "I've already had four. I'm so full I need to take a nap, and that's not going to help me finish the work I'd planned for this afternoon."

"We were having so much fun, I forgot you have work to do." She began to gather up the dishes. "I'd better get a count of how many bricks I think you need and go home. I don't want to detain you."

He didn't want their time together to end, and he grabbed her hand to stop her from loading the basket with their dirty dishes. "Don't go yet. I'm enjoying having you here."

She paused and stared at him. "Are you?"

"Yes," he whispered. He pulled one of the mountain laurel blooms from the vase, scooted closer to her, and stuck it in her thick hair. Then he arranged another one on the other side of her face. Unable to stop himself, he continued until the can sat empty, and all the blooms resembled a crown of flowers on her head.

She didn't move as he leaned back and stared at her. "There," he said. "You're just as beautiful as you were the first day I saw you."

Her lips trembled. "Am I really?"

He swallowed hard and nodded. "Yes, you are."

A nervous laugh escaped her mouth. "No one's ever said that to me before."

"Then I'm glad I'm the first." He glanced at the blooms again and frowned. "Did I ever tell you the history of that mountain laurel bush?"

She shook her head. "No, but I assumed it has something to do with your mother."

"It does. She and my father were very much in love when they first married. One day he brought a small mountain laurel plant home with him. He'd dug it up somewhere in the mountains. He planted it and told her to always think of him and how much he loved her when she looked at that plant. Even after things got so bad, she never gave up hope it would be better. When she was dying, she made me promise to come see if her mountain laurel was still living. It was the first thing I did when I rode into the Cove, and I found you here."

"I've come to that bush to pick blooms for years. Now it's special to me because we met here."

She leaned forward, and his heart caught in his throat. She wanted him to kiss her. He wanted to more than anything, but he couldn't move. After a moment he sighed, grasped her hand, and pulled her to her feet. "Come with me. I want to show you something."

He clasped her hand in his and led her past the barn and across the field behind it. He stopped before they reached the trees that grew across the back of the field. The mountains rose in the distance, and the sight thrilled him as it had since he was a child.

He tightened his fingers around Rani's and

stared down at her. "When I was a child, I explored the woods at the back of our farm and thought it was some kind of magical forest. Then when I worked for Little River, I saw all the tourists who are beginning to flock to the Smokies. But none of them were coming to Cades Cove. I had an idea, and for years I've been working on a plan for bringing visitors here."

A frown puckered Rani's brow, and she stared from the woods to him. "I don't understand."

He took a deep breath. "I haven't told anybody this, but I want to build a small lodge here at the edge of the woods for visitors."

"But why would they want to come here?"

"For the same reason we love living here. The mountains, the wildflowers in the spring and summer, the leaves in the fall, the fish in the stream, the wildlife."

Understanding dawned, and her eyes grew wide. "You want to share your love of the Cove with other people, don't you?"

"Yes."

"Tell me more about this plan. What will you do once people come?"

He smiled and shrugged. "It depends on what they want. For fishing, I can take them to Abrams Creek and any of the other streams that are filled with rainbow trout. For hiking, there are trails all over the Cove that offer some of the most beautiful sights in the Smokies. I could take groups on short or longer hiking trips—whichever they chose. For longer trips we could go up the Anthony Creek trail to Spence Field, set up a campsite there, and spend days hiking all the trails in the area. Then there're places to explore like Gregory's Cave. I think it could really open the Cove up to visitors who are willing to pay for such trips."

Her eyes danced with excitement. "Oh, this sounds wonderful—but how will you get them to come in the first place?"

His heart raced at the realization that she shared his excitement of the idea. "I'll advertise in Knoxville or Asheville or newspapers all over. The beauty of the Cove and the seclusion will be a draw for people wanting that kind of vacation. Once they come, they'll tell their friends, and word will spread."

He still held her hand, and she covered his with her free one. "Oh, Matthew, this sounds wonderful, and maybe I can help you with it. If we could attract enough visitors, then they might see what the lumber companies are doing to the forests and help us put a stop to it."

"Maybe so."

"But you have a lot of work to do before that can happen. Have you thought about how many people you'll have to hire to make this work? You'll need a cook and someone to clean the lodge, and you'll need someone to help you lead fishing or hiking trips. How long will it be before you'll be ready for this?"

He laughed and shook his head. "Whoa. You make it sound like it's going to happen overnight. I need money, and right now I have very little left. I'll have to put in a few crops first so I can get some money to build the lodge. I'm giving myself five years before I start building the lodge."

She stared at the woods as she was envisioning the lodge he'd described. "I see the perfect spot for the lodge. And maybe you should build a separate cabin for the kitchen and dining room." Her voice grew more animated. "And maybe you could have a spot in the dining hall where I could sell my bowls and vases." She stopped, clamped her lips together, and turned to him. "I'm sorry. This is your dream. I didn't mean to take over."

In that moment, he knew why he'd told her what he'd kept hidden from everyone else. He wanted more than anything he'd ever desired to share it with her. He wrapped his arms around her and pulled her to him. She stared up at him, and the mountain laurel blooms in her hair filled him with a longing like he'd never known.

"You're not interfering," he whispered.

With a groan he lowered his mouth and pressed it against her trembling lips. His heart pumped, and he tightened his hold on her when her arms encircled his shoulders and her fingers caressed the back of his neck.

He released her mouth and pressed his cheek next to hers. "Oh, Rani," he murmured, "I never dreamed I'd meet anyone like you when I came back here."

"And I never thought someone like you would enter my life." She pulled back and stared up at him. "But I'm glad you did."

He swallowed hard. "I'm glad I did too. There's still a lot you don't know about me, though. And I'm so much older than you. I want to take this slow and see where it leads us. I don't want you to be hurt."

She smiled, reached up, and stroked his cheek. "The difference in our ages makes no difference to me, and I know you could never hurt me."

He didn't respond but clasped her hand and led her back toward the barn. He hoped she was right, but in his heart he feared she was wrong. Rani was still young, and the years he'd been gone were filled with too many mistakes—ones that might make it impossible for him to ever have a normal life. If that proved to be true, he would never allow Rani to be hurt because of it.

Chapter 9

In the days following the kiss Matthew and Rani had spent every spare minute together. So far she didn't think her parents had noticed, but Granny had. One morning a week after Matthew told her of his plan for his farm she was busy packing their noon meal in a basket when Granny hobbled into the kitchen.

Her eyebrows arched when she saw what Rani was doing. She dropped into a chair at the table. "Are you goin' over to Matthew's again today?"

Rani didn't glance up, but nodded. "Yes. He works so hard, and I can't stand to think of him being hungry. It's really no problem for me to take him some food."

Granny snorted. "I reckon it ain't no problem except that you been mighty hush-mouthed about it, and you've gone over there for the last three days. Do your ma and pa know what you been a-doin'?"

Rani gave a nervous laugh and tucked the cloth around the food she placed in a basket. "No, but I'm sure they wouldn't mind. Both of them have been gone every morning this week either visiting or waiting for a baby to be born."

"Well, they been here at night, and I ain't

noticed you and Matthew a-tellin' them about all your private time together." Granny crossed her arms and snorted. " 'Course I don't know why they so blind. Anybody with good sense can see the way you and that boy look at each other. I ain't never seen nobody as lovesick you two."

Rani's face burned, and she glanced up at Granny. "We aren't lovesick, and there's nothing wrong with us having some private time, as you call it. We've just become good friends."

Granny shook her head. "Good friends, huh? That's not what it looks like to me. And if you're sure that's all it is, then you need to let your folks know." Granny was quiet for a moment before she spoke again. "Tell me one thing, though. Have you and Matthew talked about marriage?"

Rani shot a surprised look in her direction. "No. I told you we're just getting to know each other."

"Well, I don't feel good keepin' this from your ma and pa. If Matthew has any intentions toward you, he needs to tell Simon."

"Intentions?" Rani dropped to her knees beside Granny's chair and grasped her hand. "Please don't say anything to Mama and Poppa yet. I don't know what's going to happen between us. I just know I'm happier than I've ever been in my life."

Granny reached down with her other hand and caressed Rani's cheek. "Darling, I want you and

Matthew both to be happy, but this all happened so sudden. You ain't lived out in the world like Matthew has, and you don't understand how different it is from life here. I worry because I don't want you to get hurt."

"I know you do." She took a deep breath. "But, Granny, I think I'm falling in love with Matthew. All I want is to be with him."

Granny tilted her head to one side and smiled. "Back when your ma come to this valley, she was full of life just like you are now. The only dif'rence is she had her heart set on going to New York. Didn't want to fall in love, but she did. With you it's not the same. I know you been lookin' for somebody to love ever since Josie got married, but you ain't found him. Now this handsome man who's lots older than you and has seen lots more than you'll ever see comes along, and you fall head over heels. Maybe you need to get out of the Cove and see what's out there in the rest of the world before you make any big decisions."

"I don't want to leave home. Besides, where would I go?"

"You can always go visit your Uncle Charles over to Maryville. He'd love to have some comp'ny."

Rani shook her head. "I love him and enjoy seeing him, but I don't want to go right now. Maybe this winter I will."

Granny snorted. "By this winter you'll change your mind. You need to go before you git more involved with Matthew."

"Please understand, Granny. I'm making the bricks for Matthew's chimney, and I want to help him any way I can. I know you worry about me. And I also understand there's a lot about him I don't know, but he's a good man. And he has big dreams for his farm. I want to be a part of it with him."

Granny squeezed her hand. "Yeah, I reckon he is a good man, but I don't want either one of you to git hurt. I 'spect all I can do now is pray for both of you, but I don't want you to keep your folks in the dark about this much longer. When you planning on telling them?"

"I wanted to wait until Stephen got home so he could meet Matthew."

Granny nodded. "Well, Stephen will be here next week." She glanced at the basket and smiled. "Now get on out of here before that boy wonders what's keeping you. And remember I'm a-prayin' for you both."

Rani jumped to her feet and hugged Granny. "Thank you. I should be back before Mama and Poppa get home."

"You be careful now."

"I will," Rani called over her shoulder, and she ran out the back door.

As she headed toward the road that ran in

front of their cabin she glanced around for Scout, but he was nowhere in sight. He was probably off on one of his rambling trips. He'd just have to miss going with her to Matthew's today.

Humming a song they'd sung in church the Sunday before, she stepped into the dirt road and began the mile-and-a-half trip to Matthew's farm. She'd come to look forward to the time they spent talking about his plans for the farm. At night when she was in bed, she would recall all the things Matthew had told her about his plans, and she could see herself as having a major role in his dream.

About halfway to the farm, she was so engrossed in her thoughts that she didn't notice a horse and rider in the thick forest on the right side of the road until they emerged and blocked her path. The man reined the horse to a stop and leaned on the saddle pommel.

"What you doin' out here, Rani?"

She shaded her eyes with her hand and stared in surprise at the sight of George Ferguson trying to keep his balance on the horse. She didn't know which shocked her more, the fact that George had deliberately blocked her way or his slurred speech. She narrowed her eyes and stared at him weaving back and forth in the saddle.

She lowered her hand and took a hesitant step forward. "George, are you all right?"

A shrill laugh erupted from his throat. "That's a

good question. I thought I was last night until I woke up with this headache this mornin'."

Her mouth gaped open, and she sucked in her breath. "Have you been drinking?"

He laughed again and started to dismount, but his foot slipped, and he tumbled to the ground. Before Rani could reach him, he pushed himself to his feet and laughed. "I guess I missed the step."

Rani stopped in front of him and almost gagged. The stench of liquor and perfume combined with the smell from his vomit-stained shirt sent her reeling backwards. "You smell like you've spent the night in a tavern. Where have you been?"

A silly grin covered George's face, and he swayed on his feet. "Over to Wear's Valley, if it's any of your business. I found out there was some women in the world who like me even if you don't."

Her eyebrows shot up. "You *have* been in a tavern!" She shook her head in disgust. "Those women over there only like you for what you spend on them, George. I can't imagine what your pa is going to say when you get home. And your mother. Did you stop to think how this behavior is going to hurt her?"

He took a step toward her, but his legs wobbled so she feared they would collapse. "Don't you say nothing about my folks," he snarled. "They always treated you nice."

"I know they did, but I doubt if they'll be happy with you when you get home." Her gaze raked him once more and she took a step forward. "I can't stand to see you like this. Now get out of my path so I can be on my way."

He grabbed her arm and clamped his fingers around it. "You ain't walkin' away from me, Rani. Not until I say you can."

She tried to tug free, but he tightened his grip. "George, you're hurting my arm. Please let me go. I don't know what's come over you. I've never seen you like this before, and I don't like it."

He gritted his teeth and glared at her. "Well, get used to it. I expect this is all you'll get from me from now on."

Her eyes widened in fear, and she tried to pull away again. "George, have you forgotten that we're friends?"

"Friends? Is that what you think? Well, friends don't treat each other the way you done me."

Rani quit struggling against him and stared up into his face. "I am your friend, George. I've only tried to be honest with you. I didn't mean to hurt you."

His eyes glazed, and he released her. He staggered backwards a step and stared at her. The pain in his eyes pierced her heart. "Hurt me?" he murmured. "You nearly killed me, Rani. I feel like somebody done carved my chest up with a big knife and cut my heart right out. I've loved you since we were young'uns, and you acted like it meant nothing to you."

She reached out toward him, but he swatted her hand away. "It does mean a lot to me, George. When you're sober, you'll understand I did it for your own good."

"I ain't never gonna feel better, and it's your fault." He grabbed hold of the saddle and pulled himself back up. When he was seated again, he pointed his finger at her. "I hope someday you know how I feel. I reckon your time's a-comin' if you think Luke Jackson's son is gonna make you happy. It ain't gonna happen, Rani, and I'm gonna be there to rub it in."

Before she could respond, he grabbed the reins and dug his heels into the horse's side. She watched as they galloped down the road. George had been a part of her life for as long as she could remember, and now it was as if he'd turned into someone she didn't know.

Suddenly she didn't want to share the noon meal with Matthew. All she wanted was to go home and talk to Granny. She would deliver Matthew's food, but then she was heading right back to the cabin where her life had always been peaceful and filled with love. Maybe she could find help for her troubled heart there.

Matthew had no idea what was troubling Rani, but he could tell something had happened. When he'd left this morning for his farm, she'd met him at the barn and told him she would bring the noon meal for him. But when she'd arrived, she had been elusive and wouldn't talk. Then she'd left without eating.

Now with supper over, she had disappeared. For the past week they'd spent the time after supper on the front porch. Scout would lie between their two chairs, and they'd talked at length about the mountains they loved, the progress he was making at his farm, and his future plans for the lodge.

Tonight, though, she didn't join him, and it worried him. Alone, he listened to the voices of Simon, Anna, and Granny drift through the open front door. Rani hadn't joined them either. Where could she be?

Scout, who lay beside him, suddenly rose, shook his body, and ambled down the front steps. Matthew rose and followed Scout around the front of the house and into the field next to it where the smell of burning wood drifted on the night air. Their destination now obvious, Matthew moved toward the spot where he knew Rani would be.

He found her sitting beside the fire pit, the glow from the embers giving a soft glow to her body. She turned and smiled when he eased down beside her. "What are you doing out here?"

"I missed you after supper and couldn't figure

out where you'd gone. Scout seemed to know, though."

She laughed and rubbed the dog's head before he settled on the other side of her. She stared into the sky. "Aren't the stars beautiful tonight?"

He followed her gaze and nodded. "They are."

"I like to sit out here at night sometimes and look at the stars. I wonder about God and how He made such a beautiful creation for us, and I thank Him for letting me live in this valley. And I try to sort out things in my head."

"What kind of things?"

"Oh, just things that worry me."

He reached for her hand and clasped it in his. "And what are you worried about tonight? You were so quiet at supper I could tell something was wrong. Can't you tell me what it is?"

"I don't want to upset you."

"I want you to be able to tell me anything. If something's bothering you, I want to know what it is."

She sighed. "It's George."

His body stiffened, and he straightened his shoulders. "George?"

"Yes. I met him on the road to your farm today." She turned to him, and the fire reflected in the tears in her eyes. "He was drunk, Matthew. I know his parents are upset, and I don't know what to do."

"But why was he drunk in the middle of the day?"

"I think he must have been drinking for a long time. He smelled awful, and he couldn't even stand up." She slipped her hand free of his and wiped at her eyes. "But that's not the worst part of it. He told me it was all my fault."

"Your fault? But why?"

"He said I had cut his heart out." She spoke the words without looking at him, and then fell silent.

"Oh, I see. He wants you to think because you won't marry him you've turned him into a drunk."

"I guess so."

He stared into her eyes. "Rani, you didn't hold a gun to his head and make him drink. He made that choice. You can't accept the blame. It sounds like he wants you to feel sorry for him."

She thought about that for a moment before she nodded. "I think you may be right. He's always sulked when he didn't get his way. But I never meant to hurt him. I only wanted to be honest with him. I don't love him, and I don't want to marry him."

His heart leaped at her words. "I'm glad," he whispered.

"So am I." She leaned forward, cupped her hands around his face, and stared into his eyes before she brushed her lips across his cheek in a feathery kiss. "Thank you, Matthew."

He swallowed and willed himself not to pull

her into his arms. He didn't want anything to ruin this tender moment. "For what?"

"For listening to me and helping me find some peace. My Uncle Charles always did that before he left the mountains."

"I have a lot of respect for Doc. I don't think I could ever be the man he is, but I'm glad I was here to help you now."

"So am I. I can't wait for him to see you and for Stephen to meet you."

She smiled, laid her head on his shoulder, and turned her attention back to the fire. He stared up at the stars again and said his own silent prayer of thanks to God for bringing him home.

Then he placed his arm around her waist, and they sat side by side staring into the fire, flaming around the bricks that would soon be a part of his home. He had begun to hope that the woman who'd made them might also have a place in his future. She already had a place in his heart.

The day Anna had looked forward to for weeks had finally arrived. Stephen and Uncle Charles would arrive any minute. It had been too long since she'd had them together at one time. It could only be better if her brother Robert and his family and her mother were also coming. Maybe she could plan a family reunion of sorts in the fall.

She pulled her dress from the wardrobe in her

bedroom, slipped it over her head, and moved to the mirror her brother had given her when she married. As she squinted at her reflection, her gaze traveled over the tiny wrinkles around her eyes. Her skin no longer resembled that of the young girl who'd come to Cades Cove. The years had transformed her into a person that at times she hardly recognized.

Where was that girl who had jumped out of a buggy twenty years ago ready to take on whatever life threw at her? Sometimes she wondered how that girl who'd led such a sheltered life on her family's farm in Strawberry Plains had survived the hard years in the Cove.

The door opened, and Simon walked in. A warmth filled her, and she knew it would never have been possible if he hadn't been with her. She pulled her hands away from her face, took a deep breath, and began to button the bodice of her dress. Simon's reflection appeared behind her in the mirror, and she smiled.

He put his arms around her waist and nuzzled her neck. "Don't you look pretty this afternoon."

Her fingers stilled, and she stared into the mirror. "Do you really think so?"

He chuckled. "I do. I wouldn't trade you for any other woman in the world."

His arms tightened, and she leaned back against him. "But I'm getting older, and I don't look like the girl I used to be."

He kissed her ear and then laughed. "I'm not the young man I was twenty years ago either. I like to think that we're just getting better with age."

"I do too." She turned in his arms and hugged him. "We're getting older, and our children are grown. Sometimes I wonder where the years went."

"Me too."

She took a deep breath. "But this is a happy day. I can hardly believe Stephen will be here soon. It seems like ages since we've seen him and Uncle Charles too." She pulled away, turned back to the mirror, and smoothed her hair into place. "What time is it?"

He pulled out his pocket watch and opened it. "It's three o'clock. What time are John and Martha coming?"

"Martha said they'd be here about five. She's bringing her blackberry pie and green beans and squash from her garden. I've got the chickens roasting in the oven, and the peas and new potatoes are simmering on the stove. We have the jam cake Granny made yesterday, but I still have to cook the corn and slice the tomatoes." She bit down on her lip. "Do you think that will be enough food for everybody?"

Simon laughed. "As long as you don't invite the rest of the neighbors to eat." He laughed and smiled at his wife. "I think I'll go find Rani.

Have you seen her lately? I couldn't find her before I came in here."

"I think she's checking on the bricks out at the pit. Why are you looking for her?"

He put his watch back in his pocket and sat down on the edge of the bed. "I'm worried about her."

His tone of voice stirred a warning in Anna. She turned around from the mirror and walked over to where he sat. "Why? Has she said anything?"

He shook his head. "It's just a feeling I have. She's seemed a lot happier lately, and she smiles a lot like she has a secret. Do you think she's up to something we don't know about?"

Anna propped her hands on her hips and laughed. "Simon Martin, quit looking for trouble. You should be glad she's happy. After the way she moped around here all winter and fussed about Little River Lumber, it's time she perked up. You know she's always happier when summer comes. And she's really excited about Stephen and Uncle Charles coming."

Simon pushed to his feet. "Maybe it's nothing, but still . . ."

Anna held up her hand to quiet him. "Let's not think about anything except Stephen's homecoming today. Are you still planning to talk to him while he's here?"

"I am." Simon took her hand and pulled her

toward the door. "Let's go wait with Granny. Maybe Rani will come inside soon."

Granny sat in her chair in front of the unlit fireplace just as she had all winter. She smiled when they walked into the room. "Now I know what you're a-gonna say. Of course there ain't no need for a fire in July, but I shore do like a-sittin' here and thinkin'. And today I'm a-thinkin' 'bout Stephen and Doc a-comin' home. Reckon when they gonna git here?"

Anna laughed and walked to the front door. "I don't know, Granny. Uncle Charles told me in his last letter that his train got into Townsend before Stephen's. He was going to have the horse and buggy rented and waiting by the time Stephen arrived. I hope their trains were on time."

Simon ambled over to stand behind her. "I do too. But I felt better knowing Stephen could drive Doc here. A man sixty-five years old doesn't need to be making that trip by himself."

Anna turned to him and arched an eyebrow. "Tell that to him. He still insists he had to retire because his horse Toby, not him, wasn't able to make it over the mountain roads anymore."

Simon and Granny both laughed. "I've heard him say it many times, but we all know . . ."

Before he could finish, Anna whirled back to stare out the door. "They're here!" she cried as she rushed onto the front porch and down the steps.

Simon ran after her, and they came to a stop just as the buggy rolled into the yard. Stephen pulled the horse to a stop, handed the reins to his uncle, and jumped to the ground. He ran to them, wrapped his arms around his mother, and lifted her in the air.

She squealed in delight just as she'd done ever since Stephen had gotten big enough to pick her up. She hugged him, and he set her down on the ground. "Mama, you're prettier than you were when I left last fall."

Tears of happiness filled her eyes, and she patted his cheek. "And you look more like my father every day. I'm so glad I gave you his name. He'd be so proud of you."

Stephen glanced at Simon and swallowed before he stuck out his hand. "Hello, Poppa. It's good to see you."

Simon stared at his son, and Anna wondered how he had ever allowed the gulf to develop between them. Had he been so grief-stricken over Willie that he had ignored the boy who was growing into a man right before his eyes? Tears glistened in his eyes, and he pushed the outstretched hand away and pulled Stephen into a bear hug. "It's good to have you home, son. I think we have a lot to talk about while you're here."

Stephen's arms encircled his shoulders, and Anna felt as if her heart would explode with joy at the sight of her husband and son embracing.

"I have a lot I want to tell you, Poppa. I've missed you."

"I've missed you too."

"Well, land's sakes," Granny called out from the porch. "Are you gonna keep Doc a-sittin' in that buggy all day, or are you gonna help him down?" She held out her arms. "Come here, boy, and give your ole Granny a hug."

Stephen pulled away from Simon and smiled. "Granny, did you make me a jam cake?"

She propped a hand on her hip and sniffed. "You think I'd let you come all the way home and not have your fav'rite cake a-waitin'?"

He laughed and rushed up the steps to Granny. Anna turned back to Simon, but he was already on the other side of the buggy helping her uncle climb down. "Wait a minute, Doc," he said. "I'll help you."

Simon held the reins in one hand and the other gripped her uncle's arm. Anna reached for his other arm and helped him step to the ground. When he steadied himself, she put her arms around his shoulders and gave him a hug. "Uncle Charles, I'm so glad you're here. It seems like ages since I've seen you."

His mouth curled down in the familiar smile that reminded her of her father, and he pushed his spectacles up on his nose. "I've missed all of you and couldn't pass up this opportunity to come back to the place I love."

Simon stepped around him and climbed into the buggy. "And we're glad you did. Now I'm going to take care of your horse. You go on inside with Anna and Granny, and I'll be back shortly."

Anna looped her arm through her uncle's and guided him to the porch where Stephen and Granny still stood. As they approached the steps, he frowned and glanced down at her. "Where's Rani?"

"Probably out at the fire pit getting ready to fire her next batch of bricks. She's making them for the chimney at Matthew's cabin."

Uncle Charles chuckled. "That girl never ceases to amaze me." He reached over and chucked Anna under the chin. "But with the mother she has I shouldn't be surprised."

Anna stared up into the faded eyes of the man who had brought her to Cades Cove all those years ago, and her heart filled with gratitude. "I was lucky. I had a wonderful uncle to guide me after my father died. Sometimes I shudder when I think what my life might have been like if I'd been accepted to nursing school the first time I applied. You never would have brought me here, and I never would have experienced the happiness I found in these mountains."

He smiled. "I was only God's instrument to let you find out the plan He had for you. I'm thankful you listened to Him."

"I am too, Uncle Charles. I am too."

Chapter 10

Simon leaned back in his chair and smiled. The buzz of conversation drifted through the room and filled him with a contentment he hadn't felt in a long time. Besides Stephen and Uncle Charles, John, Martha, and two of their children had joined them for supper.

He studied the faces of each person seated around the table tonight. Rani was laughing as Matthew leaned over and whispered something in her ear. A rosy glow covered her face tonight, and he wondered if it was because her brother was home or if it was something else. After Stephen's visit, he needed to find out what had caused her newfound happiness.

Then there was Stephen, the son who had stayed away from home this past year because of heated words between the two of them. No one would ever know how he regretted the words he'd spoken and how much grief it had caused Anna. It was time to do something about it.

He cleared his throat. "Could I have your attention for a moment?"

The conversation halted, and everyone turned their heads to stare as Simon rose to his feet. He let his gaze drift over each one. When he didn't speak, Anna frowned. "What is it, Simon?"

He cleared his throat and tried again to speak. "All the people I love most in the world are seated at this table tonight. I'm thankful for Anna and my two children, for my brother and his family, for Doc who brought Anna to me years ago, for Granny who's taken care of all of us, and for Matthew—who returned just as he promised."

He paused and blinked back the tears filling his eyes. "I've tried to be the kind of man God wanted me to be, but sometimes I've failed. All of you know how hard I've been on Stephen about wanting him to follow me in the ministry."

Stephen's eyes grew wide, and he leaned forward. "Poppa, we don't need to talk about this in front of everybody."

Simon shook his head. "No, I have to say this, Stephen. After much soul-searching and prayer, I have realized what I should have known all along. God's plans for Stephen don't lie in guiding people in their spiritual lives. The gifts God gave him are for a different ministry, for helping heal their bodies. I'm sorry I didn't listen to you, son, and I want you to know I support your decision to pursue medicine."

Stephen's eyes grew even wider. "You . . . you do?"

"Yes. You did what I asked and completed a year at Milligan College. Now if you still want to go to Vanderbilt, I'll help you get there."

Stephen pushed to his feet and rushed toward Simon. He grabbed him and hugged him, then held him at arm's length and stared into his eyes. "Poppa, thank you so much. I'll work hard and make you proud of me."

Simon squeezed his son's arms. "I've always been proud of you. All I want is for you to be the best doctor you can be and take care of me when I'm old and sick."

Laughter echoed around the room, and Simon glanced at Anna. She wiped a tear from the corner of her eye and smiled. Her mouth formed the words *I love you,* and he let out a deep breath. *I love you too,* he mouthed before he released his son and glanced at Granny.

"Now how about some of that jam cake, Granny, and maybe a helping of Martha's blackberry cobbler? I feel like celebrating tonight."

Granny chuckled as Anna and Martha rose and began to clear away the plates and prepare for dessert. "When it comes to eatin', preacher boy, you celebrate ev'ry night. But I always liked to see a man with a healthy appetite, and yours is 'bout the healthiest I ever seen."

He laughed and clutched at his heart. "Wounded again by one of the women in my house. I don't know if I'll survive to old age."

He rose, picked up some of the plates, and carried them to the dry sink where Anna stood. When he set them down, Anna reached out and squeezed his arm. "Thank you for doing that in front of everyone, Simon. You've made Stephen very happy. Uncle Charles says he's going to make a great doctor."

He leaned over and kissed her on the cheek. "Never let it be said I doubted Doc. After all, I wouldn't have you if he hadn't talked you into staying with me."

She laughed and punched him playfully on the arm. "He didn't talk me into it. I decided on my own because I loved you so much." She glanced over her shoulder at the people gathered around their table. "And God has really blessed us, Simon."

He followed her gaze and nodded. "Yes, He has."

When Stephen returned to his seat, Rani leaned across the table and stuck out her hand. Stephen grabbed it, and they squeezed their hands tight together.

"I can't believe Poppa did that in front of everybody, Stephen, but I'm glad he did."

"I am too," he said. "I had come home intending to tell him that I had already been accepted at Vanderbilt for the fall. Uncle Charles had promised to help me with the expenses, but we were afraid of how Poppa would react."

She smiled. "It doesn't look like you have to worry anymore."

Uncle Charles laughed and slapped Stephen on the back. "I told you that God would work it all out, and He did."

Stephen nodded. "He sure did."

Uncle Charles glanced at Matthew and smiled. "Matthew, how's the rebuilding coming along?"

Matthew shifted in his chair. "It's slower than I'd like. But Simon thinks in the next few weeks he'll be able to get a group of men together to come and help me. Cecil Davis is going to build the fireplace."

Uncle Charles's eyebrows arched. "And I hear Rani is making the bricks for it. How's that going?"

"I'm just about finished," Rani said. "I dug an extra pit so I can bake more at a time. I'll have them ready by the time Mr. Davis comes to Matthew's farm."

Uncle Charles shook his head. "Your brother has a gift for medicine, and you have a gift for making pottery. I'm very proud of you both."

Matthew glanced at her, and the smile on his lips made her pulse race. "She's quite a woman all right. I've never seen anything like the pottery she makes."

"Which reminds me," Uncle Charles said. "I wish you'd come to Maryville and visit me soon. The grandson of an old friend of mine has moved to town and opened a studio. He makes pottery and fires it in a kiln he built in the back yard. He's making quite a name for himself at the resorts in the mountains."

Rani's mouth widened. "He has a kiln? I've read about them and wished that I could see one."

"Well, come visit me, and I'll take you to his studio."

Matthew swiveled in his seat. "I told you there were people who wanted to buy mountain-made crafts. Maybe you should go to Maryville and meet him. You might be able to sell some of your pottery through him."

She waved her hand in dismissal. "I've told you mine aren't good enough to sell."

"Well, I think they are," Matthew said.

A slight smile pulled at the doctor's mouth. He looked from Rani to Matthew before he pushed his spectacles up on his nose. "Well, if you ever come to see me, I'll take you to his studio."

She nodded. "All right, but I don't know when I'll be able to get away. I have too much going on here right now."

Uncle Charles's mouth twitched. "That's what I thought."

She started to ask him what he meant, but her mother's voice caught her attention. "Rani, come help us serve dessert."

She jumped up from her chair and hurried to help her mother and aunt. She didn't think about Uncle Charles's words again until she was in bed later that night. Had he detected something

199

between her and Matthew? If so, he was more observant than her parents. Granny said she couldn't understand why they couldn't see it, but neither had asked her about it.

She smiled and slipped under the covers. For now, the fewer people who knew how she felt the better for her, but she had promised Granny she would tell her parents when Stephen left. She wanted to keep the secret tucked away in her heart for now. Maybe Matthew would declare his intentions, as Granny said, before long. Then they would tell her family together.

Sighing in happiness, she closed her eyes and said a prayer of thanks to God for bringing her brother and uncle home. Tonight had been one of the best nights she'd had in a long time, and she was glad Matthew had been there to share it with her.

With breakfast over, Matthew stepped out the back door of the cabin and stared at the dark clouds hanging over the mountains. Even the threat of rain couldn't dampen his spirits this morning. He was still thinking about the good time the family had enjoyed the night before with Stephen and Doc. The laughter and the love he'd seen around the supper table made him wish that he could really be a part of the Martin family, not just a guest in their home.

He shook the thought from his head and walked

toward the barn. He would have liked to linger at the breakfast table longer and listen to the stories Doc and Granny were telling about their early days in the Cove, but he needed to be on his way.

He'd almost reached the barnyard when a wagon rattled into the front yard, and a woman's voice rose in a scream. "Anna! Anna! I need help!"

Matthew turned and ran back to the cabin and around the side to the front yard. The front door flew open, and Simon and Anna ran onto the porch at the moment he rounded the corner of the house. He stopped in surprise at the sight in front of him.

Laura Ferguson pulled back on the reins of the team pulling a farm wagon and set the brake with her foot. He shook his head in disbelief that a petite woman like Laura had been able to hook the horses to the wagon, much less drive them here. But mountain women were used to filling in where they were needed. And from the fear on her face, he knew she was in great need today.

Anna and Simon ran down the steps. "Laura, what's wrong?"

She wrapped the reins around the brake and scrambled over the seat into the back of the wagon. "It's Pete. He's hurt bad. Help me, please."

Matthew ran to the back of the wagon, released the tail gate, and peered into the bed of the wagon where Pete lay unconscious. His stomach roiled at the pool of blood that surrounded Pete's body. Anna was already climbing in, and he and Simon gave her a boost.

"What happened?" she asked.

"Pete was outside a-cuttin' wood this morning when he made a mislick with the axe. It came down and cut his leg real bad. I didn't know what to do, but I brought him here to you and Granny 'cause it's closer than Doc Harrison's house. Kin you help him?"

Anna raised the blood-soaked cloth that covered Pete's leg. She bit down on her lip and replaced the cloth, then reached out and grasped Laura's shoulder. "You did right, Laura. He might have bled to death before you could have driven all the way to Dr. Harrison's house. Besides, Uncle Charles is here, and he'll help us."

Laura glanced toward the house and breathed a sigh of relief. "Thank the Lord for Doc a-bein' here. I reckon I done the right thing."

Matthew glanced toward the house and saw Doc and Rani step onto the porch. "It's Pete Ferguson. He has a bad axe wound."

Doc pursed his lips and turned to go back inside. "Bring him in the kitchen, Simon, and I'll get my bag."

Anna motioned for Matthew and Simon. "Pick him up, but be careful of his leg."

Stephen ran down the steps and joined them as

they pulled Pete's limp body from the back of the wagon. The three of them carried him up the steps and into the kitchen where Granny waited with the table ready for them to lay him down.

When Pete was settled, Stephen turned to his mother. "Can I stay and assist? This is my first time to see an injury like this, and I want to help out."

She and Simon exchanged quick smiles. "I hope you make out better than I did the first time I had to help Granny with a similar case. But Matthew, why don't you go on to your farm? I know you've got a lot to do today."

He shook his head. "I'll wait to see how Pete makes it."

Granny poured some hot water from the kettle into a pan. "Then go on out on the front porch and help Rani settle Laura down. We don't need her bustin' in here while we're working."

He nodded. "All right, Granny. Call me if you need me."

He cast one last glance at Pete before he turned and hurried back to the porch. Laura was seated there, and Rani knelt in front of her and held her hands. "Mrs. Ferguson," she was saying, "would you like something to eat or drink while we're waiting? We have some coffee left from break-fast."

Laura shook her head. "Thank you kindly, Rani, but my stomach is just tied up in knots right now. I heared Pete a-screamin' for me, and I nearly fainted when I seen what had happened." She cast a worried glance in the direction of the front door. "He's gonna be all right, ain't he? I don't know what I'd do if'n anything happened to him. He's all I got now."

Rani patted Laura's hand. "Now, now. Don't talk like that. You have a wonderful family. There's Ted and Lucy and George. They love you so much and you know they'd do anything for you."

Laura's eyes filled with fresh tears. "Lucy and Ted done moved out of the Cove. I won't hardly ever see them again. And only the Lord knows where George is."

Matthew and Rani exchanged surprised glances. "What do you mean?" Rani asked.

Tears trickled down her cheeks. "George ain't been home much lately. He's taken up with a bad crowd, and he came home drunk a few times. The last time it happened Pete told him not to come back 'til he was ready to settle down and act like a man."

"Oh, Mrs. Ferguson, I'm so sorry."

The woman wiped at her eyes. "Pete's been real upset about it, and he's a-blamin' me for a lot of it. Says I was always too easy and always made excuses for George 'cause he was my baby." She leaned forward and gazed into Rani's eyes. "But you know he's a good boy, Rani."

Rani nodded. "Maybe he's just lost his way right now. But I know you raised him right, and he'll come around in time."

A sob escaped Laura's mouth. "If'n he don't get killed first. The last time he come home drunk Pete found bottles of moonshine in his saddle bags. He said it was for a feller over to Wear's Valley. Pete asked him if he was a-workin' at somebody's still, and they had a terrible argument. George said what if he was making moonshine, it paid better than scratching out a living in the dirt. That's when Pete told him to leave, and we ain't seen him since."

Rani's face paled, and she swallowed. "I'm so sorry, Mrs. Ferguson."

Her lips trembled. "I'm so a-feared the sheriff's gonna ride up one day and tell us he raided a moonshine still and George is in jail for making illegal liquor. Or worse yet, that he was shot and killed trying to get away from the law. I don't know what I'll do if that happens."

Rani cast a helpless glance in Matthew's direction. "You can't think like that."

Laura nodded, and then clamped her hands over her eyes. "That's what Pete says, but I cain't help it, and now Pete's hurt real bad." She took a deep breath. "Oh, Lord, please don't let him die," she wailed.

Matthew eased down into the chair next to Laura. "That's what we're all praying right now.

But he couldn't have a better team working on him than Doc and Granny, and Anna. I think God led you to bring Pete here today because He knew this is where he'd get good care. I know they'll do everything they can for him."

Laura lowered her hands to her lap, and a brief smile flickered on her face. "That's right nice of you, Matthew. I seen you at church a few times, but I ain't talked to you since you come home. Are you glad to be back?"

"I am."

Rani grasped Laura's hand and leaned closer to her. "And we're all going to sit here and pray until Mama comes out and tells us how Mr. Ferguson is."

Laura looked from one to the other. "Thank you for bein' so good to me today. I guess we just have to leave this all up to the Lord."

Rani nodded, leaned back, and closed her eyes. Her lips moved, but Matthew couldn't make out the words she prayed. He wondered how Laura's words about George had affected her. He'd tried to tell her George's choices weren't her fault, but he didn't think she had accepted that yet.

After a moment he closed his eyes and offered his own prayer for Pete Ferguson's well-being. As always he ended with the words he'd prayed every day since childhood. *Don't let me be like my father. Make me a better man.*

Matthew opened his eyes a few minutes later

and smiled at the steady gaze Rani directed at him. Laura still sat with her eyes closed, and neither he nor Rani spoke. They didn't have to. She stared at him with an intensity like he'd never experienced. And in her gaze he recognized what he'd been missing in his life. Rani loved him, and the thought almost took his breath away. He hoped she could see the same in his eyes.

He smiled, and she nodded. Their silent communication confirmed what he'd known was taking place in their lives. Now he just had to figure out what they were going to do about it.

Laura opened her eyes and sat up straight. "How long has it been since they carried Pete inside?"

With the moment shattered, Matthew turned his attention back to Laura. "They haven't had time to finish yet. We'll just have to be patient."

An hour later, Matthew didn't know how much more patient he could be. He had paced up and down the porch for the last fifteen minutes and paused at the door from time to time to listen for sounds from inside the house. So far he hadn't been able to make out anything.

He walked to the opposite end of the porch from where Rani and Laura sat and had just turned to walk back when Doc stepped out of the house. All three of them hurried to him before he could take a second step.

Laura clutched at Doc's arm. "How is he?"

Doc smiled and patted her hand. "He's doing fine, Laura. The cut wasn't nearly as bad as the blood made it look. We were able to stop the bleeding and sew up the wound. He's going to have to stay off his feet for a few weeks, but I think he'll be back to normal before you know it."

Laura's body sagged, and Matthew slipped an arm around her waist to steady her. "Thank You, Lord, thank You for sparing Pete's life."

"I don't want to move Pete today," Doc continued. "We've got him settled in the bed in Stephen's room. You can go in and see him, and you can stay in there with him tonight. If he does all right by tomorrow, we'll help you get him home. I'll be leaving for Maryville in a few days, but Anna will continue to come each day and check on him."

Laura wiped at the tears on her face and smiled. "I reckon there ain't nowhere on earth folks would be so good as they are in the Cove. The Lord sure blessed me to put me among such friends." Her brow wrinkled into a frown. "I reckon as soon as I see Pete I need to go home and tend to our livestock. Then I'll come back."

Matthew shook his head. "I'll do that for you, Mrs. Ferguson. In fact, while Pete's laid up I'll come by in the mornings and afternoons to take care of your animals. And I can chop wood for you and, well, do anything else you need."

Laura turned her head and stared at him. "That's real kind of you, Matthew. Your ma had a good heart, and I reckon she'd be real proud of you for offerin' to help me. You must be a lot like her."

Matthew couldn't speak as Laura followed Doc into the house. When they'd disappeared inside, he turned back to Rani. A slight smile pulled at her lips. He swallowed hard. "Did you hear what she said, Rani? She said I was a lot like my mother."

She smiled. "I heard, and I think she's right. Your offer to Laura meant a lot to her. I think you're a very good man, Matthew Jackson. Now you have to believe it too."

"I'm trying," he murmured. "But it sure is nice having someone believe in me."

"I'll always believe in you."

The look she had directed at him earlier returned to her eyes, and it filled him with a renewed hope for his future. Now all he had to do was convince the rest of the people in the Cove he was more like his mother than his father.

Chapter 11

A week later Matthew emerged from the Martins' barn and headed toward the fire pit in the field. Life had returned to normal at the Martin cabin. Pete had gone home two days after his accident, and Doc and Stephen had left a few days later.

Matthew had done as promised and had gone by the Ferguson farm every day to do what he could to help. Pete, true to his mountain-bred nature, was determined to return the favor by helping to rebuild Matthew's cabin.

As Matthew approached the fire pit, he could see Rani sitting beside it. He dropped down beside her and grinned. "How's the latest batch coming?"

She glanced up from studying the glowing embers in the shallow pit and brushed her hair back over her shoulders. "They're fine. We're getting closer to having enough for the chimney." She picked up a stick and stirred the coals in the bottom of the pit. "I didn't expect to see you this morning. I thought you'd already left for the Fergusons when I came out here."

He shook his head. "No, I was in the barn getting ready to leave when I saw you come out of the cabin. I thought I'd see if the latest bricks fired all right."

She let her gaze drift over the charred bricks for a moment before she sat back on her heels. "They look fine. They should be cooled down enough by the time Poppa and I get back with the clay this afternoon. By tonight I'll have the new ones ready to fire. Do you want to help me put them in and get the fire going?"

He chuckled and nodded. "Haven't I helped you every night for the last week? I think I've become an expert at pit firing."

She laughed and gave him a playful punch on the arm. "I'll remember that. I can always use a good assistant."

He rose, reached down, and pulled her to her feet. "Anytime, ma'am. I'm at your service."

She stood so close he could easily wrap his arms around her, but he hesitated. He had kissed her, but he hadn't spoken of a commitment. He wanted to tell her how he felt, but something kept him from speaking the words. There were still too many unanswered questions about his past that he had to resolve, and it was unfair of him to keep those things hidden from her.

He took a deep breath. "You'd better get back to the house, and I need to get over to the Fergusons. I'll see you at supper."

She frowned and shook her head. "You're not leaving here without breakfast. I'm going to be too busy today to bring you anything to eat, so you'd better let us feed you and send something with you for later." Her frown changed to a smile. "Besides I want you to stay for a while longer. I miss having breakfast with you when you leave early."

His heart kicked against his chest at the glint in her eye. "Then you've talked me into it. I can't think of a better way to start the day than having breakfast with you and your family."

She smiled. "Good. I'll tell Mama you're staying after all. She was in the kitchen when I left, and Poppa was getting ready to go over to Uncle John's."

He rubbed his hand over the stubble on his chin. "I guess I do need to wash up some and shave before I go back inside. I wouldn't want you to regret asking me to stay."

"That would never happen."

She turned and headed back to the house. He watched her go and chuckled at how easy it had been for her to talk him into staying this morning. The truth was, though, he treasured every minute he spent with her.

Thirty minutes later, even though Simon had already left for his brother's house, Matthew couldn't tear himself away. He knew he had a full day's work waiting for him, but he was enjoying being with Anna and Granny and Rani this morning.

With one piece of ham and a few biscuits left on the table, Matthew drained his coffee cup and set it down. "I've been leaving so early every morning to go over to the Fergusons that I've missed this time with all of you." He glanced over at Rani. "But Rani has been good about bringing me something to eat later in the day."

Granny covered her mouth with her hand and coughed. "I reckon Rani has been right good 'bout takin' care of you, Matthew."

"She sure has, and I've enjoyed her company." He leaned back in his chair and patted his stomach. "I don't have to worry about being hungry here, that's for sure. It's been a long time since I've had cooking like this, Anna. With all the good eating you and Granny put out, I may decide I want to live here instead of at my farm."

Anna chuckled and rose. "Like we said, you're welcome to stay as long as you want. We think . . ." She hesitated and frowned. "Was that someone at the front door?" She rose to go to the door.

Granny sighed. "I don't think there's a baby due. I shore hope nobody else is sick or hurt. We've had 'bout all the excitement we need for a while."

Matthew could hear Anna's voice, but he couldn't tell what she was saying. Within moments she hurried back into the kitchen. Matthew glanced at Rani in surprise. The boy

Rani had given the cookies to at church trailed behind Anna.

Rani jumped up and stared at the boy. "Noah, what are you doing here?"

Noah's blond hair looked as if it hadn't been combed in days and the cowlick at the back of his head stuck straight up. He wore no shoes and his feet and ankles were covered in dirt. But it wasn't his appearance that concerned Matthew as much as the fear in his blue eyes. His lips trembled as if he was trying to keep from crying.

Rani glanced at her mother. "What's the matter?"

"Noah's mother is very ill. From what he tells me, she's been sick for several days, but she wouldn't let him come for me. This morning he couldn't wake her up, so he came anyway."

Granny pushed to her feet. "Child, where's your pa?"

Noah wiped his nose on his sleeve and shook his head. "Don't know, Granny. He's been gone a long time. He come home one day last week, but he took off ag'in 'bout three days ago—right after Ma got sick. Said he'd be back, but we ain't seen him."

Anna pulled her apron off and hung it on a peg by the stove. "I have to go check on her, and Rani, I may need you to go for Dr. Harrison." She turned toward him. "Matthew, can you hitch the horse to the buggy for us?"

He nodded and jumped to his feet. "Of course, and I'll go with you."

Granny and Anna exchanged quick glances, and Anna shook her head. "You don't have to do that. You have a lot to do at your farm. I can manage the buggy on my own."

Matthew shook his head. "I don't mind. If you need the doctor, I'll be glad to go for you."

Anna placed her hand on Noah's shoulder. "You may not want to accompany us. We're going to Wade Campbell's place. This is his son."

Matthew's eyes grew wide, and he grasped the back of the chair. Memories of years ago tumbled through his head. Just like Noah, he had run to Anna when his mother needed help. He stared into the boy's frightened eyes, and his heart dropped to the bottom of his stomach. He understood exactly what Noah was feeling. He swallowed hard. "Do Mr. Ben and Miss Virgie still live there?"

Anna shook her head. "No, they both died some years ago. Now Wade and his family live in his parents' cabin."

"Then I'm going, Anna. I don't want you and Rani there alone."

He turned and rushed out the back door toward the barn. Halfway there he stopped and raised a trembling hand to rub his eyes. Of all the people in the Cove, he had hoped he could avoid seeing Wade Campbell, but his hopes had just been dashed.

With a shake of his head, he inhaled and ran toward the barn. It didn't make any difference if he saw Wade today or not. The past couldn't be changed, and it did no good to dwell on it. All he needed to think about now was helping a young boy get help for his sick mother. If he encountered Wade in the process, he'd just have to deal with it.

Rani had no idea what had just taken place between her mother and Matthew in the kitchen, but she knew it had upset Matthew. She directed a questioning look at her mother, but she just frowned and held out a chair for Noah. "Sit down, Noah, and Granny will get you some breakfast while Rani and I are getting ready."

The boy eyed the ham and biscuits on the table. "Thank you, Miss Anna. I ain't had anything since yesterday when I ate the last of the biscuits Ma made 'fore she got so sick."

Granny hobbled over to the cabinet and pulled a plate out. "Well, you gonna eat now. How 'bout some milk to go with that there ham?"

Before Rani could question her mother about Matthew's reaction to Wade Campbell's name, she rushed from the kitchen toward the room where her medical supplies were stored. Rani hurried after her and entered to find her mother already inspecting the contents of her medical bag.

"Mama, what did Noah say is wrong with his mother?"

Anna rifled through the bag for a moment before she looked up. "He just said she had pains in her side and has been vomiting. He also said her skin was very hot."

"Do you have any idea what it might be?"

Her mother shook her head. "There's no need to guess at this point. But we do need to hurry."

Rani nodded and took a step closer. "Mama, why did Matthew get upset when you mentioned Noah's father?"

Her mother closed the medical bag and picked it up. "Twenty years ago Wade Campbell was about the age you are now. His parents tried to keep a rein on him, but they couldn't. He drank and gambled and was always into some kind of trouble. And he thought he could best any man in the Cove when it came to a fight."

Rani bristled at the memory from her Sunday school class a few months earlier. Noah had flinched when he sat down, and he had confided in her that his pa had whipped him with a razor strap. "Well, he hasn't changed much. I've often wondered how his wife lives with him."

"Yes, Bertha has had a hard time, but she's stayed because she had nowhere else to go. And she loves Noah."

Rani crossed her arms and frowned. "Well, his father must not or he wouldn't beat him so. But I still don't understand about Matthew."

Her mother sighed. "Like I said—Wade thought he could beat any man in a fight. One night he was in a tavern over in Wear's Valley. He was drinking with Luke Jackson. They got into an argument, and when it was over, Luke was dead of a gunshot wound."

Rani's eyes widened, and she gasped in surprise. "Wade Campbell is the man who killed Matthew's father?"

"Yes. All the witnesses said Luke drew his gun first, so Wade wasn't charged with murder. I'd hoped Matthew would have some time to adjust to life here before he had to see Wade. And I hope he doesn't come home while we're there."

Rani turned her head at the rattle of the buggy drawing to a stop beside the house. "Matthew's outside," she said.

Anna hurried from the room with Rani close behind. They stepped into the kitchen just as Matthew appeared at the door. "I'm ready whenever you are," he said.

Her mother motioned to Noah before she headed to her bedroom. "Noah, finish eating while I get something from my room." She glanced over her shoulder at Matthew. "I won't be but a minute."

Noah jammed the last bite of biscuit in his mouth and picked up the glass of milk. Rani looked around for Matthew, but he had disappeared back outside. She hesitated before she hurried to catch up with him.

Matthew waited for them beside the buggy. He stared at the ground but looked up when she approached. She stopped in front of him and stared into his eyes. "Mama told me about Wade. Are you sure you're all right?"

The muscle in his jaw twitched, and his dark eyes reminded her of angry storm clouds. He looked very different from the man who had been laughing with her at the kitchen table just moments before. "I'll be okay, Rani. I guess I was foolish to think I could avoid seeing Wade. I know I'll have to see him sometime."

Rani frowned and inched closer to him. "Do you hate him?"

He shook his head. "I don't hate him. It's my father I hate, and everything he put our family through. Wade just did what I wanted to do many times."

Her breath caught in her throat, and she flinched at the anger lining his face. "You can't mean that, Matthew."

"Oh, but I do," he snarled. "You have no idea how it feels to have your mother put herself in front of you and take the blows your drunken father meant for you. My mother did that so many times I lost count. I would try to pull him off her, but he was too strong. After he'd finished, he'd pass out, and I'd think how easy it would be to shoot him."

She reached for his hand and cupped it in both of hers. "My parents have always told me you endured a lot from your father, but all of that made you into the man you are today. The man who kissed me doesn't have it in him to kill anyone."

He looked down at the hands covering his and let out a ragged breath before he pulled free. "You don't know me at all, Rani. And I guess it's better if you never do."

Before she could respond, Anna and Noah rushed from the house and toward the waiting buggy. Matthew helped Anna climb into the front seat before he turned to her daughter. When he clasped Rani's hand to help her into the buggy, his fingers tightened around hers, and she glanced up at him. The anger she'd seen earlier was gone, and in its place sorrow clouded his eyes.

Noah jumped in next to Rani, and Matthew grabbed the reins and wrapped them around his hands. "Everybody ready?"

Rani nodded, and he flicked the reins across the horse's back. As they headed onto the road that led toward the Campbell's cabin, Rani stared at Matthew's rigid back. Gone was the warmhearted man who had comforted her at Willie's grave. The man who had kissed her and spoken

220

with excitement about his dreams had also disappeared. Instead she saw the tormented face of a stranger.

She had witnessed the first glimpse of how past events had affected Matthew, and she realized he was right—she didn't know him at all. It appeared there were many different aspects of Matthew's personality she didn't understand. But much to her surprise, they didn't frighten her. Instead she felt protective of him. He needed someone to help him face the memories that still haunted him. She could be that someone.

She closed her eyes and prayed for Bertha Campbell, praying that her mother would be able to help her. And she prayed that nothing would happen at the Campbell cabin to awaken Matthew's dark memories.

When they pulled off the road and onto the trail leading to the Campbell cabin, Matthew's hands tightened on the reins. It had been twenty years since he'd come down this path, but he remembered it as if it were yesterday.

He still recalled how his shoes and pants were wet from running through the dew that sparkled on the grass that morning, but he didn't mind. He only had one thought in his head. Find his father, who had left home three days ago to go hunting for some game to feed the family. Now with all the food gone and his mother nearly exhausted from tending his sick brother, Matthew had slipped away to come to the home of Ben and Virgie Campbell, Wade's parents.

They had been cordial, but they didn't know if his father was off with Wade or not. Mrs. Campbell had even offered him a biscuit and a cup of milk, but he had refused. He didn't have time to eat when his mother and Eli were hungry. He had run most of the way home and had arrived just as the sheriff rode his horse into their yard.

Matthew heard his mother's scream at the sight of his father's body draped over the back of another horse the sheriff led, but he couldn't move. He stood still and stared at the man who had caused their family so much pain. His mother wouldn't receive any more beatings from his father, and relief had coursed through Matthew's body. But then he'd looked at his mother, and he'd regretted his thoughts.

In a few minutes time, her appearance had changed. Grief had carved hollowed-out lines in her face, and she looked like an old woman. Her wail split the air, and she fell to her knees, her hands lifted toward heaven as she cried out her agony to God. He'd never been able to rid himself of that picture. It had been seared in his mind. Every time he thought of his mother, he remembered how she'd looked the day the sheriff brought his father's body home.

Then resilience born of the hard life she'd

endured took control. She pushed to her feet and pulled her apron up to wipe away her tears. Taking a deep breath, she straightened her shoulders, and her features melted into the impassive look she would bear until her death five years later. She turned to him, and in that mountain twang he loved she said, "Son, I reckon you better be a-goin' for Miss Anna and Granny."

And that journey had now brought him to the one he was making today. Back to the place he'd come twenty years ago looking for his missing father, because today another young boy had come in search of help for his mother.

Matthew pulled the horse to a stop at the front of the cabin and climbed down. Anna and Rani were out of the buggy and rushing through the front door before he could walk around to help them down.

He tied the horse to a tree at the side of the yard and turned back toward the cabin. Noah stood facing the door on the front porch. His arms dangled at his sides, and his small fingers flexed. Matthew stepped up next to him and touched his shoulder. "Noah, do you want me to take you inside?"

The boy stared up at him, and his eyes filled with tears. "I'm a-feared to go in. My ma is mighty sick. What if she dies?"

Matthew started to assure him that his mother was going to be all right, but he thought better of it. He had no idea how sick Noah's mother was, and the last thing he wanted was to offer him false hope. He put his hand on the boy's shoulder. "Let's not think like that right now. Miss Anna will let us know something before long. In the meantime, how about if we sit down here on the steps and get better acquainted."

Noah nodded and took a seat on the top step. He tilted his head to one side and squinted up at Matthew. "I seen you in church."

Matthew dropped down beside the boy, stretched his legs out, and crossed his right foot over the left. "I remember that. You're the boy who ate my cookie. My name's Matthew Jackson. I used to live in the Cove, but I moved away. Now I've come back."

"Do you know my pa?"

"Yeah, I know him, and I knew your grandparents. Your grandpa was a mighty fine man."

Noah shrugged. "I don't remember him. I kinda have a picture in my head of my granny, but I'm not sure." They sat in silence for a moment before Noah spoke again. "I sure wish Miss Anna would come let me know about my ma."

"She will. Give her time."

The words were barely out of his mouth before the door opened, and Anna stepped onto the porch. Noah jumped to his feet and ran to stand in front of her. "How's my ma, Miss Anna?"

Anna knelt down and placed her hand on

Noah's shoulder. She smiled and stared into his eyes. "Your mother is very sick, Noah. But she is so proud of you because you came to get me. She told me you are the best son any mother could ever have."

Noah frowned and stared past Anna to the door. "When can I go in and see her?"

"She's resting now and doesn't need to be disturbed. But I need to ask you some questions about your mother's illness. So I want you to think real hard before you answer. Do you understand?"

Noah nodded. "Yes'm."

Anna smiled. "You told me your mother got sick about the time your father left three days ago. Do you remember if she said anything before that about not feeling well?"

He twisted his mouth to one side and thought for a moment before he answered. "I came inside the other day, and she was bent over and a-holdin' her stomach. When I asked her what was wrong, she said she had a pain. My pa come home that night, and I heard her tell him she'd been hurtin' for a few days and needed to go see Dr. Harrison. Pa told her he was tired of her complainin' and layin' around all the time and he didn't have money to pay no doctor."

Anna's lips pulled into a straight line. "Do you remember what day that was?"

"It was the day we got the big rain that afternoon."

Anna smiled. "Thank you, Noah. That helps me a lot. Now I need you to do something else to help your mother."

His eyes grew large in his small face. "Tell me what you want, Miss Anna, and I'll do it."

She stood, placed her hands on his shoulders, and turned him to face Matthew. "We need to get Dr. Harrison for your mother, and Matthew doesn't know where he lives. It's way on the other side of the Cove. I want you to go with Matthew and show him where Dr. Harrison lives so he can come help her. Can you do that?"

Noah nodded. "Yes'm. I reckon I know where he lives. It won't take us long."

He turned, dashed down the steps, and headed to the buggy. Matthew stepped closer to Anna. "How bad is it?"

She bit down on her lip and shook her head. "Very bad. Tell Dr. Harrison to hurry. If Noah's right about his mother being sick the day of the big rain, then she's been ill for over a week. If Bertha has appendicitis like I suspect, it may have already abscessed and burst."

Matthew glanced at the boy seated in the buggy and then back to Anna. "Is there anything you can do for her?"

"No, I'm not qualified to operate. And I'm afraid that's all that will save her life at this point. Get Dr. Harrison back here as quickly as you can."

"I will." He jumped down the steps and ran to untie the horse.

Within minutes the buggy was bouncing over the ruts left in the road from the winter storms. Noah didn't speak but stared straight ahead as if he were willing the horse to go faster. When the turn-off to Dr. Harrison's home finally came into sight, Noah pointed to his right. "The doctor's house is down this here path."

Matthew turned the horse into the narrow lane leading to a cabin at the end. Noah was out of the buggy and onto the porch before he had pulled the buggy to a complete stop. Matthew tied the reins to a hitching post in front of the house and bounded up the steps. Noah doubled up his fist and pounded on the door.

The door opened, and a young woman holding a baby in her arms stood before them. "May I help you?" The baby gurgled, and she bounced him in her arms.

Matthew removed his hat. "Morning, ma'am. I'm Matthew Jackson. I'm sorry we had to come banging on your door so early."

The woman smiled. "That's not unusual, Mr. Jackson. I'm Lettie Harrison. How can I help you?"

"Anna Martin sent us for Dr. Harrison." He glanced down at Noah and grasped his shoulder. "This is Noah Campbell, and his mother is very sick. Miss Anna says she needs a doctor right away."

A frown creased her forehead. "Oh, I'm sorry. My husband isn't here right now. He left yesterday to go over to Gatlinburg."

"Do you know what time he'll be back?"

She shook her head. "I'm not sure, but he should be home sometime this afternoon." She stepped back and motioned for them to come inside. "You're welcome to wait if you'd like."

Noah looked up. Big tears filled his eyes.

Matthew put his hand on the boy's shoulder and smiled. "Noah, I'd better get on back and let Anna know the doctor's coming later. But you can stay here and bring him to your cabin when he gets back."

Noah's lips trembled, and he shook his head. "I 'spect I need to git on back home too. My ma might need me to do something for her."

Matthew nodded. "I understand." He turned to Mrs. Harrison. "When your husband returns, please tell him to come to Wade Campbell's cabin. Anna says it's urgent."

Mrs. Harrison bent over and looked into Noah's face. "I will send my husband the minute he gets home. And I'll pray that Anna will be able to help your mother in the meantime."

Noah clamped his lips together and took a deep breath. "Thank you kindly, ma'am. We'll be a-lookin' for the doctor."

Noah turned and ran down the steps to the buggy. Matthew watched him climb in before he leaned closer and whispered. "Tell your husband Anna thinks it's appendicitis, and she believes it may have already abscessed."

She gasped and hugged her baby tighter. "Then I know I'll be praying for her. And tell Anna I'm praying for her too."

"Thank you, ma'am." Matthew shoved the hat back on his head and hurried to join Noah in the buggy.

As they raced over the road on the way back to the cabin, Matthew studied Noah out of the corner of his eye. Just as he had done on the trip to the doctor's house, he remained silent and stared ahead.

Matthew could only guess what was going through the boy's head, but he knew the anguish he was in. He too, had felt helpless the day his mother had died during the influenza outbreak in Pigeon Forge. The disease had already claimed his brother, and he held onto his mother's hand as if he could pump his own life into her. In the end it hadn't done any good, though. She had left him, and he had been alone ever since.

From the moment Noah arrived at Anna's wanting help for his mother, Matthew had seen the love Noah had for her. Just like he'd had for his mother. If Bertha Campbell died, he wondered what would happen to Noah. From what little he knew about Wade Campbell now, he didn't seem too different from his own father.

Noah hadn't mentioned his father other than to say he'd been gone for days and hadn't returned with food for them. There had been no concern for his safety or where he might be. He had acted as if his father's absence was normal.

Matthew couldn't stand to think about what Noah's life would be like if he didn't have his mother to care for him. He snapped the reins to urge the horse on and breathed a silent prayer that the doctor would arrive in time to save Bertha Campbell's life.

Chapter 12

Rani hadn't been able to sit still ever since Matthew and Noah left to get the doctor. She had no idea how much time had passed because there was no clock in the Campbell cabin, but she thought it must have been well over an hour. Since it took about half an hour to reach Dr. Harrison's home from here, they should be back any minute.

Her mother hadn't needed her in the room with Mrs. Campbell, and she was glad. It wasn't that she didn't feel sorry for the sick woman, but she felt so inadequate when it came to helping someone who was ill. As she had often told Granny, she wasn't as smart as Mama and never would be. All she knew how to do in situations like this was to follow her mother's instructions.

She sighed and hurried to the window for what must have been the tenth time in the last few minutes. She pulled the curtain back and stared down the road in hopes of seeing their buggy come into view, but the road was as deserted as it had been earlier.

Rani turned and stared at the closed door to the room where her mother tended Mrs. Campbell. What was going on inside? She eased to the door and placed her ear against it, but she could hear nothing. Pushing it open just enough to peer inside, she peeped around the door and into the room. Her mother sat in a chair beside the bed. Bertha lay motionless on the bed's cornhusk mattress.

"Mama," she whispered, "do you need anything?"

Her mother rose, placed a hand on Bertha's forehead for a moment, and then tiptoed to the door. She glanced over her shoulder at her patient before she answered. "Bertha appears to have gone into a coma. I haven't been able to rouse her for the last thirty minutes or so."

Rani gazed over her mother's shoulder at the still figure. "Was she able to take any of the willowbark tea?"

"Yes. Thank you for making it. I thought it might bring her fever down some and give her some relief from the pain, but it didn't." Her mother bit her lip and shook her head. "She was really suffering when we first got here. And now with her so unresponsive, well . . . I'm very concerned. I wish the doctor would get here. She needs more than I can give her."

Rani jerked her head around at the sound of a horse coming to a stop outside. She grabbed her mother's hands and squeezed them. "They're back."

"Thank heaven," her mother said as she hurried back into Bertha's room. "Send Dr. Harrison in the minute he comes inside."

Rani ran to the door, jerked it open, and stepped onto the front porch. The smile on her face faded at the sight of Matthew and Noah climbing from the buggy. She glanced around in hopes the doctor had followed them, but the road was empty.

Noah jumped out of the buggy and lunged up the steps. "How's my ma?"

Rani looked past him to Matthew, who was tying the horse to the tree. From the look on his face, she knew he didn't bring good news. She glanced down at Noah and took him by the hand. "She's sleeping now."

"Can I see her?"

"Not just yet." She waited as Matthew climbed the steps. He stopped at the edge of the porch and shook his head. "What's the matter? Where is Dr. Harrison?"

Matthew glanced down at Noah. "Dr. Harrison had gone to Gatlinburg. His wife said she would send him as soon as he gets home this afternoon."

Rani sucked in her breath and nodded. "I see. I'd better go tell Mama."

She hurried back into the house, cracked the door to Bertha's room open, and motioned for her mother. A worried expression crossed Anna's face. "Where's the doctor?"

Rani shook her head. "He wasn't home. His wife will send him as soon as he gets back."

Her mother's eyes grew wide, and she reached behind her to close the door to the bedroom. She glanced at Matthew. "Did she have any idea how long it would be?"

Matthew shrugged his shoulders helplessly. "She said he was supposed to be back this afternoon."

Anna started to say something but paused when she looked down at Noah. She seemed to be deep in thought for a moment before she stepped around Rani and went to the boy. "Noah, your mother is in a deep sleep right now, but I know she would want to see you. Would you like to go into her room?"

Noah swallowed hard and nodded. "Yes'm, Miss Anna. I reckon I would."

She smiled. "Then why don't you go sit by her bed for a few minutes while I talk to Matthew and Rani?"

Her mother took Noah by the hand, led him into the room, and motioned for him to sit in the chair beside the bed. When he was settled, she came back into the front room and closed the door. "Bertha's condition has worsened in the last hour. Her breathing rate has gotten faster, and her skin is clammy and pale. She complained of chest pains before she lapsed into a coma. I think she's in shock at this point. We need to pray that the doctor will get here soon and will be able to do something to help her."

A loud cry split the air, and Anna whirled to open the door. They rushed into the room to find Noah standing by his mother's bed. Tears ran down his face. "Miss Anna," he wailed, "something's wrong. There's a funny sound coming out of my ma's throat."

Rani grabbed Noah's hand and pulled him away from the bed as her mother bent over Bertha. "Noah, come with me into the other room."

"No!" He screamed and struggled to pull away from her.

Matthew's arms circled the wriggling child and lifted him up. "Do as Rani says, Noah. Let Miss Anna take care of your mother."

Noah's body went limp, and he sagged against Matthew. Rani followed them into the other room and closed the door behind her. Matthew dropped down into a chair at the kitchen table and cradled the boy in his lap. She went to them and knelt in front of them.

"Noah," she said, "do you remember how we talked in Sunday school about God being with you when things happen that make you sad?"

His big blue eyes stared into hers. A tear slid down his check, and he nodded. "Is God here now?"

Rani nodded. "He is, and He's so sorry your mama is sick. But He wants you to be a brave boy because that's what your mama would want. Can you do that for her?"

"I . . . I'll try." He laid his head against Matthew's chest and pressed his lips together.

Rani glanced up at Matthew and detected a hint of tears in his eyes. He blinked, looked down at Noah, and swallowed hard. Rani rose and slipped into the chair across the table from them. They sat without talking for what seemed an eternity before the door to the bedroom opened.

Her mother eased out of the room and closed the door behind her. The look on her face told them she didn't bring good news. She walked to the table, and her eyes softened as she looked down at Noah.

She bent down and placed her hand on Noah's shoulder. "Noah, I'm so sorry, but your mother has passed away."

The boy's lips trembled, and tears filled his

eyes. "Has she gone to be with Jesus?" he asked.

She nodded. "Yes. Do you want to see how peaceful she is now?"

He didn't answer but slipped out of Matthew's lap and placed his hand in Anna's. Together they stepped into the bedroom. Rani stood at the door and watched Noah approach the still figure on the bed. He stared down at his mother for a moment then bent and kissed her forehead. He turned to leave, then broke into a run, dashing through the house and out the front door.

Rani and Matthew ran onto the porch, but he had disappeared. "Noah, come back!" Rani cried out as she started down the steps.

She'd reached the bottom step when Matthew caught up with her and grabbed her arm. "Let him go, Rani. He needs some time alone. I'll go look for him in a few minutes."

Rani nodded and stepped back onto the porch. She looked over her shoulder for Matthew, but he wasn't behind her. He had walked to the corner of the house and stood looking toward the mountains in the distance. She started to go to him but hesitated.

As she stared at his straight back and broad shoulders, she knew Noah wasn't the only one needing some time alone. Matthew wanted it too. Perhaps Bertha's death had stirred memories too painful to be shared. Later he might need her, but not now.

• • •

Matthew had no idea where to begin looking for Noah. He could have secret hiding places anywhere in the thick tangle of vegetation that covered the fields around the cabin. It pained Matthew to look at those overgrown fields that once had produced some of the best hay crops in the Cove. An apple orchard Matthew remembered from his childhood had vanished from the field behind the cabin as if it had never been. Gone also was the open-sided shed that had sheltered Mr. Ben Campbell's beehives. Once they'd been said to yield the sweetest honey in the Cove.

Matthew shook his head in disgust. Wade hadn't been any better at taking care of the land his father had passed to him than he had been at providing for his family.

He pulled his hat off and wiped his shirt sleeve across his forehead. The day had warmed up, and Noah might be anywhere. He tried to think where he would have gone to be alone when he was a boy. Somewhere that would conceal his whereabouts but would allow him to keep an eye on what was happening around him.

Of course.

The hay loft.

The ramshackle barn behind the cabin would be the ideal hiding place. Matthew didn't glance up at the opening of the loft above the barn door as he ambled across the hardened earth of the former barnyard. A feeling that he was being watched from above reminded him of the times he'd kept an eye on his drunken father while the man staggered around yelling for him to come out of his hiding place.

Matthew stepped into the barn and closed the door behind him. He glanced around in the dim interior. The absence of any animal sounds or smells and the deserted stalls confirmed the notion that Wade no longer kept livestock in the building. Near the other end of the aisle he could see a ladder that led to the hay loft. A rickety bench sat beside it, and he sauntered toward it and eased down. The bench creaked and swayed, but it held his weight.

Matthew sat still for a moment and listened for a sound from above. A floorboard creaked, and he smiled to himself. A piece of wood lay on the ground. He picked it up and hummed a tune as he pulled out his pocket knife and began to whittle.

After a few minutes, he heard a rustling sound from above. "Hey there, Noah," he said. "I wondered where you'd gone off to." He waited for a reply but none came. "Miss Anna didn't need me right now, so I thought I'd come out here and sit awhile. I like to pass the time by whittling sometimes. Come on down, and I'll let you take a few swipes with my knife."

"You will?"

The soft voice came from right above Matthew's

head, and he looked up. Noah was peering at him through the opening to the hay loft. Matthew smiled and motioned for him to join him. "Sure will. I hate to whittle alone anyway. I suppose it won't be a treat for you, though. You probably whittle all the time."

"No, I ain't never done it before. I ain't got no knife."

"Well, you can use mine. Come on down and sit a spell with me."

Noah swung his body around to the ladder and climbed down. When he hopped off the last rung to the ground, he paused and took a hesitant step. He glanced down at the knife Matthew held and then back up. "Who taught you how to whittle?"

Matthew shrugged and slid the knife down the wood again. "I reckon I just picked it up on my own. But I'll teach you if you want me to."

A big grin pulled at the boy's mouth. "I shore would like to learn."

"Then come over here and let me show you." Noah settled on the bench beside him, and Matthew handed him the knife. "Now you have to be real careful not to cut yourself. Hold the knife in this hand and the wood in the other."

Noah wrapped his right hand around the knife handle and turned his left hand up to take the stick. When Matthew had positioned Noah's hands, the boy looked up. "Now what do I do?"

"Slide the blade down the wood away from

the fingers of your left hand. I don't want you to cut a finger off."

Noah laughed. "Me neither."

For the next fifteen minutes Noah whittled the wood until he had shaved it into a sharp point. Matthew took the piece, held it up, and nodded. "I think this is the best first job at whittling I've ever seen. No telling what kinds of things you can make as you get better. But you have to remember not to use a knife unless a grownup is with you. It's too dangerous for a boy to do by himself."

Noah's smile disappeared and tears filled his eyes. "Then I guess I won't never git to do it. I don't have a ma no more, and my pa don't hardly ever come home. I 'spect I'll be by myself all the time."

Matthew closed his knife, stuck it in his pocket, and put his arm around the boy's shoulders. "My mother died too, Noah. I know how you're hurting right now. You need to think about the good times and how much she loved you. That'll help you feel better."

He shook his head. "I don't reckon I'm ever gonna feel better."

"Yes, you will. Your pa will be home soon, and he'll take care of you."

"My pa don't never pay me no mind," said Noah. "I reckon he won't like having to take care of me." He stared up at Matthew a moment, and he tilted his head to one side. "Do you have a boy at your house?"

"No, I'm not married."

"Would you like to have a boy?"

"Well, yes, I would, but . . ."

Noah directed a pleading look at Matthew. "Then how 'bout I come to stay with you? I'd work real hard."

"I'm sure you would."

"And I don't eat much. I wouldn't give you no trouble."

Matthew swallowed hard. "I know you wouldn't, Noah, but I don't even have a cabin. I'm staying at Simon and Miss Anna's house right now."

"Maybe I could stay at their cabin with you."

Matthew shook his head. "I don't think that would be a good idea."

"Why not?"

Matthew put his hand on Noah's shoulder and exhaled. "Because your pa wouldn't let you. You're his son, and he wants you with him."

Tears ran down Noah's face. "My pa won't care. He's gone all the time, and I'm scared to stay here. It gets real dark at night. What if a bear or a bobcat comes up to the cabin and tries to get in?"

Matthew shook his head. "I don't think . . ."

Tears welled up in Noah's eyes and threatened to spill over. "Please, Mr. Matthew," he whispered. "I don't want to stay by myself."

Matthew reached out and put his arm around Noah's shoulders, and the boy threw his arms around Matthew. Noah's body shook with wracking sobs, and Matthew remembered how he'd cried the day his mother died. "Don't worry, Noah," he whispered, "I'll talk to your pa. We'll work something out."

The door to the barn crashed open, and a flash of sunlight lit the aisle. Matthew glanced over his shoulder at the doorway and saw a man holding the reins of a horse. He led the horse into the barn and stopped a few feet away from Matthew and Noah.

"Who are you, and what you done to make my boy cry?" the man bellowed.

Matthew released Noah and rose to face the man he'd thought about for twenty years. He'd known the time would come when he would meet Wade Campbell, but he'd never dreamed it would be at a time like this.

"Your son is upset, Wade. I was trying to calm him down."

Wade frowned and walked toward them. He stopped in front of Matthew and directed an angry glare at him. "How come you know my name when I ain't never seen you before?"

Matthew's stomach roiled at the strong odor he'd often smelled on his father. He might have been away for years, but he still remembered the smell of moonshine whiskey. "You've seen me before. You just don't recognize me. I'm Matthew Jackson."

Understanding dawned in Wade's eyes, and a taunting grin pulled at his mouth. He stroked his scraggly beard for a moment before he spit a wad of tobacco to the ground. "Well, well, well. I been gone for a while, but I heared you done come back to the Cove. I wondered when I'd git the chance to meet up with you again."

"I wondered the same thing, but I didn't think it would be under these circumstances."

"What do you mean, circumstances?" Wade snarled.

Noah huddled closer to Matthew. His body trembled, and Matthew reached down and clamped his hand on the boy's shoulder. "I was at the Reverend's home when Noah came for Anna. He said his mother was sick. I came with Anna and Rani to check on her."

Tobacco juice trickled from the corner of Wade's mouth, and he wiped it away with his sleeve. "Ain't nothing wrong with Bertha 'ceptin' she's lazy. If she'd git up and do somethin', she wouldn't have time to think 'bout doctors and things that are gonna cost me money."

Matthew shook his head. "You're wrong about that, Wade. I'm sorry to tell you Bertha passed away just a little while ago."

Surprise flashed across Wade's face, and he glanced back at his son who slipped behind

Matthew. "Now if that just ain't the last thing I needed to hear today. What am I gonna do with that there young'un? I ain't got time to be taking care of no boy."

Matthew's hands balled into fists, and his body stiffened. "He's your son, Wade. He needs a father."

A smirk pulled at Wade's mouth. "I guess you know all 'bout what a father should do, seein' as how you had such a good one."

Matthew took a step toward Wade, but he stopped when he felt Noah tug at his arm. He glanced around, and his heart slammed against his chest. Noah's face registered the terror he had often felt at the boy's age. He turned back to Wade. "It doesn't matter now what kind of father I had."

Wade laughed and sauntered over to a stall. He dropped the reins he still held, pulled a rifle from the back of the saddle, and opened the stall door for the horse to enter. When he turned around, he propped the rifle on his hip and glared at Matthew.

"I reckon I done ev'rybody in the Cove a favor the night I killed your old man. When you and your ma left, I figured we were through with the likes of Luke Jackson in these parts. Never figured his son would have the gumption to come back."

Noah clutched at Matthew's back, and he put a

hand behind him to pat the boy's shoulder. "I didn't come back for any trouble, Wade. All I want is to live in peace on my old farm."

Wade threw back his head and laughed. "And you ain't got no hankerin' to even things out with me for what I done twenty years ago?"

"No, and I don't have a gun, Wade. You can't claim self-defense this time." He shook his head. "Like I said, I don't want any trouble."

Wade's eyes narrowed. "Boy, you had trouble the minute you rode across the ridge into the Cove. You think I don't know you come back here all ready to settle an old score? Now step away from my boy."

Matthew's heart hammered, but he reached to push Noah away. The boy only tightened his grip on Matthew. "Noah, you need to let go."

"No!" Noah's cry pierced Matthew's heart.

"Boy!" Wade's voice thundered through the barn. "You git away right now!"

"No, Pa," Noah wailed. "He's my friend."

Wade raised the gun. "Noah, I'm warning you . . ."

"Mr. Campbell, what are you doing?" Wade whirled at the voice from the door, and Matthew gasped at the sight of Rani stepping into the barn. He wanted to rush to her, but he feared any sudden movement would cause Wade to pull the trigger.

Wade stared at her. "This ain't no concern

of yours, girl. This is between the two of us."

She glanced from Matthew to Wade. "It looks like you're the only one with a gun. If anything were to happen here today, I'd be glad to testify to that in court."

Rage blazed in Wade's eyes. "Don't you go a-threat'nin' me, girl. You better git on out of here if you know what's good for you."

Anger boiled up in Matthew, and he stepped forward. "Don't talk like that to her, or there *will* be trouble between us."

Wade jerked the butt of the rifle to his shoulder and stared down the sights. "Don't come any closer, Jackson, or you're a dead man."

Rani rushed past Wade and headed toward Matthew and Noah. Wade's finger twitched on the trigger, and Matthew's heart leaped into his throat. He held out a hand to warn her off. "Rani, get out of here before you get hurt!" he yelled.

She narrowed her eyes, pursed her lips, and shook her head, still walking steadily toward him. When she reached him, she whirled to face Wade. Matthew grabbed her shoulders to push her away, but she planted her feet in the soft dirt of the barn and struggled to shake free of him. "No, I will not let him do this."

Matthew looped his arms around her waist and picked her up, but she kicked his shins and slipped from his grip. She clenched her fists and took a step toward Wade. "Now I suggest you put that gun down and get up to the house. You need to take care of your dead wife and son instead of acting like you think you're the toughest man in the Cove. My father just arrived, so you need to get out of here before I yell for him to come out here. I'm sure you wouldn't like for the preacher to tell everybody you know how you acted on the day your wife died."

"You got a smart mouth on you, girl." Wade glared at Rani for a moment before he took a deep breath and lowered the gun. He glanced at Noah and shook his head. "Git yourself over here, boy. Now!"

Matthew grasped Noah's arm and pulled him around to face him. His hand shook so he couldn't control his grip. He released Noah and stared down into the child's face. "You've got to go with your pa, Noah. I'll see you later."

Before Noah could say anything, Wade rushed forward and grabbed Noah by the arm. "Don't come near my boy agin, Jackson. You hear?"

Matthew swallowed the fear that still burned in his throat and nodded. "I hear."

Wade turned and stormed from the barn with Noah in tow. The boy looked over his shoulder before they disappeared out the door. Big tears rolled down Noah's face. Matthew groaned and turned away.

He closed his eyes and tried to forget how

he'd felt when his father turned on him. The same anger he'd seen in his father's eyes had been in Wade's eyes today, and he feared what consequences Noah would face when they left.

"Matthew, are you all right?"

Rani's voice sent renewed anger surging through him. Rage like he'd felt many times in the past boiled up in his soul. He spun to face her. "Why in the world did you do that?"

Her eyebrows arched. "Do what?"

"What made you think you had the right to interfere?"

A puzzled look shadowed her eyes. "Interfere? I was trying to save your life. When I walked in, I thought Wade was going to shoot you."

"So you thought you'd let him shoot you instead?"

"He was angry, but not angry enough to shoot the preacher's daughter."

Matthew raked a hand through his hair. "You can't be sure of that. He was too angry to think clearly."

Her lips tightened and her eyes narrowed. "All I wanted to do was help you."

"Help me? Like you helped me with George?"

Rani's mouth dropped open. "What are you talking about?"

Matthew gritted his teeth and shook his head. "You stepped between Wade and me just like you did when George found us at the cemetery. I can handle my own problems, Rani. I don't need a woman to protect me."

Her face grew red. "I was afraid he was going to shoot you, Matthew. I couldn't stand by and let that happen."

The hurt look on her face hit him like a kick in the stomach. She couldn't possibly understand. His words had pained her, and he regretted them. He exhaled. "That's just what my mother used to say every time she stepped in front of me to take the beating my father intended for me. I won't live like that again, Rani. I won't watch someone else I love get hurt because of me. Do you understand?"

She sucked in her breath, and tears flooded her eyes. "All I wanted to do was protect you."

He nodded. "I know. But you can't protect me from everything I have to face. I have to do it on my own."

A tear slid down her cheek. "I'm sorry if I offended you. I won't do it again."

He took a deep breath. "I'll see that you don't. When we get back to your cabin, I'm going to tell Simon and Anna that it's cutting into my workday to keep traveling back and forth. There's a spot in the barn where I can sleep until the cabin's rebuilt. I think it would be better if I stayed there."

Her face grew pale, and she swayed on her feet. "Are you doing this to get away from me?"

He bit his lip and nodded. "Yes."

"Please don't." She held out her hand and inched forward. Another tear slid down her cheek, and he longed to wipe it away.

"I have to stand on my own two feet and take whatever's coming my way. I won't have you hurt in the process."

He wasn't going to take her hand. She lowered it and swallowed hard. She stared at him, and the hurt look in her eyes shattered his heart. "I hoped there might be something special happening between us. When you told me about the lodge and . . . and kissed me, I thought you loved me. A minute ago you said you wouldn't let someone else you loved be hurt. Did you mean that?"

He closed his eyes and shook his head. "Rani, please . . ."

When he opened his eyes, she clenched her fists and stepped closer. "Answer me. You may not have spoken the words, but you've made me believe you love me. Do you?"

He wanted to lie to her, to tell her she was just another woman and that the kiss meant nothing to him, but he knew he could never say the words. "I care for you, Rani. I love you, but I'm never going to do anything about it. There's too much in my past for you to have to live with. It's better if I step away now before you get hurt worse."

Tears spilled over onto her cheeks. "But

Matthew, I love you too. How can I forget what you said?"

"It would be best if we pretended we'd never spoken the words we've said today."

"I can't do that," she sobbed.

He grasped her shoulders and stared into her eyes. "Yes, you can. There's no future for us, Rani. Your parents are the most respected people in the Cove, and I'm the son of Luke Jackson."

"But you're also Naomi Jackson's son. Have you forgotten what Laura said about how you were kind like your mother?"

"No, I haven't forgotten, but Laura is one person. There are a lot of other folks around here who are going to judge me because of my father. Today it almost got you killed, and I won't put you in the middle of my problems again."

She lifted her chin in defiance. "I don't care what *some* people think. I love you."

Her words pierced his heart, and he released his grip on her shoulders before he relented and wrapped her in his arms. But after a moment he stepped back and shook his head. "It's no use, Rani. You're not going to change my mind. From now on I'm only going to think of you as the daughter of two of my oldest friends. Nothing more."

"But . . ." The words she meant to say never came out. After a moment she wiped her eyes and nodded. "Fine. I suppose there's nothing I can do to change your mind. Maybe in time I'll come to see that you're right. For some reason we bring out the worst in each other. I say and do things that anger you, and you lash out at me. It's taking too much energy for us to have a relationship, and I'm tired of all the tension."

He struggled to keep her from seeing how he regretted hearing her agree with him. "Me too. All I need to think about right now is getting my farm in shape. I don't have time for anything else."

"Then I guess we're agreed." Her words held a hopeful hint that he would contradict her.

Instead he nodded. "We are."

She whirled and ran from the barn. He willed himself to stand still and not chase after her like his heart demanded.

When she was gone he sank down on the bench, propped his hands on his knees, and buried his face in his hands. His body trembled, and he silently berated himself. The things he'd said to Rani were unforgiveable, and he doubted if she would ever speak to him again.

If she only knew what those words had cost him. He'd almost begun to think she could help him find his way back from the lonely path he'd followed since his mother's death.

He closed his eyes and pictured her throwing her arms around him and telling him she loved him just as she had done a few minutes ago. But that would never happen now. That hope had died the minute she stepped in front of Wade Campbell's gun. His stomach roiled at the thought that in his anger Wade might have shot her, and it would have been his fault.

The memory of his mother stepping in front of him and receiving the blows meant for him had haunted him for years. At least he'd been honest when he told Rani he loved her, but he wouldn't let another woman he loved be harmed because of him.

He had never thought he would find someone who would love him, but Rani said she did. No one had ever loved him but his mother and Eli, and they were both gone. And now, so was Rani.

Chapter 13

Rani trudged up the steps of the Campbells' cabin and stopped on the front porch. Even with the door closed she could hear the angry voice of Wade Campbell inside. She wiped the tears from her cheeks before she opened the door.

"I'll take care of my wife, Simon. I don't need the help of no do-gooders from your church to come in here a-prayin' and carryin' on. And there ain't no need for no funeral. I'll get my cousin to help me dig a grave right here on my land."

"Wade," her father said, "you can do what you want about burying Bertha, but I wish you would reconsider letting me read some Scripture and say a prayer. Bertha was a fine woman, and she would have wanted that."

"Ain't no need for that either. It don't make no difference to her now."

Rani glanced at her father and saw the muscle in his jaw twitching. She knew how many times he had tried to talk to Wade about trusting Jesus, but Wade had never wanted to listen to him. She recognized the sorrow on her father's face, knowing that once again Wade was turning his back on God.

Her father started to speak again, but her mother laid her hand on his arm and shook her head. She clasped her hands in front of her and smiled. "Wade, I think you know how much I loved Bertha. I'll never forget the day I helped bring Noah into the world. She was one of the bravest women I ever assisted, and she became one of my dearest friends."

The glassy stare in Wade's eyes didn't waver from her mother's face. "I reckon she liked you a lot too, Miss Anna."

"Then please allow me to do something for my friend. Let me tend to her body and put her Sunday dress on her. She would want you and Noah to remember her that way, not looking like she's been suffering from all the sickness and pain."

Wade swallowed, and his Adam's apple bobbed. "I reckon it would be all right for you to do that."

She nodded. "Thank you, Wade. I know that's the way she would have wanted it. And I know you and Noah will miss her."

A frown pulled at Wade's eyebrows. "Miss Anna, you're a good woman. I reckon Bertha would be pleased to have you tend to her."

"I'll call you when we're ready for you to see her." Anna glanced at Rani. "Get a pan of hot water and come into the other room."

Rani didn't look at Wade Campbell but hurried to the woodstove, lifted up the kettle, and poured some water into a pan. When she carried it into the other room, her mother was already stripping the soiled dress from Bertha's body.

Anna looked up when Rani entered. "Put the water here and close the door."

Rani did as she was told and returned to her mother's side. For the next few minutes they worked without speaking as they bathed Bertha's body. Her mother pointed to a dress hanging on a wall peg. "There's the dress Bertha wore to church when Wade would let her come. Would you get it for me?"

Rani pulled the dress from the peg and stared down at the black cotton dress. She ran her fingers down the thin channels of sewn-together fabric that ran up and down the bodice. The needlework was exquisite. Tears filled Rani's eyes, and she smoothed out the decoration Bertha had sewn with such care into the simple dress. "Mama, what's going to happen to Noah now?"

Anna shook her head. "I don't know, Rani. Your father and I will talk to Wade about him."

Rani handed her mother the dress and looked around the room. "I wonder if there's a brush or comb in here."

Her mother pointed to a table on the other side of the room. "There may be one over there."

The table her mother pointed to held a few personal articles that must have belonged to Bertha. An ornate ivory hair comb and a brush with a tarnished silver handle lay next to the tattered Bible Rani had seen Bertha carrying in church. She opened the flap and stared at the page that contained several generations of names. "This must have been Bertha's family Bible. The names date back more than a hundred years."

Her mother glanced up from dressing Bertha. "We need to make sure it's saved for Noah. That may be all he'll have to remember of his mother."

She flipped over a few pages and stopped at a daguerreotype wedged in the pages. A somber young woman in a black dress stared at her. Rani picked up the picture and noticed the ivory comb sticking in her hair. "Look at this. The woman in this picture is wearing the comb that's beside Bertha's Bible."

Her mother moved over beside her and looked at the picture. "Bertha showed me this picture once. It's her mother when she was a young girl, and the comb was given to her by her father. Bertha would never wear it because she was afraid she might lose it."

Rani closed the Bible, placed it back on the table, and picked up the brush. Tears flooded her eyes. "A black dress, a hairbrush, a comb, and a Bible. Some people might think Bertha was just a poor mountain woman, but she wasn't. She was always the first one to arrive at someone's cabin when the wife was sick. She'd cook and clean and care for the children. And I saw how she loved Noah and how he loved her. She might have had a hard time with Wade, but she was rich with friendships of those who knew her."

Her mother put her arm around Rani's waist and hugged her. "You're right, darling. She reminded me a lot of Matthew's mother. I saw how much Naomi loved her children the first time I met her. I'm glad you have a heart that lets you see the good in people. Don't ever lose that."

The mention of Matthew took the wind from her lungs, and she wiped at the tears that spilled down her face. "I'll try not to. Now let's get Bertha ready."

She and her mother walked back to Bertha's

bed and stared down at the woman. The face that had been wracked with pain when they first arrived now looked peaceful. "She thanked me over and over for bringing cookies for Noah to Granny's birthday gathering. I didn't think about that being the last time we would talk."

Her mother nodded. "We should never take anything or anyone for granted. We have no idea what the future holds."

Rani's heart lurched at how her future had changed in the last hour, but she shook the thought from her head. There were other matters —more important ones—to be addressed now. "Mama, you were so kind when you asked Mr. Campbell if we could dress Bertha. I wish I knew how to talk to people like you do. You can convince people to do things they really don't want to. My words have the opposite effect. How do you do it?"

Her mother smiled and patted her cheek. "I was once an outspoken young woman too. I thought I knew what I wanted, and I intended to have it no matter how it hurt anybody else. I alienated my brother and hurt my mother. And I broke your father's heart before I realized that all I was doing was fighting God. He wanted me to let go of my stubborn will and place my trust in Him. When I did, I found out God had better plans for me than I could ever have made for myself."

"I try to let God lead me too, but it seems I

always do something to get in His way." Rani glanced back down at Bertha. "But right now I'm concerned about what God has planned for Noah. I love that child, and I don't want to leave him here with Wade."

Her mother sighed. "Neither do I. But we need to complete the job we came here for before we decide how we're going to address that situation."

They set to work and didn't speak again until Bertha was dressed in her Sunday best and the tangles had been brushed from her hair. "She looks beautiful, doesn't she?" Rani said.

"Yes. Let's go tell Wade and Noah they can come in now." Anna opened the bedroom door, and they stepped into the other room.

Wade, Noah, and Simon rose to their feet. "Are you finished?" Wade asked.

Her mother nodded and smiled. "We are. You and Noah can go in now."

Wade clenched his fists and strode into the room. Noah's eyes grew wide, and he stared at the open bedroom door as if he was afraid to enter. Rani walked over to him and took his hand in hers. "Do you want me to go with you, Noah?"

He nodded and tightened his grip on her hand. "Yes'm."

Rani led the boy into the room and stopped by his mother's bed. Wade glanced down at his son but didn't speak. Noah stared at his mother for a moment before he wrapped his arms around

Rani's waist and began to sob. After a moment Wade turned and strode out of the room. Rani, her parents, and Noah trailed behind.

Wade walked to the window, stuck his hands in his pockets, and stared outside. Gone was the defiant man she'd encountered in the barn. Simon stepped up behind him. "Wade, if you'd like, I'll bring my brother John back and we'll build a coffin for Bertha. Then we'll be glad to help you dig the grave for Bertha."

Wade shook his head and sighed, then turned to face her father. "Ain't no need for that, Preacher. Like I said, I'll get my cousin to help me."

"If that's the way you want it, I'll not insist," Simon said. "But I want you to know that God is with you in your grief. He's reaching out to you now."

A small smile pulled at Wade's mouth. "I reckon you been trying to get my soul saved ever since I shot Luke Jackson, but I keep tellin' you that God don't want no sinner like me."

Simon shook his head. "You're wrong about that, Wade. He loves you and wants to give you the peace He offers."

"I reckon there ain't no peace that's gonna help me at this point, but thanks for trying." Wade glanced over at Noah, whose arms were still wrapped tight around Rani's waist. "Maybe you can help my boy, though."

"How?"

Wade took a deep breath. "I cain't stay too long in one place. Have to be movin' around. That ain't no life for a boy. Do you know any family that might take him in for a while?"

Anna hardly hesitated before she spoke, her eyes soft. "We would be glad to have him stay with us, Wade. He knows us, and he loves Rani. Of course you'd be welcome to visit him any-time."

His bushy eyebrows drew down into a frown. "Ain't Luke Jackson's boy stayin' at your place right now?"

Before her parents could answer, Rani spoke up. "Matthew is planning on moving to his cabin today after we get back home. So we have an empty room for Noah."

Her father frowned, and her mother's mouth gaped open in shock. "When did you find out about this?" her father asked.

"I'll tell you later," she answered.

Her father studied her face a moment before he turned back to Wade. "Well, everything seems to be worked out. We'll take Noah with us when we leave."

Wade nodded. "Good." He stared down at the floor for a moment before he continued. "I guess I'm doin' what's best for him. You'll tell folks that, won't you?"

Her father smiled. "I will indeed, Wade."

Noah still huddled next to Rani, and she felt

his sigh of relief. She smiled down at him. "Let's go get your clothes together. You're coming home with us."

Her mother held out her hand to stop them. "Don't forget those other things we talked about. Noah will want them later."

Rani nodded and led Noah into the bedroom. He pulled a pair of pants and two shirts off a wall peg and turned to her. "I'm ready."

She grabbed the brush, comb, and Bible and stuck them in the basket her mother had brought into the room earlier. "Then let's go."

A few minutes later Rani and Noah, followed by her parents and Wade, stepped onto the front porch. Matthew stood by the buggy and didn't look up as they exited. Rani bit down on her lip and blinked back her tears. She forced a smile to her face and gave Noah a nudge.

"Tell your father goodbye, Noah."

He turned to Wade and swallowed. "Bye, Pa. I guess I'll be a-seein' you."

Wade nodded. "Don't make no trouble for the preacher and his family. You hear?"

Noah glanced back in the house. "What about Ma?"

Wade closed the door and stood in front of it. "Don't you worry none 'bout her. I'll take care of ev'rything."

Noah released Rani's hand and ran down the steps toward the buggy. She followed him and hopped in, followed by her mother and Matthew. As they pulled out of the yard, Rani glanced back at her father. He was still standing on the front porch with Wade. Whatever he was saying, Wade was having none of it. He shook his head, walked back into the cabin, and closed the door.

Simon stared at the door for a few moments before he trudged down the steps and mounted his horse. He trailed behind the buggy as they made the journey toward home.

Rani settled back against the seat and closed her eyes. The day had started off so well, sitting with Matthew beside the fire pit, but it had disintegrated into the most heartbreaking day of her life.

She peeked at Matthew's straight back and almost dissolved into tears. Not too long ago she had worried she would never find a man she could love. Now she had found him, but he was determined there would be no relationship between them. His rejection of her today had shattered her heart into tiny pieces. She wished Matthew Jackson had never come back to Cades Cove. It would be better never to fall in love than to be hurt like she was now.

No one spoke on the way back to Simon and Anna's cabin, and Matthew was glad. He didn't think he could have managed to make conversation with Rani after what had happened between them today. He could feel her presence, though, and that disturbed him almost as much as it would to talk with her.

He breathed a sigh of relief when the cabin finally came into sight. He pulled to a stop in the backyard for Anna and Rani to get out. Simon rode past him toward the barn.

Anna hopped out and motioned for Noah to come with her. The boy climbed down, took her hand, and walked with her into the house. Rani didn't move.

Matthew swiveled in his seat to glance over his shoulder. She hadn't moved from the back seat, and her dark eyes bored holes into him. He would have expected to see anger in her gaze, but he didn't. Instead she had the look he'd often seen on wounded animals, and it broke his heart.

"Rani . . ."

She held up her hand. "I just wanted to tell you that I will finish making all the bricks for your chimney. I should have them completed in the next few weeks. If you want Mr. Davis to begin laying them then, I suggest you get to work on the cabin. You need to be in it by fall."

"Thank you for doing that. I don't want to put you to any trouble, though."

"Maybe you should have thought about that before you told me you loved me. Compared to what I'm feeling now, making a few bricks won't be any problem at all."

"Rani, please know I never meant to hurt you. I'm doing this for your own good."

"Well, excuse me if I don't thank you," she sneered. "I'm afraid I can't see how the way I feel right now is better for me. But I'm not going to belabor the subject. You don't have to worry about me begging you to change your mind. I will never do that. I'm just sorry that you've thrown away what could have been the best thing in your life."

Before he could answer, she jumped out of the buggy and ran into the cabin. His head drooped, and he closed his eyes. She was right. She was the best thing he'd ever had in his life, and he had thrown it away. He'd done it for her good, but even knowing that didn't make the hurt any easier for him.

He flicked the reins across the horse's back and headed toward the barn. Simon was waiting for him when he climbed from the buggy. "What's this I hear about you moving back to your farm today?"

Matthew busied himself unhitching the horse from the buggy and tried to keep from making eye contact with Simon. "I don't want to overstay my welcome, and I have a lot to do there. I'm using up a lot of time traveling back and forth."

Simon placed his hand on Matthew's arm. "Has something happened to make you feel unwelcome? I know Rani was a little hard on you at first, but I thought the two of you had become friends."

"We have. I just think it's time for me to go. Besides, you have Noah now. He can sleep in Stephen's room."

"Matthew, quit unhitching that horse and look at me." Simon's voice vibrated with the authority Matthew had often heard him use when he was a child. Matthew turned to look at him. "I know something's happened, and I'm not letting you leave here until you tell me what it is."

Matthew swallowed hard. "Please, just let me go."

"No. What has caused this sudden decision? Maybe I'm wrong, and you and Rani aren't friends. Are you leaving because of her?"

"Yes, but . . ."

"What has she done? Tell me, and I'll make her apologize. I won't have you leave here because she's done something to make you feel unwelcome."

Matthew raked his hand through his hair and groaned. "Simon, please don't . . ."

Simon took a step closer and glared at him. "I know she's headstrong, but I won't have her being rude to guests in our home."

Matthew sighed and rubbed his hand across his eyes. "She hasn't been rude to me, Simon. In fact, it's just the opposite."

A puzzled look flashed across Simon's face.

"Just the opposite?" Then his mouth dropped open, and his eyes widened. "You're not saying that you and Rani . . ."

"I love her, Simon."

A confused expression flitted across Simon's face, and he blinked his eyes. "But when did this happen? You barely know each other."

"It may seem like it's sudden to you, but not to me. I've never known anyone like her."

Simon shook his head in disbelief, and then his eyes darkened. "You've been a guest in our home for weeks, Matthew, and you haven't said a word about this to Anna or me. Rani is still a young girl with romantic notions, but you're a man. You shouldn't have kept this from us."

Regret washed over Matthew. Now he had something else to add to his list of mistakes. "You're right, Simon. All I can say is I'm sorry. I hope you'll forgive me."

The stern look on Simon's face relaxed, and he exhaled. "Of course I'll forgive you, but I'm still having trouble taking this in. When did this attachment between the two of you begin?"

"For me, from the beginning. I think I fell in love with her the first time I saw her at the mountain laurel bush at my cabin. Can you understand that?"

Simon's stern expression gave way to a smile. "Yes, I can. I knew I loved Anna the first time I saw her."

"As for not telling you, we decided to take it slow and see what happened. I know I'll never love anybody like I love her."

Simon blinked and shook his head. "Then I don't understand. If you love each other like you say, why are you leaving?"

"I'm leaving because I'm Luke Jackson's son." Matthew almost spat the words from his mouth. "And like my father I've done a lot of things I'm ashamed of. Things I don't want her to ever know, but they've made me what I am. Rani is your daughter, and she deserves better than being tied to somebody like me."

Simon let out a sound that was half laugh, half cry. "Oh, Matthew, have you forgotten all I taught you? God stands willing to forgive whatever we've done. He doesn't want us to live in the past. He wants to give us hope for a better life."

"And that's why I came home. I wanted a better life. I thought it might be possible until today at Wade's cabin."

Simon frowned. "What happened?"

Matthew took a deep breath. "I knew there were folks in the Cove who wouldn't forget my father, and today I found out for sure. I was in the barn with Noah when Wade came home. When he found out who I was, he pulled a gun on me. He said he knew I had come for revenge. I tried to tell him he was wrong, but then Rani walked in.

She placed herself between me and Wade's gun."

Simon's face paled. "She did what?"

Matthew gritted his teeth. "I was scared he was going to shoot her, but she wouldn't move. I tried to pick her up and move her out of the way, but she fought me. Then she faced Wade and gave him a tongue-lashing. I thought Wade was going to shoot us both."

Simon let out a long breath and slumped down on the buggy step. He rested his elbow on the wheel and covered his eyes with his trembling hand. "When Wade's been drinking as he was today, there's no reasoning with him. She could have been killed."

"I know. When he finally left, Rani and I had an argument. I told her how my mother would stand in front of me and take the beatings my father intended for me, and I vowed I would never put another person I love in danger again. I love Rani too much for her to be hurt because of me."

Simon didn't move for a moment. Then he straightened and rose to his feet. "Thank you for telling me this, Matthew. And thank you for wanting to protect my daughter. But we both know how determined she can be. She may not accept your decision."

"She'll have to because it's final. I won't do anything to encourage her, and I'll stay away from your home. She said she would finish the bricks. Maybe you can bring them to my cabin or let me know when they're ready, and I'll come get them."

Simon shook his head. "I'll bring them over. What about your clothes?"

"I only have a few left inside. Just bring them when you do the bricks. I don't want to run into her again."

Simon grasped Matthew's shoulder and squeezed. "I'm sorry about all this. I remember how it hurt when I thought I had lost Anna. I'll pray that God will show you what He has planned for you and Rani. It may not be His will for the two of you to be together, but He may also have plans we know nothing about."

"Thank you, Simon. I appreciate that." Matthew inhaled. "Now I'll put your horse up and get out of here."

Simon shook his head. "No need for that. I'll put the horse in the barn. You go on. You've already missed out on a day's work. I'll be over to check on you in a day or two."

Matthew nodded and turned toward the barn. "I'll look forward to seeing you."

"One more thing, Matthew," said Simon, reaching out a hand to the young man. "If you ever want to talk to me about what happened after your mother died, I'll be willing to listen. I'm not a judge, just a preacher who's loved you since you were a boy. Maybe you've judged your actions too harshly because you're afraid you're going to be like your father. I'm willing to help any way I can."

"I know you are, but I don't think there's anything that can help me. Just take care of Rani. She needs you more than I do. I'm sorry I've hurt her so. I should never have come back here." He turned toward the barn but stopped and faced Simon. "And I really am sorry about not telling you and Anna about my feelings for Rani. I guess I always knew nothing was going to come of it. It always turns out that way for me."

He hurried into the barn to saddle his horse. When he reached the stall, he covered his face with his hands and sagged against the wall. He'd had such hopes the day he rode back into the valley. He knew there would be those who wouldn't welcome him, but he'd never dreamed he'd meet a woman who would capture his heart the moment he saw her.

Now he had made a mess of that like he had everything else in his life. He hadn't been able to protect his mother and brother, he'd made enemies everywhere he'd worked, and now he'd broken Rani's heart. Simon was wrong. God didn't have any plans for him. He was destined to make the same mistakes over and over again. Just like his father had done.

Chapter 14

Simon's legs were shaking so hard that he didn't think he could make it to the cabin without falling. He stared at the back door and counted each step until he stumbled into the kitchen and sank down at the table. He propped his elbows on the tabletop and buried his face in his hands.

How could Rani have been so foolish as to put herself in Wade's line of fire? The very thought sent chills down his spine and made him sick to his stomach. *Oh, God,* he silently prayed, *I did it once, but I don't think I could survive the loss of another child. Thank You for sparing Rani's life.*

He sat there with his shoulders shaking for several minutes before he heard footsteps and looked up to see Anna standing in the door from the front room. Concern lined her face. "Simon, are you all right? What's the matter?"

He took a deep breath and pushed to his feet. "Where's Noah?"

"He's in the other room with Granny. She's telling him a Bible story. Did you want to see him?"

He shook his head. "No, I want to see Rani. Do you know where she is?"

"She headed for her room the minute we came inside. I haven't seen her since. Why do you want to see her?"

"We both need to talk with her."

Anna frowned. "You look upset. Has she done something?"

"Yes."

She closed her eyes and shook her head. "I was afraid of that when she said Matthew was leaving today. If she's offended him in some way, I want to know what it is."

He reached out, grasped her hand, and held it for a moment. He didn't know if he could say the words or not. Finally he took a deep breath. "I had a talk with Matthew, and he told me what happened at Wade's farm. It has shaken me to the bone, Anna. I wish I didn't have to tell you this, but I feel I must."

Her eyes grew wide. "Simon, you're scaring me. Tell me what happened."

"All right." He licked his lips. "It all began when Wade came home and found Matthew in the barn with Noah."

As he continued his story, he watched her face change from puzzlement to shock to fear. When he'd finished, she reached out and grabbed the back of one of the kitchen chairs. She closed her eyes and held onto it for a moment. Her lips were clamped together, and her body shook as if it were experiencing spasms.

"She could have been killed," she finally whispered.

He put his arm around her to steady her. "Yes."

They held each other for a few minutes, each lost in thought of how they had almost lost another of their children. After a few minutes, Simon released her and cleared his throat. "We need to talk to her right away. Let's go to her room."

Anna wiped the tears at the corners of her eyes and followed him down the narrow hallway. They stopped at the closed door to Rani's room and knocked. "Rani," Simon said, "are you in there?"

He could barely make out her muffled reply. "Yes, Poppa."

"Your mother and I want to talk with you. We're coming in."

He eased the door open and they stepped into the room. Rani lay facedown on the bed, but she pushed into a sitting position when they entered. She wiped at her eyes, but couldn't disguise the fact that she'd been crying.

"Wh-what d-do you want?" she stammered.

They walked to the bed and sat on either side of her. Anna glanced up, and Simon knew she wanted him to take the lead in the conversation. "Rani," he began, "I had a talk with Matthew after we got home, and he told me what happened at Wade's house. I have to tell you that your mother and I are very concerned. You could have been killed today."

Her eyes grew wide, and she looked from one to the other. "I'm sorry if I've caused you any worry, but I really don't think I was in danger. Wade was just trying to scare Matthew. Besides, Noah was there, and he wouldn't have shot his son."

Simon shook his head. "You don't know that for sure. But we're thankful you're safe and that no one was hurt." He paused for breath. "However, that was a very foolish thing for you to do. We love you and don't want you to place yourself in a situation like that again. Your mother and I don't want to lose another child." His voice cracked. "You're the only daughter we will ever have, and I don't think we could survive if something happened to you."

A sob ripped from Rani's throat as she threw her arms around her father. "Oh, Poppa, I didn't think about that. I'm so sorry. But it scared me so when I opened that door and saw that gun pointed at Matthew." She then turned to her mother and hugged her. "I'm sorry, Mama. I won't do any-thing like that again."

A tear slipped from Anna's eye, and she hugged Rani close. "You act before you think sometimes, darling. You have to be more care-ful. I love you so much."

"I love you too, Mama. And I'm sorry I upset you."

Simon cleared his throat and glanced at Anna. "Good. Now that we are agreed about your future safety, let's talk about your happiness. Matthew tells me that the two of you have feelings for each other."

A surprised look flashed across her face. "I can't believe he told you that."

"Well, he did," Simon said, "and I have to tell you I'm disappointed you didn't feel like you could tell your mother and me. You and Matthew should have been honest with us."

Fresh tears ran down her face. "Maybe I was afraid you wouldn't approve. But I was happier than I've ever been, and I wanted to enjoy it without hearing why Matthew might not be the man for me."

Anna reached for her hand. "He is a bit older than you, Rani, and he has a lot of memories that have scarred him. If we had disapproved, it would only have been because we love you and don't want to see you hurt."

Rani squeezed her mother's hand. "Well, after the hateful things he said today, I know how wrong I was not to tell you."

Simon reached for her other hand and covered it with his. "He wasn't being hateful, Rani. He was honest. He has a lot in his past that causes him pain, and he doesn't want you hurt because of it. He's only trying to protect you."

Her body began to shake, and tears poured from her eyes. "But I love him so. I just want to be with him. He has a wonderful plan for his farm, and I wanted to be a part of it. Now he's turned his back on me." She turned to face Anna. "Mama, how could he do that if he loves me?"

Anna shook her head. "I don't know what's in his heart, Rani. I only know the journey toward the one you love is often filled with heartache. But you're young. You'll meet someone else, and you'll fall in love again."

Rani's eyelids drooped, and she shook her head. "I guess I shouldn't be too surprised that things didn't work out with Matthew. I've always known God wouldn't let me be happy in life."

Anna's eyes grew wide. "What are you talking about?"

Rani clasped her hands in her lap and stared down at them. "It was my fault Willie died," she whispered. "I took him from you and Poppa, and I've always known God would take something from me. I . . . I didn't want it to be Matthew, though."

Her last words died with a wail before she fell into Anna's arms and buried her face against her mother's chest. Anna's face had paled, and Simon knew his must look the same. He touched Rani's shoulder. "Rani, Willie's death wasn't your fault."

"But it was," she cried out. "I should have watched him like Mama said, and then he wouldn't have died."

Anna gritted her teeth and pushed Rani into a sitting position. "No, Rani, it wasn't your fault. It was mine. Willie came in the kitchen and wanted to stay and watch me work. I told him I didn't need him underfoot while I was so busy. I made him go outside. If I had kept him with me, he'd still be alive. I've always blamed myself, not you."

Simon stretched his arms to embrace them. "No, you're both wrong. I was going fishing with John that morning, and Willie begged me to let him go. The last time I took him he'd thrown rocks in the water and scared all the fish off. So I told him he had to stay home. There's no way I'll ever forgive myself for not taking him with me. If I had, he'd still be alive."

The three of them sat there hugging each other and crying as they grieved for the child they each felt they had failed. After a few minutes, Simon pulled his handkerchief out and handed it to Rani. "We've each carried a burden for ten years, and I'm glad today we've finally spoken it aloud. We could spend the rest of our lives asking *what if,* but that's not going to bring Willie back. He's with our heavenly Father, and I know he'd want us to be happy."

Anna nodded. "He would. He loved his family."

Simon patted Rani's shoulder. "Now we have to figure out a way to help you deal with this new hurt. Do you want me to talk to Matthew again and see if I can change his mind?"

Rani stood up, walked to the window, and looked out. "I don't think he'll change his mind," she said. "And maybe it's for the best. My attachment to Matthew has caused George to hate me, and that's hurt too. He's drinking a lot, and I can't stand to think how his parents must be hurting."

Anna rose to her feet and gasped. "George is drinking?"

Simon stood up. "Pete told me all about it while he was here after his accident. He and Laura are devastated. George isn't staying at home anymore. They don't know where he's living, but Pete suspects he's working at a still."

Anna put her hand to her throat and groaned. "Not George. How could he do this?"

Rani turned from the window. Fresh tears rolled from her eyes. "So I have that to add to my past mistakes. I can't stay here and see what's happening to George and then run the risk of seeing Matthew. I can't see him and act as if he means nothing to me."

Her mother moved toward her. "What do you want to do?"

She took a deep breath. "I want to go to Maryville and stay with Uncle Charles for a while. Maybe I can forget about Matthew and come back home a new person."

Simon glanced at Anna, then to Rani. "Are you sure you want to do this?"

She nodded. "Yes."

Anna swallowed hard before she spoke. "Uncle Charles will be glad to have you, but you have to promise me you'll come back. I need at least one of my children close by."

Rani moved to her mother and hugged her. "I'll come back, Mama. I just need to get away for now."

"When do you want to leave?" Simon asked.

She thought for a moment. "I told Matthew I'd finish the bricks. I should have enough ready in two weeks. I'd like to leave after that."

Simon nodded. "All right. We'll write to Uncle Charles and tell him you're coming. I'll drive you to Townsend in the buggy, and you can take the train to Maryville. I'll also take the last load of bricks over to Matthew's for you so you won't have to see him."

Her lips tightened into a thin line. "Thank you, Poppa. I don't ever want to see him again."

"Rani," Anna said, "don't say that. Please pray about this and try to forgive Matthew. Try to understand what he's feeling right now."

She shook her head. "I'll pray, Mama, but I'll pray that God will help me forget him and will keep him as far away from me as possible. Maybe then I can find some happiness."

Matthew hung the harness on a peg in the barn wall and turned just in time to see Scout dash through the open door and head straight to him. Matthew dropped to his knees and grabbed the wriggling dog in a hug. "Where did you come from, boy?"

He stood up, walked to the door, and smiled at the sight of Simon climbing down from his wagon. With Scout trotting alongside him, Matthew stepped from the barn. Simon turned as he approached, took off his hat, and wiped his arm across his forehead. "This is one of the hottest days we've had so far this summer. But you expect a few like this in August."

Matthew stuck out his hand, and Simon grasped it. "It's good to see you, Simon."

"Good to see you too." He nodded his head in the direction of the wagon. "I brought the last of the bricks. This ought to do it for the chimney."

Matthew walked to the wagon and glanced into the bed that was stacked high with bricks. The sight of them pricked his heart, and he swallowed. "Rani did a good job on them."

Simon nodded. "She did. And I talked to the men at church on Sunday. They'll be here tomorrow to help rebuild your cabin. With all the help I've got coming, we ought to be able to get it up in a few days. We'll at least get the walls and roof on, and Cecil can get the chimney laid.

I figure you can work on the inside and get it finished by fall."

"I really appreciate you asking them to come."

Simon chuckled. "They were all glad to do it. Especially Pete. He says he doesn't know how he would have made it these last few weeks without all the help you've been to him. He plans to be here even if all he can do is sit in a chair and oversee the work."

"That's awfully nice of Pete. I didn't mind helping out a bit while he was so bad, and I got to know the Fergusons a lot better." He paused a moment and bit down on his lip. "I guess you wonder why I haven't been at church lately."

Simon shook his head. "No, I had an idea why you stayed away."

Matthew stuck his hands in his pockets and stared down at the ground. "I'll come back. I thought for now it might be a good idea for me not to see Rani. And I didn't know how you and Anna feel about me after learning about Rani and me."

"If that's what kept you away, you can come next Sunday. Anna and I have forgiven you for not telling us. And as for Rani, she won't be there for quite a while."

Matthew frowned. "Why not?"

Simon sighed and pushed his hat back on his head. "She's gone to stay with Doc over in

Maryville for a while. I don't know when she'll be back."

Matthew swallowed hard and tried not to let Simon see how his words had shocked him. "That's good to know. Maybe being with Doc can help her through this rough time."

Simon shook his head. "I don't know about that. She sure did cry a lot before she left." He reached out and clamped his hand down on Matthew's shoulder. "What about you, Matthew? What do you need right now to help you?"

Matthew stared at the man he'd wished could be his father when he was a boy. Maybe wanting a stable family and a father he could respect had been part of the attraction to Rani, but not all of it. He gave a slight shake of his head. "I don't know, Simon. Hard work is helping a lot, but I sure miss being with all of you in the evenings."

"And we miss you too. I want you to know I'm here for you if you ever need to talk. I want to help you any way I can."

Matthew exhaled. "You can't change my past, Simon. Just take care of Rani."

"We will." He pointed to the bricks in the back of the wagon. "Now let's get these unloaded so I can make some visits this afternoon. And by the way, Anna said to tell you to come for supper tonight. She and Granny have been missing you."

He shook his head. "Thanks, but not just yet. I

need some time to work through things in my head before I come back there. Tell Granny and Anna I'll see them soon."

Simon sighed. "All right. But let me know if I can help."

"I will. And, Simon, thank you for not holding it against me about Rani. I'll try to make it up to you and Anna."

Simon nodded, and they didn't speak anymore as they set to work unloading the bricks. When they were all stacked beside the others at the side of the cabin site, Simon climbed in his wagon and drove out of the yard. Scout stood beside Matthew and looked from him to the departing wagon. After a moment Matthew snapped his fingers and pointed in the direction of the wagon.

"Go on, boy. That's where you belong."

Scout looked up at him, whined, and pawed at the ground as if uncertain what to do. After a moment, he glanced back at the wagon that was disappearing in the distance and ran after Simon. Matthew watched him go and thought of the first night Scout had allowed him to approach him, the same night Rani had declared to him she wasn't a girl but a woman.

He could feel the muscle in his jaw twitching, and he pulled the brim of his hat lower. He wondered what she was doing right now in Maryville. Had she already put any thought of him out of her head? Was she on her way to a new life? He'd told himself that's what he wanted for her. But in his heart he knew that wasn't true.

More than anything he wanted her with him to share in the building of his cabin, but he had put an end to that. Maybe in time he could live with his decision, but right now it was more difficult than he could ever have imagined.

"I declare, Miss Rani. What's happened to your appetite? When you stayed with us to go to school, I couldn't fill you up. Now you eat like a bird. I never let nobody I cook for starve to death, and I don't intend to start now. We've got to put some meat on those bones."

Rani looked up from where she sat at the dining room table into the face of Uncle Charles's housekeeper, Mrs. Miller. The woman's round face always seemed to have a rosy tint, probably because of the time she spent hovering over the stove in the kitchen. Streaks of gray ran through her once dark hair, and kindness sparkled in her brown eyes.

Rani glanced at Uncle Charles, who was focused on devouring a piece of fried chicken. "Your food is wonderful," Rani said to Mrs. Miller. "In fact it's some of the best I've ever eaten. It's just that I haven't felt well since I arrived."

Mrs. Miller clucked her tongue and shook her

head. "Then we have to do something about that." She shoveled a big piece of cornbread onto Rani's plate and stepped back. "We'll start with cornbread. Eat that, and you'll feel better."

Uncle Charles laughed and placed the chicken bone back on his plate. "You can't argue with Mrs. Miller, Rani. She's been taking care of me ever since I moved to Maryville, and I don't know what I would do without her."

Mrs. Miller beamed and straightened her shoulders. "It's a pleasure helping out where you're appreciated." She stared down at Rani and frowned. "But we gotta do something to get some life back into this girl, Doc."

He nodded. "I agree with you. That's why I've planned a little trip for us this afternoon."

Rani laid her fork on her plate and leaned forward. "What kind of trip?"

"Well, not a long trip. Just downtown, really. Do you remember I told you about my friend's grandson—the potter?"

"Yes. You said he had a kiln. Are we going to his studio?"

"We are. He's working on the pieces he's going to show in Knoxville next spring, and I thought you might like to meet him."

Rani's eyes grew wide. "Oh, Uncle Charles, I would love to meet him and see his work. When are we going?"

He glanced at Mrs. Miller and then down to

Rani's plate. "As soon as you finish your cornbread."

Rani's eyes filled with laughter, and she reached across the table and grasped Uncle Charles's hand. "Thank you—and you, Mrs. Miller—for all you've done for me. I appreciate both of you so much, and I promise I'm going to be better company from now on."

Uncle Charles squeezed her hand and smiled. "We just want you to be happy, darling."

Mrs. Miller sniffed and wiped at her eyes. "We sure do. If you think of anything you want to eat, you tell me, and I'll cook it for you."

Rani smiled. "I will, Mrs. Miller, and I promise to work on regaining my healthy appetite."

She picked up her fork, scooped up some green beans, and popped them into her mouth. She closed her eyes and smiled. "Um-m-m, these are good." She chewed for a moment and then swallowed. "See? I'm already eating better."

Mrs. Miller laughed and turned to go back to the kitchen. "Just wait until you see the egg custard pie I made for dessert."

She hurried toward the kitchen, and Uncle Charles watched her go before he glanced back at Rani. "That woman is a jewel. She has such a kind heart, and she sure takes good care of me."

Rani swallowed and wiped her mouth on her napkin. "I like her very much. You were lucky to find her."

"I sure was. I don't know if I ever told you or not, but when I moved into this house, her husband was very sick and couldn't work. She'd used up all their money on medical bills and needed a job. I offered to pay her to clean my house and cook for me and to treat her husband for free, and she agreed. He died about a year later, and she's worked for me ever since."

"I'm glad she didn't move away. Mama feels better knowing you have her looking after you."

Rani directed one last glance toward the kitchen before she picked up the cornbread and took a bite. As she chewed, a new resolve began to form in her mind. She'd moped around Uncle Charles's house ever since she arrived, but she wouldn't mope any longer. She had come to Maryville to forget Matthew, and that was what she intended to do. From now on she would concentrate on keeping herself busy so she wouldn't have time to think about the man who had broken her heart. There had to be all kinds of things to interest her in a town this size, and she intended to find them all.

The visit to the potter's studio this afternoon was a good way to begin.

A bell over the door jingled when Uncle Charles opened the door for Rani to enter. Rani stepped into the artist's showroom and looked around in wonder at the assortment of bowls and vases displayed. The bright colors of the pieces that sat on shelves around the walls and tables across the floor made her pit-fired pieces look like dingy rejects.

"Look around and make yourself at home," a man's voice called from a room at the back of the shop. A curtain hung over the door that led to the room and blocked her view of what lay beyond. "I'll be with you in a minute."

"David, it's Charles Prentiss. Take your time. We'll just browse," Uncle Charles called back.

Rani wandered to the far side of the room and gazed down at the pieces in a locked glass case but turned just a moment later when a man walked into the room. A long apron covered him from his chest to his knees, and specks of clay clung to the material. He stuck out his hand and hurried toward Uncle Charles.

"Dr. Prentiss, I'm glad you came in today. I've been working on some pieces for the exhibit in Knoxville, and I wanted you to see them. After all, you've encouraged me so much since I opened my studio."

Uncle Charles waved his hand in dismissal. "That's because I recognize a gifted artist when I see one. You deserve all the accolades you're going to get in Knoxville."

"Thank you. So, are you shopping or just visiting today?" the young man asked.

"Both, I guess. I've been meaning to get

another of your pieces, but today I've brought someone who's very interested in seeing your work." He motioned for Rani to join them. "This is my niece Rani Martin from Cades Cove."

He turned toward Rani, and his eyes blue widened. His Adam's apple bobbed up and down and he took a deep breath as she walked toward them. When she stopped next to her uncle, his gaze traveled over her. "I'm David Brann, Miss Martin. I didn't see you at the display case. I'm delighted to meet you. Your uncle has spoken of you often."

"He's told me about you and your studio too, Mr. Brann." She swept her arm in an arc. "This is wonderful. I've never seen so many beautiful pieces together in one place before."

He smiled and brushed the shock of blond hair that hung over his forehead out of his eyes. "Thank you, Miss Martin, but you are a very accomplished potter also."

Her mouth dropped open in surprise. "How do you know that?"

He laughed, and the corner of his eyes crinkled. "Your uncle has quite a bit of your work in his home. I've admired it ever since I first saw it."

She felt her cheeks flush, and she returned the young man's warm smile. "They look rather primitive compared to yours."

A frown creased his forehead. "Oh, you musn't think like that. Every artist has their own special gift they bring to their work, and your pit-fired pieces are some of the best I've ever seen."

She laughed. "Thank you for the compliment." She glanced around the shop again. "Mine are all handcrafted, but I imagine you use a potter's wheel."

He nodded. "I do, and I fire my pieces in a kiln I have out back of the studio."

She clasped her hands in front of her and sighed. "A potter's wheel and a kiln sound like such luxuries to me. I dig my clay from a pit in a hollow near our home and fire it in a field next to our house. I've always wished I could learn to use a potter's wheel."

"I'd be glad to teach you."

Her eyes grew wide with excitement. "You would? I would be so grateful, and I'd be glad to pay you for lessons. When could you start?"

"There's no need for you to pay me. Doc has done a lot for me since I came to Maryville, and it would be my pleasure to return the favor. How about if we start this afternoon? I'm caught up for the day and don't have anything pressing."

She turned to Uncle Charles, who had remained quiet through her exchange with Mr. Brann. "Do you mind if I stay, Uncle Charles? I can find my way back to your house when we're finished."

Uncle Charles smiled. "Stay as long as you like, darling. I can come back for you later this afternoon, though."

"There's no need for that," David said. "I'll be glad to drive Miss Martin back to your home." He turned and faced her. "That is, if you don't mind riding with me."

For the first time since coming to Maryville, Rani felt a surge of excitement. She was going to learn to use a potter's wheel, and something in the easy manner she and David Brann spoke reminded her of the ease with which she and George had once spoken.

She smiled at him. "I think you look perfectly capable of handling a horse and buggy, Mr. Brann."

His eyes sparkled, and he leaned closer. "I'm afraid the only horses I own are under the hood of my car."

She gasped. "You own an automobile?"

He laughed and held up his hands. "Guilty. Do you still want to ride with me?"

She threw back her head and laughed. "More than ever. I've never ridden in a car before."

Uncle Charles laughed and turned toward the door. "Then I'll leave you two artists to your work. Thank you for bringing Rani home later, David, and we'll expect you to stay for supper."

His gaze swept Rani. "I would be delighted, Doc."

When he had left, David turned to her. "My wheel is in the back room. I have another apron you can wear. I'd hate for you to get that pretty dress dirty."

She laughed. "Don't worry about that, Mr. Brann. I'm used to having clay all over me."

He cocked an eyebrow and studied her for a moment. "It is a rather messy medium. Before we start, however, there's one thing we need to get straight."

"And what's that?"

"I'm not an old man yet, just turned twenty-six. And you're definitely not an old woman. So let's not have any more of this Mr. Brann and Miss Martin stuff. I want you to call me David, and I'd like to call you Rani. Is that agreeable with you?"

She smiled and stuck out her hand. "Hello, David. My name is Rani."

He took her hand in his and squeezed. "Hello, Rani. It's good to meet you. I'm glad you came to my shop today."

Chapter 15

Even though Simon had said the men planned to come help build his cabin, Matthew doubted they would show up this morning. After all, they had too much to do on their farms, and it cut into a farmer's workday to put aside his chores. The fact that it was Luke Jackson's son needing help would probably keep them away too.

When Cecil Davis pulled his wagon to a stop at the cabin site, Matthew hurried to welcome the man who would lay the bricks Rani had made. Cecil climbed down from the wagon and nodded. "Morning, Matthew. Looks like a good day for workin'."

Matthew remembered how Cecil's tall, muscular frame had always seemed at odds with the man's soft-spoken words. Matthew stuck out his hand and nodded. "I appreciate your help, Mr. Davis. Simon said he and John would be here, but I'm really not expecting anybody else."

"No need to worry. They'll be along in a while. I passed by Pete Ferguson's place on my way here. It looked like he was loadin' up to come."

"I told him he didn't need to push himself. He's still not over that accident."

Cecil nodded. "I reckon he'll know how to pace himself. He's not one to pass up somebody a-needin' he'p." Cecil paused and narrowed his eyes. "Just like you wasn't when you he'ped him."

"I was glad to do it."

"Well, Pete's been a-tellin' ev'rybody 'bout how you done come over there ev'ry day. I always knowed you was a good man, Matthew. I'm right glad you came on back home where you belong."

Matthew realized Cecil had probably just made one of the longest speeches of his life, and the words felt like a soothing ointment applied to an open wound. Simon, Anna, Granny, and even Rani had told him he'd done the right thing in coming home, but he had thought them biased in their opinions. To have a member of the community voice those same words gave him hope that maybe he did have a place in the Cove.

He stuck out his hand. "Thank you, Mr. Davis. I'm glad to be back."

Cecil shook his hand and nodded. "Cecil. Just call me Cecil."

Matthew smiled. "I will."

Two other wagons pulled into the yard and rumbled to the site. Simon and his brother John climbed down from one, and Howard Ledbetter and his son Edward from another. Within minutes Pete Ferguson had arrived as well as Joshua Whitson, William Carter, and his son Sam.

Matthew could hardly believe how quickly the men set to work. Before he knew it, Pete had organized the men into teams with different jobs and had sent them off in all directions. Then he had taken his place in a chair underneath a tree at the edge of the cabin site.

Matthew walked over to Pete and glanced down at him. "Are you making it all right?"

He chuckled. "I feel fit as a fiddle. It's good to be out ag'in."

Matthew stared after the men who were walking toward the tree line at the back of his property. "I've said it a hundred times this morning, but I'll say it once more. I really appreciate what all of you are doing for me."

Pete leaned back in his chair and shook his head. "Just helping a neighbor out. That's what we do in the Cove."

Matthew closed his eyes and inhaled the sweet mountain air. "I guess that's right. We've always done that."

He turned, picked up the axe that he'd propped beside a tree, and headed after the men who were on their way to chop down trees and strip them into logs for the home he'd dreamed of having. This was developing into one of the best days of his life. Everything would be perfect if his mother, Eli, and Rani were here to share it with him.

Rani studied the piece she'd just made on the potter's wheel. After a minute she shook her head, grabbed the wet clay, and dumped it back into the tub at her feet. "I'm never going to get the hang of this," she cried. "Why won't it work for me?"

Across the room David looked up from the glaze he was painstakingly applying to a large bowl. "You're being too hard on yourself. Don't expect perfection at first. Keep trying."

She jumped to her feet, grabbed a towel, and wiped the clay from her hands. "I've tried for three weeks, David, and it's not getting any better." She wadded the towel into a ball and hurled it at her chair. "I might as well give up. I'm never going to be any good at this."

David laid down the brush he held and wiped his hands on the front of his apron. He crossed his arms and leaned against the table beside him. "I'm beginning to think you may be right."

Her eyes grew wide, and her breath caught in her throat. Even though she had voiced the words, it surprised her that he agreed. "S-so you think I don't have any talent for working with clay?"

He shook his head, dropped his arms to his side, and straightened. "I didn't say that. I said you may never be any good at it."

She frowned. "But . . . I don't understand what you mean."

He walked over to her, and she almost flinched at the disappointment she saw in his eyes. "I was impressed the first time I saw one of your pieces at your uncle's house. But you've been here for a month now, and I've begun to wonder if you have what it takes to be a successful artist."

His words stung like a slap in the face. She had worked so hard to impress David, but she had failed as she always did. "I've always doubted I had the talent for it. It just hurts a little to know you agree with me."

He frowned and shook his head. "I don't agree that you lack the talent. You are very gifted, Rani, but you may never be successful because you don't believe in yourself. Why would you doubt yourself when you are so blessed? Do you really believe perfection is the mark of a true artist? If you do, then you're wrong. Nothing is perfect in this life. Not me, not you, and not one of the pieces either of us will ever make. We all have our imperfections, but we learn to adapt."

"I know that."

He frowned. "You don't act like you do. I've watched you try over and over. You've destroyed pieces that were on their way to being beautiful works of art. I think for some reason you have it in your head that you're not worthy of the gift God has given you, and you intend to show Him. Why is that?"

Rani lifted her chin and glared at him. "You're wrong, David."

"Am I?" He tilted his head to the side and stared at her. "You're the daughter of a minister. I'm sure you know the parable Jesus told about the man who entrusted his servants with an amount of money. To one he gave five, to another two, and to another one. The first and second man went to work and increased their fortune. The third one hid his money and did nothing with it. When the master returned, he was angry with the third man. He took his money and gave it away."

"I know that story. I've heard it dozens of times."

"But have you ever thought about what it means, Rani? God has given each of us some special gift, and we're accountable to Him for how we use it. He's given you the ability to make beautiful pottery that could bring joy to people all over the country. Instead of working to improve that gift, you complain and feel sorry for yourself. Nothing in this life comes easy, Rani. If you want to learn from me, I'll teach you. But you have to work hard, and you have to quit acting like a spoiled schoolgirl."

Willie's face flashed into her mind, and she blinked back tears. She remembered how he had watched her dig her first fire pit and helped her gather the wood for it. Had her guilt over his death caused her to doubt the gift God had given her?

Rani's lips trembled, and she turned away from David. She wiped at the tears in her eyes and took a deep breath before she turned back to him. "You're right, David. My family has always encouraged me to push myself more, but I've been afraid to do it."

He frowned. "But I don't understand why. You have ability like few I've ever seen. If you would just trust yourself and open yourself up to the gift God wants you to share with others, you would find great pleasure in your work."

"I've always found pleasure in it, but I've told myself it was something I do for myself and my family. Someone told me once that he thought people would pay to buy my pieces, but I didn't believe him. Do you think they would?"

"I know they would. In fact if you'd agree, I'd like to include some of your pieces in my exhibit in Knoxville next spring."

She gasped and shook her head in surprise. "You'd really take some of my work with you?"

"I would. I think it would be a great addition to the show. We've got eight months until then, and that's enough time to do something really extraordinary. And you and your uncle can accompany me to Knoxville for the exhibit. Would you like to do that?"

"Go to Knoxville? Oh, I would love that." Before she realized what she was doing, Rani threw her arms around David's neck and hugged him. "Thank you. Thank you for everything." She pulled back and stared up into his eyes. "You're a good man, David, and you've been so kind to me. I want to learn everything you can teach me. Will you help me?"

"I will." The muscle in his jaw twitched, and his gaze traveled over her face. "I only want you to be honest with yourself and with me." He paused a moment and stared into her eyes. "Rani, why did you really come to Maryville?"

She started to say that she had only come to visit her uncle, but he had asked her to be honest with him. She took a deep breath. "I came to get over a man."

"Is he the one who encouraged you with your pottery?"

"Yes," she whispered.

His arms encircled her and drew her closer. "I'd like to help you forget him."

The desire to kiss her sparkled in his eyes, and Rani knew she only needed to give the slightest encouragement. Instead she laid her cheek against his chest, closed her eyes, and wished it were Matthew holding her instead.

"Maybe you can," she whispered. "Maybe you can."

To some people it might seem like little more than a room with log walls, but to Matthew it meant home. He stood in the middle of his one-room cabin and let his gaze drift over the rough wooden walls. Since he'd moved in a few weeks ago, he'd worked on finishing the inside walls and making sure the cabin was ready for the coming winter, but there was still a lot of work to do. At least he had a roof over his head. He hoped one day he'd be able to do something to help out the men who'd given their time to build his home.

He walked over to the fireplace and lifted the lid on the black pot that hung over the glowing embers. His stomach growled at the smell that drifted up. Maybe by next year he'd be able to afford a wood stove and wouldn't have to cook over an open fire any more.

A knock sounded at the door, and he replaced the lid before heading across the floor. When he opened the door, he smiled at the sight of Simon, Anna, and Noah standing outside.

"Come in. It's good to have visitors."

Anna held up a basket. "And we've come bearing gifts. Granny sent an apple pie, and I've baked you two loaves of bread."

"I can't think of anything I'd rather have than some of your and Granny's cooking."

They stepped into the cabin and he closed the door behind them. Anna looked around for somewhere to set the basket and frowned. "Don't you have a table?"

He chuckled and ambled over to stand beside her. "Not yet. And no chairs either. I guess we'll all have to stand, or sit on the floor."

Noah plopped down on the floor and grinned up at Matthew. "Suits me fine."

Matthew squatted beside the boy and chucked him under the chin. "How've you been, Noah? I thought you'd come help build my cabin, but you didn't."

Noah frowned and glanced at Simon. "I wanted to come, but he said it was too dang'rous a place for a boy to be."

Matthew laughed and stood. "Then you'll have to come visit me now that it's finished. Maybe you can help me make some chairs."

Noah's eyebrows arched. "You gonna whittle 'em?"

Simon reached down and ruffled the boy's

hair. "No, he won't whittle them, but we'll come back to help." He turned to Matthew. "And that reminds me, John and I are coming over next week to help you pick your corn. It looks like it's ready to be harvested."

"Thanks, Simon. I just have that one field I planted for grain for my livestock. Next year I hope to have more land cleared and a bigger crop. I was lucky I could get that one field in before it got too hot."

"And I'm coming too," Noah said. "I'll bring Scout. He follows me ev'rywhere I go."

Matthew placed his hand on his heart and staggered backward. "Oh, no, you've taken Scout's loyalty away from me. What am I going to do?"

Noah jumped up. "I didn't mean to, Matthew. I'll tell him to like you ag'in."

Matthew laughed. "I'm teasing you, Noah. I'm glad Scout's got somebody to play with. Since Rani and I are both gone, I guess he's mighty glad you came to live with the Martins."

"I reckon I'm right glad too. I miss my ma, but I sure don't miss seein' my pa." He sighed. "I just wish Miss Rani would come home. Sunday school ain't the same without her."

Before Matthew could reply, Anna took Noah by the hand. "I've got some plates and forks in my basket. Why don't you and I try to find something to cut Granny's pie with? I know you

303

were begging her for a piece before we left home."

Noah's grin revealed the gap where his two front teeth had been days ago. "I'd like that."

Matthew watched Anna and Noah settle on the floor in front of the fireplace before he turned back to Simon. "I guess the rest of you are missing Rani as much as Noah is."

Simon sighed. "It's just not the same with her gone. I'm like Noah. I sure wish she'd come home."

Matthew stuck his hands in his pockets and rocked back on his heels. "Have you heard anything from her since she left?"

"We had a letter yesterday. She says she's enjoying being with Doc, and she's working with a potter there in Maryville."

"Is he the one Doc was telling us about when he was here in July?"

"I think so. His name's David Brann, and he has a studio there. She's learning how to use a potter's wheel, and she's really enjoying working with all the glazes he uses. She's all excited because he's doing a showing of his work in Knoxville next spring, and he's going to include some of her pieces."

Matthew smiled. "Rani's pottery in a show. That's wonderful. Maybe working with this man was just what she needed to help her believe she has a gift."

"Hey, you two," Anna called out, "what are you talking about over there? Come and join Noah and me for a piece of pie!"

Matthew glanced in the direction of her voice and smiled. She had spread a cloth on the floor in front of the fireplace, and she and Noah had sat down on the floor. Simon chuckled and nudged Matthew in their direction. "It looks like we're having a picnic in front of your fireplace."

"It sure does."

Simon walked over to them, dropped down beside Anna, and accepted a plate that held a piece of pie. Sitting here with Simon and Anna reminded Matthew of the day he and Rani had eaten under the oak tree and he had shared his dream with her.

Now she was pursuing her dream somewhere else. From what Simon said, she must be enjoying her new life. There wasn't a day that went by that he didn't wish things could have been different for them. But wishing didn't make it happen, and he was glad she was moving on. He had no idea how he would do that.

A pounding at the door jerked Matthew from a sound sleep. He bolted into a sitting position on the pallet he'd made in front of the fireplace and listened for another knock. Had Simon and Anna returned? No, they'd left hours ago. He strained to hear another knock, but none came.

He eased into a standing position and reached for the rifle that lay on the floor beside him. He tiptoed toward the door but stopped when a floorboard creaked beneath his feet. He waited a moment before he took another step.

He reached the door and pressed his ear against it, listening for movement outside. Hearing nothing, he cocked the rifle and reached for the door latch. He pulled the door open and stared into the black night before he stepped onto the front porch. The wind blew down from the mountains and ruffled the leaves on the trees.

In the distance he heard a dog howl, but there was no one in sight around the cabin. "Must have been the wind knocking something up against the wall," he muttered, and turned back toward the door.

He'd only taken a step when he stopped. In the darkness he could just make out a piece of paper with a nail through the center of it hanging on his front door. The wind hadn't left that unless it had used a hammer to pound the nail into the wood.

He pulled the paper from the door and carried it back inside. An oil lamp sat on the floor next to his pallet. He dropped to the floor, lit the lamp, and held the paper up to the flickering light. It was difficult at first to make out the crude handwriting, but there was no mistaking its message:

GIT OUT OF THE COVE WHILE YOU KAN
STIL WALK.

Matthew read the note several times, then
wadded it into a ball and tossed it in the fireplace. The flames licked at the paper before it
vanished in a ball of fire.

He didn't move for a long time. He'd just begun
to think he was going to be accepted in the
Cove, but now it didn't seem likely. Somebody
wanted him gone. He had his suspicions about
who it could be, but there was no way to prove it.
All he could do was keep a sharp lookout for
trouble and watch his back at all times.

He laid the rifle next to the pallet, blew out
the lamp, and settled back down in front of the
fireplace. Outside the wind blew around the
cabin, and he listened for any strange sounds in
the night. He'd worked hard to get this piece of
land back, and he wasn't about to let anybody
run him off of it.

Chapter 16

Simon and John had shown up just as Simon
promised, and they had worked with Matthew
from early morning until late afternoon picking
the hardened ears of corn from the dry stalks in
the field. They loaded bushel after bushel on

Matthew's wagon, and Noah had sat perched atop the pile as they'd hauled it to the barn.

Now with the three having left for home, Matthew stood inside the barn and thanked the Lord for the blessing of the abundant harvest and for having good friends like Simon and John. He could be assured his horse, mules, and cow would eat well this winter. With all the wildlife in the Cove, he knew he would as well.

Several times today he had started to tell Simon about the note he'd received the night he and Anna had visited, but he knew if he told of that one he'd also have to tell him of the two that had followed. With the threats having been leveled against him, he'd become even more cautious than before.

He left the barn and headed back to the cabin. His gaze darted from side to side as he trudged along. When he entered the house, he closed the door and walked over to the fireplace. He propped his foot on the hearth and stared down at the smoldering coals.

Rani's face flashed in his head, and he wondered what she was doing tonight. Each day he missed her more than the one before, and he wondered how he was ever going to put her from his mind. To him she would always be the girl who'd stolen his heart.

He sighed and straightened. Tonight he didn't need to think about Rani or how someone had been close enough to shoot him. He needed to eat something and go to sleep. He walked over and bolted the door as he now did every night—a small measure of protection against an enemy who was intent on doing him harm.

He grabbed a piece of cornbread and the fried chicken Anna had sent with Simon this morning, gobbled it down, and stretched out on the floor in front of the fireplace. He closed his eyes and tried to push Rani's face from his mind, but he couldn't. He was still thinking of her as he felt himself drift into sleep.

He had no idea how long he'd been asleep when he shot up into a sitting position. He listened for the sound that had awakened him, and his blood turned cold at the high-pitched yell piercing the night. It was coming from the direction of the corn field.

Grabbing his gun from beside him, he jumped up and ran out the door. The fire racing across the dried stalks in the cornfield lit the night sky. Fear rooted him to the spot as he watched the flames slowly devouring the field. At the moment the wind was blowing in the opposite direction of the cabin and the barn, but if it shifted, as it often did in the Cove, both buildings could be in danger from flying embers.

Intent on getting his animals to safety before the barn ignited, he raced down the steps, threw open the heavy door, and rushed inside. As he opened the stalls, he drove the animals from the barn into the fenced yard. When the two mules, his horse, and the cow stood outside the barn, he locked the gate behind him and headed toward the field. If the barn caught fire, he would come back later and drive the animals out of the enclosure.

He stopped at the edge of the field and stared at the blazing fire. What could he do? He was only one person, and the fire was a raging inferno.

Before he could decide how to proceed, Simon and John rode into the yard, dismounted from their horses, and rushed toward him. "What happened?" cried Simon above the roar of the fire.

"I don't know. I woke up, and the field was on fire. How did you know?"

"Didn't you hear the bells ringing? We keep a lookout for fires. When somebody spots one, they ring the dinner bell in their yard, and ev'rybody comes running," John said.

Matthew shook his head. "I didn't hear anything."

At that moment several wagons rolled to a stop, and men with shovels in their hands jumped to the ground. Several riders appeared on horses, dismounted, and ran toward the fire. Pete Ferguson began to shout orders.

"Men, git your shovels and spread out around the field. Don't let no spark get by you. We gotta keep this blaze contained to this field, or we're gonna have ourselves a mess to take care of."

Matthew watched in amazement as the men rushed to do as commanded. He hesitated only a moment before he ran back to the barn, grabbed his shovel, and rushed to join his neighbors on the fire line. For hours the men stood united as they pounded the embers that tried to escape the field.

As the sun rose over the mountains, the soot-covered group trudged to their wagons and horses. The last spark had been extinguished, and the weary firefighters were on their way to their homes and waiting breakfasts.

Matthew stood in front of his cabin and shook each man's hand as he prepared to leave. Over and over he expressed his gratitude to his neighbors who'd saved his house and barn from being destroyed. As Pete Ferguson prepared to climb into his wagon, Matthew walked over and stood next to him.

"Do you need help getting in?" he asked.

Pete bit down on his lip and winced as he pulled himself up. Matthew could only guess how much pain Pete must have suffered as he battled the blaze throughout the night, but he had persevered until the end.

A muffled groan escaped Pete's mouth as he settled on the wagon seat and stretched out his leg in front of him. Perspiration trickled down his face and left trails on his soot-covered skin. "I'm 'bout back to normal, Matthew. Be sure and keep an eye on that field. We could've overlooked a spark. We don't want it to blaze up agin."

"I'll do that, Pete. And thanks for all your help. You've been good to me since I've been back."

Pete stared at the reins he held before he looked up at Matthew. "I don't reckon I ever thanked you proper-like for all you done for me after I got hurt, but I want you to know I appreciate it." He took a deep breath. "And I want you to know somethin' else. When you came back here, I thought you wouldn't last. I guess I figured you was like your pa. But you ain't. If you ever need anything, just let me know."

Matthew stood in stunned silence as Pete snapped the reins and guided the team of horses from the yard. He watched the wagon roll into the distance before he turned back to Simon, the only man who remained. "Where's John?"

"He left a few minutes ago," Simon said, "but he'll come by later. I thought I'd stick around for a while in case you needed some company."

Last night as he'd battled the fire, he'd decided what he had to do. Now Pete's words made him doubt his decision. He did need help, and who better to give him advice than Simon? He shook his head in resignation. "You always could tell when I needed help, Simon, and I reckon I do right now. I don't know what to do."

"Want to talk about it?"

"Yeah. Come on inside, and I'll fix us some coffee. And I have somewhere for us to sit this time. There were some boards leftover from building the cabin, and I made a bench so I could sit in front of the fire. I think it'll hold us both."

Simon followed Matthew inside the cabin and looked around before he laughed. He walked over, placed his hands on the bench, and pressed down. "We've really got to get you some chairs."

Matthew picked up the coffeepot, filled it with water, and dumped in some coffee grounds before he set it in the coals. His gaze drifted over the bricks that Rani had made, and he closed his eyes as her face drifted through his mind. After a minute he turned to face Simon.

"I'm beginning to think I may not need any furniture, Simon. Maybe I made a mistake in coming back."

Simon's eyes grew wide with surprise. "What are you talking about?"

Matthew sank down on the bench, and Simon eased onto the other end. Matthew stared at the fireplace again before he spoke. "I thought I could come back here to live, but I think I was wrong. Everywhere I turn I see something that reminds me of Rani. Now with this fire, it just doesn't seem worth staying on anymore."

"Matthew, you can't give up because you had

a fire. Just be thankful we'd harvested the corn before the field was destroyed."

"Oh, I am. But it won't stop there. Whoever did this won't rest until I'm run out of the Cove."

Simon leaned forward and frowned. "You think the fire was set deliberately?"

"I know it was. Three different threatening notes have been left lately, and then I wake up in the middle of the night when someone yells to me from my field. Whoever it was meant for me to wake up. I'm lucky everybody showed up, or my house and barn would be gone now too."

Simon was silent for a moment. "Do you have any idea who might be behind this?"

Matthew snorted. "Of course I know. It's Wade Campbell. He thinks I have a grudge against him, and he's determined to see me gone, one way or the other."

Simon jumped to his feet. "Then we have to go to the sheriff."

"And tell him what? That I suspect Wade? I don't have any proof, and it'll be my word against his. And I don't think he's going to stop until something happens that's worse than a cornfield fire."

"But we can't let him get away with this. We have to fight for your right to be here."

Matthew clasped his hands in front of him and sighed. "It seems like I've been fighting for something all of my life. Mostly to survive, and

I'm tired. I want some peace in my life. I hoped I would be able to find it back here, but I don't think I will."

Simon stuck his hands in his pockets and stared down at Matthew. "You had to know it wasn't going to be easy to return."

"Yeah, I knew there would be folks who couldn't forget the things my father did. How can I expect them to forget when to me it still seems like it happened yesterday?" He let out a deep breath. "I know there had to be some good times. I try to remember them, but all I see is how I tried to survive the beatings and keep him from hurting my mother. I thought we'd be fine after he died, but it didn't work out that way."

Simon dropped back down on the bench beside Matthew. "I know. When I heard your mother and Eli had died, I went to Pigeon Forge to find you, but Mrs. Johnson said you left right after the funeral. Why didn't you come back here then?"

Matthew shrugged. "I don't know. All I could think about was getting as far away as I could."

"Where did you go?"

"North Carolina, Virginia, Kentucky. For the next few years I drifted from place to place. By the time I was eighteen, I'd been working in a coal mine in Kentucky for a year. I stayed to myself a lot and made it all right for a while until something happened one night that set me on a different path."

"Do you want to tell me about it?"

Matthew closed his eyes for a moment and let his mind drift back to a time he'd tried to forget. He didn't want to tell Simon. The truth was he didn't want to see the disappointment and disgust in Simon's eyes when he found out about the years he'd tried so hard to forget. But he needed to tell someone—to try to explain to Simon how his life had spun out of control and left him with only shame as a companion.

"I think it's time you found out what kind of person I really am. It was cold that winter night in Kentucky, and I'd just gotten paid. I was walking down the street in the town the coal company owned, and two fellows staggered out of a saloon. I guess they thought a skinny boy like me was easy pickings, and they wanted my money. That little bit of money was all I had in the world. When one of them hit me, something came over me. It was like I was that boy being beaten again, and I tore into them like a wild man. They were so drunk it didn't take much to knock both of them down, but I didn't stop when they fell. I kept kicking them in the stomach and face until several men who'd come outside grabbed me and held me until the sheriff got there."

"What happened?"

"He arrested me because they were hurt so bad and took me to jail. I figured that's where

I'd stay. But the next day, this fancy dressed fellow named Harry came to see me. Said he'd seen the fight the night before, and he liked the way I handled myself. Said he'd like to hire me. He traveled from town to town with a group of fighters and challenged the locals to matches which he took bets on. He said one of his men had been hurt and couldn't fight for a while. He wanted me to take his place. He said he'd pay the sheriff off so he'd release me, or I could stay and face going to prison. It turned out that the two men I'd beaten up were foremen, and the coal company had already fired me."

"So you went with him?"

"I did." Matthew rubbed his hands over his face. "The next few years are like a blur. We traveled from town to town. I can't remember how many men I fought. I didn't show any mercy to anybody, and I beat most of them to a pulp in the ring. No telling how many men's bones I broke or how many I left crippled." Tears filled his eyes. "And I liked it, Simon. When the crowd cheered for me, it was like I was finally being accepted by somebody. And for once in my life, nobody tried to take advantage of me. Even the other fighters who traveled with us were afraid of me."

Pain flickered in Simon's eyes, and he shook his head. "Matthew, you don't have to tell me this if it's too painful."

Matthew gritted his teeth and shook his head.

"No, you have to know what I was like then." He took a deep breath. "There were no rules in the kind of fighting we did, and I could figure out in the first round how I was going to put a man down. Harry started calling me the Ice Man because all I wanted was to knock my opponent senseless. Every time I walked away from some man lying in his own blood I'd think of my father and wonder how many men he'd left in the same shape. And I'd know I was just like him."

Simon's forehead wrinkled. "Oh, Matthew, you . . ."

"Then one night," Matthew interrupted, "we were in some little town in Ohio, and this boy of maybe fifteen wanted to fight me." The memories were coming too quickly now, and all Matthew wanted was to rid himself of them. "He looked scared, and I thought I'd finish him off in the first round. But I didn't. Every time I knocked him down, he'd get back up and come at me again. He wouldn't quit. Time after time he pushed back up and staggered toward me, and I'd hit him harder. Before long, blood was running in his eyes, and he couldn't see, but he'd come back at me again. The crowd started booing me, and his friends on the sidelines kept yelling for him to quit, but he wouldn't. He'd just stagger to his feet again."

"He must have had some reason to take all that punishment."

Matthew nodded. "The crowd got louder, and I got angry. This kid was making me look bad, and I didn't like it. I went after him with a vengeance, and by the time I finished, he looked like he'd been mauled by a bear. I stared down at him and couldn't believe what I'd done. His friends ran into the ring to carry him out, and one of them told me the boy had entered the fight in hopes of making some money to buy food for his mother and little sister. When I heard that, I knew I was worse than my father had ever been. That boy had been trying to do what I'd failed to do for my mother and brother. I ran out the back door of the building we were in and threw up. Then I grabbed a few clothes and headed south. All I wanted was to forget what had happened, but I couldn't."

"How far did you make it?"

"Over the next few months I slowly made my way back to Tennessee by working odd jobs along the way. One night I walked into Elkmont —into one of the Little River camps. My shoes and clothes were worn out, and I looked like a raggedy man."

"Is that when you went to work for Little River?"

Matthew nodded. "I didn't have any money, and I survived for a few weeks by eating out of a garbage can behind a restaurant. One night the cook found me rifling through the garbage. He took pity on me, invited me inside, and fed me. The next day he took me to the Little River office where his brother was hiring railroad workers and got me a job. From then on, I had one goal in mind. Make enough money to come home. I kept to myself and saved my money. I vowed I wouldn't fight a man again. Now all I fight are the nightmares of those years."

Simon clasped his hands in his lap and stared at Matthew. "Why haven't you ever told me any of this?"

"Because I'm ashamed of what I did. I didn't want you or Anna or Granny to know that I was exactly like my father."

"And what about Rani?"

Matthew's eyes grew wide, and he jerked his head up to stare at Simon. "I especially didn't want her to know, and you have to promise you'll never tell her. I've prayed every day since I can remember that I won't be like my father, but inside I'm just like him. Now somebody else knows it too, and he wants me out of the Cove."

"But you can't leave, Matthew."

"Yes, I can. I can't fight anymore, Simon. I just want some peace in my life."

Simon stood, walked to the fireplace, and reached for the Bible lying on the mantel. "Is this your mother's Bible?"

Matthew nodded. "Yes. I've always kept it with me."

Simon sat back down and flipped through the pages. "I remember when you were a boy, you told me you had put your trust in God and wanted to follow Him. Do you still believe that?"

"Yes, but for years I acted like He didn't exist. I've failed Him in so many ways."

"We all have failed at times, Matthew. But He's always ready to forgive us for faltering in our faith. You've had this fear all your life that you're going to be like your father. The truth is that all children are affected by the actions of their parents. You lived with your father's abuse and drunken rages. You convinced yourself that since his blood runs in your veins, your life would be just like his. But have you thought about Jesus' blood? He shed it to give you a life free from sin and doubt."

Matthew frowned. "I know that, but it's hard to forget what I've done in the past."

"I understand that. But you need to focus on Jesus and what He promised in the Scriptures. You've let the fear of being like your father control you for years. You need to quit dwelling on that and think on the promise we're given in 2 Corinthians 5:17. 'Therefore if any man be in Christ, he is a new creature: old things are passed away; behold, all things are become new.' "

"But Simon, how can He forgive me for injuring, and maybe crippling, all those men?"

"I wish I knew how many times someone has asked me how God can forgive horrible sins we've committed. The answer lies in one little

321

word, Matthew. It's grace. When we sin, we don't deserve His favor or His mercy, but He gives it freely. It's difficult for us to understand how He could love us that much, but He does. God stands willing to forgive you for what you did, but it sounds like it's going to be harder for you to forgive yourself."

Tears ran down Matthew's cheeks. "I don't know if I ever can."

Simon pressed Naomi's Bible into Matthew's hands. "Do you believe the words in this book like your mother did?"

"I do," he whispered.

"Then put the past behind you and become the new creature God wants to make of you. You can't run the rest of your life. It's time you faced up to the past."

"How do I do that?"

"You pray and ask God to forgive you for what you've done. Ask Him to take the guilt out of your heart and replace it with peace and strength to live your life for Him."

Matthew pushed to his feet and strode across the room. He stopped with his back to Simon and raked his hand through his hair. After a moment he turned, retraced his steps, and came to a stop in front of Simon. "It can't be that simple. There has to be more to it than that."

Simon put his hand on Matthew's shoulder and sighed. "Don't try to make something difficult out of something so easy. The Bible tells us that we're going to have tribulations in the world, but Jesus stands willing to give us the peace we need to face them. All you have to do is ask Him."

Matthew's lips trembled. "I want that peace, Simon."

"Then ask Him to help you find it."

Matthew dropped to his knees in front of the bench and clutched the Bible to his chest. "Oh, God, help me. I asked You into my life when I was a boy. But somewhere along the way, I forgot about You. Forgive me for the things I've done and the people I've hurt. Help me be the kind of man my mother would want me to be. Show me how to let go of the past, Lord. Make me that new creature the Bible speaks of."

Simon knelt beside him and placed his arm around Matthew's shoulders. "You've taken your first step toward letting your past die, Matthew. Now you need to study God's word and discover the man that's inside you waiting to be born. His name is not Luke Jackson. It's Matthew Jackson, and he's got a life to live free from guilt and the fears of the past."

Matthew stared into the face of the man he'd always admired more than any other and smiled. "I think I'm on my way to finding him, Simon."

David stopped the car in front of Uncle Charles's house and swiveled in the seat to face Rani. "I enjoyed having supper with you tonight, Rani. I hope we can do it again soon."

Rani laughed and shook her head. "David, we've had supper together nearly every night this week, and you've said the same thing every night when we've gotten home."

He grinned, and the dimple in his cheek winked at her. "It's my way of reminding you that I enjoy your company and want to spend more time with you."

"I enjoy your company too. I'm sure we will be together more. In fact, if I remember correctly, Uncle Charles asked you to come to supper tomorrow night."

David put his arm on the back of the seat, and his fingers touched her shoulder. "That he did. I suppose he thought the only way he was going to get to see you was to invite me over. I hope he doesn't think we're spending too much time together."

She shook her head. "No, he understands how hard I've been working to get ready for the exhibit, and he appreciates all the help you've been to me."

He leaned closer, and his arm slid around her shoulders. "I enjoy the time in the studio with you, but it's the after-hours time that's beginning to interest me more."

Rani's throat went dry, and she swallowed. "I've enjoyed that too."

His other arm encircled her, and he pulled her closer. "We've only known each other for a few months, but you must have figured out that I'm crazy about you, Rani."

She stared into the eyes that held her captive. "Y-you are?"

"Yes." His hand slid up her neck, and his fingers stroked her hair. "You're the most beautiful woman I've ever seen. I think about you all the time."

"I think about you too, David, but . . ."

His finger touched her lips. "Don't say it. He's gone, Rani, and I'm here. We're a good match. We have the same interests, we work well together, and we never fight."

The memory of the heated words she and Matthew had spoken at times flashed through her mind, and she realized she and David didn't clash like that. Maybe they *were* a good match. "We do seem to get along well together." Her gaze drifted over the interior of the car. "But there are other things to consider. Your family is wealthy and can afford to give you anything you want, like this car for instance. I'm a girl from a poor family in a remote mountain valley. I'm sure your family wants something better for you."

"There is no one better than you. I'm not pressuring you into anything right now, Rani. I only wanted you to know how I feel. Think about what I've said."

"I will."

He lowered his head, and she raised her lips to meet his. She closed her eyes and tried to push Matthew's face from her mind, but she couldn't.

Uncle Charles was already seated at the breakfast table when Rani came into the kitchen the next morning. His eyes lit up when he saw her, and he set his coffee cup down.

"Good morning. I wondered if I was going to see you this morning since you spend so much time other places."

She laughed and kissed him on the cheek before she settled in her chair. She picked up her napkin and spread it in her lap. "I'm spending a lot of hours getting my pieces for the exhibit finished. Maybe I'll be able to cut back on my time at the studio soon."

His eyes twinkled. "I'm only teasing, darling. I'm very proud of the work you've completed since coming here. And I can hardly wait to see the full showing."

Mrs. Miller set a plate of ham and eggs in front of her and smiled. "I'm proud of you too, Rani. I get real excited when I think about all the folks that are gonna see your work. I wouldn't doubt you selling all of your pieces while you're there."

Rani reached up and squeezed the woman's hand. "Thank you, Mrs. Miller. But this is really

David's show. I only have a few pieces in it. I have to confess, though, that I couldn't be more excited if I'd done the whole show myself. David's pieces are gorgeous."

Uncle Charles nodded. "I've seen them, and I have to agree. He's outdone himself this time." He picked up his coffee cup but set it back down. "By the way, isn't he coming to supper tonight?"

Rani swallowed the bite of ham before she answered her uncle. "He is. He'll come home with me today when we close the studio. I know he's looking forward to spending some time with you tonight."

Uncle Charles glanced up at Mrs. Miller and rolled his eyes. "I doubt if David will want to share any of his time with me. He seems intent on keeping Rani to himself."

Rani put down her fork and stared at her uncle. "Do you think I've been neglecting you?"

He shook his head. "No, darling, but it's plain to see the man's fallen in love with you." He put his elbows on the table and leaned closer. "The question is, how do you feel about him?"

"Well, I . . ." She stopped, unsure of what to say next.

Her uncle's forehead wrinkled into a frown. "Be careful, Rani. Make sure you're over Matthew before you become involved with David. It wouldn't be fair to him if you're still in love with someone else."

Rani stared into her uncle's eyes for a moment before she sighed. "Matthew made it plain there was never going to be anything for us in the future. I have to think about what's best for me now. David and I share a love for our work, we get along well, and he makes me laugh. Besides, he's a wonderful man."

"I know he is. That's why I don't want to see him hurt." The doctor laid his napkin beside his plate and reached across to grasp her hand. "Your mother wrote me and said you've mentioned working with David in your letters to her, but you've said very little else about him. That surprised me since you spend most of your time with him."

Rani bit down on her lip. "I really didn't know what to tell her. I didn't want . . ."

"Matthew to know?" he finished for her.

Her face grew warm. "What difference should it make to Matthew? He's the one who rejected me, Uncle Charles. I don't think it makes any difference to him who my friends are."

Uncle Charles stared at her a moment before he picked up his fork and speared a bit of ham. "Your mother is also upset because you told her you wouldn't be home for Christmas."

Rani concentrated on pushing the scrambled eggs around on her plate. "I thought it best not to travel in the winter. There could be snow drifts in the Cove, and it might be too cold for

Poppa to drive to Townsend in the buggy to pick me up at the train station."

"That might be true unless you go home before the first snowfall."

Her eyes grew wide. "Do you want me to go home?"

He reached for her hand and squeezed it. "Of course not, darling. But I don't want you to be unhappy because you have to spend Christmas with me instead of being with all your family."

She laughed and leaned over to kiss him on the cheek. "I'll miss Mama and Poppa, and Granny too. But I also know I'll enjoy spending Christmas with you and Mrs. Miller."

His eyebrows arched. "And David? He told me he isn't going to his father's house for Christmas."

She laughed. "And David too. I'm sure we'll all have a Christmas to remember."

Her uncle laughed. "I wouldn't doubt it. And remember, you're welcome to stay here as long as you want. I'm sure the longer you stay the happier David will be."

She smiled. "I really like David a lot, Uncle Charles. I think he's helping me get over Matthew. Now I want to get on with my life. You've always told me to look for the plan God has for me. That's what I'm doing."

"Then be careful how you interpret what God is saying to you. Don't try to substitute your desires for His will."

"I won't. I'm praying God will show me what that will is."

"Good girl," her uncle said as he picked up his fork and began to eat.

Rani picked up her coffee cup and took a sip. How could she know what God's will was? All her life her family had talked to her about it, and she had thought Matthew was the one God had sent to her. But that hadn't worked out, so it must not have been God's will. If it wasn't God's will, then why couldn't she put Matthew out of her mind?

She tightened her hands into fists, and her fingernails cut into her skin. Matthew was out of her life, and there was nothing she could do to change that. She would not think about him. She would concentrate on what David had said to her last night.

David was right. They were very much alike. They shared the same interests. Her life with him would be very different from what it would have been with Matthew. With David she would never have to worry about money, and they could work together in producing their pottery.

After all, if Matthew had really loved her, he never would have thrown their love away like it meant nothing to him. Maybe he wasn't capable of loving. If that was true, then she was better off without him.

Chapter 17

Matthew stepped out of the barn and pulled his coat tighter against the cold December wind that blew down from the mountains. The first snowfall hadn't come to the Cove yet, but it wouldn't be long. The white peaks in the distance signaled that winter was on its way.

Smoke curled up through the cabin's chimney, and he hurried to get inside out of the cold. When he approached the cabin, though, he didn't go inside but walked around to the tall chimney that stretched from the ground and up the side of his cabin to tower above the roof. Every time he passed it he thought of Rani and of the times they'd sat beside the fire pit and watched the bricks baking in the flames.

He reached out and trailed his fingers across the rough bricks. Touching them made her seem closer to him somehow. It was like she had left a part of herself with him when she went away. He put both hands against the bricks and leaned forward until his forehead rested between his hands.

"God," he prayed, "thank You for the peace that is slowly coming into my heart. Thank You for Simon, who's guided me through Your word and helped me understand how much You love me. Be with Rani wherever she is today and keep her safe. I love her so, Lord, and I pray that someday I'll have the chance to tell her I'm learning to live each day knowing You're with me. Amen."

He straightened and took a deep breath before he walked to the front door and entered the cabin. He'd just taken off his coat when he heard horses stopping in the yard. He opened the door and frowned at the sight of Simon and a man he didn't know climbing down from their horses.

They tied their mounts to a tree nearby and walked toward Matthew. "Good morning," he called out. "Come on in out of the cold and have some coffee."

"Don't mind if we do," Simon called out.

They followed him inside and walked toward the fireplace. Simon stuck his hands out to warm them at the fire and nodded toward the man next to him. "Matthew, this is Sheriff Frank Hawkins. He came by my place this morning, and I thought I'd better come over here with him. He has something to tell you."

Matthew's eyes grew wide. "To tell me? What is it, Sheriff?"

Sheriff Hawkins turned his back to the fire and clasped his hands behind him. "I hear you had a fire a while back."

Matthew glanced at Simon, then back to the sheriff. "Yes, back in the fall."

"And you'd had some threatnin' notes before that?"

"Yes."

"Had any since?"

"No. They stopped right after the fire."

"Do you know a man named Chester Goode?"

Matthew shook his head. "The name's not familiar to me."

The sheriff shrugged. "Don't make no matter. He lives over toward Wears Valley, but we caught him peddling some moonshine yesterday. When we arrested him for selling illegal liquor, he decided to tell me about the others involved."

Matthew glanced at Simon again and back to the sheriff. "I hope he didn't say I was one of them."

Sheriff Hawkins laughed and shook his head. "Naw, he said Wade Campbell was the one who owned the still, and he had a boy named George Ferguson helpin' him."

Matthew's mouth gaped open in surprise. "George? Does Pete know?"

Simon nodded. "We stopped by there on our way here. Pete didn't seem too surprised, but Laura took the news hard."

"I'm sorry to hear that," Matthew said. "I'll go over to see them later today."

"Anyway," the sheriff continued, "Chester said Wade and George were the ones who set your field on fire. Right after that, they figured the law would be after them, so they headed over to the North Carolina side of the mountains near Proctor where they set up a still. They've been over there selling moonshine to the workers of the Little River Lumber Company for the past few months. That explains why your night visits stopped."

Matthew frowned. "If Wade's making liquor in North Carolina now, where did Chester get the moonshine he was selling?"

The sheriff hooked his fingers in his gunbelt and exhaled. "Well, it seems they've come back to Tennessee, and Wade had a new still in his barn. We went over there, and sure enough there it was. But it had been abandoned. He must have found out we were onto him."

"What about Wade and George? Did you find them?"

"Not a sign of them anywhere. There were no clothes or food in the cabin, so I figure they cleared out. Chester thought they probably went back to North Carolina. If they did, then I reckon the sheriff over there can worry about them."

"But you can't be sure?"

Sheriff Hawkins shook his head. "No, but since Chester didn't show back up with the money, Wade probably suspects we're after him. I don't expect he'll be showing his face around here for a while. He spends most of his time running from the law in Tennessee, North Carolina, and

Georgia. I don't think you'll have to worry about any more fires."

"That's good to know." Matthew stuck out his hand. "I appreciate you coming by and telling me this."

Sheriff Hawkins shook Matthew's hand and glanced at Simon. "Well, if you need me for anything, you know where to find me."

Simon nodded. "I do. Thanks again, Frank."

Matthew walked the sheriff to the door, then turned back to Simon. "Maybe we've seen the last of Wade Campbell around here. But I sure hate to hear that George is mixed up with him."

"Me too. Pete's been worried about him for months."

"I don't understand how George could suddenly turn his back on everything he's always known. Do you think he did it because Rani wouldn't marry him?"

Simon sighed and sank down on the bench that sat to the side of the fireplace. "I thought so at first, but Pete tells me they've had trouble with George for a long time. That surprised me because nobody in the Cove would have believed it. He seemed like the perfect son."

Matthew sat down beside Simon. "I wish I could talk to him. I'd like to share with him what you've helped me to see these past few months."

"That's what serving the Lord is all about, Matthew. Once we turn our lives over to Christ, we want everyone else to know the peace He brings us. I'm glad you've come to understand that."

Matthew stared into the fire for a moment before he spoke. "I wish I could tell Rani what's happened in my life. I know she probably hates me after the way I've hurt her, but I just want her to know I'm finally at peace with my past. I thought maybe she would come home for Christmas, and I could talk to her."

Simon sighed and slapped him on the shoulder. "I'm afraid you won't get to do that. She's staying in Maryville for Christmas. We sure are going to miss her."

Matthew's heart dropped to the pit of his stomach. He'd thought she wouldn't miss Christmas in the Cove. He must have hurt her a lot more than he realized for her to stay away from her family at such an important time. "I'm sorry, Simon. I guess this is my fault too."

Simon shook her head. "Don't worry about it. She'll have to come home sooner or later. I just wish she'd hurry up and do it."

Matthew and Simon sat in front of the fire, each lost in their thoughts. Matthew closed his eyes and thought of how Rani had looked in front of the mountain laurel bush the first day he'd seen her.

He wished she would come home soon. He wanted to beg her forgiveness for hurting her and to tell her he'd never stopped loving her. It was too much to hope that she might still return his feelings, but that didn't matter so much. He only wanted her to be happy.

Anna set the last of the clean Christmas dinner dishes in the cupboard, untied her apron, and hung it on a peg next to the stove. She turned and smiled at Granny, who was sitting at the kitchen table. "Did you enjoy our Christmas dinner, Granny?"

Granny's eyes twinkled. "You outdone yourself this time, darlin'. Ev'ry year I wonder how Christmas can get any better, but it does. Maybe it's because I'm gittin' older and don't have as many left as I'd like."

Anna laughed and shook her finger at Granny. "Now, now, none of that talk today. This is the day we celebrate the birth of our Lord, and we have a lot of blessings to thank Him for."

"We have been blessed this past year," Granny said. "The crops were good in the Cove, Matthew came home, and Stephen got to start to school at Vanderbilt. Rani's going to have her pottery in an art show in a few months, and the good Lord sent a lot of laughter back in this house when Noah come to live with us. The only thing that would have made today better was to have Rani and Stephen at home."

Anna sighed. "You're right about that. I've

been thinking about all my family today. My mother isn't doing well right now. I thought I might take Noah to Strawberry Plains for a visit with her and my brother's family in the spring."

"Maybe you can go when Rani's in Knoxville and go to her art show. Noah would love that."

Anna shook her head. "I don't know. There are several babies due at that time, and I may not be able to get away." She laughed and walked over to help Granny to her feet. "I should have realized before I took over for you that a midwife's life is controlled by when a baby decides to make an entrance into this world."

Granny arched an eyebrow and grunted as she rose from the chair. "If I remember right, I told you that when you first come to the Cove."

Anna laughed. "I think you did too." She guided Granny toward the door to the front room. "Let's see what the menfolk are doing."

Granny snorted and hobbled toward the door. "They're prob'ly sleepin' in front of the fire. I declare I never seen two grown men put away as much food as Simon and Matthew did."

As they stepped into the room, Noah jumped up from his chair by the fire and ran toward them. "Is it time to open presents yet?"

Simon turned a bleary-eyed stare in Noah's direction and smiled. "Not just yet."

As Anna guided Granny to her chair, she

338

glanced at the small tree Simon and Noah had cut in the woods and brought home. The decorations they'd used for years hung from the limbs of the little fir tree. There were the paper stars Stephen and Rani had made when they were children and the tinsel she had bought years ago and carefully wrapped away each year after Christmas. This year Noah had added his contribution by helping her string the popcorn that looped the tree.

The most precious ornaments of all, though, were the pictures of toys Willie had cut from the Montgomery Ward Catalog the last Christmas of his life. He had brought them to her and told her someday he would make a lot of money and buy himself all the things he'd wished for in the book. Anna blinked back a tear, and let her hand brush against several of the pictures as she led Granny to her chair.

Then she settled on the sofa and motioned for Noah. "Come sit by me while Simon reads the Christmas story, and then we'll see what's under the tree."

Noah climbed on the seat beside her and snuggled close. For a brief second she closed her eyes and remembered other times Willie had done the same. Then she opened her eyes and smiled down at the child who'd brought so much joy into her life in the last few months. She hugged him close as Simon began to read.

" 'And it came to pass in those days, that there

went out a decree from Caesar Augustus that all the world should be taxed . . .' "

Anna's mind wandered to Christmases past and the three children who were no longer here. The years had passed too quickly. It seemed only yesterday that they were all at her feet. How she longed to have them all back again. Next to her Noah stirred, and she pulled him closer and rested her cheek on top of his head.

Simon's voice quieted, and she glanced at him. He smiled at her from across the room, and she realized he knew what she was thinking. He too longed for days past.

She released Noah from her arms with a smile. "Are you ready to see what's under the tree?"

Noah jumped to his feet, his eyes round. "I sure hope there's something for me."

Anna laughed, reached down, picked up a brown paper package, and handed it to him. "I think this is for you."

Noah ripped the paper apart and sucked in his breath. His lips moved as if he was trying to speak, but no sound came out. As if he held the greatest treasure he'd ever seen, he stared at the baseball glove and ball in his hand. After a moment he turned to Anna and swallowed. "Is this really for me?"

She smiled and nodded. "It is."

He turned his head to stare at Simon. "I ain't never had nothin' like this before."

Simon blinked from the tears in the corners of his eyes. "They belonged to our little boy a long time ago. Now they're yours."

Noah cradled the gift to his body. "Just for me?"

"Yes. I have a bat I used when my brother John and I were boys. I'll teach you how to catch and bat. By next spring you ought to be able to hold your own with any of the boys in the schoolyard."

Noah jumped up, ran to Simon, and hugged him. Then he hurried to hug Anna. When he pulled away from her, he looked up into her eyes, and for a fleeting second it was as if she looked into Willie's face again.

"You ain't never told me what to call you."

"No," she said. "I thought I would let you decide on your own."

His forehead wrinkled, and a serious expression clouded his eyes. "I reckon I cain't call you Ma, but maybe I could call you what Miss Rani calls you. How about Mama?"

She squelched the hiccup of emotion that rumbled in her throat. "I think Mama sounds fine."

He turned to Simon. "What does Miss Rani call you?"

"Poppa," he said.

Noah smiled. "Mama and Poppa. That sounds good. Now I guess I'm a part of the fam'ly."

Anna laughed and hugged him again. "I guess you are."

Grinning, he sat down on the floor and slipped the baseball glove on his hand. Anna watched him for a minute before she reached down, picked up a few more packages she had placed there, and handed them to each one.

Smiles lit the faces of Simon, Granny, and Matthew as they tore their brown packages open. Simon grinned as he pulled out the muffler she'd knitted. "This will keep me warm all winter."

Matthew pulled out one like it. His fingers caressed the wool. "Thank you for making this for me, Anna. I haven't had a Christmas present in years. I'll think of you when I wear it."

She smiled. "And I'll feel your good thoughts."

Granny chuckled. "Well, would you look at this? I got me one too. I 'spect Anna means for us all to be warm this winter."

Anna laughed. "Or it means it's the only thing I can knit."

Granny waved her hand in dismissal. "No it don't. I reckon I taught you right well."

Simon cleared his throat. "Since I can't knit or sew, I couldn't make anything for you. But when John went over to Pigeon Forge a few weeks ago, I asked him to pick up a few things for me." He handed a package to Anna. "This is for you."

"For me?" She directed a stern glare in his

direction. "You didn't spend money we don't have on something for me, did you?"

He laughed. "Open it and see."

Her breath caught in her throat as she pulled a leather journal from the paper. She ran her hand over the smooth cover and blinked back tears. "A new journal. Oh, Simon, you knew I had filled up the other one."

He nodded. "I figured you could use a new one." He glanced over at Matthew. "Anna started writing in a journal when she first came to the Cove, and she's filled up a lot of them through the years. But I have some other things too." He handed a small sack to Granny, one to Matthew, and another to Noah. "For the three of you, I have something for your sweet tooth."

Noah's eyes lit up. "Candy too? This is the best Christmas I ever had."

Granny's eyes grew wide. "You sure do know what I like too."

Matthew grinned. "Thanks, Simon. But I feel bad. I don't have anything for all of you."

Granny reached over and patted his arm. "You done given us the best present you could when you come home to us."

Anna nodded. "You'll always be like a member of our family, Matthew. We want you to remember that."

Tears pooled in his eyes. "Thank you," he whispered.

Granny straightened in her chair. "Well, if truth be told, I ain't really no member of this fam'ly, although I'd fight any man who said I wasn't. So I have a gift to give to Simon and Anna, my son and daughter."

She pulled an envelope from her apron pocket and handed it to Simon. He and Anna exchanged surprised glances before he tore into the envelope and pulled out a sheet of paper. His face grew pale as he read what was written on the page.

"Oh, no, Granny, we can't accept this."

Anna stepped closer and peered down at the paper. "What is it?"

Granny settled back in her chair and crossed her arms. "It's the deed to my farm. I'm a-givin' it to you. I wrote Robert, and he took care of ev'rything for me at the courthouse. It's all legal, and now my land belongs to you. I feel like we ought to keep it in the family."

Anna knelt beside Granny's chair and clasped her hand. ".Thank you, Granny. I don't know what would have happened to Simon and me if you hadn't been by our sides all these years. We love you."

Granny's eyes filled with tears. "And I love all of you, darlin'." She sniffed and straightened in her chair. "Now I know you just got them dishes washed, but I sure would like to have another piece of that chocolate cake you made. I ain't never tasted anything like it. How about you, Noah? Want some more cake?"

Clutching his ball and glove, he jumped to his feet. "I'll race you to the kitchen, Granny!"

She frowned. "Well, hold your horses, boy. I ain't as spry as I used to be. You can help me up, and we'll go together."

Anna laughed and pushed to her feet. "Everybody come back in the kitchen, and we'll all have another piece."

She hurried back to get the cake and some plates out of the pie safe. She set it on the table and began to place slices on the dishes. As she did, she closed her eyes and thought once again of her children and Christmases past.

She glanced around the kitchen. To some people their small cabin might look like something only the poor could call home, but to her it was the castle her prince had brought her to over twenty years ago. She had never regretted her decision to stay here instead of going to New York. She closed her eyes.

When I came to the Cove, Lord, I didn't know what You had planned for me. Thank You for my wonderful life with Simon and Granny. You gave me three wonderful children, and I thank You for each one of them. I pray that Rani and Stephen have had a wonderful Christmas, and let them know I'm thinking of them. Lord, You've heard my prayers of heartbreak through the years for the loss of Willie, but I've always felt Your strength flowing through me. Now You've sent me another child, and I find he's healing the hole in my heart. Help me to be worthy of Your love.

Movement at the door signaled the entrance of someone from the other room. She opened her eyes and smiled at Noah leading Granny into the kitchen. He glanced up at Granny and grinned. "Look, Granny, Mama's already got the cake cut for us."

Tears filled her eyes. "I sure do, son."

Simon and Matthew followed them into the room, and Simon walked over and put his arms around her. Together they watched as Noah sat down and began to devour the cake in front of him. Simon's arms tightened around her.

"Merry Christmas, Anna."

She looked up into the face that was still as handsome as the first day she saw him and smiled. "Merry Christmas, Simon."

Mrs. Miller set the silver tray on the parlor table and glanced over at Rani, who was sitting on the sofa. "Miss Rani, here's the coffee and my special Christmas cake. Do you want me to cut it before I go?"

Rani scooted to the edge of the sofa and frowned. "Where are you going?"

"Home. I don't want to be in the way."

Rani stood up and pointed to a chair. "You are not in the way. You are going to sit down in that chair and have dessert with us. I won the battle to make you eat dinner at the table with us, and I'm not going to give in on this, either."

Mrs. Miller smiled. "Well, if you think Doc wouldn't mind."

Uncle Charles and David walked into the parlor at that moment from the dining room. "Uncle Charles, tell Mrs. Miller we want her to have dessert with us."

He directed a shocked look in his housekeeper's direction. "Why would you not want to join us?"

"I didn't want to intrude."

Uncle Charles took her by the arm and guided her to a chair. "You are not intruding. Now have a seat."

David laughed and plopped down on the sofa next to where Rani had been seated. "I don't know about you, Mrs. Miller, but I can't wait to get a bite of that coconut cake you made. I haven't eaten any since I was a boy."

Mrs. Miller frowned. "Then at least let me serve everybody."

When everyone had been served, Mrs. Miller took a seat opposite the sofa and joined in the conversation. Rani smiled and nodded from time to time, but her mind kept wandering. She imagined her family gathered to read the story of Christ's birth. She could see Granny nodding in her chair as she listened, and she wondered if they had invited Matthew for Christmas dinner. She hoped so. He probably hadn't celebrated Christmas in years, and she wanted his first one back in the Cove to be a good one.

Later, when the dishes had been cleared away and Uncle Charles and Mrs. Miller were in the kitchen, she turned to David. "I hope you aren't missing your family too much today."

He shook his head. "I'm not, but I imagine you are. You haven't been away from home as long as I have."

"I have had a few moments when I wished I was home, but I've really enjoyed being with you."

He smiled. "I'm glad." He pulled a small package from his pocket and handed it to her. "I wanted to get you a present to let you know how much I appreciate all the help and encouragement you've given me as I've prepared for the show. And also to let you know how important you are to me."

She stared at the box wrapped in white tissue paper with a red bow on top. "I'm the one who should be thanking you for all you've done for me. I don't know what to say."

"You don't have to say anything. It's not much, just something I saw and thought you would like."

She tore the paper from the box, opened it, and stared in wonder at the gold locket nestled on black velvet. A four leaf clover made from small emeralds decorated the front, and small diamonds sparkled at the top and bottom of the clover. She shook her head. "I can't accept this. It's too expensive."

She started to hand it back to him, but he shook his head and reached inside the box. He pulled out the necklace. "No, I want you to have it. Let me put it on you."

She hesitated for a moment, but the look on his face told her he wouldn't give in. With a sigh she turned away from him and lifted her hair off her neck. As he slipped the necklace around her neck and fastened it, his breath fanned her back. A tingle ran down her spine at the touch of his lips grazing her skin.

"You're so beautiful," he whispered. "You know I've fallen in love with you. I'd like to give you much more than a necklace."

She let her hair drop back to her shoulders and swiveled to face him. Her fingers touched the locket that rested in the hollow of her neck. "I'm flattered that you think of me that way, David."

His eyebrows arched. "But?"

She smiled and touched his cheek. "Give me some time."

His eyes darkened. "All right. I can be patient. I'm going to show you I really am a great guy."

She clasped his hand in hers. "I already know

that. But you're too good to me, David. I've been hurt before, and I don't want to do that to you. Like I said, just give me some time."

He stood and pulled her to her feet. His arms encircled her waist, and he drew her closer. "I've been in love with you since the first day you walked into my shop. I've waited a long time for a woman like you, and I don't intend to let you get away."

She smiled. "I'm not going anywhere."

Matthew shivered in the saddle and urged his horse to go faster. This had been a wonderful Christmas, but he was ready to get home and sit by his own fireplace.

He'd never spent a Christmas like the one he had with Simon, Anna, and Granny. From the look on Noah's face, he'd never had one like it either. The only thing that could have made it better was if Rani had been there with him.

He wondered what she had done today. Had her Christmas been as peaceful as his? Anna said she might come home in the spring, but that was a long time off. At least four or five months. She'd already been gone for five months, and it seemed like an eternity.

He touched the muffler Anna had made and tucked it tighter around his neck. Although he treasured the gift Anna had made for him, he wanted the one Granny and Noah had been given. He wanted to be a member of Simon and Anna's family.

A pang of regret shot through him. If he hadn't held onto the guilt about his past for so long, that might very well have happened. When he'd sent Rani away, he had dashed that dream forever.

He stared up into the sky and prayed as he had for months since Rani left. "Keep her safe, Lord, wherever she is, and please help her not to hate me too much. I love her so."

Chapter 18

Rani looped her arm through her uncle's and stepped into the showroom of the Knoxville gallery. She stopped inside the door and let her gaze drift over David's displayed pieces around the room. Her breath caught in her throat at the rich colors and unusual shapes David had produced. After nine months of hard work, the day she and David had looked forward to had finally arrived.

"Oh, Uncle Charles, aren't David's pieces beautiful?"

David appeared at her side before Uncle Charles could answer and laughed. "Thank you, ma'am, but I suggest you look at the pieces my assistant made. They're quite exquisite too."

She glanced up into David's smiling face and arched her eyebrows. "Could you guide me to where this budding artist's wares are being shown?"

His eyes softened. "It would be my pleasure. If you and your uncle will follow me, I'll lead the way."

They crossed the room and came to a stop at a table where her pieces sat. As she studied each one, she recalled the hours she'd spent working on them and how patient David had been with her. Her eyes filled with tears, and she turned to him. "When I visited your shop for the first time last August, I would never have believed that nine months later I would be showing my work in a public exhibit. I'll never be able to thank you enough for all you've done for me, David."

He cleared his throat and smiled. "You really didn't need my help all that much once you decided you could do it. I'm very proud of you, Rani."

"And so am I," Uncle Charles added. "Now I think I'll leave you two artists alone to greet the guests who are entering, and I'll browse around." He winked at Rani. "I might even find a piece I wish to purchase."

Rani laughed and stared after him as he strolled across the floor. When she turned back to David, he smiled and inched closer. "Do you think your uncle would mind if I stole you away from him tonight for supper? Something has happened that I want to discuss with you."

"I'm sure he wouldn't mind. But now I'll be in a stew all afternoon trying to figure out what the big mystery is all about. Can't you give me a hint?"

He threw back his head and laughed. "It's no big mystery, just a business proposition I've been offered. I want to get your reaction to it. Will you have supper with me?"

She smiled. "Of course I will. After all you've done to help me, I want to do whatever I can for you."

His eyes sparkled. "Thank you, Rani." He glanced around and took a deep breath. "Now we need to do as your uncle suggested and meet our guests. I want everyone to get a chance to see your pieces."

He took her by the arm to lead her across the room, but she held back. "David, this is your show. I want you to be successful. You've worked hard, and you deserve it. Don't worry about trying to promote me. I want you to be the star today."

He swallowed hard. "Thank you, Rani, but you've been the brightest star in my life since the day you walked into my studio."

"I'm glad, David," she whispered.

He smiled down at her and led her to where a group of men and women stood at a display table.

She stared up at him and thought how handsome he looked today. His fair skin and blond hair were very different from Matthew's dark eyes and hair, but maybe that was good. At least she wasn't constantly reminded of the man she had once loved.

Rani scraped the last bite of strawberry shortcake from her plate and popped it into her mouth. Across the table David lowered his coffee cup and smiled.

"Did you enjoy your dinner?"

She swallowed the last bite and wiped her mouth on her napkin. "Oh, David, this place is wonderful. How did you know about it?"

"My father brought me here once when we visited Knoxville. I thought you might enjoy it."

She glanced around at the waiters in their black suits and the flute and cello players who provided soft music from a raised platform at one end of the room. "But this place must be so expensive. We could probably feed our family in the Cove for a year on what you'll pay for this meal tonight."

He chuckled and shook his head. "It doesn't matter what it cost, Rani. I wanted it to be special for you."

She arched her eyebrows and nodded. "Well, it's certainly been special. I never thought a mountain girl like me would get to eat in a place like this."

He glanced around the room before he looked at her again. "I suppose I've taken things like this for granted because of my family's money. But I learned a long time ago that wealth doesn't bring happiness. I didn't know what being happy was like until I met you."

"You've never talked about your family much."

He settled back in his chair and shrugged. "My grandfather made a lot of money in railroads, and my father expanded the business into other areas. My brother works with him now, but they're content for me to pursue my art."

"I'm surprised they didn't want you in the family business too."

"I think it was my mother who convinced my father to let me follow my dream. She was an artist too, and painted. Before she died, she made my father promise not to interfere in my life, and he never has. He's generous with his money and very supportive. I feel very fortunate."

"You are." She pushed her dessert plate out of the way and clasped her hands in her lap. "But you must have some business leanings in you if you're thinking about a new venture. Are you going to keep me in suspense, or are you going to tell me what it is?"

He laughed and sat up straight in his chair. "I met a man at an art exhibit last year when I visited St. Louis. It was a chance meeting. He was in town visiting family, heard about a young artist who had an exhibit, and decided to attend. I had gone because I knew the artist. We happened to meet and struck up a conversation. He was from a small town in upstate New York."

"Is he a potter too?"

"Yes. As we talked, we discovered that we both had ambitions to develop new glazes and techniques that would set our work apart from anyone else's."

Rani smiled. "It sounds like you have a lot in common."

He nodded. "I told him how I'd been working on a glaze that would give the piece a crackled look when fired, and he was very interested. We've kept in touch ever since, and now he's offered me a great opportunity."

Rani's eyes widened. "What is it?"

"He says there's a large kiln works for sale not far from where he lives. He wants us to go in as partners on it. We could continue our separate work on pottery, but we could collaborate and experiment with different glazes. He thinks in time we could establish a line of pottery that could be sold in the best shops in this country and abroad."

Rani reached across the table and grasped his hand. "Oh, David, this is what you've wanted for a long time. It sounds perfect for you. I think you should do it."

He glanced down at her hand holding his and

covered it with his other one. "You realize, of course, I'd have to move to New York to work. I couldn't stay here."

She hadn't thought of that. For a moment regret that he'd be going away washed over her, but she shook it from her mind. The important thing was for David to follow his dream. "I know. But, David, you have to do what is best for your career, and this sounds like the perfect opportunity."

His hand tightened on hers. "Would you miss me if I went away?"

"Of course I would."

"Would you come with me if I asked you?"

She frowned and tried to pull her hand free, but he held her in a tight grip. "I . . . I don't understand."

"Marry me, Rani, and come with me to New York. You know I'm in love with you. Think of the wonderful life we could have there. We could work together in our studio, and you could help me develop the glaze that we will use."

She frowned. "New York? That's so far from Tennessee. I never thought about leaving the mountains."

"You're not that mountain girl who walked into my studio nine months ago. You're quite a sophisticated young lady now. I've seen the way the men in this restaurant have looked at you tonight. They're all envious of me. Please marry me, Rani. I don't think I can go without you."

"M-marry you?" His grip on her left hand tightened. She wrapped the fingers of her free hand around the napkin in her lap and crushed it into a ball. "This is such a shock. Are you sure you want to marry me?"

He chuckled and nodded. "I'm positive. I've never wanted anything so much in my life."

She glanced down at her new flowered pink silk dress decorated with tied French knots. When she'd seen it in the shop in Maryville, she had thought it the most gorgeous dress she'd ever seen. No one in Cades Cove had ever owned anything like it. Uncle Charles had purchased it for her, and the woman who'd shown it to her had assured her it was perfect to wear to an art exhibit. She could have dozens of dresses like this if she married David, and she wouldn't live in a cabin anymore.

But this was all happening too fast. Her family hadn't even met David yet, and she would want her father to perform the ceremony when she got married. She needed to think about what she was doing before she gave him an answer.

"Do we have to decide right now?"

Disappointment flickered in his eyes. "Maybe not right this minute, but soon if I'm going to be in New York in time to complete the deal."

"When do you have to be there?"

"I have to be in New York by the first of June. We could be married the middle of May and have a short honeymoon maybe at Niagara Falls." He reached in his pocket and pulled out a gold ring set with a swirl of diamonds. "This is my mother's ring. I want my wife to have it. Will you please make me the happiest man on earth and agree to marry me?"

She stared at the sparkling diamonds and thought of how her parents had struggled in Cades Cove to provide for their family. If she married David, there would always be money. She would also be free to pursue her love of pottery. As she had told Uncle Charles, David was a good man, and she respected him. And best of all, he loved her. When she added all his good attributes together, she couldn't think of a single reason to say no.

Still she hesitated. "Will your family approve of me, David? I'm sure they would want you to marry someone with more social standing than I have."

"My family will love you. We can visit them on our way to New York."

She took a deep breath. "Then I have one request. I've always wanted my father to perform my marriage ceremony at our church in the Cove. Would you be willing to go home with me and get married with my family and friends there?"

He nodded. "That would be perfect. Then we could go back to Townsend and take the train to New York."

David seemed to have an answer for everything. Maybe that's what she needed, someone who loved her and wanted to take care of everything for her. And they didn't clash as she and Matthew had seemed to do all the time. Being married to David would be good for her.

"Spring is my favorite time of the year in the Cove. The first of May would be a beautiful time to have a wedding." She smiled and glanced down as he slipped the ring on her finger. "It would be my honor to be your wife, David."

Matthew stepped onto the porch of Simon and Anna's cabin and stomped the mud from his feet. The ground was saturated from the spring rains, but that meant good news for the farmers who would be planting their crops soon. This year he would plant more than one field of corn, and he could hardly wait.

He raised his fist to knock on the door, but it opened before he connected with it. Noah grinned at him from inside. "I seen you ride up, Mr. Matthew. Granny says for you to come on in. It's still cold outside."

Matthew stepped into the cozy room where Granny sat in front of a roaring fire. He walked over, leaned down, and kissed her on the cheek. "Good morning, Granny. How are you feeling today?"

She reached up and patted him on the cheek. "Right tolerable, Matthew. It's good to see you. You need to stop by more often."

He pulled another chair over beside her, slipped his coat off, and hung it on the back of the chair before he sat down. He held his hands out to the fire and smiled. "It seems like there's always something to do on the farm. I spent the winter building furniture for my cabin, and now it's time to think about spring planting."

"How's that bed you built working out?"

"Fine, Granny. That feather bed you and Anna made for me makes sleeping on corn shucks a lot easier."

She laughed and nodded. "I know what you mean."

He glanced around the room. "Where are Simon and Anna?"

"Lucy Whitworth is having her baby today. She and Simon went over there. It's just me and Noah here."

"I really came to see you. I missed you at church last Sunday, so I thought I'd check on you."

Noah sat down on the floor between the two chairs and stared up at Matthew. "I been sick, and Granny stayed home with me."

Matthew reached down and tousled the boy's hair. "I'm sorry to hear that. What was the matter?"

"Just a sore throat, but Granny fixed me up right good. I feel better now."

Granny shifted in her chair and glanced at Matthew. "I thought Anna or Simon prob'ly told you why I wasn't there."

He shook his head. "No, I didn't talk to them. I started to speak to them after church, but they were in a deep conversation with Pete and Laura, and I didn't want to interrupt."

Granny sighed. "Yeah, they 'bout to go crazy 'cause they ain't heared from George in months. The sheriff comes by ev'ry once in a while." She glanced down at Noah. "He thinks George and you-know-who are prob'ly still in North Carolina. Land's sakes, I never would have thought that boy would give his ma and pa so much grief. He was always so nice when he was a-callin' on Rani, but Pete says even then he was a-slippin' out and drinkin' a lot."

Matthew nodded. "I've been over to see Pete and Laura several times. I wish there was something I could do for them."

Granny started to respond, but before she could Noah glanced up at him. "Did you know Miss Rani's comin' home?"

Matthew's eyes grew wide, and he glanced up at Granny. "She is? When?"

362

Noah grinned and nodded. "The first of May, and she's a-gonna get married."

Granny reached down and grasped Noah's shoulder. "Noah . . ."

Matthew frowned and shook his head. Surely he hadn't heard Noah right. "What did you say?"

Noah glanced up at Granny as if he didn't understand the glare she was directing at him. He twisted from her grip. "I said Miss Rani is a-gonna get married in May. At the church."

Matthew slumped back into the chair, his eyes wide. "Noah," he heard Granny say, "go on in the kitchen. I need to talk with Matthew."

Noah pushed to his feet and glanced from Granny to Matthew before he trudged toward the kitchen. At the door he turned and looked back at Granny. "Did I do somethin' wrong, Granny?"

She smiled at him. "No, child. I just need to talk to Matthew. Now you run on and play."

When he'd disappeared through the door, Matthew lowered his hand from his forehead and stared at Granny. "Why hasn't Simon told me about this?"

"I'm sorry you heard about it this way, Matthew. We just found out about a week ago. She wrote Anna and told her she'd accepted David Brann's proposal, and they were coming home to be married. Simon was going to come tell you today before they came back from the Whitworths."

His mind reeled from the news, and he shook his head. "David Brann? Is that the potter she's been working with?"

"Yes. It seems he's gonna buy into a business up in New York. It's a kiln works, and he and another feller are gonna experiment with dif'rent glazes to use on pottery. Rani says they think they'll soon have a line of pottery that they'll sell all over the world."

She was going to leave the Cove for good. He couldn't believe it. "New York?" His voice cracked on the question. "That's a long way from here."

"I know. But she says it's a great opportunity for them to work together on this new line."

Matthew stared into the fire and nodded. "I knew she had a gift for creating beautiful works of art. I'm glad she's found someone who can help her develop it. It sounds like she's going to have a wonderful life. I'm happy for her."

Granny reached out and touched his arm. "What about you, Matthew? How's your life these days?"

He pushed to his feet and propped his arm on the mantel and his foot on the hearth. He closed his eyes and sighed. "I'm doing all right, Granny. I miss Rani, but I've finally gotten some peace about my past. Simon has been a big help to me. I spend a lot of time at night studying the Bible, and I know God's going to take care of me."

The same concern for him he'd seen as a child flickered in her eyes. "And you think you can accept Rani marrying somebody else?"

He took a deep breath and faced Granny. "I guess I don't have a choice. If she's fallen in love with another man, I don't have anybody but myself to blame. I know I hurt her, and I'm sorry about that. Maybe I'll have the chance to apologize and wish her well when she's home. Her happiness is more important to me than mine."

A sad smile pulled at Granny's lips. "That's the way love is, Matthew. You want the best for the other person."

"I suppose so, Granny, because I really do love her. I let my past get in the way of having a future with Rani. Now it looks like hers doesn't include me." He walked over and squeezed Granny's shoulder. "But I'll be okay. Now, I'd better be getting on home. Tell Simon and Anna I'll see them later."

He pulled his coat back on and headed for the door. It was time to move on.

Chapter 19

Rani had hardly been able to catch her breath since they rode into Cades Cove. She didn't know if it was because she was wedged between David and Stephen in the back seat of the buggy or if it was because she was home again.

All around her the Cove was coming back to life after another hard winter. Her favorite time of year had arrived again, and she realized for the first time how much she had missed the familiar places they passed on their way home. She wanted to urge the horse to move faster, but her father appeared content to let the mare amble along. Perhaps Poppa was enjoying his conversation with Uncle Charles too much to notice how eager she was to get home.

She grasped her brother's hand and squeezed. "I'm so glad you could come home from school early. I don't think I could have stood it if you had missed my wedding."

He returned the pressure on her hand and smiled. "My professors were very understanding when I told them I had to be home for my twin sister's wedding."

David leaned around Rani to address Stephen.

"When do you plan to go back to Nashville?" David asked.

Stephen darted a look at their father's back before he responded. "I don't have to be back until August, so I thought I'd stay at home until then."

Their father cast a startled look over his shoulder. "You're staying home this summer?"

Stephen nodded. "I thought I'd give you and Uncle John a hand on the farm for a few months. That is, if you don't mind."

Her father's face broke into a big smile. "That's the best news I've heard in months. Your mother will be thrilled too. With our only daughter moving off to New York, it'll be good to have at least one of you home." He chuckled. "Of course, Noah thinks he runs the place now. So you may have some competition for your mother's attention."

Rani reached up and patted her father's shoulder. "I'm so glad you and Mama took Noah. Have you heard anything from his father?"

"No. The sheriff thinks he and George are still in North Carolina. I don't doubt it because Matthew hasn't had any trouble since last fall."

A silence covered the inside of the buggy, and Simon glanced over his shoulder at Rani. Remorse filled his eyes.

She frowned. "What kind of trouble did he have?"

Her father turned around and concentrated on the road. "Oh, just some threatening notes that were left, and his cornfield was burned one night."

Rani's heart pounded, and she clasped her hands in her lap. "Was he hurt?"

"No, nothing like that. Anyway, everything's fine now."

Rani settled back in her seat and glanced at David, but it appeared as if he hadn't heard the exchange. His attention appeared riveted on the mountains in the distance. "I've never been to this part of the Smokies before. I understand why you love this place so much, Rani." He pointed toward the mountainside. "What's the name of those flowers I see in the distance?"

Rani swallowed. "That's mountain laurel," she whispered.

"I really like that shade of pink. Maybe we can copy it for some of our pottery."

"That would be nice," she said.

She stared straight ahead and tried to concentrate on her upcoming wedding. In two days she would be Mrs. David Brann, and she would be on her way to New York. She didn't need to worry about nighttime fires at Matthew's farm or the mountain laurel bush where they'd met.

The buggy trundled forward, and she held her breath. They were approaching Matthew's cabin, and her father had finally urged the horse to move faster. Maybe he wanted to spare her the sight of what she had hoped would be her home.

As they rolled by, she turned her head and stared at the cabin set back among the trees. The yard wasn't overgrown as it had been a year ago. A tulip poplar shaded the neat house, but it was the chimney that sucked the breath from her. Tears filled her eyes, and she turned her head away so David wouldn't see.

Stephen leaned closer. "Did you see your bricks?"

She clamped her lips together, nodded, and grasped the front of her skirt in her hands. She could not think about what had happened a year ago. The present was all that mattered, and she was about to be married.

Matthew had kept a watch all morning for Simon's buggy. Granny had told him this was the day Rani was coming home, and all he wanted was one glimpse of her. He'd paced the cabin floor for hours and listened. Every time a horse approached, he'd inched the door open to peer outside.

He was about to give up hope when he heard what sounded like a buggy approaching. He hurried to the door and cracked it enough to see outside without being seen.

Simon's buggy came into view, and he waited

for that one glimpse he wanted. Then he saw her. She sat in the back seat between Stephen and a man he'd never seen. She wore a blue dress and a matching hat that was pinned on top of her head.

He'd told himself he could be satisfied to see her once. That's all he wanted. But when the buggy had disappeared from view, he knew it wasn't enough. It would never be enough. He wanted to see her every morning when he woke and every time he walked into his cabin.

He groaned and slammed the door. She was about to be married. He had no right to think this way. She belonged to another man now.

He fell to his knees. "Oh, God," he cried, "tell me what to do."

Rani swallowed the last bite of her blackberry cobbler and glanced around at her family gathered around the supper table. It had been nearly a year since they had all been together. The last time, though, Matthew had been with them. Now David had taken his place.

David had made a good impression on her family the minute he arrived, and she was glad. After all, she'd known few men with the qualities he possessed, and he was dedicated to making her happy. He'd brought small gifts for Mama and Granny and had captured Noah's undying devotion when he presented him with a set of tin soldiers. Noah had been so engrossed in playing that Mama almost hadn't been able to drag him away for supper.

Now with everyone through eating, Rani pushed to her feet and began to help clear away the dishes. She leaned over and kissed her father's cheek as she took his plate. "Thanks for catching me up on all the gossip in the Cove. I hope David wasn't too bored, though."

David grinned and shook his head. "On the contrary, I find it quite interesting to hear all of you talk about life here. I hope Rani is going to like it where we're going to live. It's very different from her life here."

She smiled. "I'm sure I'll adjust in no time. After all, I won't be alone. You'll be there with me."

David turned toward her father and cleared his throat. "I wanted to tell you, sir, that I'm very sorry I couldn't come to you and ask for Rani's hand in marriage in person. It just wasn't possible. We were too far away, and I needed to give my friend a reply about the kiln works purchase. But I assure you and Mrs. Martin I will always take care of her and cherish her."

Rani put her hand on his shoulder and smiled. "Mama and Poppa know what a wonderful man you are, David. And even if I hadn't told them, Uncle Charles would have."

"That's right," Uncle Charles said. "I know David's going to take good care of Rani."

Her mother placed the dirty dishes in the dry

sink and walked back to the table. "I can't believe we're having a wedding the day after tomorrow! Rani, you and I need to go to the church tomorrow to make sure everything is in order. I think we're going to have a big crowd come to see you get married."

Rani's eyes grew wide. "That's wonderful. I've missed the people from church. I can hardly wait to see all of them."

Her father leaned back in his chair and hooked his fingers in his belt loops. "Yep, I think everybody in the church is coming."

Noah, who'd been concentrating on shoveling blackberry cobbler in his mouth, shook his head and wiped blackberry juice from the corner of his mouth. "I don't think ev'rybody's coming."

Granny reached over and dabbed at his mouth with a napkin. "Now what makes you think that, child?"

" 'Cause I asked Mr. Matthew if he was coming, and he said he didn't think so."

Rani stared in stunned silence at Noah. He tilted his head to one side and closed one eye. "What's the matter, Miss Rani?"

"N-nothing, Noah. Finish your pie."

She turned and hurried to the dry sink. Behind her, she heard her mother's voice. "Noah, I think it's time you were getting ready for bed."

"Bed?" he whined. "It's not even dark outside yet."

"Then when it gets dark, you'll be ready. Come with me."

She turned and watched her mother pull Noah down the hallway toward the bedrooms. After a moment her father spoke. "Well, why don't the rest of us go in the front room for a while?"

The chairs scraped on the floor as they rose. Then she felt David standing behind her. He leaned over and whispered in her ear. "Hurry and join us. I'd like to spend some time alone with you tonight."

A wobbly smile pulled at her lips. "I won't be long."

As soon as the men and Granny had left the kitchen, her mother touched her arm. Rani turned to stare at her. "I'm sorry about what Noah said. He didn't realize he was saying anything wrong."

Rani smiled and covered her mother's hand with hers. "It's all right. I knew it might be awkward at times while I was home, but I'm fine. I didn't really think Matthew would come to the wedding. In fact, I doubt if I'll see him at all."

"I doubt it too," her mother said.

Rani plunged her hands into the hot dishwater and began to scrub the plates her mother placed in the pan. After a few minutes of silence she took a deep breath. "How is Matthew?"

Her mother dried the plate she held and placed it in the cupboard before she responded. "He's doing well, Rani. He's finally faced up to his past, and he seems happy. He isn't the man you knew a year ago."

Rani reached for a cloth and dried her dripping hands. "What do you mean?"

Her mother led her to the table, and they sat down. She reached across and clasped Rani's hand. "Your father has had the opportunity to guide him in Bible study this winter. I know he has told him about the years after his mother died, but Simon hasn't revealed anything to me. Whatever happened, Matthew seems to have peace about it now. He's mentioned several times that he would like to see you to ask you to forgive him. Granny said he was very upset when Noah told him you were getting married."

"Why would he be upset? He rejected me as if I meant nothing to him."

Her mother's eyes grew wide. "All your life I've told you to follow God's will in your life. Did you ever think when Matthew turned his back on you it might have been because God had something better for you?"

She nodded. "I've thought about it, and I know David is a wonderful man. I'm thankful God brought him into my life. We're going to be happy in our work and in our marriage. He loves me so much."

"And what about you? Not once in the letters you've written home have you talked about loving David. It's always about his feelings for you. He's a good man, Rani, and deserves to be loved for who he is. You'll only end up making him miserable if you don't share his love."

Rani pushed to her feet. "You're wrong, Mama. I do love David. Who wouldn't? Any woman would be lucky to have him, but he wants me."

"And who do you want?" Her mother's stony gaze made her heart thud.

Her lips trembled, and she threw the towel she still held to the table. "I want to marry David. Now if you'll excuse me, I'm going to find him and spend some time with him."

David glanced up and smiled as she walked into the front room. "There you are."

She took his hand and pulled him to his feet. "Come sit on the porch with me. I want you to see what our mountains look like at night."

He nodded to Simon and Granny. "If you two will excuse me, I'll go outside with Rani for a bit of air."

They stepped out the door and stopped at the edge of the porch. David put his arm around her waist and drew her closer. She leaned against him and listened for the night sounds in the Cove. Neither spoke for a few minutes.

"My family likes you very much," she finally said.

"Good. I like them too. They're the kind of people you meet and feel like you've known for years. I'm glad they're going to be my family too."

"I think you won them over with the gifts you brought. Noah especially," she chuckled.

He tightened his arm around her. "Rani, who is Matthew?"

She stiffened. "Why do you ask?"

"You've never told me the name of the man you were in love with. Then tonight when Noah said Matthew wasn't coming to the wedding, I figured that must be him. Is it?"

"Yes," Rani said, letting out a deep breath. "Yes, it's Matthew."

David turned her to face him. "Do I have anything to worry about?"

She swallowed. "Why would you have anything to worry about?"

"Don't answer my question with one of your own. Maybe coming back here to get married wasn't such a good idea. You can't seem to talk about him to me."

Rani wrapped her arms around him and laid her head on his chest. "I'm sorry. It's just that he's part of my past. You're my present and my future. We're going to be married the day after tomorrow."

He kissed the top of her head and then held her at arm's length. "If you have any doubts, please let me know."

She smiled. "If I have any, I will. Now quit talking like a silly fool and kiss me."

He lowered his lips toward her, but before he could kiss her a loud barking interrupted them.

Scout charged onto the porch and jumped on Rani. He bounced, yelped, and licked her like he'd gone mad.

Laughing, she dropped to her knees and clamped her arms around the dog's trembling body. "Where have you been, boy? Off chasing rabbits again? I missed you when I got home today."

David bent over and reached out to pat Scout's head. A growl ripped from the dog's throat. Scout's lips curled back from his bared teeth, and he snapped at David's outstretched hand.

Rani grabbed the dog and pulled him backward. "No, Scout! Bad dog!"

David straightened and raised his eyebrows. "Did I do something wrong?"

Still holding Scout, she stood and shook her head. "No. He's very protective of me. He'll warm up to you before long."

David held out his hand once more, and the dog tried to lunge at him. David backed away. "Maybe I'd better leave you with your dog for tonight."

Rani tightened her hold on the wiggling dog. "I'll calm him down and then come inside."

David stared at Scout once more before he backed away. "I think I'll get ready for bed. I'm going hunting with Stephen early in the morning, and I need to get some sleep. We should be back before noon." He grinned. "Talk to your dog while I'm gone and tell him I'm really a nice person."

"I will."

David opened the door and entered the house. As soon as he disappeared, Scout whined and licked her face. She laughed, put him down on the porch, and propped her hands on her hips. He cocked his head to one side and sat back on his haunches. "What am I going to do with you? You've always scared off all my suitors."

As soon as the words were out of her mouth, the truth hit her. She dropped down in the chair where she'd sat so many nights in the past. Scout settled on the floor beside her, and she reached down to pet him. "All of them except one."

Matthew poured himself a cup of coffee and slumped down in the chair in front of the fireplace. He'd been awake all night trying to decide what he needed to do. Now that the sun was up, he was still as confused as he'd been after catching that brief glance of Rani yesterday.

One minute he wanted to charge up the steps of the Martin cabin and tell her she wasn't going to marry anybody but him. The next minute he berated himself for such thinking. She'd made her decision to marry David Brann. That had to mean she loved him.

But what if she didn't? He shook his head and jumped to his feet. She had to love David if she'd promised to marry him. He slammed the coffee cup down on the table he'd built and strode to the door. There were chores to be done, and he couldn't waste any more time trying to decide what he needed to do.

He stormed down the front steps of the cabin, stuck his hat on his head, and rounded the corner of the cabin. The sight of the chimney stopped him in his tracks. Could it be possible that she had only agreed to marry David because she thought Matthew had quit loving her? If so, he had to let her know that wasn't the case. That he would never stop loving her—not until he took his final breath.

Matthew spread his palms on the bricks Rani had made and leaned his weight against the structure that reached from the ground to high above the roof. "God," he whispered. "Tell me what to do. I'm afraid of losing her, but I'm afraid to go to her and tell her how I feel."

The LORD is my light and my salvation; whom shall I fear? the LORD is the strength of my life; of whom shall I be afraid? The psalm he'd read a few nights before drifted into his mind.

Matthew inhaled and straightened to his full height. The fear he'd felt a moment ago had vanished, and he knew he had to see her. If she rejected him, he would be all right. The Lord was now the strength of his life, and with God's help he could face whatever life threw at him.

• • •

Rani wrapped the shawl around her shoulders and stepped onto the front porch. The crisp morning air did little to clear her head after a sleepless night. Being back home in familiar surroundings should have relaxed her, but for some reason she'd lain awake most of the night, her mind in a whirl.

Perhaps it was bridal nerves. She'd heard all women had them before they married. In fact, Josie had told her she hadn't slept for weeks before she married. Rani's heart lurched, and she sank down in one of the porch chairs. Of course, Josie probably hadn't slept because she was marrying a man she didn't love.

The door opened, and her mother stepped onto the porch. "I thought I heard you get up. Don't you want some breakfast?"

She shook her head. "In a little while. When did Stephen and David leave?"

Her mother chuckled. "Hours ago I'm sure. You know Stephen likes to get an early start. They should be back any time now. What are you doing out here?"

Rani smiled and pulled her shawl tighter. "I wanted to sit on the porch for a while and, as Granny would say, 'soak up them mountains.' "

Her mother laughed and sat down beside her. "I never tire of it either. The first time I saw the view from the Cove of those peaks, I knew this was where I wanted to live." She shook her head. "Of course, I fought against it until it was almost too late."

Rani swiveled in her chair to face her mother. "I know you love Poppa and you wouldn't trade your life for anything. But have you ever thought how different your life might have been if you had gone to New York to school instead of staying here?"

"I've thought about it, and thanked God a thousand times He helped me see what was best for me. New York didn't have anything to offer like what I found here. We don't have much money, but I have a husband I love, a family I'm proud of, and friends who trust me to treat their loved ones. I could never have found such a rich life in New York."

"And now I'm going to New York. Not the big city, but a small town."

Her mother reached over and patted her hand. "I never thought my daughter might end up there. I'll miss you."

Tears filled her eyes. "I'll miss you too."

Her mother leaned closer. "But you can have a good life there, Rani, if you really love David. Do you?"

Rani pulled her hand away. "Why do you keep asking me if I love David? I've told you how I feel."

"No, you haven't. You've talked about how

much he loves you, what a good person he is, how great your life will be working with him, all the money he has—all of those things. But you have never said to me you love him so much you hurt when you're away from him. You don't talk about how you want to make him happy. It's all about what he's going to do for you."

Tears filled Rani's eyes. "Mama, I love you and Poppa, but we're poor. We live in a remote mountain valley with only the bare necessities for life. Out there in the world there are all kinds of wonders waiting for me, and David can give me all that. Don't you want me to have a life with all the things you never had?"

Her mother stared at her for a moment before she shook her head. "I'm your mother, and of course I want you to have a comfortable life. And you're right about your father and me being poor. But I'm more concerned with you missing out on what I've had."

"What's that?"

"The great love your father and I have shared. It can't be one-sided, Rani. It has to be shared. I couldn't care less about what's in the outside world. All I want is the love that I've experienced inside the walls of this little mountain cabin. If you don't have that, it won't matter how much money you have or how many people buy your artwork. You will end up living a miserable life."

Rani jumped to her feet and whirled to face

her mother. "I won't be miserable. I will be happy. You'll see."

Her mother pushed to her feet and stared over Rani's shoulder. "Tell that to the man riding into the yard."

Rani turned and gasped at the sight of Matthew sitting tall in the saddle on his horse. His gaze didn't waver from Rani's face as he approached the porch. When he pulled the horse to a stop, he glanced at Anna.

"Good morning, Anna. I've come to talk to Rani. Do you mind?"

"Not at all," she said. "I'll be inside if you need me."

When she'd disappeared into the house, Matthew climbed down and tied his horse to the tree at the corner of the house. Then he slowly walked up the steps toward her.

Rani wanted to run—to hide—but she felt glued to the spot.

She held her breath as he walked closer.

Chapter 20

Matthew climbed the steps without taking his eyes off Rani. In the nine months since he'd seen her she had grown even more beautiful. She regarded him with a steady, confident stare that told him she was no longer the young girl who had captured his heart. During her absence she had acquired the self-assured demeanor of a woman who possessed the ability to face whatever problems came her way.

She didn't look the same either. Her long, dark hair was pinned on top of her head, not loose around her shoulders like he had always liked. The memory of how she'd looked with a crown of mountain laurel blooms washed over him, and he stumbled on the last step.

Regaining his balance, he stopped in front of her and took off his hat. "Hello, Rani."

She clasped her hands in front of her, pursed her lips, and gave a slight nod. "Hello, Matthew."

"I hear you're getting married."

"I am."

He glanced toward the front door. "Where's your fiancé? I'd like to meet him while I'm here."

"He's not here right now. He and Stephen went hunting this morning. Did you ride over here to meet him?"

He took a deep breath. "No, I came to see you. Do you mind if I talk to you?"

She arched an eyebrow. "Have you come to pay a social call on the daughter of two of your dearest friends?"

"No, I came to see the woman I got to know last spring when I came back to the Cove."

She lifted her chin and glared at him. "I'm afraid that woman doesn't exist anymore."

He held his hat in front of him, and he gripped the brim with both hands. "I'm sorry to hear that. She was very special to me."

Her eyes widened. "If I remember correctly, she was so special that you threw the love she gave you back in her face and walked away. You wanted nothing else to do with her and told her so in no uncertain terms."

He swallowed. "I know I did, Rani, and I'm sorry about that. If you only knew how many times I've regretted what I did, you would know I hurt like I had a knife in my heart."

She blinked and started to say something. Instead she shrugged. "Good. I'm glad I wasn't the only one suffering."

He threw his hat in one of the chairs and took a step closer to her. "I'm trying to talk to you, Rani, and you're making it difficult. Please at least be cordial while I tell you why I'm here."

She frowned. "Why are you here?"

He took a deep breath. "I'm here because I've spent the last nine months trying to deal with my past. I thought if I could ever forgive myself for all the things I'm so ashamed of, I might be worthy of you. I've lived for the day when you'd come back so I could tell you how sorry I am I hurt you. But I did it for your own good, Rani. You deserved somebody better than me."

She straightened her shoulders. "I told you I only wanted you, Matthew."

"I know, and I made a mess of everything like I always do." He reached out and placed his hands on her shoulders. "But I'm a different man now, Rani. Your father helped me see how much God loves me and how He wanted to forgive me. Now I've forgiven myself also, and I feel like I can have the kind of life I've always wanted."

Her lips trembled. "Then I'm happy for you, Matthew."

His fingers tightened on her shoulders. "But it's no good without you," he rasped. "I've never quit loving you, and I need you."

She shook her head. "No. Don't say that to me. I'm going to marry David."

"Do you love him?"

"I'll be happy with David."

He gritted his teeth and glared at her. "But do you love him?"

"Let me go." She twisted free from his grip. "I'm going to have a wonderful life with him."

"What makes you think you can have a better life with him than you can with me right here in the Cove?"

Her face grew red, and she frowned. "He's a wonderful man who happens to have a lot of money, and we share a love for our work. He can help me get my pottery sold all over the world. And we'll lead an exciting life. I won't live among hillbillies on a dirt farm in the middle of the nowhere."

Her words hit him like a slap in the face. "Hillbillies? Dirt farm? Where did those words come from? Have you changed so much that you think the people who live here are ignorant and not as good as you? If so, I suppose I'm the worst of them all."

"If I think you're the worst, it's because that's what you told me the day you walked away from me. *I'm not good enough for you, Rani,* you said. Well, I went out and found a man who is good enough for me." She spat the words at him.

Anger boiled up inside of him, and he clenched his fists at his sides. "It sounds to me like you found him at the expense of losing everything you held dear before you went away."

"What are you talking about?"

He waved his arm in an arc. "The mountains, Rani. When I came home, I couldn't believe I'd found someone who loved these hills as much as I did. You were ready to take on the biggest lumber company in the state to protect the land you loved. Now it's dirt farms and hillbillies to you. What happened to you while you were gone?"

Her chin trembled. "Nothing happened to me. I still love the Cove, but there's a big world out there. I want to be a part of it. I've outgrown this valley."

He shook his head in disgust. "Outgrown it? The truth is you're not worthy of it anymore."

She gritted her teeth. "How dare you talk to me that way!" she hissed.

He stared at her for a moment before he groaned and raked his hand through his hair. He grabbed the post of the porch and stared at the mountains in the distance. Then he took a deep breath and turned back to her. "I didn't come here to fight with you, Rani. I came to let you know I'm a different person."

The anger on her face slowly dissolved into sadness. Tears filled her eyes. "I'm sorry I yelled at you, Matthew. It seems we always end up fighting, and my mouth takes over before my brain can stop it. We bring out the worst in each other at times. David and I never disagree on anything."

Matthew picked his hat up from the chair, shoved it back on his head, and nodded. "I think our disagreements were good for our relationship. You're a strong-willed woman, Rani, and you need someone to tell you when you're wrong. I was never afraid to do that. I doubt if you'll like living with someone who agrees with everything you do and say."

"I'm sorry, Matthew," she whispered. "It's too late for us."

"It's not if we love each other." He took a step toward her, but she shrank away from him.

"I can't. I promised David, and I can't hurt him."

"But you can hurt me?"

Tears flowed down her face. "Please, don't do this to me. Just go."

He nodded. "All right, I'll go." He walked to the porch steps, stopped, and glanced back. "I'll pray you have a happy life, Rani. I'll never quit loving you."

Matthew trudged down the steps and walked to his horse. When he was in the saddle, he glanced back. She still stood where he had left her, but she didn't move as he turned the horse and guided him to the road.

Matthew glanced up at the sky as he headed toward home. "Thank You, Lord, for helping me get through that. I'm gonna need You an awful lot from here on out. It'll be hard, but I know You'll be there."

He dug his heels into the horse's side and galloped away from Rani.

Rani stared after Matthew until he'd disappeared down the road. Then she walked back into the house. Her mother and Granny glanced up from where they sat at the kitchen table as she walked in.

"Where's Matthew?" her mother asked.

"He left."

Her mother and Granny exchanged quick

glances before Granny frowned. "Child, are you all right?"

She nodded. "I think so."

Her mother pushed to her feet. "Do you want to talk about your conversation with Matthew?"

She burst into tears and covered her eyes with her hands. Her mother ran to her side. "Rani, what is it?"

Her body shook from deep sobs, and all she could do was shake her head. She collapsed against her mother and wrapped her arms around her waist. "Oh, Mama. It's not fair. Just when I'm about to be married, Matthew shows up and says he still loves me."

"I knowed that, darlin'," Granny said. "That boy's been like a sick puppy ever since you left. I ain't never seen nothing like it. But the question is, how do you feel about him?"

Rani pulled back from her mother and stared at Granny. "It doesn't matter. I'm going to marry David."

Her mother's eyes grew large. "It matters a lot. You should only marry David if you love him."

Granny nodded. "And if you love David, then it ought not to make no dif'rence to you what Matthew says."

"But if Matthew loved me, why did he break my heart?"

Her mother shook her head. "I can't tell you

why Matthew acted the way he did. All I know is that he thought it was for your own good at the time. Remember—he said it after Wade Campbell had been pointing a gun at you."

Rani wiped her tears away and sat down at the table. "Last night you told me that Matthew might have turned his back on me because it wasn't God's will and that He might have had something better in mind for me."

Her mother nodded. "Yes, and I believe that's true."

"So, you're saying that God had Matthew turn away from me so I could meet David and marry him?"

"No, Rani, that's not what I'm saying."

"Then what do you mean?"

Her mother slipped into the chair next to her and clasped Rani's hands on top of the table. "When you met Matthew, he wasn't ready to have a life with any woman. He had too many problems from his past to overcome. But you fell in love, and he probably would have wanted to marry you, but you would have been miserable living with all his anger and guilt."

Granny leaned across and patted Rani's hands. "And you were dif'rent too, Rani. All you did was rant about the lumber companies and make folks mad tellin' them how they was disloyal to their friends. And you didn't have no confidence in yourself when it came to your artwork. You go off to Maryville, and you come back a confident young woman who's done had an art show in Knoxville. Matthew's not the only one changed. You are too."

Her mother squeezed her hand. "Maybe that's what God wanted. He had to work on both of you before He could let you be together."

"But how do I know for sure what God's will is for me? I'm afraid I'll do the wrong thing."

"It's not always easy to know," Granny said. "You know the story of the prophet Elijah in the Bible. When ole Queen Jezebel wanted to kill him, he ran away 'cause he was so scared. God told him to go up on a mountain, and He'd tell 'im what to do. Elijah went up there, and God sent a wind and a earthquake and a fire. But God didn't speak to him in those things. He spoke to Elijah in a still, small voice. Then Elijah knew what God wanted him to do."

Her mother put her finger under Rani's chin and turned her face toward her. "Maybe you need to quit protesting too much that you don't know God's will and listen for His still, small voice inside your heart. He'll let you know what you should do."

"You think I'll really know?"

"I do," her mother said. "And when He speaks to you, don't think about how either Matthew or David are going to feel. You do what God tells you is the right thing."

Granny nodded. "And you'll find the great things God has planned for you."

Rani took a deep breath and pushed to her feet. "I think I'll go sit by my fire pit out in the field and look at the mountains. Maybe when I'm out there alone, I can hear His voice."

Her mother stood up and hugged her. "I know you can if you listen."

Granny reached out and squeezed her hand. "And we'll be a-prayin' for you, darlin'."

She kissed her mother's cheek, then leaned over and kissed Granny. "Thank you. I love you both so much." At the back door she turned back toward her mother. "When David comes back, tell him where I am."

"I will."

She stepped outside and headed into the field toward the fire pit she'd first dug when she was a child and the other one she'd dug to fire the bricks for Matthew's cabin. The spring rains had brought the grass around the pits back to life, and it looked as if a green frame had been placed around the holes.

She dropped down and stretched her legs out in front of her. It felt good to be back where she'd spent so many hours. A rustling beside her alerted her to another presence, and she smiled as Scout lay down beside her. He looked up and whined before he laid his head on his outstretched paws.

"We've spent a lot of time out here, boy," she

said. "I'm glad you're here today instead of off with Stephen and David. But then you've always preferred hunting your own rabbits instead of helping anybody else."

Scout whined again, and she stroked his head. "Maybe you knew I needed you more than they did."

She stared at the mist-covered mountain peaks in the distance and thought about what her mother and Granny had said. Could it really be as simple as what they'd said? Be still and listen. That's what she'd do, and she wasn't leaving this spot until she felt God speaking to her heart.

Her fingers smoothed the soft fur on Scout's head, and he gave a contented whimper. Her hand froze in place, and her heart pounded at the memory of walking a dusty road a year ago. Then she heard it—a small voice that whispered, "Remember the promise you made."

The sun had climbed higher in the sky, and the temperature had grown warmer. Neither Rani nor Scout had stirred from their positions beside the fire pit. Her stomach rumbled with hunger, and she remembered she hadn't eaten any breakfast. It had to be almost noon by now.

She heard footsteps approaching, and she turned to see David striding toward her. Scout raised his head and growled. Rani put her hand on his head. "No, Scout. Be still."

David smiled as he neared and then dropped down beside her. "Your mother said you were sitting out here." He glanced down at Scout. "Do you think he'll bite me today?"

She shook her head. "I don't think so."

"Good." He pointed at the pit. "Is this where you fired your pieces?"

"Yes. I dug my first pit here when I was a child. Over the years it's gotten bigger, and I dug another one last year to fire the bricks for the chimney at Matthew's cabin."

He stared into the hole again. "Well, you won't have to use a pit when we get to New York. You'll be able to use any kiln you want to."

She turned to him. "David, what did you really think about the pieces I made for the show in Knoxville?"

"I thought they showed a lot of promise. You still have a ways to go, but they were very good." He leaned over and nuzzled her neck. "I'd buy anything you made."

She twisted away from him and looked into his eyes. "Did you think they were unique?"

He frowned. "What are you asking, Rani?"

She shrugged. "I had the feeling that they were more like copies of your work, not what I would have produced if I'd pit-fired them."

He laughed. "Of course they didn't look like pit-fired pieces. That's not the kind of pottery we're going to develop for our buyers."

She frowned. "But why not?"

He sighed and reached for her hand. "Because those type of pieces are more primitive. They won't sell in the markets we're planning to produce art work for. We need to concentrate on making our glazed works the main focus."

"I see," she said. She stared toward the mountains again. "Aren't the Smokies beautiful?"

"They are," he said. "I've never seen another range like them. They seem to roll on forever."

She smiled. "I've always called them my mountains, but they've been here since time began. The Cherokee lived here before anyone else, and they called them Shaconage. It means 'place of the blue smoke.' I love these mountains. And the valley."

He nodded. "I understand that. I promise you we'll visit often."

"My father's family goes back generations here. They scratched out a living for years and planted a deep commitment to the land in their children. I'd forgotten until I came back that I'm a child of the Cove, and my roots run deep in the earth here. My pottery is a part of the land too. I dug the clay from a hollow not too far from here and fired it in a pit in the dirt God placed here. It's as much a part of the Cove as I am."

His face had turned pale. "What are you saying, Rani?"

She took a deep breath. "I'm saying I can't

marry you, and I can't go to New York. My heart is here with the land and the people I love."

He shook his head. "No, you're not thinking rationally. You've come home after being gone for months, and you're about to move hundreds of miles away. It's natural that you should be scared. You'll be fine once we're settled in our own home. You'll be so busy you won't have time to think about Cades Cove and what's happening here."

"You're wrong. I thought I had put it out of my mind, but I was only fooling myself. I belong here, not in New York."

He swallowed hard. "Is it the Cove you want, or is it a man named Matthew?"

A tear trickled down her cheek. "I'm sorry, David. I haven't been honest with you. I thought I was over him, but I'm not. I gave him my heart a year ago, and he still has it."

"But I love you, Rani. I can give you a life so much better than what you can have here."

She nodded. "I know you love me, and I'm honored. I love you too, but not in the way a wife should love her husband." She slipped his mother's ring from her finger and held it out to him. "Please take this back. Someday you're going to find a woman who deserves to wear it. I'm not that person."

She dropped the ring in his open palm, and he closed his fingers around it before he slipped it in his pocket. "Is there anything I can do to change your mind?"

She shook her head. "No."

"Are you going to marry Matthew?"

"I don't know. I'm letting God lead me today. I have no idea what He has planned for me tomorrow or the next day. I'll have to see what He intends for me in the future."

"If you need more time, I'll wait. I can go on to New York, and you can join me later if you decide you made the wrong choice."

She shook her head. "I won't come to New York, but I wish you the best in your new venture. Truly I do. Maybe someday you'll send me one of your pieces."

He stared at her for a moment before he leaned over and kissed her cheek. "I love you, Rani. I hope you'll be happy."

She blinked back tears. "I hope you will be too."

He cleared his throat and pushed to his feet. "Now if you'll excuse me, I think I'll go ask your father if there's any way I can get back to Townsend this afternoon. If I can, I'll check the trains for the first one going east and be on it."

"You don't have to leave today, David."

"I think I do. It will be too uncomfortable being around you."

She nodded. "If that's the way you want it."

A sad look crossed his face. "None of this is the way I wanted it, Rani."

He turned, and she watched as he strode across the field. Tears streamed down her face, and she closed her eyes. "God, please forgive me for hurting David, and I pray someday he'll find it in his heart to forgive me also. Be with him and take care of him."

Scout whined again, and she stroked his head. Now she had to decide what she needed to do next. Should she go to Matthew and tell him about her broken engagement or not? She sat still and waited for the answer.

She had no idea how much time had passed when she heard someone approaching. She glanced around and saw her father walking toward her. He dropped down beside her and put his arm around her waist. "David told me what happened. How are you feeling, darling?"

She laid her head on his shoulder and sighed. "I feel awful about hurting David, Poppa, but I would have hurt him much worse if I had married him."

"Yes, you would have. I realized at supper last night that you didn't love him."

Surprised, she straightened and looked into his face. "How did you know?"

He grinned. "Because you didn't look at him the way your mother looks at me."

She threw her arms around her father and

hugged him. "You remembered I said that's what I wanted when I married."

He nodded. "Yes. I was shocked last summer when I found out you and Matthew had fallen in love. But as I thought about it, I realized I shouldn't have been. You looked at him that way all the time."

Tears filled her eyes. "Oh, Poppa. I tried to hate him, but I couldn't. I still love him. What should I do?"

"Maybe you need to go talk to him. Your mother said he came here today."

"He did, and I was rude to him. I'm afraid he may not want to see me."

He put his finger under her chin and tilted her face up. "Where's that girl who wanted to tackle Little River Lumber singlehanded? She wasn't afraid of anything."

Rani wiped at her eyes. "I don't think I know her anymore."

Her father laughed. "I hope you can find her because I really liked her. Maybe if you took a short ride in the buggy, you could find her somewhere."

Rani frowned. "What are you talking about?"

"When David got back to the house from talking with you, he asked if we could take him to Townsend. He didn't want to wait until morning. John was at the house, and he volunteered to drive him there. It gave John an excuse to spend the night at Annie's house. He and David left a few minutes ago for Townsend."

"So he's gone."

"Yes, and I thought you might like to take a drive in our buggy. Maybe you need to go check out those bricks you made. Matthew's chimney is something to see. So, I hitched up the buggy for you. It's waiting back of the house."

She threw her arms around her father and hugged him. "Thank you, Poppa. Don't you want to come with me?"

He shook his head. "In this case I think three would be too many people. Besides, you've been handling that horse and buggy since you were a child." He chucked her under the chin. "Every Cove girl can handle a horse."

She grinned and jumped to her feet. "You're right. As I told David, my roots run deep here, and I'm never leaving this place again."

She ran to the waiting horse and buggy behind the house and jumped in. As she guided the horse onto the road, she turned her face up to the sun and welcomed its warmth on her face. She was on her way to Matthew.

Chapter 21

There were chores waiting, but Matthew couldn't make himself get outside and do them. All he'd done since he'd returned from seeing Rani was to pace the cabin floor or to sit in his chair and stare into the fireplace. He couldn't shake the image of her from his mind.

He stopped in his latest trip across the floor and grabbed a cup from the shelf on the wall. Some coffee might give him the boost he needed to get on with his work. With his mind still focused on the things Rani had said earlier, he reached into the fireplace for the coffeepot and wrapped his hand around the handle.

Too late he realized what he'd done. The hot metal seared the palm of his hand, and he dropped the pot at his feet. Coffee poured out the spout and the open top across the floor.

He cradled his burned hand in his uninjured one and rushed across the floor to the water bucket. He plunged his hand into the cold water. Berating himself for being so distracted, he reached for a cloth to clean up the mess, but he hesitated. A buggy had rattled to a stop in his front yard.

He wrapped the cloth around his hand and headed to the door. A knock sounded before he could reach it. He opened the door and gasped at the sight of Rani standing on the front porch. He tried to speak, but his throat had suddenly gone dry. He swallowed and tried again. "Rani, what are you doing here?"

"I came to talk to you. May I come in?"

His gaze swept over her, and his heart pounded at the sight of her hair cascading around her shoulders. He nodded and stepped back for her to enter. She moved past him into the cabin, and he struggled to keep from touching her to see if she was real and not a dream. She stopped inside the door and glanced around before she turned back to him and looked at the cloth dangling from his hand. "What happened?"

He frowned and glanced down at his forgotten injury. He shook his head. "I burned it on the coffeepot, but I'll be all right."

"Let me see." She stepped closer, took his hand, and unwrapped the cloth.

When she bent her head to study the burn, he raised his other hand to caress her hair, but he let his arm drift back to his side. "It's really nothing," he said.

She straightened to her full height and smiled at him. "This doesn't look too bad. I'm sure Mama has something to take the pain away." She let go of his hand and smiled. "You have to be more careful when you're cooking in a fireplace."

His mind whirled with questions, and he

narrowed his eyes. "Rani, what are you doing here?"

"I wasn't very cordial this morning, and I'm sorry. I thought we needed to talk some more."

He shook his head. "What's left to say? I think you said it all."

She inched closer to him. "No, there's something else I've never told you. I should have this morning."

"What's that?"

"It's a promise I made to Scout."

He arched his eyebrows. "You made a promise to your dog?"

Her dark eyes stared at him. "Last summer when we met, I had been to my friend Josie's cabin to tell her goodbye because she was moving out of the Cove. That afternoon while we were talking she told me for the first time that she had married Ted when she was really in love with someone else. I couldn't imagine how she could do that."

His heartbeat quickened. "Rani, what . . ."

She held up her hand to stop him from speaking. "On the way home I told Scout I would never have that problem. I promised him that I would never settle for second best even if it meant I would never get married." Tears filled her eyes. "I forgot that promise until after you came today. When I remembered it, I knew I could never marry David, not when my heart belonged to the man I met that day at the mountain laurel bush."

His mouth dropped open, and he stared into her eyes. "Rani, are you saying you love me too?"

"I was so angry with you when I left the Cove that I told myself I didn't love you, but I knew it wasn't true." She began to cry. "Oh, Matthew, I'm so sorry for the things I said today. I love you so much, and all I want is to be with you."

"That's all I want too." He pulled her to him, and she wrapped her arms around him. She raised her lips to meet his, and he thought his heart would explode with happiness. He'd dreamed of kissing her night after night, and he had to almost pinch himself to believe the lips pressed against his were real. He released her mouth and stared down at her. "Don't you ever leave me again."

"I promise I won't." Her face lit up with happiness. "I can't believe this is happening. I thought we'd lost our chance."

He hugged her tightly and pressed his cheek against hers. "This is just the beginning. I want you by my side when I wake up in the mornings, and I want you here every time I walk in this cabin. Marry me, Rani. I need you."

"Yes, yes," she whispered. "I'll marry you."

A sudden thought struck him, and he pulled back from her. "What about David?"

"David's gone. I realized I would hurt him

more in the long run if I married him when I didn't love him. Uncle John has taken him to Townsend to catch the train to New York."

Matthew held her at arm's length and frowned. "But what about your pottery? Are you sure you're willing to give up the opportunity to work with him?"

Her fingers stroked his cheek. "I want to create mountain-made pottery that visitors to the mountains will buy. I've learned a lot working with David, and I think I can create a market for pit-fired pottery right here in the Smokies. I already have a name for my line—Mountain Laurel Pottery." She grinned. "If it doesn't work out, I can always open a brick factory."

He laughed, picked her up in his arms, and whirled her around in a circle. "I love you, Rani. We're going to have a great life together."

She threw back her head and squealed with delight. "Put me down, and let's go tell Mama and Poppa we're about to have a new member of the family."

He stood her in front of him and cupped her face in his hands. "A member of the Martin family? That's too good to be true. I can't believe how God has blessed me. I have the woman I love, and I'm finally going to have a family."

She raised her lips to his. "We're going to have a great life, Matthew."

He leaned forward to kiss her but froze in

place at the sound of a shout from outside the cabin. "Jackson, you in there? Come on out. I got somethin' for you."

Matthew looked down into Rani's startled face and saw fear in her eyes. She recognized the voice too. He stepped back from her, and she grabbed his arm. "No, Matthew," she cried. "Don't go."

He took a deep breath and pulled away from her. "I have to."

He walked to the door and glanced back at her. "You are not to step in front of me. Do you understand?"

Tears rolled down her cheeks. "Yes," she whispered.

He closed his eyes and said a quick prayer before he opened the door to face Wade Campbell.

Rani grabbed the back of a chair to keep her legs from buckling underneath her. The tone of Wade's voice reminded her of the day last summer when she and Matthew had encountered him in the barn after Bertha's death. That day she thought she'd lost Matthew forever. Now when they had found their way back to each other, Wade showed up again. She couldn't let him take Matthew away from her a second time.

She took a deep breath and followed Matthew onto the porch. Her breath caught in her throat at the sight of Wade leaning against the wheel of her buggy with George Ferguson standing next to him. Wade held a rifle in his hands. George's eyes grew wide when he saw her, but Matthew didn't seem to sense her presence.

He clenched his fists at his side and walked to the edge of the porch. "I'm surprised to see you, Wade. I thought you were in North Carolina."

"I was, but I come back home to take care of somethin'."

Matthew's fingers twitched, but he didn't move. "Why are you here, Wade?" he asked.

Wade straightened and spit out a wad of tobacco. His legs wobbled, and he staggered against George. "I got myself in a little trouble last night, and I gotta clear out of this part of the country. Thought I'd come see you first, though."

"What kind of trouble are you in, Wade?"

Wade looked at George and laughed, but George clamped his lips together and looked away. "It don't matter what kind of trouble," Wade said. He took a deep breath and curled his fingers tighter around the gun. " 'Fore I go, I need to take care of some unfinished bus'ness 'tween the two of us."

Matthew's body tensed. "I don't know of any business between the two of us, Wade. You're drunk. You need to go somewhere and sleep it off."

Wade's upper lip curled back from his teeth,

and he aimed the rifle at Matthew. "I'm not drunk enough to be scared off by the likes of you." He closed one eye and peered down the sights of the gun. "It's been a-stickin' in my craw ever since I heared you come back to the Cove. I done told you once you shouldn't've come back here. You oughta listened to me, boy."

Matthew shook his head. "I've never done anything to you. Why would you leave me threatening notes, burn my cornfield, and now show up here to kill me?"

" 'Cause I knowed right from the start why you come back. You wanted to get even for your pa's death, but I ain't gonna give you the satisfaction. Ain't nobody gonna say Luke Jackson's boy got the best of me."

Rani's heart thudded, and she eased up next to Matthew. "Mr. Campbell, please get out of here and leave us alone. All Matthew wants is to be left in peace."

Matthew jerked his head around and cast a startled look at her. "Rani, I told you . . ."

"I'm not standing in front of you, Matthew," she interrupted. "I'm standing beside you, and that's where I always want to be."

The muscle in his jaw twitched, and he grabbed her arm and pulled her behind him. She peeked around his back so that she could see Wade's face. "You're wrong about me wanting to get even, Wade," Matthew said. "I never blamed you for killing my father. You were only protecting yourself, and anybody else would have done the same thing in your place."

Wade laughed. "Yeah, you'd say anything to keep me from shootin' you."

"No, I wouldn't. I know how my pa was. He was a bully and drunkard. Nobody had any respect for him. All I want is for folks to know I'm not like him. I shouldn't have to take the blame for things he did. Do you want that for Noah?"

Wade's eyes narrowed. "What're you talkin' about?"

"If you kill an unarmed man, then everybody in the Cove is going to know it. Do you want them to blame Noah for what you did and make him miserable for the rest of his life? He's just a child. He has no control over you just like I couldn't make my father do right. But Noah shouldn't be blamed for your bad choices."

The gun wavered in Wade's hand, but he jerked it back up. "Don't go tryin' to confuse me, Jackson. Now move away from Rani."

Rani threw her arms around Matthew's waist and held tight. "No!" she screamed. "George, do something!"

Wade cocked the gun. "All right. Have it your way."

Matthew tried to push Rani aside, but she clung to him. He held up a hand to stop Wade. "Wade, think what you're doing!" he yelled.

"George!" Rani screamed again.

George, who had appeared paralyzed with fear since Rani had stepped onto the porch, suddenly came to life. He lunged for Wade and grabbed the barrel of the rifle. He pushed downward until the barrel pointed toward the ground. "Wade, you can't do this. That's Simon's daughter standing up there. It won't just be the sheriff after us— it'll be every law man in the country if you hurt her."

"I don't care. I ain't leavin' Jackson alive." Wade tightened his grip on the gun and pushed against George, but George held on. They fell back against the buggy wheel as they wrestled over the gun. The horse, startled by the commotion, reared up and tried to break free of his reins. The motion of the buggy shoved the two across the front yard, but neither relaxed their grip in the struggle.

Matthew broke free of Rani, leaped off the front porch, and ran toward them. Before he could reach the two, Wade pulled one hand free and punched George in the face. As George stumbled backward, Wade jerked the gun to his shoulder and fired. Rani screamed in horror as George collapsed in a heap.

Wade turned toward Matthew and leveled the gun at him. Rani screamed again, but before Wade could fire, Matthew sprang at him like a man possessed. The sound of a cracking bone split the air with Matthew's first punch, and the rifle dropped from Wade's hands.

Rani jumped off the porch, ran toward Matthew, and picked up the rifle just as Matthew delivered another bone-crushing blow to Wade's jaw. Matthew clutched the front of Wade's shirt in one hand, pulled him into a standing position, and drew back to hit him again. He held his shaking fist in midair and frowned. As if debating whether to deliver the blow or not, Matthew didn't move. Then he relaxed his grip on Wade, and the unconscious man sank to the ground.

Matthew turned toward Rani, and she gasped at the wounded look in his eyes. "I thought he was going to kill you, Rani," he whispered. "I didn't want to hurt him."

She nodded. "I know, Matthew."

He shook his head and reached for the rifle. "There's some rope hanging on a nail just inside the barn door. Go get it, and I'll check on George."

She glanced at George before she turned and ran to do as Matthew said. When she returned, she handed Matthew the rope. "H-how is George?"

Matthew knelt beside Wade and began to tie his hands behind his back. "He's pretty bad off. The bullet hit him in the side, and he's losing a lot of blood. We need to get him to your mother and Granny right away. I'll put Wade in the buggy and go see if I can find something to press against George's wound before we load him."

"All right." She hurried over to where George lay and bent over him. "George, can you hear me?"

He opened his eyes and stared up at her. "I-I'm s-sorry 'bout this, Rani. I w-wouldn't've come with Wade if I'd knowed where he was goin'. H-he said we was going back to North Carolina."

She patted his hand. "Don't try to talk. We're going to get you to my mother. She'll get you fixed up in no time."

He tried to raise his head, but he sank back to the ground and grasped her hand. Fear flickered in his eyes. "If'n I don't make it, tell my ma and pa I'm sorry. I wish I could go back and do it all over again."

"You'll be able to tell them, George. They want you back home."

Within seconds, Matthew had reappeared and dropped down beside her. He handed her a tablecloth. "This is all I could find." He glanced down at George. "Your mother made this for me. I think she'd be glad to know we used it for her son."

A weak smile pulled at George's mouth. "Thanks."

Matthew slipped his arm around George's shoulders. "I have Wade in the buggy. Now we're going to lay you down in the backseat, and

Rani is going to press this on your wound. Are you ready?"

George nodded, and together Rani and Matthew pulled him to his feet and supported his weight as they stumbled toward the buggy. When George was on the backseat, Rani squeezed in beside him and pressed the table-cloth to his side. Wade, still unconscious, sat tied to the arm rail in the front seat.

As Matthew started to climb in, George stirred. "Matthew, wait."

Matthew stopped and stepped back to face George. "What is it?"

George coughed and then groaned in pain. "I-if'n I don't make it, t-tell the sheriff I saw Wade kill Chester Goode last night."

Matthew frowned. "Is that the man who was selling moonshine with the two of you?"

George nodded. "Wade knew Chester had sold us out to the sheriff. I thought we'd gone to his house to talk to him, but Wade wanted to get even with him. He shot Chester down in cold blood when he stepped out of his house to go to the barn. Wade told me if'n I ever told anybody, he'd find me and kill me the same way. Wade said we had to git back to North Carolina 'cause Chester's wife saw us before we rode off. I reckon the sheriff is after us by now."

Matthew squeezed George's arm. "You can tell the sheriff that yourself. Now let's get to Anna."

Matthew jumped into the driver's seat and snapped the reins on the horse's back. As they turned onto the road, George moaned and closed his eyes. Rani placed her finger on his neck and sighed in relief when she felt a pulse. Perhaps it was a blessing that George was unconscious. He wasn't feeling any of the bumps as the buggy skimmed the ruts.

Rani glanced at Matthew's straight back from time to time as they raced toward her home, but he didn't speak. When her cabin came into view, she almost collapsed against George. When she'd left to go to Matthew's cabin, she would never have dreamed what would occur before she returned.

As they drew nearer, she saw several horses with riders in the front yard. When they pulled to a stop, she recognized the sheriff standing next to her father at the foot of the steps. The men on horseback wore badges, and she supposed them to be deputies.

Her father's eyes grew wide with alarm as they pulled into the yard, and the sheriff stared in disbelief. Matthew jumped from the buggy the instant it came to a stop. "Sheriff, you may be looking for these men. George Ferguson is badly wounded, but Wade Campbell is just unconscious."

The front door flew open, and Anna and Stephen dashed onto the porch. "Mama," Rani called out, "George is hurt and needs help."

The sheriff's deputies jumped from their horses and assisted her father, mother, and brother as they carried the unconscious George into the house. Matthew reached for her hand, and she climbed down from the buggy. Her hands and arms as well as her dress were covered in blood.

She stopped in front of the sheriff. "Do you need to ask me any questions, or is it all right for me to get cleaned up?"

The sheriff shook his head. "You go on, Miss Martin. I think Matthew here can tell me everything I need to know."

She glanced up at Matthew, and he nodded. "You go on. I'll wait on the porch for you after I get through talking with the sheriff."

There was something in the tone of his voice that frightened her, but she nodded and walked toward the house. As she mounted the first step, Stephen rushed out the front door. "Mama wants me to go for Dr. Harrison. She says George has lost a lot of blood. And she wants me to stop and tell Pete and Laura to come over here. I'll be back as soon as I can."

She nodded and turned to watch as the deputies pulled Wade from the buggy and Stephen jumped in. Then she entered the house. When she walked into the kitchen, her mother and Granny already had George on the kitchen table and were studying his wound. They didn't look up as she walked down the hallway to her room.

As soon as she closed the door, she undid the buttons of her blood-stained dress and let it fall to the floor in a heap at her feet. She stepped out of it, walked to the washbowl on a table across the room, and poured some water from the pitcher into it. She dipped her hands into the water and watched as it turned red.

She scrubbed her hands and arms before she reached for a towel and dried them. Then she walked to her bed, sank down on the edge, and buried her head in her hands. The fear and panic she'd held in since hearing Wade's voice call out to Matthew bubbled to the surface, and she began to shake.

Tears streamed down her face, and she jammed her fist into her mouth to stifle the sobs. She'd never been as scared in her life as she had been when Wade aimed his gun at Matthew and her. They had just found each other and had come so close to losing each other forever.

She lay down on her bed and buried her face in her pillow. *Thank You for protecting us, Lord.*

Matthew reached down and scratched Scout behind the ears. The dog had settled down next to him as soon as he sank into the chair at the end of the porch. Matthew stretched his legs out in front of him and closed his eyes.

He didn't know when he'd ever been as tired as he was at this moment. But it wasn't a physical fatigue, it was an emotional one. The day had been filled with more twists and turns than any he could ever remember. Now he had to try to come to grips with the feeling that had come over him when he attacked Wade Campbell. For a fleeting second it had been almost like being back in the ring, and the old urge to destroy an opponent had threatened to make him forget everything God had been teaching him.

The front door opened and Rani stepped onto the porch. She had on a clean dress, and she was no longer covered in George's blood. She eased into the chair next to him and patted Scout's head. Matthew laced her fingers with his and smiled.

"It seems natural for us to be sitting here with Scout between us. I've missed this."

She snuggled in the chair and gripped his hand tighter. "Me too." She glanced back at the house. "I saw Dr. Harrison when I came through the kitchen. He's still working on George, but Mama says she thinks he's going to be all right. Pete and Laura are in the front room with Noah. Did you see them when they arrived?"

"Yes. I told them what happened and what George said. They hope he'll get to come home."

Her eyes widened. "Do you think the sheriff may arrest him?"

"I don't know. There's still the problem with him and Wade selling moonshine. Maybe if George will testify against Wade about Chester's death, the law will go easy on him. I'd like to see him get a second chance."

Her eyelashes fluttered, and a contented expression covered her face. "Like us. I can't believe we're getting a second chance."

He directed a somber gaze at her. "I want that more than I've ever wanted anything, but I think there are some things about me you need to know before you marry me."

She sighed and shook her head. "Matthew, there isn't anything you could ever tell me that would make me love you less."

He swallowed. "I hope not, but I have to take the chance. You know that your father has helped me face up to my past, and I've told him everything. I never wanted you to know, but after what happened today, I think you should."

She sat up straight, and a puzzled look crossed her face. "Then tell me."

He released her hand and stared toward the mountains in the distance. "After my mother died, there was nobody who cared about me, and I had nowhere to go. So I struck out on my own."

The story of the years between that time and when he arrived back in the Cove began to tumble from his lips. He left nothing out and told it with graphic descriptions of the places he'd been and the things he'd done. He told her how he'd taken pleasure in leaving men in a bloody heap on the floor.

When he ended with the story of the young boy whose face had haunted his dreams for years, tears ran down his cheeks. He buried his face in his hands and shook his head. "And today when I attacked Wade, I felt that same urge. It was like I was that person again, and he was going to pay for thinking he could best me."

Matthew wanted to look at her, but he was afraid of what he might see. Would she hate him because of his cruel actions of years ago? Perhaps she would even change her mind about marrying him because she was afraid he might become that man again in the future.

"Matthew, look at me." Reluctantly, he raised his head. He expected to see disappointment and maybe fear in Rani's eyes, but he saw only love. "I'm glad you told me this," she said. "Now I understand why you sent me away last year. But you've made your peace with the past. It doesn't have a hold on you anymore."

"That's what I thought. But today . . ."

She reached over and put her fingers on his lips to stop him. "Matthew, today was very different from when you were fighting for a living. Wade intended to kill us, and you were protecting us. Protecting me. I feel like the luckiest woman in the world."

He frowned. "How's that?"

"I may not be your wife yet, but I know that when I am I won't have anything to fear. The

Bible says for husbands to love their wives like Christ loved the church and gave Himself for it. Today when you charged toward a man with a gun, you were willing to give your life to protect me. I know you'll always do that in the future."

"But I hit him awfully hard."

Rani laughed. "Yes, twice. But I watched your face when you drew back for the third blow, and you didn't take it. You realized he was unconscious, and you released him. From what you've told me the old Matthew wouldn't have stopped with two punches."

He thought for a moment before he nodded. "I think you're right. I did stop."

"Yes, you did—because you're not the man you were before. With God's help you really have become a new creature."

He smiled, pulled her to her feet, and wrapped his arms around her. "I need to be sure that you'll never be afraid of me."

She reached up and caressed his cheek. "How could I ever be afraid of you? There's a part of you that is still that little boy who wants to be accepted and loved. You don't have to look any further. I'm here, and I've promised I will never leave you. I love you too much to do that."

He hugged her close and whispered in her ear. "I'll make you a good husband, Rani. I promise I will."

"I know you will, Matthew."

They stood locked in each other's arms, each lost in their own thoughts. It had been a long day, but God had seen them safely through. Matthew breathed another prayer of thanks and looked past her into the distance. "Look at that sunset, Rani."

She turned and stared toward the mountains and the sun that was slowly disappearing behind the peaks. Streaks of orange and red fanned out across the sky in a breathtaking picture. "It's beautiful, and we have a lifetime to share the sunsets in our valley."

His arm circled her waist. "A lifetime with you sounds good to me." He pulled her closer and let out a contented sigh. "I finally feel like I'm home."

Chapter 22

On a warm June afternoon four weeks later Matthew stood next to Stephen at the front of the church and waited for his bride to enter. Josie, who'd returned for the wedding to stand up with Rani, faced him and Stephen. With the church packed with well-wishers, the temperature had grown hotter in the building.

Matthew ran his finger around the edge of his shirt collar and wiped at the perspiration that dotted his forehead. With a grin on his face, Stephen leaned forward. "Are you nervous?" he whispered.

Matthew nodded. "A little."

Stephen laughed under his breath. "You ought to be. I'm sure glad it's you and not me that's going to have to put up with Rani from now on. She can be quite a handful."

Matthew smiled and nodded. "That she can be."

He glanced around at the people present and smiled at Anna, Granny, and Noah sitting in the front pew. Behind them, George Ferguson sat between his parents and nodded when he caught Matthew's eye. Matthew glanced at Laura and smiled at the happiness on her face. She had to be thankful her son was back and would soon be free of charges because of his testimony against Wade. With Wade on his way to prison, he supposed Noah would be a permanent member of the Martin family, and Anna appeared happier than she'd been since he'd come home.

His thoughts were interrupted when the church door opened, and Rani and her father appeared. The sight of her sucked the breath from him, and his heart pounded against his chest. She'd pulled her hair up today, and the veil her mother had worn on her wedding day covered her head. She carried a bouquet of mountain laurel blooms.

She and Simon walked slowly down the aisle, and Matthew couldn't take his eyes off her.

God had blessed him far more than he'd expected when he rode back into this valley a year ago. When she finally stood beside him at the altar, Simon reached for his hand and joined it with Rani's. Then he stepped in front of them and opened his Bible.

"Dearly beloved," Simon read, "we are here today to join this man and this woman in holy matrimony."

Holy matrimony. The words sent a thrill through his soul, and he squeezed her hand. He knew Simon was still speaking, but he could only concentrate on the woman at his side. He answered Simon's questions with a hearty *I do!* when asked and remembered to slip the ring on her finger. But most of it was a blur until he heard the words he'd been waiting for.

"I now pronounce you husband and wife. Matthew, you may kiss your wife."

He froze at the words. His wife? Rani was really his wife? He stared at her, and she smiled. "Aren't you going to kiss me?" she whispered.

He exhaled and nodded. "Oh, yes—for the rest of my life."

He leaned forward and brushed his lips across hers. Then they turned and exited the church. Once outside they stopped at the bottom of the steps, and he put his arms around her. She gazed up at him. "I love you, Matthew."

"I love you too, Mrs. Jackson."

She laughed and threw her arms around his neck. Stephen and her father rushed out of the church door and hurried down the steps. "No time for standing around," Stephen said. "Folks are coming out, and they're expecting a piece of cake."

They laughed and headed toward the tables Anna and Simon had placed there earlier. Several women guarded the cake Granny had made and waited for the arrival of the guests. Before Matthew had time to thank them, the guests poured from the church and crowded around them.

Laura Ferguson was one of the first to congratulate him. "Matthew, I want to thank you kindly for what you done to save my boy. I ain't never gonna forget you for it."

He shook his head. "No need to thank me, Laura. I'm just glad things are looking up for George. He's a good boy at heart."

Laura nodded. "I reckon he is. Just thought he'd show his pa and me that he knew more than we did. I don't think he'll stray far from home from now on."

"I'm glad to hear that."

"God bless you, Matthew." She reached out and gave him a quick hug before she hurried away.

Matthew watched her go and thought of how her shy ways reminded him so much of his mother. He could only imagine the courage it had taken for Laura to hug him. It was a gesture he would always treasure.

"We's right happy for you, Matthew."

He turned to see Cecil and Pearl Davis standing next to him. He stuck out his hand. "Thank you, Cecil. I'm glad you came today, and I'm really glad Josie got to come. I don't think Rani would have married me if Josie wasn't here."

Pearl smiled. "We's right glad she's home too. It's been awful nice havin' little Jimmy with us for a few days."

Matthew glanced across the crowd and spied Rani and Josie talking. Rani juggled Jimmy in her arms. She smiled at the toddler and planted a kiss on his cheek. Matthew stared at her and thought of how many nights he'd sat by his fireplace and envisioned Rani beside him holding their child. Now she was his wife, and he might become a father before long.

Before meeting Rani, he'd never given that prospect much thought, but now he knew that's what God had been preparing him for this past year. God had changed his life and given him the chance to prove that he could be a better husband and father than his father had been. The thought humbled him.

With a smile, he walked toward his wife.

Matthew and Rani stood on the porch of their cabin, and she watched her father's buggy disappear down the road. He'd driven them here after the wedding, and now he had left her to begin her new life with her husband.

She stared up at Matthew and smiled. "I enjoyed seeing all our friends after the wedding, but I was ready to come home."

"I hope you can think of it as home, Rani. Right now it's a simple one-room cabin, but I'll make it better for you. I promise I will."

She laughed and kissed him on the cheek. "I don't care what it's like. As long as we're together, that's all that matters."

He stared in the direction of the buggy. "But I'm poor. I don't even have a buggy. Your father had to bring us home from the church."

"Oh, Matthew," she said, "I don't need a buggy. I've been riding a horse all my life, and I still like walking. Don't worry about the things we don't have. I'm looking forward to the good times we're going to have as we build our life together."

He shook his head. "I still don't know what I did to deserve you." He took her hand and pulled her down the steps. "There's something I want to do before we go inside."

He led her around the cabin and into the field behind the house. He stopped when they reached the mountain laurel bush.

She smiled at the sight of the blooms that covered the bush. "This is where we met."

He nodded. "I wanted to bring you back here today." He walked over and picked a handful of blooms. When he returned, he began to arrange them in her hair. She remained motionless until he stepped back and smiled. "There. It's just like it was a year ago when I first saw you here."

She shook her head. "Not quite. Scout's not here."

Matthew laughed. "No, he didn't want me near you that day." He led her over, and they sat down beside the bush. He put his arm around her shoulders and pulled her close. "I fell in love with you the minute I saw you. Some folks might think that's not possible, but I knew that day."

She twisted in his arms and stared up at him. "Do you remember what I was doing when you first saw me?"

"Yes, you had your arms stretched out, and you were whirling in circles while you sang some strange words."

She nodded. "Yes, it was a prayer a Cherokee woman taught me when I was a child."

"A prayer? I remember I asked you what you were saying, and you wouldn't tell me. What was it?"

She reached for his hand and held it. "When I was a little girl, I loved to hear the Cherokee woman who lived on the next farm talk about her people and how they loved the land. One day she taught me a prayer of thanks. The day we met, I'd just come from saying goodbye to Josie, and I was so sad. All my friends were leaving, and I just felt empty inside. When I stopped at the mountain laurel bush, the blooms were so beautiful, and I knew God had made them. I felt His presence there, and I began to give Him thanks."

"And what were you thanking Him for?"

Tears sparkled in her eyes, and she squeezed his hand tighter. "It was like God whispered to me that my life was going to get better. So I closed my eyes and began to sing the words I'd learned years ago—words of thanks for unknown blessings already on their way. I opened my eyes, and you were standing there. I fought against it at first, but in my heart I knew you were the unknown blessing that was already on its way when I first began to pray. God had sent you to me."

Matthew's eyes were full of tenderness as he reached out and pulled his wife toward him. "I love you, Rani Jackson," he whispered in her ear.

Rani snuggled against her husband and silently thanked God for the unknown blessings He was already sending to her and Matthew. She could hardly wait to see what they were.

About the Author

Sandra Robbins and her husband live in the small college town in Tennessee where she grew up. They count their four children and five grandchildren as the greatest blessings in their lives. Her published books include stories in historical romance and romantic suspense. When not writing or spending time with her family, Sandra enjoys reading, collecting flow blue china, and playing the piano.

To learn more about books by Sandra Robbins
or to read sample chapters,
log on to our website:

www.harvesthousepublishers.com

Center Point Large Print
600 Brooks Road / PO Box 1
Thorndike ME 04986-0001 USA

(207) 568-3717

US & Canada:
1 800 929-9108
www.centerpointlargeprint.com